WHEN THERE WERE HEROES

By the same author:

Gate of Hope
Titus

First published in the UK in 2003 by
Dewi Lewis Publishing
8 Broomfield Road
Heaton Moor
Stockport SK4 4ND
+44 (0)161 442 9450

www.dewilewispublishing.com

ISBN: 1-899235-59-0

Design & artwork production: Dewi Lewis Publishing
Printed and bound in Great Britain by
Biddles Ltd, Guildford and King's Lynn

2   4   6   8   9   7   5   3   1

WHEN THERE WERE HEROES

Elon Salmon

DEWI LEWIS

PUBLISHING

For Blodwen, Nella, Mollie, David and Becca.

... On that path from Deganiya to Kinnerth,
Stood the loaded harvest of my life ...

From a popular early Israeli song

1

Sometimes I sleep with my eyes wide open. And although I am in Muswell Hill, north London, I see the starry sky of Jezreel in my sleep. And then my father speaks to me in a faraway biblical voice. I seldom remember his words when I wake up. But a vague sense of his presence always lingers with me for a good part of the day.

This morning I'm up earlier than usual. It is dark outside. I go to the kitchen which is open-planned, adjoining the living room. My flat is on the top floor of a converted Edwardian terrace house. As I stand at the bay window drinking a mug of coffee, I see the taxi that has come to take to work the girl who lives in the house across the street. Her name is Rosalind, I've heard a friend call her that. She works for the BBC. Attractive, you might say, in a media executive style.

The taxi pulls away. Rosalind already has a wad of papers in her lap, not a moment wasted. I try in vain to remember what my father said before I woke up. I do remember, though, that it is the First of September, his birthday and a private beginning of the year for me.

Yesterday I had a troublesome going to press day for *Kadima*, the weekly I edit. Now that it is behind me, an idle day stretches ahead. The only entry in my office diary, as I remember, is an invitation to a reception sometime in the afternoon.

Silence returns to the street, not for long, I know. When Moon rises from his feline slumber to demand breakfast, my day will begin for real. I turn on the radio: Richard Strauss's *Ein Heldenleben*. Once again I think of my father, this time with a practical sense of purpose: there's a box in my work room containing his diary notes. I feel I am at last ready to go through them, put them in order and in so doing stitch together my own life's fragmentation.

Moon has arrived in stealth to rub against my naked calf. His purring goes up my leg like sonar massage. In my mind – past ablution and breakfast cereal – I'm halfway through Highgate Wood to the tube station and thence on to Whitefriars Street, where my office is. A vacant morning with nothing much to do; a still autumnal semi-darkness for the dream cinema of recollection.

* * * * *

Two police cars stand in front of the Daily Telegraph building in Fleet Street. Beside them an ambulance, its backdoor thrown open, the roof beacon flashing. Barriers have been put up along the pavement on both sides of the street. The traffic, however, flows on unhindered. A crowd gathers, ignoring the police instruction to move on. I too, stop to look.

Sitting on the roof above the imperial Roman-Victorian entrance, now demonstratively closed with a heavy padlock, is a man. He is middle-aged, with a humpty dumpty body. A pin-striped suit strains to contain his belly. A pink shirt and a dark red tie flung aside by the breeze, suggest vocational attention to appearance. He sits stock still, legs dangling over the parapet, staring blankly, seemingly oblivious to the people below, who stare at him in expectation.

Another man in a khaki anorak – a plain-clothes policeman, a medic perhaps? – appears at the far end of the roof. Slowly he moves towards Humpty Dumpty, talking to him. The latter tenses, and wiggles forward, hands tightening on the edge of the roof. His feet tremble; small delicate feet, shod in shiny black shoes. The policeman, or medical man, stops dead. Stretching his arm to the man, he appears to plead with him.

'I wonder how he got up there, what with him being so fat and all,' says a girl who stands with her boyfriend not far from me.

'Some blokes will do anything for a bit of publicity. C'mon you silly bugger, jump!' the boyfriend says.

'That's a horrible thing to say,' the girl breathes.

'Bloody exhibitionist, that's what he is. Pissed as a newt after a fat lunch, I'll bet. And not a thought for the poor sods who'll have to clean up the mess. He won't jump. No way!' says the young man with a sneer.

The anoraked policeman or medic reaches the man. Putting his arm round his shoulders, he grips his wrist. Slowly they both move away from the edge.

'There, what did I tell you?' says the young man, and begins to peel a Mars bar.

Grey autumnal light dims over the salvaged suicide and his salvager. The crowd disperses. Double decker buses trundle to and fro in Fleet Street. It begins to drizzle.

My father Gideon's birthday: born at the onset of autumn, he died with spring, like the life cycle in reverse of an ancient fertility god. I've grown accustomed to mark the passage of time by these two dates.

'Birth out of death. Death out of birth. And for all the beautiful things in life, everything ultimately gets devoured', were the last words he had written to me.

A shaft of light spears the street, touching invisible water. I can almost feel the secret River Fleet seep through the old macadam as it courses down to Ludgate, not far from where Gideon, in a twilight of a passing era, had his photo snapped in the arms of a pretty fellow student, underneath Love Lane street sign.

If an heroic epic poem told the story of modern Israel, Gideon would get a line or two. His death, however, should be re-written, for the sake of poetic impact: it was shadowy, unheroic.

But what a funeral it had been! Not at the cemetery on Mt. Herzl where the heroes of Israel are buried, yet still in Jerusalem, a city where funereal dolour is soaked into the stone. The great of the land were there in full attendance like mafiosos in a gangster film coming to make sure a former colleague was truly dead.

I did him justice at the graveside. Dutifully recited the Kaddish then cutting short a congress of eager obituarists, gave my own impromptu oration. Magnified and sanctified in the name of the Lord, one sporadically brilliant, remorsefully flawed warrior, builder of a nation, would-be statesman, father, lover, here laid to rest on the 17th of March, 1967, Amen. At heart, a pagan to the last.

But what was that attenuated cadaver shrouded in a prayer shawl, being lowered into a freshly-dug grave? My father? His body was never conclusively identified. Was he somewhere else? Free at last, having a good laugh?

My sister Tali stood arm linked through our mother's. Eyes lowered, having taken count of who was here and who absent. Mouth puckered to a point. I could hear her thoughts: 'What has he left? Anything not on the list? Anything we don't know about?'

And Beth? No widow's tears under the veil but a hard glint of a newly-found persona. Ashes to ashes. Liberation from disgrace... Honour which was, at last, hers for keeps.

* * * * *

Stationer Hall in the City is beautiful. Dark timber, rows of escutcheons beneath high leaded windows, and a ringing floor. There is mellow medieval jollity about the place which, on this occasion, works for a flash purpose of public relations. The reception is to launch a book about the Jews, about the genesis of modern Israel, by a decidedly un-Jewish author, whose career has spanned several diplomatic posts around the world, including two in the Middle East. A review I read described the book as a 'seasoned diplomat's apprehension of national destinies'.

A table stands by the entrance, laden with copies of the book, hefty tomes in orange and purple, exuding gravitas.

I fumble for my invitation card.

The reception is already well under way. The sound of chit chat and laughter bounces about the space of the hall like a huge slow ball. I recognise some of the faces. There is uniformity of cheer. Hands grasping glasses or else gesticulating. A vast congress of mouths emitting and ingesting. I suddenly become aware that I am inadequately dressed. They'll think I'm an accountant or something. I concentrate on becoming invisible; I summon music to mantle me.

And then, as if from nowhere, there's this radiant woman facing me. A total stranger. I've never seen her before and yet somehow she is crucially familiar, as though she has always been there in my imagination, near yet far, ever changing yet essentially unchanged. A part of my inner landscape. And in an instant I can accept the absurd notion that all my past fallings in love were in reality with her.

She looks me straight in the eye, she's friendly. She smiles. 'How do you do it?'

Her voice too, is evocative of something I cannot immediately identify. It is a cultured, quiet voice, the kind of voice foreigners, Americans in particular, consider very English. She's slender... on a more relaxed occasion I would find words to describe her looks. Good bones! That is all I can think of for the moment. Her hands are exquisite. The diffident authority of her manner suggests a life-long awareness of her own worth. Perhaps also of the responsibilities that come with being beautiful.

'Do what?' I reply, trying to appear serene.

'Look so serene,' she laughs. 'I've had three gin and tonics to no avail. How many have you had?'

She is rocking slightly on her feet; we meet in the sway of an illusory sea.

'I've lost count,' I tell her.

She looks at me, head a little aslant. I can see the tiny pulse in her lovely neck which for all its loveliness is somewhat past youthful perfection.

'I have this trick of making myself invisible,' I say.

'I don't believe you,' she says.

'Why not?'

'Perhaps because I've no faith in improbabilities.' Her eyes are laughing. She lowers her gaze to her empty glass.

'Well, I thrive on them. Besides, I don't know a soul here. It helps.'

Her name is Imogen Dowland, she tells me. And then, 'Get me another gin and tonic, and I'll run through who's who for you complete with the pecking order.'

'You're on. Stay right here. I'll be back in a wink.'

But she isn't where I left her when I return. I see her at the far end of the hall, talking animatedly to a group of friends. As our eyes meet, she doesn't seem to recognise me. Her brow furrows for a moment when I hold up her drink. Then she smiles. She detaches herself from her friends and comes towards me.

She looks different now: focused, reflexes restored. Can a brief alcohol-free social intercourse do this? Her beauty now has hard edges; she seems altogether far less accessible. I take her in more comprehensively. Her walk is graceful. Her movements fluid. Is there something imperious, or unforgiving about her splendid head? An area of unkind light exposes silver in her auburn hair. Is she wearing contact lenses, I wonder. Her dress is a modest black and white cotton number, unassuming to the point of plainness. She might have bought it in some upmarket Oxfam shop. I know with certainty she could wear rags and still look magnificent, like the goddess Athena revealed in disguise.

At last she is facing me, hand extended to receive the gin and tonic I carried to her from across the hall. No makeup. The only adornment is a ring with a dark oval stone on her right hand. It must have taken centuries of privileged living and selective marriages to produce someone like her.

'I am sorry. I got drawn away. Some people I know, whom I haven't seen for years. Thank you so much for getting my drink,' she says. Her eyes, which are very blue and intelligent, are luminous from fatigue.

'Don't mention it. But should I keep you from your friends?'

'Oh absolutely,' she laughs, adding as an afterthought, 'Oh dear, you no longer look serene.'

'My defences got subverted. Anything can get to me now,' I admit.

'Oh dear,' she says once again and drops her gaze to her glass. There's a moment of awkward silence. I can't think of anything to say that would rekindle her interest. It is she who breaks the silence. She asks what I do. More precisely, why I'm here. I make my job seem more important than it actually is, because although I don't know her and therefore haven't the faintest idea what might impress her and what not, I cannot bear the thought of not seeing her again.

She is a lecturer in Sociology at the London School of Economics. Her diffidence, contrasting with my own lack of it, makes me blush inwardly: I've made a fool of myself. Better to disappear instantly!

Imogen Dowland has no affinity with Jews whatsoever other than general interest – they are, after all, an interesting people, are they not. She is here because her cousin is the book's publisher, and she happens to know the author with whom she had been chatting a while ago.

'I said I'd point out who was who. Are you still interested?' she asks.

'No, that's okay. Thank you all the same.'

It must take an awful lot of fair-mindedness as well as expert knowledge to make people understand why Israel was behaving in such an ugly way, she comments. And I feel that any moment she will drift away from me.

'Are you a descendant of the celebrated Elizabethan lutenist?' I ask.

'Very indirectly. Alas, I'm not musical. Though I do enjoy listening to music.'

'What a waste of valuable heritage.'

She laughs. 'Isn't it just. In my salad days, when I was student, I did make an effort.'

'Where was that?'

'Cambridge,' she answers, as though I had asked an indiscreet question.

'To think we might have met.'

Her mouth crinkles at the corner. 'I'm a little older than you seem to think,' she says.

Not far off a male voice declaims in faked American: 'You who have passed the pillars and outward from Herakles when Lucifer fell in North Carolina.'

Imogen raises an eyebrow. 'Well, when you've heard that, you've heard everything.'

'He's got it wrong. It's N. Carolina.'

'Really? What's the difference?'

'Probably nothing. But that's the way the Canto goes.'

'I don't understand Ezra Pound,' she says as if asserting a virtue.

'Neither do I. But I know about Lucifer. Where and how he fell. It wasn't in N. Carolina nor anywhere near it.'

I want to know more about this tantalisingly reticent woman who is already sneaking glances at her watch. I will say anything, do anything to delay our parting.

'Tell me,' she says.

'About Lucifer?'

'No. About you.'

* * * * *

Gideon towers over me. Behind him, the kitchen's open window. The light floods in through the blossoming passion flowers on the wire fence outside and illuminates Gideon's shoulders. A hero, a lion of a man. My father.

In one hand he holds a handkerchief stained with my tears and the blood which had flowed from my nose. His other hand rests on my head. I feel the comforting warm weight of it. 'I named you after a great Jew. Not a bible prophet, not a mere king, nor a tribal hero of the sword. A philosopher. A man of wisdom, culture, and temperance,' Gideon says. 'He lived in Alexandria a long, long time ago, when Rome was mighty. He might have changed the world. Rome might have survived because of him. And we would've been a part of it. Forever!' He pauses magisterially. The grandeur of that lost opportunity seems to move him. 'A well-ordered world, Philo. No ghettos, no persecution. No pogroms... No Jews going to slaughter like sheep,' he says gravely. The war and the terrible things that happened to Jews in Europe are vivid in his mind.

'Would we still be here?' I ask, because my faith falters, because I'd been thumped on the nose by the class bully who had taunted me about my name. Because for once the scheme of things Gideon expects me to apprehend, is too much for my childish grasp. Gideon laughs, 'Yes. Without doubt. Nothing and nobody can destroy us *Ivrim*. We'd still be here all right, as we shall be when everybody else is gone.'

Gideon uses the term *Ivrim* to distinguish us, who live here, in *Eretz* Israel, who when threatened by the German Nazis from Syria to the north and Egypt to south, stood our ground and prepared for battle, from Jews of the Diaspora about whom he has ambivalent feelings. There is missionary fervour in his eyes, for my sake. For

Mother's sake too, because she doesn't take easily to ideals. Also for Tali's sake, although Tali is too little to understand anything.

Then, remembering what had began all this, Gideon continues in a matter of fact voice, 'I could have called you Yehuda, Moshe, Chaim, anything. Would you have liked that better?' Tears well up in my eyes again. I look down, I say nothing. 'Names like that come a penny a dozen. One day you'll be proud of your name, believe me. All worthwhile things in life come with a bit of suffering.' 'Give me that handkerchief, Gideon,' Mother says. He hands it to her without as much as a look.

'And I've taken the family name of Jerusalem. So that we may always remember who we are and where we come from. A dignified meaningful name, Philo. Wear it with pride.' 'We live in Haifa,' I foolishly protest. 'Makes no difference, Philo. Jerusalem is our soul, symbol of our being, what we are, have been, shall be. Always...'

Imogen Dowland repeats my name. 'There's a lot to live up to with a name like yours. Have you been able to?'

We are sitting in this Italian restaurant in the Strand. She is no longer impatient to go. Premises have been established between us. She is older than me. And successful. And well-connected. And married although separated from her husband who is an anthropologist and broadcaster. There's a son who is at Oxford and a daughter at home who aspires to be an actress. Mrs Dowland is kind. She's formed the impression that I need to be listened to. But I can sense that her own unhappiness makes her receptive to confessions.

'Philo Jerusalem,' she says again. 'It sounds medieval, not a bit Israeli. Israel,' she continues after a pause, 'makes me think of endless wars. And Palestinian refugees, and fanaticism... And toughness which I've never admired. When did he die, your father?'

'1967.'

'Before or after the Six Days War?'

'Before. On the Ides of March.'

'It must have been a terrible year for you,' she says flatly, intimating a conversation stopper.

We've only started on the coffee. I won't give up yet.

* * * * *

14

A camel lies dead at the main cross-roads in Ya'bad. Its carcass, already bloated and buzzing with flies, blocks the traffic of military vehicles through the village. No one in the battalion knows who killed the camel, or why. Only that it seemed to have happened sometime after the fighting had come to an end. When the back-up units arrived and the looting began.

Radios are playing the hit of the day: Jerusalem the Golden, a song which moves soldiers to tears. The song was actually written way before the war. Now that the unbelievable has happened and Jerusalem is ours, it has become a hit and the songwriter is being hailed as a prophetess. Like Deborah of the bible.

Ya'bad is deserted. Its peasants, tradesmen, officials, school teachers all fled before the invading army. Us. There had been three frightened horses in the police station stables. A sergeant from Brigade Headquarters wanted to shoot them, but on the day a man from a kibbutz across the border, not far from the site of ancient Armageddon, arrived with a lorry and carted them off.

Only this camel is left. And while its diminishing presence is ravaged by death and fought over by clouds of scavengers, the head is strangely clean, composed in a kind of stoic acceptance, as though the animal had registered a last dignified protest against its pointless killing. The eyes are open and moist. Gideon once told me of an Arab saying: when camels understand they are about to be slaughtered, they weep like humans.

Two soldiers on sanitation duty arrive. They douse the camel with petrol and set it alight. Smoke creeps through the alleys. The stench is unbearable. It brings the medical officer to the scene. He stands there, hand clapped across his mouth, incredulous that anyone could be so idiotic to have done that. Then an armoured half-track is summoned. It tows the smouldering corpse out of the village, to the hillside where for the remaining days of our stay in Ya'bad the site is marked by congregations of carrion crows and buzzards.

Fortunately, my company is not billeted in the village but camped in the olive grove on the facing hill. In its fourth day, the war is virtually won. Our troops are sitting on the bank of the Suez Canal. Israeli flags fly over the Old City of Jerusalem. The West Bank is occupied. Cowed and confused, its people try to comprehend the alien energy of the occupier. Only the Golan Heights remain to be dealt with.

Our Brigade, made up of veteran armour and infantry units, is now fragmented. The main part of it has gone north to join a task force

15

assembled somewhere at the foot of the Golan Heights. Left here is one battalion, and not the best one at that. We sit around on the hills, doing what soldiers do to keep up a familiar routine. We watch the stream of vehicles and cars 'commandeered' from the conquered, whiz past in the narrow valley below. The men are beginning to grumble. They are not youngsters; they have families, farms, shops. Fighting when you have to is one thing. Sitting on a bloody hill in the middle of nowhere, doing bugger all, is another.

This morning I saw one of my men, an ophthalmic technician from Afula, at his morning prayers. The talith flapped about him. A gentle, self-effacing man, the tefilin on his forehead and arm made him look fierce. Rocking back and forth, he was reciting as he has been doing ever since we crossed the border:

'Hear, O Israel, ye approach this day unto battle against your enemies: let not your hearts faint, fear not, and do not tremble, neither be ye terrified because of them; for the Lord your God is he that goeth with you to fight for you against your enemies...'

A battle which raged far away from us. An enemy he never saw, never tried to understand. I called Avner, my platoon sergeant. I said to him: 'Av, in ten minutes I want the whole platoon on parade. In their underwear. With all their belongings spread on the ground in front of each man. Every scrap. Understand?'

He looked at me, stupefied.

'You and I and the corporals are going to inspect. Anything that shouldn't be there will be confiscated. After that, if any man takes as much as a button from here, there'll be a proper sentencing by the CO.'

He stared at me. 'Are you crazy? What d'you think they are, fresh meat recruits you can push around?'

'Ten minutes, Avner.'

'Like hell,' he retorted.

Nevertheless, he did as he was told. Trying not to sound pompous, I gave the men a short talk about the purity of arms, about looting. Then we carried out the search. In stony silence. Among the men were two teachers, a social worker, an engineer. We found not a thing. No one said a word. Afterwards Avner came to my tent. 'Satisfied?' he sneers.

'I did it for the good of us all,' I reply.

'And what if someone takes a little souvenir, when you see officers, all sorts of jobnicks from non-combat units drive off with television sets and fridges?'

'Precisely for that reason.'

He shakes his head and sighs. 'Philo, these fellows have been with you in *miluim* year in year out for nearly ten years. How can you treat them like that?'

'Don't preach to me, Av. I know what I'm doing.'

As he turns to go, he gives me one of those lugubrious gazes of his which make him resemble a horse. 'You've got a new nickname. "Jerusalem the Golden". That's what the boys are calling you. I hope it makes you feel real good.'

It doesn't. As a matter of fact, I feel lousy, not least because I've been constipated since we crossed the border. And now, in the blazing heat, I'm called for a briefing at Command Headquarters in the village. I walk down the rocky slope into the valley, past the dead camel whose ribs are beginning to gleam through the darkening cadaver, and up towards Ya'bad. I remember how easily I might have been killed already on the second day of the war, without having fired a shot. Stupidly. Wastefully. And an Army official would have notified my wife Mimi. And I would have been buried steeped in honour, among the heroes who fell. Perhaps side by side with my friend Dedi, an officer in the Paratroopers, who was shot to bits outside the Lions Gate during the assault on the Old City.

At the briefing an Intelligence officer from Central Command warns us against booby traps, against being shot at by seemingly harmless Arab civilians. 'Take no chances', he tells us, 'touch nothing. Keep your eyes skinned. Be alert.'

Our own battalion commander, an engineer from Haifa, enjoins us to uphold discipline. It is imperative to avoid looting so as not to tarnish our army's reputation. My mind is on another matter. I remember a villa at the far side of the village, set in grounds crowded with vines. No Arab would think of booby trapping a lavatory. I can see nothing reprehensible to tarnish the army's good reputation if I took uninvited some Ya'bad hospitality. In fact, I look on it as a *droît de seigneur* of a sort, modest and totally harmless.

The quiet dignity presented by the villa's façade is dispelled the moment I step in. A broken chair lists over in the hall. A line of discarded items pours out of the bedroom like torn entrails. The large bed stands lop-sided, one of its legs missing. Those pieces of furniture that have been left behind are mindlessly ravaged. On a dresser in the living room a colour family snapshot has been overlooked by the raiders. It shows an old man wearing a kefiya sitting on a chair, holding a stick. Beside him a matronly woman, and around and behind them, young people, children.

I harden myself to the violated privacy of this home. I concentrate on my purpose. There is a commodious bathroom. But I find no lavatory. Until I reach the back of the house, and there it is, outside. A squat hole lined with bathroom tiles, and two brass handles screwed to the walls on either side.

Positioning myself over this thing, I think angrily, 'Damn them! No wonder they can't fight when they don't even know the meaning of proper, civilised shit houses!' I hear a thin laughter, Gideon's laughter; he who had ridden Israel's cloud of glory, and died on a spring night on the magical island Møn, Denmark. I laugh. Then I weep. But at last I find release.

The war is over. The country is drunk with euphoria. Listening to commentaries on the radio, we hear how the whole world admires Israel. David has knocked out Goliath in the first round, for the whole count. Miss Jacqueline Du Pré the most gifted and passionate of cellists, is giving concerts round the country with her pianist husband Daniel Barenboim. Nasser is finished. Do the bewildered Arabs of Jerusalem understand who is David and who Goliath? Or where they fit in that showdown?

Rumours circulate: we are to be demobbed; we are to be transferred to Jerusalem. A letter arrives, from Mimi. She is well, and as always, very busy – so many new exciting things to do, so much to see. Our three years old son Jacob is fine, and missing me. Mimi is taking him to her mother in Haifa, because she herself is too busy. My mother Beth sends greetings, they had lunch together, she and Mimi, that day.

Busy busy busy...

So much to see. So much to do. I read her deceit between the lines, and I know, without regret, without feelings, that our marriage is dead, and that she too knows it.

Sitting on the hill on top of my packed gear, while Avner musters the platoon towards the waiting lorries, I suddenly, just like that, for no obvious reason, remember Alison Leeming, met surprisingly in Alaska Café, Jerusalem, two weeks before the war. The last person on earth I'd have expected to see in Israel. But there she was, not quite so blonde and a little stouter, about to marry a Tel Aviv dentist called Aharon Feingold whom she had met three months before in Swiss Cottage. She got a job with Israel Radio, broadcasting in English. They loved her accent, she laughed: *Towery city and branchy between towers. Cuckoo-echoing, bell-swarméd, lark-charméd, rook-racked, river rounded...*

Alison, Alison, O the mind, mind has mountains... You make me long for England too unbearably.

* * * * *

'I must go,' says Imogen.
'I've talked too much.'
'Oh no, absolutely not.'
'Will I see you again?'
She hesitates. 'Yes, why don't we meet sometime.'
'When?'
'Not before too long,' she says smiling.
My first taste of her English opacity, which can simultaneously raise and dash hopes.

2

Jacob my son. Sometimes, like now, I feel you in me; bone of my bone and blood of my blood. An ache in a severed limb...

I hear you sneer: 'too late for all this crap. Where were you all those years of my growing up, when I needed you?'

I stretch my arms out to you again. Blame me for anything you like, but be fair. Don't turn your back on me with that hard expression on your face. Listen to me! You were not "an accident"; wherever did you get such a notion? No. I wanted you more than I realised at the time. And I need you. We need each other so that we can make sense of our lives.

Jacob, I did not desert you. I had to go. There was no other way. The restlessness I inherited from my father is irresistible and contagious. That's his legacy from which I sought to protect you. And dreams, Jacob. Not good dreams. Your mother will tell you – even though she never understood – that I couldn't live in Gideon's shadow. That's why, she believes, I ran away. Away from responsibility, away from you. There's a lot more to it than that, believe me. One day I shall explain.

Simple Mimi. And good, for all her deceit. How could she understand, being what she is? And you, Jacob, who accepts and demands without guilt and without calculation. Your inner voice is monophonic, like a hunter's horn. Excluding half-said things and hidden implications: right, wrong, yours, mine. Your name should have been Esau – pure, brave, uncomplicated Esau. Not Jacob, who was full of contradictions, forever harried by God, by responsibilities, wives, and, when he laid his head to rest on a stone for a pillow, by his own dreams.

Even though you returned from Lebanon on a tank, not a hero but confused, betrayed, your mind fuddled with hashish, and aged beyond your years, do not yield to bitterness. Rather, set your anger to purpose. Then forgive. Anything else is futile.

Do I sound fatuous? Listen to me, Jacob. Don't ever quit Israel no matter what. You will never strike root anywhere else. Exile will destroy you. Your toughness is of a different nature. Exile is Gideon's speciality. And mine. Mine through temperament. His through pride. When you understand this I know we shall be father and son again.

From your mother I hear that you want to become a computer engineer and leave Israel. Become an engineer with my blessings, and be a good one. Every country needs computers and engineers to serve them. Travel the world, work in different countries if you like. But return home. This is my advice, and warning. I know, whether you believe me or not.

What shall I bequeath to you? I've drawn up a will. Left all I own to Greenpeace. Let them, with my tiny contribution, try to save this spent and ravaged world. What use to you is one unexceptional flat in Muswell Hill in an unexceptional Edwardian terrace, an assortment of utility furniture, and books? I look at dwellings people build to house their pretensions, and the baggage they accumulate and I say to myself: vanities, all is vanity. Better travel light. Better be small, so as to apprehend vastness.

What magic can this now tired, over-crowded and dirty city, conjure up for you?

To you, Jacob, I leave a story – at once a map and a compass. Use it well with my blessings…

This, I hasten to say, is an imaginary letter which I shall never write, let alone send.

I'm lying in bed feeling dreadful and increasingly sorry for myself. My head is beating like a gong; I can't listen to the radio because it hurts so much. The sheets are damp with my perspiration. I've heard at work there's a new flu bug in town that makes *Moloch ha'moives* (the ever-present Angel of Death of the Jews) look like an amateur part-timer. Any moment I shall become delirious…

I stand here, in an hour of uncertain light, feeling shaky. Drizzle curls around the huge Church of St. James – my local, so to speak. The street where I live heaves up a steep slope like a dark shiny slug. Veiled in greyness, the City in the distance might be confused with the barrier of cloud. I flap metaphorical wings like a fat park goose atavistically remembering migration time. Let people stare. Let a watchful copper place a hand on my shoulder and say, 'move along now, mate.'

I shall rise… rise…

Gideon speaks to me: 'Like a soufflé. Clap, clap, clap. What a performance! Just look at you, soaked to the skin. A tramp, an alley cat!'

'Where did you come from?'

'Your flu-infested fantasy. Didn't you summon me?'

'Jesus! I must be dead!'

'Jesus indeed! Don't panic. You've come through much much worse before, remember?'

'No, as a matter of fact I don't. That was a long time ago anyway, in another country. Why have you come?'

'To help you, of course. You need that unbecoming moisture of self-indulgence drained out of you, as always. Confidence my boy. Positive thinking, that's what is called for right now. I'm going to give you a flying lesson!'

'What?'

'Do as I tell you. It's piece of cake! Get into St Jim's. Use the side entrance. The main one's locked.'

'One of us is crazy, Abba!'

'Tell me that an hour from now. Until then, trust me. Don't you know that allegorically speaking the church is a ship? An airship, let's say. You, son, are going to pilot it above London. No one, Jew or gentile, has ever performed such a feat. You'll be a hero. But hurry, we must dock safely in time for the Sunday service. Up you go, mind your step. Right up to the belfry. Now then, the truth. Have you ever seen such a control room?'

'Abba, I can't fly. All these switches, levers, dials and screens scare the shit out of me.'

'Don't talk like this and don't worry, I'm with you. Stand by the helm wheel facing the navigation screen. There. Now pull the red switch down.'

'Abba. The noise, the vibrations. It's all falling apart!'

'Nonsense. Concentrate on the take off. Release the anchor lever on your right. More power, more, I say. There! Steady as she goes. Here comes British Telecom's Radio Tower! Watch the altitude gauge, we don't want to knock this landmark down, do we? How about some music? Track selection on your left below the booster. The stereo system on this baby will blow your mind.'

'Bach's *Toccata and Fugue in D Minor*, the great Dorian, played by the incomparable Helmut Walcha. Full volume!'

'I couldn't have chosen better. Sail through the sky, above the cloud. Who do you think is looking up in awe, wondering what in hell is this? Your beautiful Imogen. Peering through her bedroom window, she hears your great Hallelujah music. And in a voice like the Queen talking to her corgies, murmurs, "My goodness, what can this be! Is it possible I've already had one too many at this time of day?"

'The Chief Rabbi, the whole of Golders Green and Hendon are at a standstill. Gazing up, incredulous. Leaning on his hoe among his over-ripe roses, Mr Fink rubs his chins. "Well, I never!" says he, "Miracles again. As it was in the beginning is now and ever shall be, world without end. Gentile and Jew, rejoice."

'Bank gently to the east, Philo. Bring her back now, to a soft majestic landing. Let the tall spire of St Jim's once again inform lost motorists where they are. Well done, son, well done. So, how does it feel?'

'Abba, are you really dead? Are you not perhaps living it up somewhere? Costa Rica? Liechtenstein? A secluded farm in Jämtland? Tell me how you died. I'll never have peace until I know.'

'No! I die my way, you die yours. Good bye.'

'Don't go! Don't leave me here! This thing is getting into a spin. I'm crashing!'

* * * * *

The telephone ringing wakes me up not a moment too soon. I'm shaking all over. The room is in semi-darkness. Nothing seems real, except Moon, bless him, who looks at me in anxiety from the foot of the bed.

I reach for the telephone. It takes me a few seconds to recognise Imogen's voice.

'Philo, would you like to come over for tea if you aren't doing anything?... Philo? Are you all right?'

'I feel terrible. Got the ague. Maybe the Black Death. Maybe the dibbuk's got into me."

'Is that all?' she laughs. 'Shall I come over?'

'And risk contagion?'

'I'll be over as soon as I can. In a couple of hours probably,' says Imogen, and hangs up.

3

Mount Carmel, Haifa

The war broke out two days after Gideon's twenty fifth birthday. I don't remember it, I was only two years old at the time. However, with retrospective conceit of the imagination I can recall the sombre mood of the music that filled the spaces between news bulletins on the wireless. Two years later, in August 1941, Gideon joins the British Army, along with a group of his friends. Among them is David Ornovsky. They had been to school together, he and David, and my mother Beth. Then again together in the Labour Youth Movement.

Most of the young men are keen to join up because everyone – especially Gideon and David – recognises the importance of gaining military experience for the inevitable struggle with the Arabs, perhaps with the British too. But for the time being, Hitler and his Nazis make all other considerations irrelevant.

Like so many things about Gideon, his bonds with people are rife with contradictions. Take his friendship with David for instance, which is to last – at least as far as David is concerned – to the end of Gideon's life.

Whereas Gideon is mercurial, David is steady. Predictable to the point of being boring, Gideon would often say. David's loyalty – a value he considers concomitant with honour – is to people. He believes in Ben Gurion; he would follow him even unto death. Gideon's loyalty is to values, historical concepts, measures of beauty and excellence. To ideas. But ideas change, don't they? Or is it he who keeps changing? After all, ideas do not respond to you, they are not hurt, they don't shrivel before you, or fight back. Is he, therefore, disloyal? Must that be the final judgement?

Gideon admires Ben Gurion for his qualities of leadership, for his political skill. Above all, for his vision. Yet he mistrusts him: BG is ruthless, manipulative, more Machiavellian than is necessary. Now, BG's rival Tabenkin, on the other hand, has a loftier mind and a purer soul. But Tabenkin is ineffective as a leader, and altogether too vain. These early insights Gideon is to claim many years later, in his memoirs, in the grudging implacability of middle aged disillusionment.

David Ornovsky, and my mother, hanker after a strong leadership. It's what the *Yishuv* needs, they assert. Gideon argues that a democratic society does not need outstanding leaders; what it needs are sound institutions and good laws.

'You are your own worst enemy,' Mother tells him, because Gideon, in his darker moods can be hurtfully distant with people who care for him, with friends, chiefly with us. By the same logic, however, he is also his own best friend, because no one can resist his brilliance, his charm, his deliberate effusion of warmth, and his wit which goes right to the core of things and makes you laugh. Yet it is to placid people who tend to bring out the worse in him, that he is drawn. And they in turn are drawn to him, like moths to fire. Like my mother Beth. Like David Ornovsky. To be scorched.

In our country there is no aristocracy. Our society – that part of it which is the driving force of the Zionist enterprise at any rate – is socialist, egalitarian, humanist. So we are taught from an early age. But it seems that even egalitarian socialist humanists crave for well-born families and strive for status.

Gideon's family is one of the oldest and most respected in the land. Arriving in Palestine from Lithuania early in the 19th century, they pioneered the Yishuv and prospered. They are the 'Buddenbrooks' of Jewish Palestine. Industrious, successful, stiff to their collars with civic probity, they make a virtue of being frugal. Mother's by contrast, is expansive, chaotic, and clannish. Her maternal grandfather was a hernia corsets maker from Odessa. David Ornovsky, who reveres Gideon's family, never talks about his own, arrived penniless and devoid of useful skills from some Polish *shtetle*.

That otherwise intelligent men and women can make such absurd fuss over family status, says Gideon sarcastically, reveals the inherent vulgarity of Jews. Only statehood might cure them of that. Jews are humanity magnified: the lofty and the ridiculous, exaggerated to caricature proportions. That, more than anything else is probably the underlying cause of anti-Semitism, he argues. In her oblique way, Mother is critical of Gideon for being indifferent to his relatives. On holidays, as in times of bereavement and of celebration, it is she who nourishes family ties.

Once, after he had already become a world figure and steeped in Classical Greek, Ben Gurion compared Gideon to the Athenian Alcibiades: outstanding but flawed. He had said the same of Moshe Dayan, who was actually flattered.

I know all this in retrospect, of course, from Gideon's papers. I go back now to August 14, 1941.

The party to celebrate Gideon's going off to the war with three of his friends, including David, who has just changed his family name to Oren which is the Hebrew for pine tree, coincides with the birth of my sister Tali. Our two-room flat in Sea Way, Mount Carmel, Haifa, is full of guests, all friends, neighbours. The furniture is pushed to one side. A table, laden with cakes, soft drinks, bottles of wine, stands against the wall. Mother is resting with Tali in the bedroom. Our landlady, Mrs Herman, a formidably didactic pillar of the community, and herself a mother of three whose youngest, Danny — one year older than me — is my playmate, is in charge, having provided the food.

Danny and I are under the table where, hidden by the long hem of the table cloth, we play at guessing which legs belong to whom. We take turns at peeking to verify our guesses. Since Danny is precocious in arithmetic, he keeps the score. A pale boy with beady eyes behind glasses, he has a strawberry birthmark on his cheek, which turns bright red when he is angry. He is angry now, because my score runs higher. I'm good on fat, hairy legs. And Danny is a poor loser. Also, he grudges me the fact that it is my father, not his, who is going to be a soldier and fight Hitler, even though Arie Herman is a senior member of Hagana, and owns a *jift*, a double-barrelled shot gun. But I am too disappointed over Tali to gloat over this transient ascendancy: I wanted a baby brother, not a sister. Sisters, says Danny with authority, are noisy and altogether boring. He ought to know since he has two. A further proof of their inferiority is that they can't pee in a trajectory standing up, as we do.

Talk and laughter fill the room, interspersed with loud 'Lehayim!'. Various bits of information are volunteered about Camp Sarafend in the south, where the men are to begin their basic training in two days' time. 'It is our duty to excel in everything we are taught,' I hear David Oren proclaim. 'For the sake of the *Yishuv's* good name. Let no British sergeant say "the Palestinian Jews are no damn good".'

'No one but an incorrigible anti-Semite would dare say such a thing. I mean, look, none of us is running away. If the Nazis came here they'll not find frightened refugees. They'll find men and women, old and young, determined to defend themselves with sticks and rocks if need be, to the last drop of blood. That's what they'll find. This is our home. Here is where we make our stand. Like Masada. Only the

British won't give us guns,' says Arie Herman with charged gravity.

'All the goyim are anti-Semitic, it's as clear as daylight. But who cares?' a voice chimes in, followed by laughter.

'Right now I care only about two things. Beth, and little Tali. A daughter to Gideon, a sister to Philo. What's the matter with you people? Have you forgotten? A lovely healthy baby has just been born!' Thus Nehama Herman in her stentorian contralto.

'Who's forgetting? Mazal Tov, Mazal Tov. May there be many more,' cries David.

Cheering, clapping.

The table cloth is lifted. Gideon's face grins at me, upside down. 'Hey, little squirrel, what are you doing hiding down there, leaving me all alone here? C'mon out and help your Old Man.' He grabs me by the arm, pulls me out, and hoists me up onto his shoulders.

Often, on Saturdays, Gideon would take me out on walks in the hills. Perched on his shoulders, I would feel I was riding a large, strong half-man, half-horse creature, wise and omniscient and dependable, like the centaur in the stories he tells me.

'Look after your sister Tali, and help your mother while I'm away. You are the man of the house now.' Gideon holds me by the shoulders as he looks into my eyes. Is there sadness in his gaze, for leaving us? Or is it that already he is far away, seeing things I cannot see?

In the next room Mother is nursing Tali, a wrinkled pink little animal with a gaping, screaming mouth and tiny grasping hands. Gideon's suitcase stands in the hall. That morning he had gone to Carmel Centre to have a haircut, cropped short as British army regulations require. He starts humming a tune we have both picked up from the radio. The easily remembered melody is our secret code. There is a boy down the road who is an orphan. We kids feel sorry for him, as though he were a cripple. I think of my father going away to an undefined thing called "War" where he might die. I close my eyes so that my tears won't show. I know I am not supposed to cry.

Mother comes in holding Tali, rocking rhythmically from side to side. Gideon takes Tali from her. He cradles her in his arms, murmurs to her, takes her hand in his mouth and kisses her head. Then he lowers her for me to kiss. Mother wipes her eyes. I crowd in to join them in a close family tableau.

'Take care now. Let me know if there's anything you need.'

'I won't need anything,' says Gideon.

'You can never tell. Write soon, anyway,' she says. He laughs.

'You'd think I was going to the other side of the world. I'll be back on leave before you know it. And the war will soon be over. Hitler can't last, now that he has taken on Russia. We'll have him beat before the year's out.'

'Please God,' says mother.

Outside a car is honking. 'Must go now,' says Gideon. He gives us one last hug, picks up his suitcase, and is gone.

* * * * *

If you stand on the wild hill not far from our house you see the blue sweep of Haifa Bay. Deep and wide and lined with a thick strip of powdery white sand, the bay curves horseshoe-like to the foothills of the Carmel range. In the distance, to the north, is Acre with her walls and white minarets. I love the view from our hill. It evokes a sense of adventure, of a great unknown, yet with something familiar standing guard over this great escape.

The hills are thick with vegetation – oaks, carob trees, acorn bushes, thorny shrubs, and perennial flowers with pale velvety stalk and deep red petals which we call 'Blood of the Maccabees'. But everywhere among this ever-busy growth, peep the rain-washed, bone-white time-sculpted rocks that are the unremitting heart of the hills.

Overhead buzzards soar. They edge close to the sea then bank over landward, screaming. Sometimes the sea wind is so high that facing it with your arms spread out you can almost lean against it.

Our house, No. 67, is more or less half way between Carmel Centre, where the shops and bus terminus are, and down the hill towards the sea, to Shoshanat Hacarmel (Rose of Carmel) where the British Army base of the airborne troops we call 'anemones' on account of the red berets they wear, is situated.

Surrounded by a large untidy yard, rutted from the feet of running children, are two twin white boxy houses from whose walls the paint is partially flaking off. One belongs to Arie and Nehama, the other to Arie's brother Yossef, and his wife Zena, who is a music teacher. Zena and Yossef have four children, each one a *wunderkind*, so she keeps reminding everyone. Dana, aged fifteen, gave her second public piano recital last year at the Technion auditorium in Hadar Hacarmel. Oded, at twelve, is Haifa's junior chess champion. Tamar, his twin sister, would be an outstanding recorder player, if only she would concentrate more on her work. But Nahum, Zena's favourite, is

28

destined to lead men and change the world, she says clasping her hands together. See how all the children look up to him, calling him Tarzan, no less!

Earlier in the year on his Bar Mitzva, Tarzan, to demonstrate his arboreal virtuosity, attempted a spectacular leap from one branch to another on the tall pine tree in our yard. He lost his grip, plummeted down and hit his head on a stone. So much blood on his white Bar Mitzva shirt, and what with all us kids looking on, and not as much as a groan out of his mouth... He needed thirteen stitches in his head, one for each year of his life.

His cousin Danny keeps pigeons in a dovecote on the roof. On that occasion, he let loose the lot, as they do at the Olympic Games.

Tarzan, with his new Kodak box camera, takes a snapshot of Mother, Tali and me in the yard, to send to Gideon. We pose. Mother holding Tali to the camera, I, standing beside her with my wooden scooter, a gift from Uncle Hai. But before the pictures are developed Gideon arrives on a leave. He is very lean. His hair is cropped shorter than ever. He is all luminous eyes, taut sun-baked skin, and dazzling teeth, like Zena Herman's piano, and charged with energy. There are Lieutenant's pips on the shoulders of his uniform.

A short leave, he explains, on finishing Officers Cadets Training course, and before being detailed to the Eighth Army. Soon he will be transferred to a destination he cannot reveal: military secret.

That night my sleep is interrupted frequently. A light burns in my parents' room, which is separated by a glass-panelled door from the one where Tali and I sleep. I hear a continuously repeated sequence of whispers, stifled laughter, moans. Silence. Then a sortie to the bathroom. The lavatory flushes. I fall asleep soon after the count of eight. In the morning Gideon is gone.

In summer our windows are wide open. Sea breeze carries in the fragrance of pine trees and honeysuckle from the fence, where tiny blue nectar-drinking sun birds hum at the blossoms. Music fills the evening air; we are a musical neighbourhood. Zena Herman pounds away at Beethoven's Diabelli Variations in preparation for a recital she will never give. Her pupils plod up and down endless scales, major, then minor. On the balcony, wearing pyjama tops, sits Yossef Herman, reading *Davar*, the newspaper of the Labour Party of which he is member. Along Sea Way, British jeeps come and go, reminding all that we are a country at war. Having recently heard on the radio Cesar Frank's sonata for violin and piano transcribed for the cello, I dream of becoming a prodigy.

Gideon's letters arrive at irregular intervals. We recognise the envelopes, as does the postman who always asks what news Mr Jerusalem sends from the front. On letter days, Mother reads out to us select parts, if we are good, and never before we have finished our supper without leaving a crumb in our plates.

Gideon writes about army life, of places he has been to and things he had seen. Of El Alamein, where he fought. Sometimes Mother has difficulties making out what he says because of lines cut out by the military censor. So she improvises. They are not sad, his letters. Reflective, perhaps but far from unhappy. He writes that he longs to be home, with us, for the dreadful war to finish. But he does not sound lonely, nor do his accounts of the war seem all that dreadful either.

There is a dog in his unit, belonging to one of the Jewish officers. The dog, a pointer, is called Abrasha. It goes with the troops wherever they go, sharing their food, standing guard by the vehicles at night. I write letters. I make drawings, for Gideon, and for Abrasha. I stick a crayon in Tali's podgy fist and guide her hand across the page. A drawing and a few words from her, for the dog too. When will we see him? 'Who knows?' Says Mother with a sigh, 'Thank God he is healthy and well. He loves you both very much, and misses you.'

Because Gideon is away indefinitely our lives seem bracketed in a kind of aoristic limbo where things happen haphazardly, without an ordered sequence. Tali is growing; one day she stands up and walks. Another day she begins to talk. She soon learns the devastating effect of her penetrating voice. Not a cry baby, she's a scream baby. Were it not for the war, says Mrs Herman, she would have considered turning us out, because of the noise Tali makes at all times of the day and night. We write Gideon exaggerated accounts of our clashes with Mrs Herman.

Forbidding though she looks, Mrs Herman is in fact a good, warm-hearted woman. Never would she shrink from responsibility, certainly not at times when people should stand together and help each other. If Mother needs a baby-sitter when she goes out, Nehama or her eldest daughter can always be counted on to step in. A pullover Danny has grown out of is immediately passed down to me. Discreetly but firmly, Nehama Herman governs our lives, disciplines us, makes sure our larder is full, our windows blacked out according to regulations, and rebukes us whenever we incur her disapproval.

Mother is acquiescent rather than grateful. She never rebels, but she does mount stubborn resistance against one of Nehamah's standing orders.

When the air raid siren sounds the neighbours hurry to the bomb shelter, a deep roomy cave at the side of the hill, which has been fitted with beds, benches, blankets and kerosene lamps. All go except us. No sooner is the siren wail heard than Mother puts blankets in the empty bath tub, and settles Tali and me in it. Someone had told her that the bathroom was the strongest part of the building. She herself sits in the armchair in the bedroom to read, until the all clear is given.

'Beth, you're being irresponsible, and anti-social. Think of the children, if you don't care about yourself,' Nehama Herman admonishes.

Mother smiles but says nothing. Tali and I know she hates caves and dark places. She told us once she'd sooner die than go in that cave, with all the neighbours.

When Mrs Herman is in her admonishing mode her cheeks swell and she makes a noise like a simmering kettle.

Autumn creeps upon us surreptitiously. Out on the hills crocuses are pushing their heads from among the damp rocks. We celebrate the New Year and the Holy Days with Mother's sister Vic, her Husband Hai and our two cousins Orna and Daphna, who live in Carmel Centre. Their home is always full of good food, and noise. Although we are not religious, we go with them to their synagogue.

Then all at once my big moment arrives: my first day at school. Dressed in the *Reali's* uniform – grey shorts, grey shirt, and a navy blue pullover, I wait for the terrifying moment. The triangular school badge, sewn onto the left breast pocket of my shirt, carries the school motto: 'Comport yourself in modesty'. 'That is just about the best rule you can follow, throughout your life,' says Mr Herman as he looks at me approvingly.

My new school satchel, full of books, pencils, a rubber, ruler and my lunch packed in a tin box as prescribed by the school, is strapped to my back. I am taken to school in Carmel Centre. Not by Mother.

The day before, a letter arrived from Gideon. He is in Italy. He has been wounded in a motorcycle accident. Just a short stay in hospital, nothing to worry about. Mother knows that our father is accident prone and anyway given to outrageous understatement where his personal well-being is concerned. She takes the bus to down town in order to get more details from the British Army official in charge of liasing with families of troops abroad. My initiation to school is therefore delegated to Tarzan, a celebrated personage in a senior class, who, hand on my shoulder, leads me to Class A. I am seated at a desk next to a sullen girl called Ada Barkai. She doesn't care a jot that my father is a wounded hero. Ada expresses her instant dislike of me by bursting into tears, my first ever encounter with gratuitous animosity. I am confused. I cry a little too. So do a number of other kids.

I already know many of the children from Zippora's Kindergarten which so many of us on Mount Carmel attended. But here, on the first day at Class A of the prestigious Haifa *Reali* School, we are all strangers to each other. Hierarchy of a sort evolves within a week, and I discover painfully that I lack both academic precocity and personal charisma. In no time at all I float downwards to near the bottom of the class.

One afternoon in the days running up to Passover, while Danny and I are taking turns careering down our road on my scooter, I see a man coming down towards our house. He is dressed like, and walks like, a stranger. Or maybe it is his tatty suitcase and the hat he is wearing that makes him appear so. We are growing used to seeing refugees from Europe. In fact, one of them whom we called Idoctor (a corruption of Herr Doctor) lives close by in a converted wooden removal container on the fringe of a vacant plot. Rumour has it that in his native Germany, Idoctor had been someone important, a professor. Now he does carpentry and odd jobs. He is kind. Everybody likes him. His sole companion is a fierce mongrel which he ties at night to one of the blocks that supports his makeshift home. Idoctor communicates with gestures. He never utters a word. Not because he is dumb but because, Mr Herman explains, being a scholar and "philosopher" Idoctor lost faith in words after what Germany did to the Jews.

As I see this man striding down the road towards us it occurs to me that he might be a refugee, like Idoctor, only much younger. Now he sees me, stops in his tracks, puts the suitcase down, and straightens to his full height. Hands on hip, he looks at me, smiling. It's Gideon.

I drop the scooter and run to him. I am bigger and heavier now. But Gideon catches me on the hop, swings me high above his head and holds me there as though I was no heavier than a pup. 'Philo,' he says, 'how you've changed. And grown. Have I been away that long?' Then he sees Tali standing at the roadside, sucking on the hem of her dress. He stretches his arms to her. Tali turns away, she begins to bawl.

Even before he reaches our door to take Mother in his arms, the whole neighbourhood already knows that Gideon Jerusalem has come back home from the War. By evening delegations arrive to look him over, inquire after his health, and, of course, ask questions, mostly about the situation of Jews in Europe. I sit with Danny in the other room and watch him open and shut the Sicilian clasp knife Gideon has brought me as a present. Tali is poking fingers into the hidden parts of a large Italian doll whose china blue eyes roll when you tilt her, emitting a soft, babyish moan from a device lodged in the stomach. She named her preposterous doll 'Boutzik' and wouldn't explain why. This kind of quirky taste was to stay with my sister Tali into adulthood.

'I must get out of these dreadful clothes,' says Gideon at last. 'I feel and look like a prisoner on furlough.'

'Oh they are not too bad,' says Mother, smoothing the brim of the hat.

Mother loves uniforms. She says a uniform makes a man look good, especially Gideon. Why, he is simply magnificent in it, born to be in uniform! You can tell from the way people – especially women – look at him. Mother seems to derive a smug kind of satisfaction from that. In a British Army captain's uniform Gideon does indeed cut a figure. The authority of his rank is subtly softened by a hint of spiritual intensity and reticence in his eyes, as in a portrait of Lawrence of Arabia.

Of course, Gideon knows just how handsome he is in uniform. He too enjoys the way people look at him, especially women.

In standard issue civvies – a jacket smelling of disinfectant, two coarse grey shirts, a pair of cord trousers, black hoof-like shoes, and the hat – he looks not merely ordinary but reduced. That, he says with biting irony in his voice, is the revenge the British take on you for daring to be like them. He sheds these clothes, he gets into his old ones which Mother has laundered and ironed. He tries to be his old self again.

The war, which began more or less on Gideon's birthday, ends more or less on my eighth. Gideon tells me no one could wish for a more meaningful birthday present. The war has not quite ended yet. But the Germans have surrendered. Hitler is dead. For us, that is all that matters.

Now the full horror of Hitler's evil, reaches us like a delayed tidal wave. Our teacher tries to make us understand what she herself cannot. Sometimes the ordeal becomes too much for her. She sits down, shaking her head, her eyes moist.

Paradoxically, in the constraining framework of the army Gideon had found freedom. The war expanded his horizons. It swept him triumphantly across North Africa then Europe. He had lived from day to day in a state of heightened sensibility. When the skeletal inmates of a concentration camp in Italy saw the Star of David, emblem of the Jewish Brigade, on the battle dress of Gideon and two of his comrades who went with him, they wondered if the day of the Messiah had at last arrived, even so late. Gideon might have temporarily lost faith, never the sense of purpose. He had seen death, he had walked through bombed out wildernesses, and all he had had to do was fight.

'What sort of freedom was that?' he asks. 'How can so many broken shards of humanity be put together again? How can we build from such a terrible ruin? Where are we going to store so much anger which you can neither dissolve nor put to good use any more?' He says such things in cold, impotent rage, because now, back in normal civilian life, the routine demands more resilience than he has. There is food rationing, shortages in clothes, furniture, everything in fact. The British, whom he grudgingly loves and admires, are now regarding the Jews of Palestine with unconcealed mistrust. Their manner is condescending; they seem not to remember that Gideon Jerusalem and so many other young men in their prime, have fought with distinction as officers and ranks in their army.

David Oren visits us frequently. He is already in the thick of Hagana activities which now concentrates on bringing in illegally refugees from Europe. But Gideon, unemployed, languishes at home.

'The Old Man must have forgotten. He has so much on his mind nowadays,' Oren reasons.

'One thing Ben Gurion does not do is forget,' Gideon replies stonily.

'I'll mention your name to him, when the right moment comes,' Oren promises.

'Don't even think of doing that!' Gideon snaps.

I learn at school about King Saul: pure of heart, courageous, head and shoulders above the others at first. Later, beguiled by dark destructive moods. I think of my father. He is displeased with my poor results but will not help with my homework. Often he shuts himself in his room, reading. Woe betide Tali and me if we make too much noise. Gideon will come out of the room, book in hand, and stand over us, glowering. 'Go outside, the two of you. And don't come back until you can behave like civilised children,' he says coldly. When the oppression comes down on us too heavily, I get angry at Mother for submitting to his tyranny, for not protecting us against his withering displeasure. I begin to feel unwanted; I begin to tell lies; I begin to wet my bed at night.

'You are too impatient. What do you expect, the world to come to you while you sit at home brooding? It doesn't work like that, Gideon. Why won't you let David talk to BG on your behalf?' Mother pleads.

'If you ask such a damn stupid question, it shows you understand nothing. Not me, and not what I want,' Gideon retorts.

'What do you want, of me, of the children? The world isn't perfect, you know, and even you can't change that!'

'Oh for God's sake! Why don't you take the children and go somewhere, to your mother in Jerusalem.'

We stand by, Tali and I, and witness our parents' first post-war no-holds-barred fight. Many more follow.

I cannot recall what led to Gideon hitting me. Only the hurt, the humiliation of being punished unjustly, as it seemed to me. For Gideon does not lash out at me in a moment of lost temper. No, he commands me to approach, gives me a short cold lecture on being a liar, then bends me over his knee and administers stinging blows with the flat of his hand on my behind. I scream and kick. His grip tightens savagely on the back of my neck. He goes on hitting. Mother stands by, saying not a word.

Early the next morning we run away, Tali and I. The haven towards which I captain our escape is the home of kindly friends who live in Ahuza, some distance beyond Carmel Centre. They live in a pleasant sprawling bungalow surrounded by a sunny lawn edged with flowers. The walls are painted marshmallow white. The roof is strawberry red. At the fringe of the garden there is a coppice of dark, whispering pines.

Meir and Dolly Burstein have grown up children who live in Tel Aviv. Their sole resident companion now is a lumbering old dog called Shamgar. Whenever we visit them Dolly spoils us with cakes that, to my eyes, resemble their home, and ice cream. Her real speciality, however, is story-telling, which she does with endearing animation.

Being small, Tali is not a good walker. She soon tires. I load her onto my scooter. Thus we labour up the hill. When at last we arrive at the Burstein home, after what seems an epic trek, we find the gate locked. The house is empty, I can tell because I cannot hear Shamgar's welcoming barks. Tali begins to bawl. To make things worse, it starts to rain. Big drops splatter on the road and leap into the air like transparent frogs. We huddle under a leafy carob tree. Hours later, when the police find us and bundle us into their car, we are both soaked to the skin; our teeth are chattering.

Back home, Gideon is furious. I am unrepentant. This first flight has revealed to me an exciting option which I am to seize repeatedly throughout my childhood. Because I am wet and miserable, I am spared Gideon's wrath. My punishment is meted from a higher authority than his: the next day I am ill with fever. Always more robustly constituted, Tali gets away with nothing worse than a bad cough.

How many days I am ill, I cannot tell. I dream that something heavy and dark is pressing down on my chest. I cry out in terror but no sound issues from my mouth. I am dragged down into murky depths, where I cannot breathe. Until a hand reaches out to me and pulls me up. Gideon's hand.

Eventually, I recover. But the attacks recur. Dr Mansbacher visits me frequently. After exhaustive examinations, he diagnoses asthma. As he goes away, Mother retires to the next room. I can hear her sobbing.

But it is Gideon who sits at my bedside during the nocturnal assaults of asthma, holding me, talking to me, giving me courage.

We call my asthma Grendel, after a monster in a myth Gideon narrates to me. Grendel is an English monster which lives deep at the bottom of a cold dark lake. 'You and I, Philo, will defeat Grendel. Together. It will be a great fight, and we shall win. Just as Beowulf did. I promise you,' says Gideon.

I see a new tenderness in his eyes, as though only now, after all he has seen in the war, he has at last come to terms with vulnerability, with the frailty of life, with the inhuman ferocity of Grendel, with the terror of the Erl King following you through night-black forests.

Our chief weapon against Grendel is music. The gramophone is set on a table by my bed. Next to it, a stack of records. Gideon himself is unmusical. He enters my world of sound as an ally, an attendant warrior. After Dr Mansbacher had given me an ephedrine injection and departed, Gideon puts on a record and sits by me until I drift into sleep.

'Abba,' I say, 'I don't want to be a fighter. I want to play the cello. I want to be the best cello player in the whole world.'

'You will. I know you will. The best there ever lived,' he assures me.

4

I know that my boss, Dr Fink, General Secretary of the British-Israeli Friendship Union which publishes the weekly I edit, is devious.

I can tell he has something in mind which he won't share with me. I can sense from his absurd put on formality the approaching demise of *Kadima*. Seventy years in print, the first Zionist journal in the English language, it had mutated, slimmed down, re-inflated, changed titles and editorial policies before reaching its present form of sixteen A4 size pages printed in an out-of-the-way Polish immigrants' press, and briefed to publish absolutely nothing that could conceivably be controversial.

So?

What meaningful purpose could a Zionist journal serve when Zionism, in Israel as elsewhere, has gone to the dogs? Be a refuge for otherwise unemployable dropouts and mediocrities? I see an accusing finger pointing at me.

At the last meeting of the magazine's Editorial Committee a new member from the far right challenged me. 'How can you call yourself a Zionist when you are a *yored*, a deserter of your country? Might I even say a traitor?' he asked.

I knew his faction was violently opposed to my views. I might have riposted that being born an Israeli wasn't a choice for me. But he and Dr Fink, both born in eastern Europe, might have chosen Israel instead of settling in London to feud endlessly over Israeli politics which they do not understand.

'I am a journalist. My job is to edit and turn out the journal on time, and to an acceptable standard. That's all that needs concern you,' I replied icily.

'Be more diplomatic, don't antagonise. We really don't need boardroom quarrels,' Fink later reproached me.

What do I care if *Kadima* fell back on its pathetic spine, shook its sixteen pages and gave up the ghost? What am I doing here, anyway?

But then, how would I live? From Gideon I learnt that losing can become an unstoppable trend.

I think of you, Imogen, constantly, night and day. You are my dawn and my dusk. Am I madly in love? Or madly in love with being madly in love? Mad, for sure, one way or the other. Yet sane enough to worry that my job, unsatisfactory though it is, might co-terminate with a relationship which is as yet purely imaginative, leaving me bereft and unemployed.

I am in a Scheherazade situation! The penalty for failure is, metaphorically, no less severe than hers.

A bomb has exploded in a busy Jerusalem street on the eve of *Shabbat*, when folks are out doing their shopping. We don't know yet how many people, if any, have been killed. How many wounded. What is the extent of damage to property. We don't know yet who perpetrated the deed. Crazy desperate fanatics? Arabs? Maybe Jews? You can never tell in Jerusalem where violence is timeless, endemic and arbitrary. We wait tensely for more news on the radio.

In Jerusalem, it is known, the British are squarely behind the Arabs. In Haifa they are impartial. In Tel Aviv they side with us. Whereas Tel Aviv is the head, the nerve-centre, engine of the *Yishuv*, Jerusalem is its soul. Without Jerusalem, Zionism has no point. Every child understands that.

Elevated on high hills, far away and stone-hearted, Jerusalem is also another world. A world of grandparents, of sugared almonds and secret whispering gardens surrounded by stone walls. A realm from where the radio station pulsates music and news. Our comforter; our oracle.

On holidays I sometimes get sent to Jerusalem. The dry air from the Judaean Wilderness is good for my asthma. God's breath that gave life to Adam, says my grandmother. And Grendel hates it and keeps away from me. My grandparents live in a large house set in a garden full of almond and pomegranate trees, just behind the Egged Central Bus Terminus. I come here alone. Never with Tali: Grandmother can't stand the noise Tali makes, and Grandfather is perennially ill.

It is late afternoon now. I talk about Jerusalem yet I am in Tel Aviv. On the second floor balcony of No 31, Heroes of Israel Street. Masha, Buba, Hanni, Mother and her sister Ela, are having tea; strong Russian tea, served in glasses lodged in elegant silver holders. Hanni has brought some white lump sugar, a scarce commodity nowadays. She puts a lump in her mouth. It becomes the focus of her plump, freckled face. She slurps the tea through the sugar. Below in the street, my older cousin Ohad is putting his new Raleigh Sturmey Archer three-gears bicycle through its paces. A prestige machine, better than BSA or Hercules but not quite in the same class as Peugeot.

'Ohad, dear' Aunt Ela calls over the balustrade, 'go over to the grocers and bring a packet of Frumin biscuits, a quarter of soft Tnuva cheese, 100 grams of black olives, and...'

'Halva, Imma?'

'No. No halva. Just what I said.'

Ohad wheels off, followed by a mounted posse of his peers. He is an obliging boy, responsible, sensible and loveable.

When you have a bike in Tel Aviv, you're somebody. Flat and labyrinthine, Tel Aviv rolls under you, readily surrendering her distances. Whiz along the sea front, keep the minaret of Hassan Bey in distant Jaffa smack in the middle of the handlebars as you crouch low. Speed past Shehunat Mahalul but don't stop – some rough customers hang about there. All the way to Witman's ice cream parlour in Mughrabi Street, where bike-owners, their girl passengers and hangers-on congregate on Saturday evenings. Some bikey boys run errands for the Hagana, or for Irgun. Ohad would like to do that, for the Hagana, of course.

The radio news bulletin gives sketchy details of the bomb attack. Apparently it was a big one. Brought down a whole house. Broken windows a full half a kilometre's radius from the explosion, and casualties. How many and how serious, is not yet clear.

'Husseini's gang, no doubt,' says Hanni Belkind knowingly.

'And now, no doubt Irgun will strike back,' says Masha, nodding her head.

'Thank God no one among our friends belongs to Irgun or Herut,' says Aunt Ela, who has highly-developed social instincts.

But they are worried, Mother and Ela, because Jaffa Street, where the bomb exploded, is not far from Grandmother and Grandfather's home. Grandmother might well have been out shopping at the very time when it happened. They are not on the telephone, my grandparents. Not many people are. A telephone is a mark of privilege, especially in Jerusalem.

'I cannot bear to see people eaten with anxiety,' declares Hanni. 'I myself will go this very moment to Buba's flat. I'll ring Jerusalem and find out exactly what's going on. Just so that you have nothing to worry about.'

'No Hanni, please don't trouble yourself,' Ela protests, for Hanni Belkind is a much valued friend who shouldn't be taxed needlessly.

But Hanni is adamant, even though her varicose veins hurt when she goes up and down stairs.

A nationally-acclaimed author of children's books, Hanni Belkind belongs to the Jerusalem intelligentsia. Not only does she have a telephone, she also has an impressive list of friends with whom to talk on it. And that quite apart from many important connections, friends of her husband Dolik who is destined to be Governor of Jerusalem during the terrible days of the siege.

Of the three sisters only Buba lives in Tel Aviv, almost across the way from Aunt Ela's house. Her husband is Director of Habima Theatre – the guiding star of the *Yishuv's* cultural enterprise.

Presently Hanni returns. She bears comforting news. Grandmother and Grandfather are fine. Not even a broken window. Miraculously, only one man was killed – an Arab upholsterer from the Old City. Six people were wounded, four seriously. Among the latter were two Arabs, a woman and a child.

'Thank God. There's divine justice for you!' says my mother Beth.

Hanni looks at her disapprovingly. 'When an innocent human being gets killed by a mindless act of terrorism, Beth, it doesn't matter whether he is Arab, Jew or Eskimo. There is no cause to thank God.'

'More tea, Hanni?' says Ela hastily.

The radio plays Tchaikovsky's *Winter Dream*, conducted by Toscanini. Oh, the moving, world-traversing power of a good tune, evocative even on a temperate Palestinian evening, when bombs go off and kill! And Buba, the emotional, artistic one, says in her plummy Russian voice, all tremulous with feeling: 'When I hear such music, I know in my heart that we have a homeland.' Tears glaze her beautiful eyes. Pinkie cocked, she raises a glass of tea to her puckered lips.

We are in Tel Aviv for a number of days – two, three, a week, who can tell – crammed together into one room in Ela's flat, whose husband Xan is a town-planner with the Tel Aviv Municipality. Away all day, he sits in his office on the top floor of Tel Aviv's tallest building, gazing lustfully at Jaffa in the distance, ravaging her in his hot town-planning dreams. They are modern people, Xan and Ela, European in their tastes. They like people similar to themselves, who have made something of their lives, who can look to the future with confidence.

Xan – the first to denounce Gideon when he fell out of grace and the only unashamed plunderer of his personal belongings when he died – celebrates his admiration of Gideon. Uncharitably, he also allows himself to wonder not too discreetly how come a man with such a tremendous potential who obviously has a promising future, could have coupled himself with a dull woman like Beth. In his own mono-flavoured salad days, Danzig-born Xan had dallied with a group of dilettante café intellectuals who, rejecting Judaism, sought to be spiritual inheritors of the ancient Canaanites. The mini-movement's appeal – always marginal – faded at once with the Holocaust. Xan had jumped boat in good time.

Gideon's promising future is in fact the reason for our being here, in Xan and Ela's home. Gideon has been summoned by Ben Gurion himself. Ben Gurion, it is said, files his disciples in the tidy system of his mind. When a certain situation arises, out pops so-and-so, who is just the right man for the job. Now Gideon's file had been pulled out. Why? What for? Gideon is diffident, won't say. Xan smiles; he knows the essential drift of Gideon's assignment, he hints. When you have friends in high places, secrets are shared benefits, or responsibilities. Of course, Xan would never divulge; not for nothing is he a confidant of future generals and statesmen.

A week passes. We hardly see my father. Somewhere in town, in a faceless room, where naked bulbs burn continuously except when periodically extinguished by power cuts, he sits in conclave with Ben Gurion and his lieutenants to fashion the project he is to realise. A plan that will be a hidden buttress in the edifice of Israel's nascent army.

We were all sitting round the table. A tray of cheese sandwiches in the middle. Next to it, a large bowl of pickles. D and A were devouring sandwiches all the time, leaving hardly any for the others. At least it kept them quiet for a while. BG ate nothing except a jar of Lebaniya. He drinks coffee perfunctorily. His self-discipline is awesome. From the way he kept blinking I could tell he was irritable. Then he asked me to go through the plan, briefly. BG believes everything worth saying must be said briefly and concisely, or not at all.

I got through the essential points of my proposal in less than ten minutes, because BG, the only one who matters, was already familiar with it in detail. All the while BG kept scribbling away, his mind apparently on other things. I thought he had not taken in what I said. When I had finished, he put his pen down and looked up. 'Well, let's hear some views. Speak!' he said, looking round. No one uttered a word. Then A, his mouth struggling with the last sandwich, began shifting in his seat. We all know he suffers from piles. He started mumbling something about the British, about allocation of scarce resources. I didn't want to listen. I knew what he was going to say even before he opened his mouth. A is a good administrator. A manipulator. But he has no heart, let alone imagination.

Suddenly BG cut him short in mid sentence. 'We need it,' he said brusquely. Nothing more. And I realised that he had already made up his mind long before I began to speak; he was just playing at democracy.

Then the others were chipping in, suggesting changes – "improvement" was the word A used – to make the plan workable, to involve more "factors". In reality to protect his own interests. R, a born pedant with a foolish Chekhovian mind, was only concerned about the "operational code name" for the plan.

If I believed in God I would pray for patience before wisdom. I would ask for placidity when irritation mounts. I would ask for the kind of resilient cunning needed to subvert mediocrity, which invariably tries to dull the edge of any good plan. I hope, in vain perhaps, that BG will not put political considerations before what I believe is our paramount necessity. And if he does, then I hope with all my heart that both the British and the Arabs are even less smart than A considers them to be...

From Gideon's notes. Written, I suspect, not at the time but in retrospection already stained by the bitterness and disillusionment of his decline.

I get the notion that we are to stay cooped up here indefinitely, to be fattened for some sacrifice Xan has in mind. In Tel Aviv, the sea air wraps you about like a wet towel. Radios blare out through open windows. Street noises go on unabated to the early hours of the morning.

I wake to feel Grendel breathing in my face. 'Ah, my favourite little victim! Did you imagine I would ever let go of you? Foolish boy!' he rasps.

Alone, I do battle with him. Once. Twice. My mother, aunt, uncle, sister and cousins attend my trials. Spectators and jury, they witness my convulsive wheezing in silence, waiting for an unfamiliar over-worked doctor to arrive from the Ein Geddi Hospital.

Then, at last, on a Friday morning – a lucky day, say Jews, because God, replete with creation, twice remarked that it was "good" – Gideon returns full of good cheer, his work done.

42

'We're going home,' he announces. We are just in time to catch the last bus to Haifa, before the onset of the Sabbath. At the Haifa down town bus terminus we pile into a taxi together with an elderly couple who have arrived from Tiberias. Mother carries the smaller suitcases. Nehama Herman emerges in time to lug in the larger one. Gideon carries Tali in one arm, me in the other.

'Things are going to be different from now on, just you wait and see,' he winks at me.

And they are. For one thing, Gideon gets a job with the Palestine Electricity Corporation as a cost accountant, his qualifications being a Middle Second in Economics from the London School of Economics. Dr Rutenburg, founder and Director of the Corporation, is now an old man. No longer at the helm of his chief enterprise, he devotes his time to philanthropy. He is a patriot, a source of power to the *Yishuv*, like the electricity his corporation generates. Everything about him bears the stamp of respectability, for which reason many of the Hagana people find shelter in his employ. Gideon falls into that category.

Our newly-found prosperity is modest but immediate. For me it marks a change of a kind I could only have dreamt about.

One afternoon, soon after I return from school, Zena Herman comes into the kitchen from the garden. Zena is jealous of her time; she is not given to socialising, and certainly not with Mother. 'Philo,' she says, peering over the top of her glasses, 'I have something to tell you.'

Mother's reflexive expression of appeasement floods her face. Her entire posture goes limp. Zena Herman makes her nervous. 'He has just come back from school, Zena...' she begins to apologise. But Zena ignores her. 'Philo, come to my studio this minute. I have a surprise for you.' And she walks out.

Zena Herman does not live in a room or a study, much less a kitchen. She inhabits a studio wherein stands a shiny black grand piano, its top slanted open like a rising scale. On a wall shelf, flanked by music books and scores, a large bust of Ludwig Van Beethoven frowns down on two time-worn metronomes.

Zena too is frowning, benevolently, as if trying hard to economise on emotion. 'Look over there, Philo,' she points. Propped up against the wall by the sofa, I see a cello. Its case lies open on the carpet, the bow across it. 'Yours, Philo. Take it, careful though. It's a good instrument for you to begin on.'

I touch the honey-coloured varnish, and believe I can already sense the magic vibration hidden in the wood. I am unable to speak from excitement.

'Yes, Philo,' I hear Zena say, 'I bought it for you on your father's instructions. I shall teach you, at least in the beginning. You will work hard, Philo. That is my condition. I will not waste my time on a lazy pupil, do you understand?'

I sit on a chair. I position the cello between my knees as I have seen cellists do in concerts. I pass the bow hesitantly over the strings.

'That's right, Philo. Feel it, let the cello know your touch. Relax your arm, let it swing, yes, like this. See? It isn't easy to make an ugly sound on the cello. But for real beauty, you have to work hard and long. The cello will sing for you all by itself, even when it doesn't know your song...' Her firm warm hand guides mine, presses, lets go, presses again. All of a sudden she straightens up. 'That's enough. Put it away now,' she says, a little breathlessly.

She goes to the gramophone, puts on a record. It is Gregor Piategorsky playing *The Swan*, from Saint Saëns' *Carnaval des Animaux*. Zena invites me to imagine the movement of the bird, to think in sound instead of in visual images. I have to concentrate. At last, I get it. Excited, I marvel at this new medium of amorphous language. Where had it lain hidden all this time? What unimaginable experiences will it lead me to?

'Tomorrow, Philo. Same time. And don't you be late for your first lesson. Or ever, for that matter.'

Zena is a driving, demanding teacher. One hour a day practice minimum, she dictates. No skiving! She could always tell if I loafed, she warns me. To Gideon – not Mother – she confides that I am truly gifted and, moreover, I have perfect pitch, which is very rare. When a teacher is entrusted with such a pupil, teaching becomes a mission, she says. Therefore, she will spare no effort in bringing me on. And if she realises at some point that I need a better teacher, she will swallow her pride and find me a master. Never mind the money. It's more important that talent should not go to waste. That too, is part of building our country, she adds, because, like all her family, she is committed to excellence.

In so far as my musical gift is inherited, it must be from Mother's side. Melody is a bonding lubricant in her family's expansive, demonstrative and noisy way of life. They sing, they thump out rhythms on tables, on thighs, they nod and tap feet at the sound of a catchy tune. On top of the old upright piano – now hopelessly out of tune – in Aunt Vic's flat, stands an oval framed photograph of her, prematurely attired in black bombazine, leaning earnestly over the keyboard. Mother too, when the spirit moves her, can bang out a Chopin étude passably close to what the composer intended it to be. So can one of her brothers. A feat for him verging on a circus act, since Uncle Menahem has been stone deaf from early childhood. 'It's the shape of the vibrations,' he explains, which he can make out through the soles of his feet as he sits at the piano. Vibrations are his speciality. He also boasts that forty minutes after a meal of cabbage or beans, he can outdo the great Pugol Le Pétomane and trumpet the first bar of our national anthem. My cousin Ohad swears he has heard him do it.

Gideon is unmusical, a deficiency he tries to overcome intellectually; for he recognises the supremacy of music as a mode of artistic expression. He has outbursts of ambition on my behalf: he sees my gift as a miraculous complement to his own gifts.

The first rains beat against the window pane. Staccato, arpeggio, pause, then a rush of crowded percussive chords. We call this first rain *Hayoré*, "the shooter". It comes early this year, and heavily. Good for the farmers, they say on the radio. Good also for Rutenberg's Palestine Electricity Corporation, for it swells the River Jordan which powers the Corporation's hydro-electric plant in Naharayim.

Tali squats on her pottie, rattling her ceramic money box that is full of coins she gets from *Doda* Vic, or Mother (I spend mine on sweets I buy after school, at Mrs Weiss's hole-in-the-wall shop next to *Doda* Vic's home in Carmel Centre). In the adjoining room Mother sits in an armchair by the radio, knitting Gideon a jumper of fawn-coloured English lamb wool. He is at work, accounting the debit and credit of his love-hate relationship with the British.

As I labour through the exercises Zena has composed for me – all taken from popular Russian folk songs – I listen to the rain. *Hayoré* is my time-keeper, my mnemonic vibration maker.

* * * * *

'A country,' Gideon reflects, 'cannot be better than the individuals who are in it. A country is not a scheme, you know. Nor a philosophical concept. A country is a living community. Like a herd. That's why I'm terrified of doctrines and ideologies.'

'What do you want instead?' asks David Oren.

'Oh, values, of course. Values born of recognising the supremacy of compassion, honour, excellence, beauty, justice, civility, helping each other. That sort of thing. Values, moreover, that are not imposed but grow naturally, like carob trees on the hills. Living things, not a part of a national doctrinal package.'

'Words. Nothing but words. How can you get what you say when your people have different experiences, different backgrounds, different ways of looking at things, eh? Tell me, if you can.'

'Slowly. Patiently. With humility.'

Oren asks his questions with ponderous sombreness. Gideon answers with teasing levity, which only confuses Oren. Mother serves supper and looks on uneasily.

'But do we have time to go slowly?'

'We haven't got time not to.'

'BG is always pushing us. Hurry hurry hurry, before this and that happens. Before we are overtaken by events on the ground.'

'Conceit, nothing less,' Gideon laughs.

'What Gideon means is that ideally there should be time, there should be a natural development, like sowing and reaping... Ideally, our society should be like...' Mother pauses nervously.

'Water Babies,' I call out, grinning at Gideon, who had recently given me Charles Kingsley's strangely haunting book.

Oren turns his still blue eyes on me. 'Yes, of course,' he says. 'Water is supremely important. Absolutely crucial. And so are babies.'

Gideon doesn't laugh this time. In fact, he frowns. He doesn't like it when people are made to look foolish, especially when it is not done by him. Besides, the allusion which excludes Oren suddenly reminds Gideon what an important virtue loyalty is. That morning he had been taken by two British policemen for interrogation down town in connection with alleged illegal Hagana activities. It had been a lonely experience. The memory of it now dilutes his wicked humour with protective generosity.

'Coming back to what you were saying, David, in certain circumstances, this notion of the purity of arms we boast of endlessly will vanish like a puff of gun smoke. No discipline can enforce it. Only strongly-held, deeply-rooted values. I hope.'

'And that is what you think you can instil in the men you are training?'

'Maybe. If I can't, it's not for lack of trying. And you know what? It wouldn't be at all bad if those concerned would apply some moral judgement in the shadier parts of our effort. You know what I am talking about.'

'BG says…'

'I know, David, I know. And I say this, once you compromise, you compromise again and again. Once you lie, cheat, murder for the sake of a goal, any goal, David, you'll always find excuses for doing it again.'

'Who is cheating? Who is murdering?' David protests.

Gideon smiles. 'No one, yet. Enough will. In time, given half the chance. We are human beings, aren't we?'

'Gideon can never resist the temptation to tease. It'll be your ruin one day,' says Mother.

'And another thing. I know no less than BG that we shall have a state, in the teeth of the British and Arab opposition. And I tell you this, if it is gained without regard for values, if we begin to make excuses and justify sloppiness, callousness, even wickedness, because certain things needed to be done and there was no other way, then we'll probably end up being no better than the ones we fight. We'll end up being just another unpleasant Middle Eastern state which happened to be Jewish.'

'Maybe. So what? Are you worried about what the world would say? BG says it doesn't matter what the goyim say, what matters is what the Jews do.'

'Yes, it's what the Jews do I'm worried about. And if they don't do the right things, better for us to remain as we are and forget Zionism. That's what I say.'

A long silence ensues at the end of which Oren pronounces darkly: 'That's the most terrible thing I've ever heard you say, Gideon, in all the time we've known each other. I only hope you don't mean it.'

'But I do, I do. Unlike you, I can afford to. You see, I'm not a survivor.' Gideon smiles one of those smiles which make him look so handsome, and dips his spoon into the soup.

'Philo,' Oren says as I prepare to go to bed, 'in whatever you do, always remember that your name is your life-long asset. Keep it pure, because once it is stained, nothing can ever cleanse it again.'

I nod my head in agreement. Gideon winks at me from behind Oren's shoulder.

I am too young to understand the meaning of allegory. Not yet too old, however, not to perceive that purity is an essential ingredient of magic. One tiny grain of baseness will turn magic into a cheap illusion, a mere conjurer's trick. Or ground it altogether. It is by such perception that I am able to make sense of *Water Babies*, a story that holds such alien fascination for me and conditions me already at this stage of my life to be receptive to you, Imogen.

The story, by its moods and provenance, also helps shed some light on the peculiar powers of Ori Falk.

Ori Falk is fourteen years old. He lives in the house next door. Our house's mild state of disrepair testifies to vigorous living. The Falks' house by contrast, with its faded green wooden shutters darkened by broken slats, and its dusty weed-infested poppy-dotted garden, has an air of still decay about it. As though all the living moisture of the place had been sucked dry for the blooming of Ori's beauty. For Ori is exquisite. To describe how he looks is as meaningless as to describe the brightness of a star in terms of candle light. I can only say that his beauty comes from within, self-generating and inscrutable.

Thoughtful and introspective, he is tough in his demands on himself as he is forgiving of others' shortcomings. It is nothing short of a miracle, Yossef Herman philosophises, that a brilliant boy like Ori should blossom from the tired loins of the Falks', from the last drop of their dying pith, to vindicate their unhappy rootless existence and ill health. What ringing triumph snatched out of defeat! A comfort and reassurance to us all, he says.

Ori is my friend. Why? Who can tell? I consider myself very lucky. Because although people, young and old, seek to be near him, Ori is shy. At times distant.

I open my window. Over the bougainvillaea and passion flowers barrier that separates our two houses, I can look into his shaded room. Framed against the window, Ori stands, half-naked. The violin held under his chin. He is playing a Vivaldi concerto. He has been practising it for weeks. Few people remember that the prolific Antonio composed these pieces not for virtuosi but for ordinary music lovers to play at home. Does he smile in heaven to hear Ori give the proof? See the assured sweep of Ori's bow arm, the flowing inflexion of his wrist. Behold total concentration and grace, with economy of effort.

Remember, Imogen, the concert at the Festival Hall we went to? Von Karajan conducting Mahler. Eyes closed, he seemed oblivious to the audience, oblivious also to the men and women who made up the ensemble. The music flowed out of his body, through his hands, directly to the orchestra. He played the orchestra as though it were an instrument with millions of nerve cells. But the sound, Imogen, came from deep inside him. That is more or less how Ori plays this Vivaldi concerto.

As I stand there listening in the slow, scented evening, I am drawn into a secret intimacy of magic with him.

Then, we are standing in a field on the periphery of the British army base. Perched on the hill top against the horizon, is the Arab village of Kabbabir, white and fragile, with its slender minaret and little domes like polished egg shells. The distant tinkling and lowing of the herds wash against the rude noises the soldiers are making as they kick a ball around in their dusty playing field.

Surfacing from his thoughts, Ori turns to me.

'What's that thing hanging round your neck?' he asks.

'The house key.'

'Give it to me.'

His hand passes over my face, down my arm, closes over my fist which holds the key.

'I will show you something you've never seen before in your whole life. Throw the key away as far as you can, anywhere you like.'

'But...'

'Do it.'

I'd have leapt over the edge of a precipice if he asked me to.

'There.'

'Forget it now,' he tells me.

We walk in the opposite direction, towards the camp. A soldier comes out of one of the huts. He is a sergeant, he has three stripes on his sleeve. His face is shiny red with a clipped ginger moustache. A toy face. Hands on hips he squints crossly at us.

'You boys want work? Take white bread home?' he says gruffly.

White bread is an expensive luxury. Ori shrugs his shoulders, and looks away.

'C'mon Jock. Over here, lad,' the sergeant shouts. One of the soldiers breaks from the group and comes over at a run. I have seen this one before. He is always friendly to us kids, always ready with offers of sweets. He is tall and fair, and muscular. His arms are heavily tattooed – mermaids in waves of yellow hairs, surrounded by hearts and daggers. His teeth are bad.

'Jock, take these two little fuckers to the dump. Get them busy clearing up the mess. When they're done, come and see me.'

'Yessir,' says Jock.

Jock leads us to a place near the perimeter fence. There is a whitewashed wooden shed, and close to it, a wide ditch full of rubbish. Jock gives us sacks.

'Rubbish in here. Empty sacks over there.' He points at a row of incinerators beyond the shed. 'You do good job, you get nice bread.'

We are alone. Ori smiles a strange, adult kind of smile.

'Why did we come?' I ask.

Instead of answering, he puts his hand in his pocket. He brings it out, opens it slowly, and there, in the palm of his hand is my key.

Magic? No, says Ori, a reality of a different kind. A reality created here, inside your head, which isolates and protects from other realities and keeps out ugliness.

I see the soldier's head. He is peering at us from behind the shed, an unpleasant grin on his face. His whole body is jerking back and forth, his thick knuckles pumping away behind the line of the shed wall.

'I want to go away from here,' I say.

We walk back to the side gate from which we came in and run into the sergeant. 'What, finished already?' he barks at us.

'Finished,' says Ori. And I gasp, because I had never heard him lie before.

But the sergeant is not a trusting man. 'Jock!' he yells, 'go see what the lazy little blighters have done. Bugger all, I'll bet.'

By the time Jock returns the sergeant has moved away. We see them talking together. Jock says, 'honest, Sir,' and the sergeant, 'Blimey. Give 'em each a bloody loaf, then.'

In the field, Ori unties the khaki cloth and lets the bread fall to the ground. I watch the white slices soak up the dirt.

'We don't want this,' he says.

I am silent. I don't understand. All I know is that throwing away bread is worse than sacrilege.

'Let the birds eat it,' Ori says.

He died in one of the first battles of the War of Independence. He had joined the *Palmach* – our élite fighting force. There had been a dawn attack on some remote police station in the hills of Galilee, where Palestinian irregulars had fortified themselves. A stray bullet went clean through his heart. His comrades charged on, leaving him transfixed in the branches of an olive tree.

I suppose magic failed him at last; I suppose his inner reality had been overrun by the bruising, unforgiving reality of war. What can magic do against such an adversary?

The Falks' house sank into still deeper silence. Weeds strangled the garden to death. And when death begat more death, the property was sold to a developer and razed to the ground.

At about that time, in another place, I had my first religious thought: In beginning was not the Word but the Note. And God, the supreme musician, created the heaven and the earth out of a tune which jingled in the vast emptiness of his mind. And when the universe was done, complete with the stars, the Milky Way, black holes, infinity, when all the animals and us humans were rooting about the world, copulating, then He laughed and said it was good. Good enough, anyway. So he annotated his jingle, implanted it in Man's dreams, and disappeared into the medium of his creation.

5

Imogen's Victorian house borders on a private corner of Primrose Hill. It's a large end of a terrace house, three floors high, with a small garden in the front and a larger one at the back. Both gardens are somewhat neglected. Imogen does not dislike gardening; one day, she says, she'll take it up seriously. But for the time being there are too many other things to do and too little time to do them in. A similar lack of care shows in the house itself, which nevertheless imparts a sloppy, cosy welcome. She has let the upper part of the house to her publisher cousin whose duty it is to look after the garden. Apparently the cousin prefers to spend the little spare time she has doing embroidery rather than gardening.

I soak up the atmosphere of my love's home. I want to know everything about her, absolutely everything. But whereas Imogen is an encouraging listener to my tales, she is infuriatingly reticent about her own life. 'Oh, there isn't anything terribly interesting to tell,' she says, and changes the subject. Or she will come up with a decisive conversation stopper – she's good at that. Or just smile, look enigmatic and say nothing.

I sense that she is, or was, a woman who takes being admired for granted and is displeased with that side of her character which causes her to do so. I apprehend she is kind to those who fall in love with her because perhaps in her younger days she had been unkind. I'm, moreover beginning to understand that Imogen considers her beauty a tiresome responsibility rather than an asset.

Trying to learn more about her, I befriend her less inhibited cousin. They are close yet very much apart. Claire is unmarried. 'Not all men see Imogen as you do,' she tells me magisterially in her clipped precise voice. Am I meant to understand that adoring old Imo will do me no good at all?

And again: 'When we were in Cambridge men used to say to me, "c'mon Claire, let's go to bed. You know you'll enjoy it." But Imogen they'd want to marry.' A small dry laugh.

There was a happy childhood with holidays spent at their grandparents' stately home in Suffolk. Dogs and ponies. Imogen's husband, Eddy Crewe, himself a cool 'Alpha male', had been almost casual in courting her. Their marriage had been mostly unhappy.

I decide not to tell Imogen that I was programmed at birth to search for, find, and forever love nobody else but her.

In our moments of relaxed candour Imogen has told me of affairs she has had, none of which have given her much happiness. Although unprompted, her telling of these is diffident, undetailed, more like admitting to folly lest I should think her perfect.

Are we having, rather about to have, an 'affair'? I ask myself. Am I to end as the latest addition to her list of unsuccessful suitors? It seems to me I am so very different from any of the men who have romanced her. Whereas my own fascination with her is as clear to me as anything I've ever understood, her seemingly half-hearted and undemonstrative attraction to me, is a total enigma.

Then, out of the blue, Imogen asks: 'Do you drive?'

'Yes, of course. I just don't own a car because it's such a daft thing to own in London. Why do you ask?'

'I'm going to my mother's this weekend. I was wondering if you'd like to come.'

I laugh. 'As your chauffeur?'

Imogen laughs too. 'The truth is, I hate driving, particularly on motorways and at night. You always ask about my background. Here's a chance to see for yourself.'

The truth is, I do not yet feel ready to meet her mother but I cannot say no to Imogen. I will not be ungallant and let her drive more than a hundred miles mostly on motorways which she hates. Besides, she owns a silver BMW which should be fun to drive.

* * * * *

As the narrow road reaches the top of the rise, Norton Howe comes into view through reticulations of wintry hedgerows. The breeze carries a faintly iodine smell from the North Sea. Surrounded by tall beech trees, and embraced by a grey stone wall, the house stands at the far end of a sloping, grassy stretch, undoubtedly a lawn once. A partly broken archway opens onto the grounds at the centre of which is a landscaped lake with a folly ziggurat structure in its middle. The house itself has a broad brick façade the colour of dried tomato, criss-crossed with grey rhombic patterns, gables, leaded windows and corkscrew chimneys. Its reflection shivers in the leaf-strewn grey water of the lake.

Claire had told me with diffident pride that Norton Howe had been in the family's possession for almost four centuries. Imogen's reference to the place has been only in passing, as though it were hereditary lunacy that ought to be kept secret.

Now that I see it, I begin to understand. A cold perverse dereliction attends the house and its grounds. Its defeat though not surrender, for there is an imperious stubbornness about the reduction of this great house, shows in everything, down to the tussocky meadows where a few bullocks and heifers now graze lethargically.

'Turn right by the post box. The cottage is at the end of the drive,' Imogen says, adding crisply because I hesitate, 'Norton Howe has stood empty for years. It's too large, too cold, and too expensive to run, and not in any way distinguished enough to be a tourist attraction.'

I want to stop the car to take a look. But she is impatient. 'Not now. Drive on,' she says. And then, placatingly, 'It is a bit of a white elephant, you know. Truly. A cousin now owns the place. He's a vicar in Ipswich. A few years back he tried to set it up as an exorcism centre, or something like that.'

'No luck?'

She laughs. 'None whatsoever.'

Compact in its seasonally-naked garden, the cottage is ready with a welcome. Smoke climbs upwards from the stubby chimney. Light shines demurely from the neat windows on the ground floor. The thatched roof, laminated like a biscuit cake, makes me think of Hansel and Gretel. I know intuitively that if Mrs Julia Dowland is the witch of this tale, I'm destined to be Hansel and Gretel rolled into one.

With this daunting thought in mind, I stall Imogen's car as I manoeuvre into the parking space in front of the cottage. Then, to make things worse, I touch the wrong something or other, setting the windscreen wipers whirring at full speed. All this happens under the gaze of the 'witch' whose face I see in the window.

'Oh for Christ's sake, stop that,' Imogen snaps.

The foretold trial has not yet began and I've lost the preliminary.

Carrying our overnight baggage, I follow Imogen into the house. The hall is in semi-darkness and cold and smelling of cooking.

Julia Dowland materialises, framed in the pale light of the living room doorway. Tall, slender and straight backed, she stands perfectly still, hands held together, a hint of a smile on her rather severe mouth which in her distant youth must have been very pretty.

Her beauty is as arresting as it is anachronistic. She carries the sterling authenticity of a class Imogen protests is defunct if not yet totally extinct. But how alike they are.

Julia's eyes are deep blue, almond-shaped and calm. Her hair isn't white, it is true silver and full and pinned up as in old fashioned photographs of royalties. Her hands, unadorned save for a plane marriage band, are misshapen by arthritis. They are the only part of her which looks vulnerable.

In a thoughtful mood Gideon might have said hers was the face of England that subjects of the vast British Empire at once adored and despised. In levity he would have said she was sepia through and through – the proverbial English Rose pressed for posterity between the pages of History. His sense of humour could be cruel and didactic.

'Hullo, Mummy.'

Julia Dowland offers her cheek to be kissed. 'Hullo darling. Was it awful on the roads?'

'Not at all. Philo's a wonderful driver.'

The ancient mother scrutinises me with raised eyebrows over the shoulder of the daughter whom I love. Her smile is sudden and astonishing, turning on its head the impression I have got of her to this moment: it is radiant, warm and happy.

'I am so pleased to meet you,' she says. 'So kind of you to drive Imogen here.'

Imogen says a little breathlessly, 'Philo was very impressed with Norton Howe. He likes country homes.'

'Poor Norton Howe.' Julia Dowland gives a punctuative laugh and raises her chin. 'What a ruin it has become. However, I believe Basil's leasing it to a Japanese firm which wants to use it as a conference centre, or something.'

'How exciting,' says Imogen with forced enthusiasm.

'There you are. Good stately homes will always find a good use,' I say.

'Darling, when must you unfortunately be leaving? Julia asks.

Over a glass of wine at the revitalised hearth, she is ready to demonstrate her adaptability to change. Just as she had greeted the advent of the motorcar earlier in her life, not to mention the aeroplane, so now she welcomes the Japanese. No doubt they will make excellent neighbours, she says. And what did it matter, in the final analysis, if nowadays nobody under the age of sixty read Anthony Trollope?

Half sedated with Macallan whisky, I am mesmerised by this beautiful antiquated grand dame who talks with eloquent humour of

'Progress' now zigging now zagging against the advent of universal Macdonald hamburger culture.

A picture in a gilt frame on the wall catches my attention. I ask permission to have a closer look. It is a portrait of Julia as a young woman, by the Scottish painter William Strang. It shows her in half profile: an exquisite long pale neck, bare sloping shoulders, deep-set wistful eyes, a sensuous sweep of long hair; the mouth surprisingly full, surprisingly gentle.

I look at the painting and the youthful Julia becomes the youthful Imogen, dressed for a period costume drama. The metamorphosis so moves me that I feel tears well in my eyes, which only Imogen detects. She reaches to confiscate my half full glass, a caution and a preventive measure in crisis management.

Unnecessary, as it happens for at that moment we hear the sound of tyres crunching the gravel on the drive. Miles has arrived from Oxford in the souped-up Mini Imogen had bought him when he passed his Prelims with distinction.

'Hullo Mum, hullo Gran, hi Philo,' Miles says, as he breezes in.

'Darling, what a lovely, lovely surprise!' Imogen cries as she rushes to his arms.

'Didn't Gran tell you I was coming?'

'Of course not. Mummy never tells anything.'

'Oh dear. Well, here I am. And starving! What's bubbling away in the scullery, Gran?'

'A modest fare, Miles. We'll eat in half an hour, if you can wait.' Then, turning to me, she adds, 'Forgive me, I've never been good with names...'

'Philo.'

'Quite. Philo's in the Green Room. You, Miles, please take your things to the Attic.'

Miles holds up a tattered army surplus canvass bag as though it were the Gorgon's head.

'My thing, Gran,' he says, and pulls out of it a bottle of wine.

He brings with him cheerful vigour that stimulates Mrs Dowland. Her manner becomes spontaneous. Almost the coquette, she laughs readily. He is good for her; he is good all round, like a spice, expertly applied. First thing in the morning he will be off to join friends in King's Lynn, he announces.

'Surely not before breakfast, Miles.'

Imogen laughs. 'When Miles says first thing in the morning, he means somewhere around ten o'clock.'

Miles holds the bottle up. 'St. Emilion, 19... can't read the rest. Must be a pretty old vintage, though. Does St. Emilion travel well, Mum?'

'Let it breathe for a while, darling.'

'This bottle, let me tell you, has been passed on from one dinner party to the next by generations of Oxford undergraduates. That's its pedigree. Breathe in peace,' he says, uncorking the bottle. He pours a little into a glass, holds it against the light, takes a sip and smacks his lips. 'Not bad. Probably much improved by age. Like you, Gran.'

'Probably? Why, Miles, that's only half flattery. Which gets you half nowhere.'

Imogen retreats to the kitchen and returns with a joint of roast beef.

'Imogen tells me you're something of an expert on wars,' Mrs Dowland says to me.

'Where I come from, everybody is,' I reply.

She raises a napkin to her lips. 'How sad.'

Darkness masses against the steamed-up windows. In the hearth the logs glow and hiss.

'I nearly visited Palestine once, when I was young,' Mrs Dowland says. 'A cousin was stationed in Beirut. We were all set to sail to Haifa, and from there motor to Jerusalem, when the news came of an outbreak of some epidemic. Typhus, I think it was. Isn't the Middle East always stricken with one epidemic or another? So instead, we took a boat to Alexandria and from there, up the Nile to Luxor. You've never seen the Nile, I don't suppose?'

'I'm afraid not.'

Mrs Dowland pauses and frowns. 'A much over-rated river, in my opinion. Though a good deal more impressive than the Jordan.'

'Gran, Israelis don't go to Egypt. The two countries have been at each other's throat for too long!'

'Indeed. But I do seem to remember reading in *The Times* that the streets of Cairo nowadays are crowded with Jews from Tel Aviv hunting for bargains.'

I can see Imogen wince. I say nothing.

'All I remember of Cairo is dirt, and flies, and too many people jostling against one another in too narrow streets. I simply cannot imagine it's any different now,' Mrs Dowland goes on.

'Luxor, however, was simply divine! We ran into a niece of Lady Burton, who was also staying at the hotel. Sophie Arundel. She told us the oddest thing. Among the papers Sir Richard had left, was a manuscript, some nonsense he had written about Jews. The Jews of London somehow got to know about it. Do you know, they paid Lady Burton an enormous sum just so they could lock it up in their vault to prevent it from ever being published! Isn't that awful? Ha! And to think that Lady Burton had been on the point of destroying it anyway, along with a lot of other stuff from her husband's pen.'

Her cheeks are flushed. In her Nile days she was, no doubt, a stunner!

'Why awful Gran? The stuff was probably vile. A load of anti-Semitic rubbish that deserved to be destroyed.'

'Surely that isn't the point, Miles. In England Jews aren't persecuted. Heaven knows how many of them have found shelter here, and prospered. You can't seriously think books should be destroyed because they say this or that!' Mrs Dowland retorts with a snort.

'But they didn't destroy it, did they? Lady Burton was going to. The Jews have kept it safe in a vault, isn't that what you said? '

'I can't remember the details. I never met the Arundel girl again. Unfortunately, I tend to be someone who says goodbye more enthusiastically than hullo.'

Who wouldn't delight in Miles? He is receptive, full of verve, and is having the time of his life at Oxford. After one year of Biology, he has decided to specialise in genetics. No other branch of science opened more exciting horizons, he contends. Without a show of effort or ambition he will rise to be Master of the Universe. And in the process there will be travels with his father – Africa, Amazonia, Papua New Guinea – before settling down to the serious work of improving life on earth.

Imogen dotes on him. She is a loving and knowing critic, a check against excess and sloppiness. Always, a helping hand and mind. I apprehend the intimate symmetry of their family relationship, knowing I could never be co-opted into it.

That is probably the reason why, as evening turns to night and coffee and cognac follow the pudding, I have to fight an invasion of yawns while they are in the full flow of conversation.

'Don't you see? The future of mankind hangs on a question of scale,' Miles argues.

'Really, darling? How so?' Imogen inquires.

'Population explosion. No one can stop that. In a hundred years there'll be standing room only everywhere in the Third World.'

'Must we suppose there will be a Third World in a hundred years' time?'

'All right. Anywhere in the world, then. Stop quibbling, Mum, and listen. Therefore, drastically diminishing resources is inevitable. With disastrous consequences, needless to say.'

'Oh I'm sure clever boffins will have found solutions to just about everything by then. Or we won't be around anymore.'

'That's just it. I have it! The supreme genetic engineering solution. Imagine Man no bigger than a foot. Then six inches, then smaller still. Tiny people, minuscule houses and cities. All of a sudden, lo, there's plenty room, endless food and resources. Plenty of everything in fact. And less pollution. And the world – just think – is huge again, open for re-discovery!

Imogen claps her hands. 'Imagine what an adventure it would be to encounter an ordinary domestic cat!'

'Sorry Mum, cats, dogs, all domesticated animals, in fact, will have to be reduced to manageable sizes. They must be our ecological support system. Wildlife will remain untouched, so you can still have your thrills, like being sucked into a tiger's yawn, or stepped on by a tapir.'

'Why not take it a step further?' I volunteer. 'Make man the size of an atom, and leave everything else as it is. Ergo no need for food at all in the conventional sense. Problems of locomotion instantly solved, since we'd be carried like pollen on the wind. And as an added bonus, no more wars, immunity to natural disasters et cetera...'

'Wonderful. I'll go for that,' says Imogen.

'That's metaphysics. I'm a scientist,' Miles ripostes.

'And I hope I live to reach a hundred and get a telegram from Her Majesty the Queen on my birthday before anyone realises your dreadful schemes, Miles. I shouldn't fancy being surrounded by midgets,' Mrs Dowland laughs. 'Your Grandfather was six foot three, you know. Your father is over six foot, and aren't you too? That's an awful lot of shrinking to do.'

'All right, what would you say if I told you that in Mexico they have successfully bred a cow that's only two feet tall, weighs 150 kilograms, and has a fantastic yield of milk? An animal tailor-made for the Third World?'

'Shetland ponies are no larger, without any help from scientists. And they are not much use to anybody,' Mrs Dowland counters.

'Can't win against your conservatism, Gran. I give up. Now I understand what all great discoverers had to go through. Just wait till I get my own secret lab. I'll give you the future human race. Tiny, cleverer, healthier, happier. Complete with a supporting range of livestock...'

I butt in. 'Farmers, Miles, aren't merely keepers of livestock and growers of food. Farmers are the custodians of tradition. Supreme survivors... So when you talk about reduction...'

As if accelerating on a downward course of self-destruction, I ramble on: the Arab historian, Ibn Khaldun's concept of cyclic history, the inevitable link between spiritualism and nanotechnology...

I seem unable to stop, even as I see Imogen's face turn cold with boredom and Julia yawning furiously. Why? The curse of the outsider desperately trying to wedge in? Only Miles, bless him, looks benevolently amused.

'What a pity Lucy isn't here,' says Mrs Dowland with finality. All of a sudden she is visibly tired.

On the landing Imogen kisses me goodnight. I taste the wine in her breath. I begin to say something but she cuts me short: 'I hope the Green Room isn't freezing. Good night, honey.'

"Honey"? She's never called me that, nor anybody else that I've heard. She hates the stuff, wouldn't touch it with a barge pole.

The Green Room is goose shit green. Cold as an icebox in spite of the crackling electric fire Julia Dowland has left there. And a little damp. The bed is high, narrow, sepulchral and sagging in the middle. I lie on my back, arms crossed like an effigy, and stare at the discoloured ceiling. It will take a miracle for me to sleep without which the night will be interminable and vacant. Could it be that Mrs Dowland, herself a hailing distance from the hereafter, has contrived to remind guests in the Green Room of mortality?

Eventually, tired from being cold, I sink into, rather than fall asleep. I dream of Julia. She speaks to me in a thin precise voice that sounds like the splitting of wood:

'Well, you certainly gave us a lecture, young man. Foreigners are clever, we all know that...

'Did no one tell you Englishness was a form of refrigeration? It keeps us upright, like trees even as we die. Take me, I'll pass away with a stiff upper lip on the stroke of a hundred. And a year or so would fly past before anybody noticed. We call that understatement, you see. Our English temperament will not tolerate explicit passion.

'You are confused by appearances. That's because when it comes to harmless deception, we English are supreme. Did Imogen tell you that before each general election she spends days sitting on the floor stuffing envelopes for the Labour Party? Of course not. Haven't you noticed how in London she tries to conceal her "posh" accent? She once paid some miserable down and out to teach her to speak working class. Huh!

'No need to stare like that. Two children begat on her while she turned her face to the pillow and thought of Socialism. When she murmurs 'darling, love' ice cubes drop from her mouth. Don't say I didn't warn you.

'Very well, come with me on a tour of Norton Howe. Here is the Drawing Room. An eighteenth century addition but arguably the finest room in the house. Look at the pictures on the wall. One Turner. Two Gainsboroughs. A Reynolds. The obligatory Canaletto. An assortment of undistinguished Flemish oil landscapes of undetermined authorship. No Constable, mind you. No water-colours for that matter. These were not considered good value by a succession of resident philistines.

'Now look at all that expanse of beautiful dark oak panelling. Admire, if you will, the carved plaster ceiling. And the baroque French and Italian furniture. The Persian carpets, worn but still magnificent. And here's a quaint article in the vitrine – the ancestral sword dating from the War of the Roses.

Doro, the Labrador bitch, and Jack, the English setter accidentally crossed with something else, dozing by the fire.

But what have we here, standing between a Ming vase and an Aphrodite plundered from Lesbos in 1872? A bloody fruit machine! Lights flashing, jingles chiming, the lot! And what, I hear you ask, is that vulgar contraption doing here? Why, it's Imogen's box of ideologies! Let it not be said the English upper class hasn't moved with the time. Goodness me... a second cousin, a peer of the realm, drives a thirty ton articulated lorry twice a month from Tottenham to Scunthorpe just for kicks.

'You are hopelessly in love? Ah, dear boy, what a ridiculous romantic you are. Love is like the flu. A few days in bed, and you're on your feet again. I knew a seventy-five years old marchioness from Kensington who kept a lover half a century younger than herself. That's class for you. Imogen? She would freeze with embarrassment at thought of mere nine years going against her. Give up. Cut your losses and run for your life, scram...'

I wake... *to feel the fell of dark not day*. It is two hours at least before dawn. My feet are frozen. I'm dying to go to the loo which, I remember, is way down the corridor, past Imogen's room.

The floor creaks like three haunted houses. To flush, or not to flush, that is the question. I flush the toilet and immediately regret it. The ancient plumbing roars loud enough to wake the dead. I tip-toe back along the corridor fearful of Julia Dowland emerging from her room hair loose, candle stick in hand.

Past Imogen's room, I see a faint strip of light from under the door. I hear her radio. I go in without knocking.

She sits up, instinctively pulling the duvet to her breast, and turns off the radio.

'Philo... What is it?'

I sit on the edge of the bed.

'What's the matter?' she says, taking my hand.

'It's so cold, Imogen.'

'There are blankets in the... Oh, how dreadful.'

I know she understands the cold I am talking about cannot be assuaged with blankets. She does not welcome me to her bed but neither does she protest when I get in beside her and put my arms around her. And after we have made love we lie side by side in silence, until she says, 'You'd better go back to your room.'

Mrs Dowland has risen early. She is already in the kitchen busy preparing breakfast. Miles is there too, sitting at the table, dressed, knife in hand, ready to decapitate a boiled egg. He momentarily arrests the execution to greet me, and Mrs Dowland turns from the toaster to smile.

'Good morning. What would you like for breakfast? Porridge, or eggs? I wouldn't wait for Imogen. She always sleeps late.'

'A slice of toast and coffee would be fine, thank you.'

'A grey wet morning,' Mrs Dowland announces as she peers through the window. 'Did you sleep well?'

'Well enough, thank you.'

I take a seat opposite Miles and have my breakfast.

'Well,' says Miles, getting up. 'I must be off. Thanks for having me Gran. Tell Mum I really couldn't wait, won't you? Goodbye.'

Despite the thick drizzle Julia Dowland comes out to see us off.

'Lovely to see you Mummy, take care.'

'Come back again soon, darling. And drive carefully.'

A quarter of an hour on, it rains heavily. I drive at a steady seventy mph. Imogen's head is turned to the window watching the grey fuzzy Suffolk countryside roll past.

'Won't you say something?' I say.

'What would you like me to say?'

'Anything.'

A pause. She doesn't look my way.

'I can't think of anything. Is it hard for you to drive in silence?'

By mid afternoon we reach my home.

'Come up for a cup of tea?' I suggest already knowing what she will say.

'Would you mind terribly if I didn't? I have a lot of work, and I'd rather get home.'

'I'm sorry, Imogen,' I say, because I feel awkward with her. The intimacy we experienced has raised a barrier between us.

'Good heavens, whatever for?' she says, pretending surprise.

'Doesn't matter.' I get out of the car. Imogen wriggles across to the driver's seat.

'Will I see you again?'

'Of course,' she says and touches my hand. 'I'll ring you as soon as I can. Next week probably. Bye.'

I watch her drive away until the car turns the corner and disappear. It feels good, better than usual in fact, to be home, except for Moon's absence. I make myself a cup of coffee then walk to the cattery in Archway to collect him.

6

Deep inside, says Gideon, people are still divided into two ancient categories: dwellers of the plain, and nomads of the hill and the wilderness. The first are builders of cities, law-givers, recorders of history, scientists and engineers. Achievers.

The second are makers of myth; poets, visionaries. Anarchists. Ephemeral in their ebb and flow, they are at once creators and destroyers.

The people of the plain set up idols; the nomads sweep in to knock them down.

What are we? Neither completely one nor the other, yet supremely the two together. The dual legacy is our inheritance: our strength, and our weakness. We possess the lyre and the sling shot; the spirit level and the pen. Can you, wise and beautiful Imogen, find a fitting space for these anomalies among your textbook definitions of societies?

And what of Gideon himself? A split personality, tormented in turns by the two. When the spirit of the myth-maker comes upon him, he is intense. He grows lean, has that faraway look in his eyes. It is then that his political fortunes move close to the edge of an abyss. It is then that he is most receptive to my music-making. It is then too, that women with certain susceptibilities tend to fall in love with him. Was it at such a time, in the shadow of the Himalayas, that he uprooted himself from Mother into the pale bosom of Grevinde Kerstin Dahlberg, and death?

But wait. Now, in Haifa, metamorphic cycles are carefully regulated in scope as in time. When Gideon is in The Builder phase, Mother takes his trousers to the tailor Mr Chimbaliste in Merkaz Hacarmel, to be let out. Let her have a man about her that is a fat, sleek-headed man and such as sleep o'nights... she's happier that way, she can cope.

The *Yekkes*, those immigrants from Germany whose pretty villas with ordered gardens can be seen along our street and in Ahuza, an exclusive suburb beyond Merkaz Hacarmel, are proudly and immutably People of the Plain. Without their meticulous efficiency trains would not run on time, power cuts would be more frequent, criminals would not be prosecuted, bacteria would invade hospitals, the Town Hall would grind to a stand still, and the British would not be able to say with grudging admiration 'look at the Jews how industrious and civilised they are. Why, you'd think this was Buckinghamshire, not the bloody Middle East!'

The Landaus epitomise Yekkeness. Situated half way between Merkaz Hacarmel and our home, their bungalow stands some distance away from the road, behind a large multi-coloured garden surrounded by a low stone wall. Its walls are cream-coloured. The windows are wide – always gleaming. The roof is red tiled and pitched.

Once a practising architect, Mrs Landau herself designed both house and garden. They make a clear statement: 'here is a home where European culture and elegance are upheld, regardless of time, regardless of place, regardless also of what the world has been getting up to.'

On Saturday afternoons you can see Dr Ernst Landau wearing baggy shorts and a Panama hat, pottering about among the rose bushes. As he digs and hoes, his broad backside always contrives to face the sun, as if it were a homely heliotropic plant.

Dr Landau did not come to Palestine as a refugee. Both he and his wife had been committed Zionists long before the Nazis reared their ugly heads in Leipzig, where Dr Ernst Landau was a Law Professor at the University. A vague historical imperative coupled with a robust home-making instinct made both him and his wife act on their conviction and migrate. In Palestine, after draining a marsh or two in the best pioneering spirit, they settled on Mount Carmel to build a nest more or less replicating their native environment.

Dr Landau is a successful lawyer. He has a large office in Hadar Hacarmel. Countless committees seek his membership; he is a pillar of the community. Their only daughter, Mimi, is the top pupil in a class parallel to mine. We meet at breaks in the school courtyard. She never says a word to me. When school is over for the day, Mrs Landau comes to fetch Mimi in a blue Chrysler convertible with whitewall tyres, the only one of its kind in Haifa, if not in Palestine. Also with her is a pedigree boxer dog called Theo, whom Mimi hugs affectionately.

Whenever I'm taken out to concerts or operas, I see the Landaus, always there, occupying the most expensive seats, and Mimi, impeccably dressed, perusing the programme with an air of adult preoccupation. She needs no telling what *Madam Butterfly* is about to do behind the screen in the last act.

I pass the Landau haven on a bright Saturday morning, wheeling my wooden scooter up the hill. A sprinkler is hissing on the lawn, throwing a wide arc of iridescent water into the air. The car, gleaming blue, is parked by the pavement (I once stole the valve caps off all four wheels. 'Gosh, the Landau's Chrysler!' said a boy at school and gave me half a dozen top grade marbles for them). Its canvas hood is down, it being such a lovely day.

Wearing a sailor suit of white and blue, bare-footed and bare armed, Mimi is busy hooking up a swing to a stout limb of an apple tree. Her guests, two blond boys and a girl, whom I vaguely recognise, are kicking a psychedelic rubber ball around the lawn, dodging the sprinkler's rotating jets. They are shouting and laughing. Theo is tearing around in circles, barking stupidly. Mrs Landau appears at the doorway, a soft, ample figure in pastel colours.

'Children,' she calls out, in her honey mellow voice 'not so much noise, please. Save your energy for the beach.' She smiles deprecatingly, as with a fluid gesture she removes a strand of auburn hair from her face.

I see the ball high in the air, momentarily over-laying the sun. It is coming straight at me. And following it, mouth gaping, is Theo, arched like a circus acrobat as he leaps over the garden wall.

'Oh, *Muti*...' Mimi shouts.

Mrs Landau is leaning over me, her bare arm cradling my head. She smells of lavender. I taste blood in my mouth.

'It's only a graze,' she says. Her scented handkerchief feathers my face. Satisfied that I am not really hurt, she straightens up. Mimi cups her hand over her mouth and sniggers at the blond boy, who sniggers back.

All at once, I'm crying.

'Now then, now then,' Mrs Landau croons, holding me closer, 'it's just a little graze. In a moment the pain will go away. You'll forget it all, truly...'

I have relished retrospectively the memory of her delicious innocence, and the haunting coolness of her smooth white arms.

I'm back on my feet soon enough. The blond boy brings me my scooter. Mrs Landau says, 'Take it into the garden, Robby.' Then she turns on the dog, 'Bad Theo! Bad dog. Go away, at once!' She commands in English, because genteel dogs with a pedigree like Theo clearly understand no other language.

The bathroom is vast, ethereal white; even the lavatory is a gleaming monument to domestic sanitation. Mrs Landau dabs iodine on my brow and elbow. Through the half-open door I can see into Mimi's play room. A shoulder-high doll's house stands against the wall, a schematic dissection of still life furnished with miniature furniture, inhabited by tiny Landaus, reading tiny books. Mimi's other toys are discarded haphazardly about the room – who would have believed that Model Pupil Mimi could be so untidy at home!

At the centre of the floor stands a large white swan mounted on two rockers, with a seat between its half unfurled wings. The bird's neck is imperiously curved. It wears a golden crown. A golden chain is thread through the black and yellow bill. What dark proud eyes it has. In my mind's eye I see Mrs Landau summoning this royal swan to carry Mimi hither and thither on its back.

'Children!' says Mrs Landau, 'children, you shall all have ice cream now. Not Theo, of course. That's his punishment for being naughty.'

'But *Muti*, the beach, aren't we going to the beach?' says Mimi petulantly.

'The sea won't run away if we are an hour late, Mimi.'

Mrs Landau carries into the garden a tray with five tall bowls brimming with rainbow crests of home-made ice cream, made of real cream. We sit round the garden table.

'So! One for Philo, one for Locki, one for Robby, one for Mooky, and last one for you, Mimi. Don't eat it too fast or you'll get a headache.'

Her face lights up with a sudden idea, 'Wouldn't it be so nice if Philo came with us to the beach?' she exclaims, clapping her hands.

I say nothing. The Landaus don't go to the public Hayat Beach like ordinary people. They have a place of their own right in the bay where their boat is moored. I don't really want to join them. Certainly not when I see Mimi wrinkling her nose and looking bored.

'What do you say Philo? Shall I ring your mother to ask permission?'

I tell her that we don't have a telephone, and besides, we are going out after lunch. Mimi does not try to hide her relief.

'Ach! Isn't that too bad.' Mrs Landau is serenely disappointed. 'Well, another time, perhaps?'

She sees me out 'Do let me know soon how your poor head is, Philo, won't you? It's so nice meeting you, goodbye.'

I didn't lie. We are, in fact, invited to Aunt Vic, matriarch of Mother's tribe.

Mother's family is large: four sisters, three brothers, each with their own families, distributed all over the country. Collectively they join in an expansive Russian soul governed by untidy excess, noisy jubilations and bereavements, and disregard for time and attention to detail. What they cannot remember they invent. Then believe their own invention. Therefore, there are frequent altercations, giving rise to petty feuds, followed by sentimental reconcilliations, which are lavishly celebrated.

Doda Vic is the eldest sister. Since Grandmother and Grandfather's home in Jerusalem has fallen into shabby stateliness, where death sits in attendance on Grandfather, *Doda* Vic's spacious flat in Merkaz Hacarmel has become our social focus as well as for hordes of itinerant distant relatives.

Named after the English Queen Victoria, Vic is arguably the most accomplished of the sisters. Vivacious and temperamental, in her day Vic was considered a beauty. She had many suitors whom she treated like courtiers. When it came to marriage, however, pragmatism prevailed: she opted for Uncle Hai. Gentle, diffident Hai, an older man with limitless patience, rational in judgement yet irrationally cheerful, has vindicated her choice. It is chiefly on account of his position that Vic enjoys social ascendancy.

Like Grandfather, American-born Hai is of Bucharan-Russian extraction. America has grafted onto his unassuming nature a sense for opportunity coupled with down-to-earth common-sense. America also confers upon him an aura of dependability, just as it does on everything, from ice cream to roller skates. Moreover, Hai is a qualified engineer, graduate of an American university. That is why Rutenberg had appointed him to a senior position in the Palestine Electricity Corporation.

But at home America retreats before the irrepressible vitality of Hai's ethnic temperament. He laughs thunderously, pinches our cheeks red, he falls asleep in armchairs – you can hear his snoring one flight of stairs down. He is generous with presents. Our favourite uncle, best *dod*.

Doda Vic's world occupies the middle ground between the plains and the hills. Here Gideon is but a sojourner. He comes to be indulged, to enjoy a warm uncalculating hospitality. He needs all that effusive sloppiness to dampen for a while that single-purposed, unforgiving flame which burns inside him. Here he can relax, unarm and disarm, albeit without entirely letting himself go in case the fuzziness of awareness inherent in Mother's family should prove contagious.

It was in fact Hai who got Gideon his job with Rutenberg. He never mentions this. *Doda* Vic does, frequently. Hai is a true professional career man. The Electricity Corporation is his life. He knows his worth, he has no use for clients within or without the family. Gideon, on the other hand, has his heart on other matters. For him the job is a convenient temporary occupation, until the real business of the Jews in Palestine begins in earnest. For all that, he works hard and well. Naturally, he gets promoted. Rutenberg knows (as does Hai) that even when affairs of the Hagana take Gideon away from his desk, somehow the work will be done.

The irony is that Hai the non-combatant, the easy-going unprepossessing family man, is soon to become a moving force in the Hagana's weapons-acquisition drive. With his American connections and self-effacing persuasiveness, he is destined to be one of the architects of Israel's Airforce. Another irony, with a bitter twist to it, is that Hai, which in Hebrew means 'alive', will die before his prime, before he has reaped the benefits of his endeavours, at about the time when Gideon's life takes off to rise briefly like a shooting star.

* * * * *

Passover coincides with my birthday. After a hard winter, the air is soft. The hillside is covered with cyclamens and anemones. When you look with half-closed eyes at the distant hills the colours merge into a wash of reds and purples and pinks.

Nature's recovery from the rigors of winter is faster than my own. I have been ill. Asthma, bronchitis, followed by pneumonia. They said I could easily have died. For nights on end, after the doctors had done their best, Gideon had sat at my bedside, battling alone with Grendel, who this time came to war better armed than ever. Aged relatives had mumbled prayers for me in synagogues. Litres of chicken soup had been decanted into my mouth.

Here I am, then. Frail but very much alive. A rug wrapped round my body against the vernal chill, I sit on the balcony looking down on Merkaz Hacarmel from the cockpit of a small, but secure world – *Doda* Vic's flat on the second floor. The street is dazzling from a recent shower. *Doda* Vic and Mother are in the kitchen preparing food for the Passover Feast that countless aunts, uncles, and cousins will attend.

A jeep sweeps into view. It stops outside Jacobson's barber shop. Four British soldiers get out. They look casual. Three wander off to disappear in nearby shops. The driver remains at the wheel. Absorbed in his magazine, he is unaware of a figure, a man, who departs from a nearby bus queue by the pavement, and draws near. Two shots rings out, flat reports, like cracks from a toy cap pistol. The soldier slumps forward against the steering wheel. The assailant silently vanishes in the crowd. Death at mid-morning on a busy street has the banality of a power cut.

Within minutes soldiers are all over the place. The traffic is shunted to the road sides. Sharpshooters appear on roof-tops. *Doda* Vic whisks me inside; such scenes are not for children, she says. We may expect a curfew. And to think that such an outrage has been perpetrated on our holy day of liberation from bondage!

The British are conducting a house to house search in the vicinity. They want to know if anyone has seen or heard anything. I hear *Doda* Vic talking to them at the door. 'No,' she says, 'No one here saw anything. Don't you know it's Passover today?' The two policemen are polite but firm. They come out onto the balcony, look around, then leave, apologising for the trouble.

The incident casts a thin shadow on our celebrations, so that for once the habitual silence of Elvira, *Dod* Menachem's new wife from a marriage arranged by post, seems ominous rather than vacuous. They had arrived late. The bus from Hadar on which they came was held up at a police road block. Hai's brother, his wife and two children, are not so lucky. They had driven all the way from Tiberias only to be turned back at the same road block. Now they are in a hotel down town and Hai is on the telephone, using his connections to try to get them through. Eventually he succeeds, the stranded relatives are on their way. Gideon is last to arrive. He had been detained in a meeting. A British officer on duty recognised him and let him through.

At last we are all sitting at the long table, behind *Doda* Vic's best china plates. Silver gleams against a white table cloth. The four ritual foods of the Seder in their ornamental platters are in place. So *Dod* Hai, wearing his embroidered Bucharan kippa, opens the Hagada to sing out the first prayer.

Since my sister Tali is the smallest, she recites the Four Questions. She has been practising for weeks. But the excitement is too much for her. She fluffs her lines, then begins to bawl. Mother helps her: 'How does this night differ from all other nights?' Gideon turns to me, arching his eyebrows. I do the same. On this night, of all nights, differences all of a sudden seem routine.

As expected, Hai asks Gideon to expound on the best parts of the Hagada, like the definitions of the "Wise Man", the "Wicked Man", and the "Fool who knows not what to ask". Gideon doesn't disappoint. He hams it up, interspersing the text with witty commentary. He does it brilliantly, mixing gravity with humour. All eyes are on him, and Mother looks at him admiringly, as she always does whenever he is being clever in public. She cannot sense the lack of spontaneity in his performance. Can she not see that his thoughts are far away from us, from here, in another place, on other things?

At around midnight, Hai's eyelids begin to droop. Elvira, having said not a word throughout the evening, glances at the tiny gold watch embedded in the flesh of her plump wrist. Her enormous bosom heaves above her folded arms as she sighs. *Doda* Vic's delicious food, especially the spiced rice pilau with chicken, has filled us to satiety. So Cousin Leah, who is a year and a half older than me, complains, as she always does, of a stomach ache. 'Imma,' she wails, 'my stomach…'

'That's because you eat too fast,' *Doda* Vic rebukes her, which is not true: Leah is a notoriously slow eater.

'There's nothing wrong with her stomach, she's always like that when she's tired,' says her older sister Daphna.

Now Hai rises from his torpor. In a voice charged with biblical resonance, he blesses us, prophesying that we, the young generation, shall grow to adulthood in the reconstructed Jewish *medina* 'soon, in our time, Amen!'

Leah, Hai's brother's younger son Eli, and I, get roller skates made in Birmingham for presents. We are ready to sing the last song when the telephone rings.

It's for Gideon. We watch in silence as he takes the receiver from *Doda* Vic.

'Yes,' he says, 'speaking… Not to my knowledge.' A long silence. 'I understand… Okay. *Hag same'ach* to you too.'

No one asks questions.

'Elijah the Prophet. He said he's sorry he couldn't make it. Got held up elsewhere,' says Gideon, with a mischievous smile.

Two British police officers arrive at our home in the morning to take Gideon away for questioning. Just a matter of routine investigation, they explain. Mindful of the Passover, they are demonstratively civil.

They stand in the hall diffidently trying out their few Hebrew words on the Herman kids who have gathered to see what is going on. Gideon, meanwhile, is taking his time having a bath.

When at last he emerges, already dressed, he asks the officers if he may have his breakfast before they take him away. Of course, they say, but decline politely when he invites them to join him. He sits down at the table, eats with deliberate slowness while glancing at the morning newspaper. Gideon is a master of timing: when he judges that the two policemen are about to run out of patience he folds the paper and lets it drop on the table. 'Gentlemen,' he announces, 'I'm ready.'

On the front page of the day's *Davar* there is a report of the shooting incident in Merkaz Hacarmel:

'Informed sources believe the killing was carried out by members of ETZEL... Since there is no apparent motive for the shooting, it may well be that it was perpetrated by certain extreme elements of the Irgun, without authorisation from their higher command... For some time now ETZEL has been trying, so far without success, to establish a presence in Haifa...'

The editorial leader deplores the killing, calling it 'an act of mindless terrorism by irresponsible elements, which will escalate violence to the detriment of all concerned.'

A week later, another story appears:

'Tuvia Lishanski from 18 Ehad Ha'am Street, Tel Aviv, was yesterday found shot dead in a hotel room in Hadar Hacarmel. Lishanski, a member of the Herut Party, was believed to have been active in Etzel... He leaves a wife and a son aged twelve... Mr Lishanski, a known anti-British hard-liner, had a history of pathological depression. It is thought that he died in tragic circumstances...'

From Gideon's diary:

April 23, 1946... Jewish sages of the Talmud blame the destruction of the Second Temple on the most wasteful of passions: needless internecine hatred. I can well believe it. Factionalism is our national curse, now as in the past. How can one hope to establish a state against such impossible odds, when instead of working together, just about everybody is pulling in different directions!

There have been times when I wanted to tell BG that he was fighting a hopeless battle. You can't do anything with the Jews; they even drive

God round the bend. Maybe it would have been better for us, and for western civilisation, if the Jews assimilated and disappeared into the Roman Empire when they had the chance. If I as much as uttered such a thought, all my friends in the Party and in the Hagana would wash their hands clean of me.

Y rang on Seder night. He wanted to know if anyone here knew about the shooting in Merkaz Hacarmel. I told him I didn't think so. His suggestion, which I will not commit to paper, was criminal. Simply that.

I fear for us all when men like Y are given power of decision. People like him equate violence with commitment and forbearance with cowardice. And I'm powerless against him, just as I am powerless against entrenched stupidity.

You can not commit bad things and then wipe the slate clean and start again, without debts as though nothing had happened. You pay from the start for everything you do. Sooner or later life presents you with the bill. You pay for what you do to others as well as for what others do to you. There is nothing for free... the account begins with the first scream as you come out of the womb... Poor, wretched, stupid Lishanski, aren't we all guilty of his death?

7

I magine me once on a stormy afternoon, Imogen, standing alone on
top of a large flat rock Ori had named "Cyprus", in a field not far
from our home. I turn my eyes to the sky. The rain blinds me. 'God,' I
shout, 'You are nothing! You don't exist!' The absurdity of addressing
a non-existent deity didn't occur to me at the time. 'You're lousy
anyway. Lousy lousy lousy!' I go on.

Nothing stirs. Only a flock of wild doves scurries chaotically
through the churning greyness over the ravine across the other side of
which the bone-white minaret of Kabbabir points reproachfully at the
sky. I wait in vain for the bolt from heaven to strike me dead.

I grow bolder. 'God, you're not worth a dog's puke! I spit on you!'

Silence but for the angry whistling of the wind. Surely I wouldn't
be allowed to get away with that, I think. Minutes pass. I'm still
standing, alone in a hilly rain-drenched wilderness, wet but alive.

All right, I'm a child. God, whoever or whatever he is, has better
things to do than smite hip on thigh obscenities-screaming children.
But how about a rebuke? A slap on the face, like Gideon had given
me – for no offence – earlier in the day?

At last it comes to me: God isn't aware I exist. I'm nothing to him –
a total zero. An instant later, an even more frightening conceit
follows: God really doesn't exist! He is a hoax, invented and
perpetuated by power-hungry men to frighten people into obedience.
Therefore, there's neither reward nor punishment for whatever people
do, good or evil. There is noone to appeal to for justice and in misery.
It's power all the way; I'm powerless, therefore a victim at the mercy
of Gideon's swings of mood.

Yet when he hit me that morning, I pitched into him, swinging
furiously. Surprised, then annoyed, he held me at arm's length, then
hit me again. Years later, in England, when he slapped my face, I
floored him with a hook to the jaw. He lay on his back silent, looking
at me with dilated eyes. I went to my room and wept: the hurt fear of
his gaze went into me like a knife. He had a gift, Gideon, of making
even his victors feel defeated.

How can you believe, when you are very young, that Heaven's
Number One is like a sly tax collector, slipping in the bills for past
trespasses when you are least able to remit them? And the Supreme

Arranger of Situations, to boot; Master of Accidents, a voyeur of his own contrivances?

This is how your life is meted out in the Gospel according to Gideon: God (oh, yes, he refers to God, atheist though he is) needs recreation, being omnipotent and omniscient can be boring. That's why He invented us, humans. He pulls a random card out of a bag. On the card is written a set of situations that will affect your life. The game begins. God watches. No reward, no punishment, no help.

You might see our week's holiday in Kfar Yehezqel as a move in that game. It is our first ever holiday together. Gideon announces it in a matter of fact tone of voice, to our complete surprise, the night before. No buses. Our journey will be in a car borrowed from the Palestine Electric Corporation, courtesy of Mr Rutenberg in person.

'Don't start packing now,' Gideon tells mother. 'We'll do everything in the morning.'

The box-like little black Austin is parked by the gate. Our suitcases are stacked on its roof, secured by bits of rope to the roof rack. Under the load, the car looks ridiculously insubstantial, its spoked wheels too fragile for the task at hand. All of which invests our venture with a kind of epic dimension, like a tiny barque, setting sail for the vast unknown.

We pile in, Tali and I at the back, with her pet tortoise Shabtai. The Hermans interrupt their breakfast to come out and bid us farewell. They are full of advice. You would think we were motoring to Australia, not a mere sixty or so kilometres into the heart of Jezreel. Gideon starts the engine. He raises his hand in salutation. Tali and I wave to the Hermans. We're off.

I learn a few things on the journey to Kfar Yehezqel. The land which Gideon cherishes as our nation's patrimony, for which he is ready to die, is not as intimately familiar to him as he had led us to believe. Also, he has a poor sense of direction. Our progress is, therefore, uneven. We deviate, double back, end up in unexpected places way off the planned route. Yet throughout Gideon stubbornly insists he intended it all, to show us places of biblical interest off the beaten track. Of course, we are not fooled; not even Tali who, little though she is, can nevertheless understand that we are lost.

Mother responds to Gideon's deceit with deceit of her own. She affects delight at his improvisation; she marvels at his knowledge of the countryside. He is, of course, aware of her insincerity, as I am. It is the lubricant on which our progress through Galilee is expedited.

Tali, it turns out, is hopelessly car sick. The tortoise adds his mess to hers in our restricted space. I sulk. We break the journey frequently. Thus, a trip, which at a leisurely holiday pace should take no more than half a day, lasts an agonising near full turn of the sun for us. We arrive at our destination with dusk.

I say to Gideon, 'Moses bungled about in the wilderness for forty years, so you haven't done too badly.'

He is not amused. He doesn't even smile. The thought suddenly flashes through my mind that deep in his heart Gideon probably regrets that he came back to us after the war, instead of disappearing from our lives altogether.

Yitzhak Aridor and his wife Ruth greet us on the grass in front of their square white cottage.

'We thought you got lost, or something. I was beginning to wonder if I shouldn't get together a search party, you know, like a posse in western films,' Yitzhak says in his slow bass voice.

'We were taking our time, making a real trip of it. Sorry if you were worried,' Gideon replies smiling wearily.

They face each other. Yitzhak, squat, powerful, bull-necked. Gideon, taller, slender by comparison.

'You look well,' says Yitzhak. 'It's been a long time.'

Gideon embraces him. 'You too. Good to see you. We have a lot to talk about.'

'That can wait. The main thing now is to get your circulation going again, after being cramped in a box all day. I hope you've all worked up a huge appetite, because Ruth's been all day in the kitchen preparing mountains of food, haven't you, woman?'

'Oh, you shouldn't have,' says Mother.

Ruth's dazzling white smile is contagious. 'Why not? It's a real occasion for us, Beth,' she says.

Mother thinks Ruth, with her aquiline face and shoulder length jet-black hair, is "stunningly beautiful". Which in reality means she doesn't consider her a threat.

The twins stand back looking at us quietly. They are not shy. They are not unfriendly either. They are only by nature and upbringing, undemonstrative. Wearing white shirts and shorts which show sun-tanned muscular legs, the two boys are like miniature Yitzhaks, with their mother's foxy eyes.

'Come,' says Ruth, 'Let me take you to your rooms so you can unpack. Itizik, boys, the suitcases!'

Kfar Yehezqel food is different from ours, being simpler, fresher, more immediately identifiable with things that grow and live. The bread has an appetising crispness, the butter, which Ruth churns herself from milk of her own cows, is tastier. And there is a lot more of everything. She enjoys watching us eat. Mother makes a point of stopping every now and again for a long 'Mmmm... how delicious! You must teach me how to make this, Ruth.'

The twins look at each other and giggle throatily.

Darkness falls fast in Jezreel. The scent of the fields is carried in through the open window. The only sound you hear is the distant howling of jackals, punctuated from time to time by an owl's shriek.

'Like music,' says Gideon.

'You should've stayed in Tel Yosef, not go to live in town,' says Yitzhak, referring to a kibbutz not far away among whose founding members Gideon was.

I am put in Ehud and Gaira's room. Tali, in a folding bed together with Mother and Gideon. The twins are a year older than me. I get to like them quickly. I'm anxious that they should like me too. They tell me of the farm, about the neighbouring Arab villages. Stories about guns – the twins are already crack shots with a rifle. They can also drive the John Deere tractor, and ride Thunder, the watchman's pure-bred Arab stallion. I suspect they have agreed between them to lay it on thick for my benefit, to amaze me.

At last the twins have fallen silent. In the living room our parents are still in the full flow of conversation interspersed with laughter. In the morning, Yitzhak and Gideon will shut themselves in a room to discuss Hagana plans, for that is the underlying purpose of our holiday. Mother will attend on Ruth, who will fill her in on various bits of rural wisdom. Tali will graze Shabtai on real growing lettuce. As for me, Ehud and Gaira are planning a special introduction to some of Kfar Yehezqel's main attractions.

The jackals howls in the night-cloaked groves. The trees whisper. Outlined against a pale full moon, an armed rider sits on Thunder, looking over the sleeping settlement.

'O watchman, what of the night?'

8

He is called Ra'am, Hebrew for thunder. A dapple grey stallion with a cascade of black mane, Thunder at fifteen is somewhat past his prime. No longer is he raced at the annual meeting in Afula where the farmers of Jezreel gallop their horses through the town's dusty main street. Now he languishes in the paddock, taken out on easy rides along the orchards beyond the settlement's perimeter. There is still fire in his belly. A proven stud, mares are brought to him from far and wide.

At Feast times Thunder is groomed, his mane is plaited. Caparisoned in flamboyant trappings, he is ridden at the head of the procession. For Old Ra'am, sire of generations of superb colts and fillies, is still magnificent. Age hasn't dimmed his splendour. Look at him pacing about the paddock, neck flexed, heels kicking, muscles like electric ripples under his skin, nostrils pomegranate red. Behold those distance-swallowing legs; and his mighty cock!

Admiring the horse, Gideon quotes God at his most pompous, from Job: *'Hast thou given the horse strength? hast thou clothed his neck with thunder?...the glory of his nostrils is terrible...'* he declaims.

A challenge? I tell him both Ehud and Gaira ride Thunder. He is as quiet as a lamb, if you don't get him excited.

'Really?' says Gideon mischievously, 'So why don't you ride him too?'

Is he serious? I can't tell.

'In the paddock, of course, if you must. Sit on the horse's back, then. Only make sure you don't get him excited. Feel real big. Isn't that what you want?'

'I can, too. I'll show you.'

Gideon throws his head back. He laughs at my defiance. He ruffles my hair. 'Philo, you don't need to show me or anybody, anything. Ever.'

At the mid-point of the day Thunder is sleepy. He stands in the paddock, head lowered, tail swishing, occasionally thumping at the hard-baked ground with slow, heavy hooves. Flies cloud about his eyes. He blinks at the carrot I hold out. Lethargically, he moves towards me.

We are sitting on the fence, Ehud, Gaira, and me. 'Look at poor

Ra'am. Today he looks as old as Methuselah,' says Ehud, 'His legs are sore, I can tell.'

'C'mon, Ra'am, lift your feet, you lazy old flea bag,' says Gaira, making clicking noises in his mouth.

The horse pushes against my knee with a weary muzzle. He crunches the offered carrot, spits half of it out.

'If you got on his back he wouldn't even notice,' Ehud says. 'Swing your leg over his side and ease yourself on. I'll hold him.'

It's so easy. Astride the stallion I'm king. My head flouts the sky. The imagination conjures greatness. I want Gideon to see me; I want just for once to be looking down on him from the height of this legendary horse.

'Sit straight. Legs forward. Hold on to the mane, lightly,' Ehud instructs. He takes Thunder by the halter and leads him round the paddock. I move with the horse's motion, I improve my balance. Now Gaira gets behind Thunder, urging him on as Ehud breaks into a run. The jolting motion of the trot nearly unseats me. I grab at the mane. 'No, sit back, move with the rhythm, move your hips,' Ehud shouts.

Thunder wakes up, tosses his head, snorts. Without my noticing, Ehud lets go of the halter. 'Press with your heels, push forward with your hips, make him go, that's right, now you're riding!'

The twins are on the fence again. I am riding solo, round and round the paddock. Ra'am fills his lungs... the thunder in his neck, the glory of his nostrils...

'Harder, don't be afraid, he won't do anything stupid. Don't let him slow to a walk or he'll fall asleep and you'll never get him started again...'

I am not afraid. Striving for mastery, I ignore a premonition which creeps like a shadow to stare at me from beyond the limits of the paddock. Tali has arrived at the gate. Preoccupied with me, the twins are oblivious of her. Our eyes meet. Hers are hollow. Out of them spills a nightmare, transforming her into a fearful agent of disaster. Her childish hands clutch at the gate's bolt. Jumping on the lowest bar, she swings the gate open.

'Clang!' goes the gate as it slams against the paddock's palisade. Ra'am stops dead in his tracks. A rumble gathers in his loins, I can feel it in my legs. The thunder is unleashed from his neck. He leaps forward, across the open space to the gate. A scream hangs in the air, then falls like a shot bird into the twins' gaping mouths.

Who are the two arboreal giants standing stock still in our path, with many twisted limbs and dusty feet? 'Gog!' whispers the one on the right. 'Magog!' rasps the one on the left.

'Gottcha!' says Gog. 'Stuck fast as a bullet in a beam,' says Magog.

In a fluorescent hospital-white room, a body bound up like a mummy lies in bed. It is immobile. Dark juices drip into the lifeless arm and nose from bottles suspended overhead. There is no colour in the face. An oxygen cylinder stands at the head of the bed. When the mask is eased onto the face, and the cylinder's tap turned on, there is a hissing sound. Then the chest heaves a little, the eyelids flutter in small spasms. *Malach Hamavet* looks up, sad-eyed, palms outstretched: it's no fun being Angel of Death when you're cheated out of a day's takings.

Doctors come and go. Nurses induct sustenance and abduct waste. The body receives all this attention with hardly a noticeable response.

Once a day Gideon and Mother come. They sit a little distance from the bed. Unable to communicate, I see them as if from another angle, from a space in the room where I hover, weightless, bodiless, beyond pain. I know there is pain, much of it. But it abides with the body of which I am free. The pain I do feel is the one reflected in my parents' face, Gideon's in particular.

I want to tell him, 'Don't grieve. I did what I had to do. It wasn't your fault. There are no regrets. I'm fine now, honestly.'

Bear with me as I edit in a sound track to the scene of my semi-comatose animation at the Bodenheimer Nursing Home in Ahuza, where my expensive recovery is underwritten by Mr Rutenberg himself. Giovanni Pierluigi da Palestrina's *Cycle of Spiritual Madrigals*, based on Petrarch's *Poems to the Virgin*.

Never mind the geo-cultural incongruity. This music, so angelic in cadence, creates a mood of beatitude suitable to my condition.

The ward room is sanitised to the last atom. My bed is high – the front end is raised, to facilitate breathing. Bed, bedside table, and chairs, are reflected in the grey tiled floor, which the nun-like nurses at Bodenheimer's scrub daily with pine-scented disinfectant. Clear honey and white bread with butter curlicues is my fare.

Here, every day between three and four in the afternoon, sits Mater Dolorosa receiving get well wishes on my behalf. Here comes Gideon to do penance for my smashed sternum, collapsed lungs, and six broken ribs caused by the tree branch that swept me off Thunder's back. Here, at last, spirit and body are re-united and forced into mutual responsibility by waves of unremitting pain. I hear my reawakened pulse thudding somewhere at the back of my head like a metronome.

Did Petrarch meet Laura before or after she became his poetic muse? I ask because at about the time of my illness in hospital I think I began to sketch you out, Imogen.

You've grown with me, changed with me, long before I met you, as I knew I would one day. Creating and re-creating you has been an all-absorbing secret preoccupation. There have been no models, no prototypes either. But there was Jenni Lind, who, walking into my ward one morning, began the process.

She stands over my bed, looking at me. Her eyes are dark blue, large and deep. She has a sad, humorous mouth. I sense in her a kind of understated intelligence. I think she is beautiful, like a queen in a story book.

'Shalom Philo,' Jenni says in a pleasant, somewhat husky voice that has a vestigial trace of a foreign accent, 'you look better, much better. I am so glad. I've worked hard to get you well, you know.'

Her hand is cool on my forehead. I find her foreign voice curiously soothing.

'Of course, you don't know me. I looked after you in hospital. Also, I'm an old friend of your father and mother. I know quite a lot about you.'

I try to remember. I have a faint recollection of a voice as gentle as hers, talking, not always to me. But the image that comes to my mind is not of Jenni but of another, older woman called Stella who had been in the bed next to mine in hospital. During the day Stella would tell me funny stories. At night she conversed with someone invisible. Her suffering came out of her in gasps, then stopped emphatically. Another woman – maybe Jenni – came in to pull the sheet over her face. I heard the castors squeak as her bed was pulled out of the room.

Jenni turns to Mother. They talk while looking at me. 'We shall see more of each other, Philo. And I hope we shall become real friends,' says Jenni.

Twice a week, on her afternoon off from Haifa's Government Hospital where she is Sister in charge of the ward to which I was brought after the accident, Jenni comes to visit me. As she arrives, Mother leaves. Sometimes Jenni's visits coincide with Gideon's, who comes

81

unpredictably at any odd time of the day. I can tell they know each other well.

Jenni tells me of their days in London when they were all students. I piece together her life scene by scene: born in Berlin to a Jewish father and a German mother. An only child. By the time the Nazis come to power, Jenni's father is terminally ill. Being a doctor, he knows it. Being a trained nurse and a colleague as well as wife, Jenni's mother knows it too. 'Sometimes, in special circumstances, death is a friend you call on...' says Jenni by way of vindicating her mother who had brought friendly death to her husband with a lethal injection. And after death's friendly visitation, a timely flight to London via Geneva.

While training for her vocation at Guy's Hospital, Jenni is haunted by her father's tragedy. She embraces Zionism. And Gideon, whom she meets at a gathering in Stoke Newington. I have a snapshot of them in each other's arms, smiling at the camera, under the street sign of Love Lane EC2.

'Really? How interesting,' says Gideon when I mention Jenni, adding, 'She's first class, Jenni. With a most unusual life.' Gideon is very appreciative of people with unusual lives, men or women.

I don't recollect Jenni telling me this or that in so many words. Patches from her life have somehow grafted on to mine without either of us having noticed, to a background of music from a borrowed wind-up gramophone Gideon has brought me.

'*The Pastoral*... How I love it. It brings back so many memories,' says Jenni, turning the first record of the symphony in her hands. Her fingers are faintly stained with nicotine. She goes out to the corridor for a quick smoke at the end of each movement. Or perhaps to escape her released memories. She smokes flat Turkish cigarettes called *Hassan Bey*, which come in a cardboard packet with a picture of a bearded man wearing a red fez .

We are friends, real friends, she tells me. Yet she is more economical with her friendship the stronger it grows, so as to preserve its energy over a longer period. I mature rapidly in her company, as though it were some super food.

This becomes apparent when one afternoon prompt on visiting hour, I have three unexpected visitors. Mimi and her mother Mrs Landau, escorted by David Oren, who already wears a vaguely perceptible patina of the hero he is soon to become.

'A short visit this time, Philo,' he apologises, 'I'm off to "The

Region".' By which he means Lower Galilee, his recent military fiefdom. 'I'll come again, soon. Just had to see how our hero was coming along. Hurry up and get well, do you hear? We need brave fellows like you.'

Oren, I can see, really likes Mimi and her mother, for whose benefit he heaps praises upon me, overstates my exploits, and his own influence on my audacity. I want to laugh with him, at his childish exuberance, but it hurts to laugh: my broken ribs have enforced gravity on me.

'Look what I've brought you, apart from these two lovely ladies.' Oren makes a chivalrous bow at Mrs Landau. He lays on the bed a shiny black jack-knife. I could supply cutlery for a company of hunters with all the knives Oren has given me over the years.

Looking at him through lowered eyelids, Mrs Landau attempts a gracious smile. Live heroes disconcert her, she prefers them dead, or at least in books.

After he leaves she says, 'Surprised to see us, Philo? It was Mimi's idea. She insisted that we come to visit you. She never forgot the last time, did you, dear? Everybody in Merkaz Hacarmel is talking about you, Philo. What a reckless, brave thing to have done! But I think of your poor mother who must have been worried to near death.

'Mimi, show Philo what you have brought him.'

With slow deliberateness Mimi unwraps the parcel she is holding. Off comes the golden ribbon, then the glossy crimson paper which she folds into a square before putting it away. It is a cake, a dome-shaped iced cathedral of a fruit cake, with a rearing marzipan horse on top.

'Mimi's own creation. Baked with her own hands, without a touch of help from me!' exclaims Mrs Landau full of pride.

'Oh, *Muti*, you helped.'

'*Doch*, only with the marzipan.'

Mimi smiles shyly, averting her gimlet eyes.

'It's perfectly all right for you to eat, Philo. I've checked both with your mother and with the Sister in charge. Only the very best ingredients. Just think, you can have a real party now, with something to give your guests. Oh I am so happy to see you looking so well. Doesn't he look well, Mimi?'

'Yes *Muti*,' says Mimi.

'But you must taste it, right away. Let's see. Here's a plate. I need a knife.'

I pass her the jack-knife. 'Try this, the Sword of Israel.'

'Ha ha, what a funny thing to say. Isn't it funny, Mimi? The Sword of Israel! I shall remember this.'

Mimi visits me regularly every day, except on Saturdays. She takes me through the school term's work, everything that I've missed. She guides me through intricate arithmetic exercises. I tell her that the whole idea of percentage and increment has a deeper universal meaning. She stares at me blankly, then corrects my mistakes. In her neat rounded hand, she paraphrases for me the books we have been given to read. Filtered through her vision and stripped of complexity, they enchant me, like the leafy flower-scented garden of her home; like the swan with the golden crown in her room.

We play Prokofiev's *Peter and the Wolf* on the gramophone. 'What are you, Peter or the wolf? I'm the bird,' she says.

'I know, I know,' I tell her.

We exchange confessions. When I say she is the loveliest, most wonderful being that ever came into my life, Mimi requites with a vow that now and forever I am her closest, dearest friend, even unto death. She blushes as she says this, inclining her head. How fragile her slender neck looks. Sweet Mimi, Water Baby of the purest stream, my playmate, my first happy, happy love; never, never seek to look death in the eye.

At the height of summer I return home. The heat is intense. White haze lies over the sea. The rocks in the fields gleam like bones. Mimi, whose visits were becoming less frequent, stops visiting me altogether. When eventually we meet at school at the beginning of the autumn term, she avoids me, then pretends not to see me.

Now at the zenith of his musical precocity, Ori Falk rehearses Prokofiev's *Violin Concerto Number One* which he is to play at the Technion Auditorium after Rosh Hashana. A difficult piece, it demands a high degree of virtuosity as well as musical intelligence. I lie on my bed listening to his full-bodied sound gliding over the evening's too warm and heavy air.

Or we listen together, he and I, to Szigeti playing the concerto on a record Ori has. And he explains the structure, pointing out the emphases, the advance and the retreat; like the way of water, or of light, says Ori – child of absolutes.

And to think that the great violinist Stanislav Huberman who founded our Symphony Orchestra had actually refused to play the concerto because he considered it "non-music"!

Zena Herman is away in Kiev visiting old friends at the Conservatoire. Anyway, I'm not yet strong enough to play the cello.

'Nonsense,' Ori says, 'try and you'll see that you can.'

He is right. More than right: have I pupated during my infirmity to burst out with a richer, mellower sonority?

'One day we'll play together. A piece for violin and cello which I shall compose,' Ori promises.

The sea is lascivious. It laps the sand like a lazy lover. But a red ensign flies by the lifeguard's look-out tower, to warn bathers against treacherous currents beneath the deceptively calm surface. Only a few swimmers dare cut away towards the deep. The others splash about in the shallow, or loll on the beach amidst damp sand castles, blankets and parasols, eyes shut against a backdrop of a pale Seurat sky. Arab ice cream vendors in rolled-up trousers shuttle along with wooden ice-boxes strapped to their backs, shouting *'Eskimo brehe...e... e... x!'*

Look at us. A typical seaside holiday family group, waiting for a beach photographer. Tali, wearing a red costume, digging fiercely into the sand. Gideon, a little way in front, hugging his knees, his back glistening with drops of water and salt. Mother, in a black swimsuit, under the parasol, under a straw hat, behind sun glasses. Me, at her side. Very pale, very thin. Being too much in the sun is not supposed to be good for me. Two more figures complete the picture: Jenni, sitting not far from Gideon. Against her thigh, Rob, an out-size Airedale, crouching sphinx-like with a red ball between his fore-paws.

Jenni is sheathed in a satiny blue swimsuit like you see in magazine advertisements. Her hair is put up high on her head. She looks Grecian, and modern. Her skin is richly sun-tanned. Her arms are round and slender. She is leaning backwards, legs stretched out. A tin of sun-tan lotion with a picture of a smiling glamorous woman not unlike herself, is close by, with a packet of *Hassan Bey* cigarettes and a lighter.

'Gideon,' Jenni says, 'you'll get burnt. Won't you let me put some lotion on your back?'

'No thanks. My skin's as rough as a football. I never get burnt.'

'What nonsense,' Jenni laughs.

'Honestly,' he says. 'But I'll rub some lotion on you, if you like.'

'Oh yes please, that would be lovely.'

Jenni, who is fair, wants to be dark. Mother, who is dark, wants to be fair. Gideon is neither one nor the other, yet at times tantalisingly both.

Lying flat on her stomach, Jenni slips the straps of her swimsuit off her shoulders. Gideon scoops the creamy stuff into the palm of his hand. He messages her back all the way to the nape of her neck with a slow circular motion.

'Mmmmmmmm...' Jenni purrs, eyes shut. The swell of her breast below her armpit moves in rhythm with Gideon's hand.

'I've always said Gideon should've been a doctor or something. He has such good hands,' says Mother and plucks a grape.

'That's it. I'm going in for dip.' Gideon wipes his hand on his trunks.

'But you've just been,' Mother almost protests.

'Another one.'

He gets up, stretches himself. 'Want to come?' he invites Jenni.

She shakes her head. 'Take Rob. He needs exercise.'

We watch Gideon's loping trot to the sea, with Rob at his heels. Waist deep in the water, Gideon leaps dolphin-like, and plunges momentarily out of sight. Surfacing, he shakes spray from his head. He swims away with a powerful crawl stroke. Soon he is a mere dot in an expanse of azure, whereas the dog turns back, clambers splashing to the shore where he stands barking stupidly.

'Rob, come here!' Jenni calls.

'I wish he wouldn't swim so far out, the red flag is up,' Mother says, peering anxiously over her sunglasses at the receding head. 'Is he turning back, can you see?'

'Abba isn't coming back. He's swimming to Cyprus,' says Tali without lifting her eyes from her sand architecture.

'He's swimming back now, I'm sure,' Jenni says. But she doesn't look sure. Half rising, she strains her eyes to see better.

Gideon seems to be swimming more vigorously than before, making a great agitation in the water. But he is stuck there, moving neither forward nor backward. The sea looks calm, the sky a wash of blue. Up in his look-out tower the lifeguard snoozes with a crumpled paperback open spine up on his knee. Death could be here, doing a bit of holiday moonlighting in the easiest hour of the day.

Gideon raises an arm. Is he waving? Is he drowning? Nothing stirs, except froth about his distant figure.

Jenni rises to her feet. A quick glance at the sleeping lifeguard, then she's away, sprinting to the water. Her swimsuit flashes over the cusp of a wave. Like Gideon, she is a confident swimmer. The distance between them closes. Soon they are together, embracing, turning round and round as in a dance. Her legs thrust out of the water to close around Gideon's body. His head presses against her middle. Locked in each other, they oar in unison to shore. Mother, who can't swim, smiles wistfully. She takes up the romantic novel she has been reading, removes the book mark, adjusts her glasses.

Safe on dry land, Gideon and Jenni stand doubled up, hands on knees, coughing, spitting brine. If one moved aside the other might fall down like a domino brick. Then slowly they come towards us.

'That was much too much of a swim,' Gideon says, rubbing himself down with a towel.

'I think we should be getting back home. The children have had enough of the sea for one day,' Mother decides.

Of all the things that had happened to me to that day, nothing so undermined my faith as coming face to face with Gideon's fallibility. That is why music fails me; the sound I produce on the cello is all of a sudden plangent, unpleasing. I can't bear it. I can't even listen to music. I feel I might as well be dead.

Therefore I sink in school.

Our new class teacher, Tehila, whose name means 'praise' in Hebrew, is in conflict with herself, not with me: her reason advises to give me up as a hopeless case. After all, the school has standards to uphold. Her teacher's heart rebels against such desertion. A thin pimply woman with a bobbing Adam's apple, Tehila will not accept that any child's obduracy could defeat her. But I do. I shut her out. Soon even she has to admit that the extra attention she lavishes on me is a waste. I can see, as can the other pupils, how my very presence in class frustrates her. Indifferent to her anguish, I sit silently at my desk and contemplate the ignominy of being relegated to a lower class.

'What is Heaven? What is Hell?' I ask Ori.

'Heaven,' he replies, 'is everything which isn't Hell. Heaven is difficult. Demanding. You have to work hard for it. Hell is easy. You just slide into it hardly noticing. Hell is ordinary.'

Our teacher Tehila, in her magisterial fervour, tries to make the class understand the historical significance of our national resurrection. Triumph out of destruction. Justice out of persecution.

Compassion out of oppression...

I outstare her reproachful gaze. To think that a son of Gideon Jerusalem whose family fills pages of history, who is himself at this very moment shaping our destiny at the side of Ben Gurion, a latter day Joshua no less, should be wilfully autistic is a punishment no devoted teacher deserves. She doesn't say so but I know that's what she thinks and feels.

I make my mind curl and slink away to Hell, to forbidden Eldorado with its panoramic vista of the Bay, where ships at night twinkle like tinsel tears.

Who are these people sitting at the marble-topped tables among the dark pines during hot murmuring afternoons, drinking iced coffee to the strains of *The Blue Danube*?

Who are the elderly ladies puckering painted mouths at china cups, 'oohing' and 'aahhing' as Richard Tauber's voice singing Lehár's *Du bist mein herz...* comes wafting across the coffee-scented air from loudspeakers in the tree branches?

What are those amorous couples who lean towards each other under the coloured lanterns?

Idlers all! Apfelstrudel munchers dislocated from extinct gentility. Empty souls clinging together in nothingness. Adulterers. Spies on death's mission, their victims, their masters.

Voyeurs of fantasies, like me.

For Café Eldorado is that kind of place: nostalgia's no man's land for the damned to while away their time. Here one evening, a Dutch Jew called Friis keeled over in his seat against a pepper corn tree, with a foot long knitting needle stuck through his heart. All he left was an unfinished slice of chocolate gateau.

With sundown I crawl through a hole in the fence; hide in a bush, watch the lit stage in the clearing among the pines. The lights throw out colours like seeds from a sower's swing. A six-piece band strikes up a tune. Fluorescent smiles on their faces. Quavers twinkle about their shiny midnight blue tuxedos. The dancers take to the floor, rotating or gyrating to a waltz, fox-trot, tango, pas redoublé, boogie-woogie – anything the sleazy saxophone squeezes out.

During the breaks on come the illusionists: a magician, jugglers, flame-eaters, acrobats, the Strong Man lifting half the weight of a bus with either hand.

All a prelude, nothing more. We wait for the main event, the night's star attraction, who at last is heralded by a roll of drums and a fan fare. Bathed in light, Carmen Phahdi emerges from the shadows. She undulates to the microphone at the centre of the stage. Loud cheers; thunderous applause; kisses blown across the darkness like fire crackers. Carmen Phahdi floats her curves upwards with outstretched arms. She pouts her glistening mouth, caresses the microphone in her jewelled hands. In her shimmering off-the-shoulders sequin evening gown, she is queen of the night, goddess of desires. Her blonde hair cascades to her shoulders. Hands crossed on her bosom, she waits for the passion to subside, for the music to begin.

Her voice is throaty. Letting her pall of hair fall half across her face, she croons *'Amado mio, love me forever...'* followed by a Spanish number *'Amor Amor...'* The collective ecstasy is too charged. Any moment a fuse will blow. Miss Phahdi knows when to let go, her timing is practiced and unerring. Now she launches into a sequence of pre-war Berlin cabaret numbers. The *Yekkes* are nearly swooning. Mistress of titillation, she leaves them unfulfilled as she switches to French, imitating Edith Piaf, then to Greek. Her range is a pot-pourri of ersatz cultures. She hypnotises the audience, holds hearts in the palm of her hand.

It's too simple to say that Carmen Phahdi is beautiful. She is Aphrodite of changing aspects, a blend of Hollywood glamour and Hellenic decadence. She is at once innocent and obscene. She repels and attracts. There are rumours that Carmen Phahdi is in fact, a man in drag. Man or woman, a Circe nonetheless, who, with a thrust of the hips will turn men to pigs.

* * * * *

What astrologer dare draw the horoscope of this nation, half-born in November, pushed out of a ruptured womb to face fire six months later? The prophets are silent. Strategists and diplomats sharpen their wits. Warriors unsheathe the sword. Autumnal days of awe, now and ever a time of uncertainty here, for Jews.

Soon the British will leave. Relinquishing the Mandate they claim was foisted upon them, they will throw this quarrelsome, ungracious and ungrateful province into the lap of the United Nations. A plague on both their houses – the Jews and the Arabs thoroughly deserve each other, the Governor of Haifa laconically observes to foreign journalists. We are a land that devoureth empires. A forge where ploughshares are forever beaten into swords.

Gideon might have been among those dispatched by Ben Gurion to the capitals of the world, to win support, cajole, make promises, trade favours, in preparation for the impending United Nations debate which will decide our fate. Instead he is at Ben Gurion' side, an operation room Ulysses, ready with wisdom. For like his biblical namesake, Gideon is full of cunning and daring stratagem.

Before decamping to some undisclosed retreat, he expresses his disappointment in me. My school report has been lying unlooked at on the kitchen table. Dressed in paramilitary fatigues and ready to leave, Gideon scrutinises the sheet without touching it. I know what it says. I can read Gideon's thoughts from the way his mouth sets. He raises his eyes to meet mine but he looks through me, as though I weren't there.

To my surprise he says nothing about my poor performance at school, nothing about Tehila's decision to send me to a lower class, nothing about my alleged unsociability. After a long pause he half turns. 'Might as well sell the cello, since it seems your gift doesn't amount to much after all. Buy you instead a toy mouth organ to play with, like Tali,' he tells me.

Rain pounds the shiny asphalt, but not for long. A cold sun breaks through the cloud cover. Little rainbows quiver in puddles. It is Saturday, mid November, 1947, a day Hai disengages from the rigours of office to celebrate Leah's twelfth birthday – her *Bat Mitzvah*. If *Doda* Vic's home is perennially carefree it is because Hai – even though in the thick of procuring a few more aeroplanes for the Hagana's nascent airforce – takes care to isolate his home from the turbulence of current events.

Leah's present is a new black Rudge bicycle, hastily rushed through the port customs by one of Hai's friends. It stands in the corridor for all to admire. Leah has not yet learnt how to ride a bike.

We are gathered in the living room, waiting for the radio to play Leah's special birthday request – Rimsky-Korsakov's *Sheherazade Suite*. But our minds are really on our impending flight over Haifa in a Rapid bi-plane, which *Dod* Hai has arranged for us. We are thrilled. None of the kids we know has been in an aeroplane.

The grownups are playing cards, as usual. The table is dressed in green felt, as you see in real casinos. Sitting round it are *Doda* Vic, Hai, Rosa and Albert Matalon who live across the street. The stakes are low: whoever wins the most buys the kids sweets.

Four years old Ami Matalon is quarrelling with Tali over a plastic train. Yossi, his elder brother, is arguing with Leah on the merits of various makes of bicycle. Himself bikeless, he looks forward to tutoring Leah in riding the machine.

'Children,' says *Doda* Vic, 'why don't you go out on the balcony? The rain has stopped, the sun is shining.'

We hear Daphna's friends whistling their group's call tune. 'Hey, Daphna, come down,' they shout, as she leans over the balustrade, 'let's see your sister's new bike. Does it have gears? Come down now, we'll teach you both to cycle.'

'Don't feel like it. Anyway, Leah doesn't need you lot to teach her,' Daphna shouts back.

'What about you, then?'

'I hate bicycles.'

The exchange develops into a jolly banter. Volunteering to keep a look out for Leah's request, I stay in the armchair by the radio while the others go out to the balcony.

'*Mon Dieu, quelle bruit!*' Rosa exclaims, rolling her eyes. Originally from Beirut, she and her husband have disowned their past, but not Française – *la langue de touts les Juifs du moyen orient*. Meanwhile outside, Leah and Yossi are manufacturing paper water bombs.

'Abbi, my cocki's up,' cries Ami, tugging at his fly.

Albert takes him, bounces him on his knees. 'Oh, cocki's up, is it? One day you'll cry when it doesn't go up anymore. Ha ha ha.'

'Albert! *Vraiment!*' says Rosa tight-lipped, and cuts the deck with a flick of her hand, like a card shark. '*Voila!*'

'*J'attendrai toujours, ra ra ra ra ra ra j'attendrai toujours...*' sings Albert, fanning out his hand of cards. He leans over to one side and farts. Rosa looks at him murderously.

'*Pardon!*' laughs Albert.

'Philo, Philo, come quickly! Your lady love is down below,' Daphna calls.

Carmen Phahdi is crossing the road on the arm of the Strong Man. She is wearing pale blue slacks with a matching cardigan. Her face is almost hidden by an enormous pair of sunglasses. Her hair is bundled untidily into a red kerchief. She looks small, insignificant. The strong man looks too flabby to be athletic.

'Well, Philo, do you still love her?' says Daphna, looking at me askance.

I affect indifference.

'Don't pretend, we know you're crazy about her.'

Miss Phahdi is directly under the balcony now. I see a patch of dark hair showing through the blond, like a smudge of dirt. The boys down below exchange glances and smirk.

'*Amado mio…*' Daphna croons, swaying her hips.

'Quick, a bomb! Gimme a bomb!' Yossi yells.

But Miss Phahdi and her escort are now out of range. The missile splatters on the bicycle saddle of one of Daphna's friends.

'Cheeky brat! I'll take the hide off your backside, just you wait!' The victim shakes his fist. We shout, we whoop. The water bombs fly.

Mr Grunspan from the floor below comes out to his balcony. Ever since his wife died of cancer three months ago, Mr Grunspan has been wearing his pyjamas like a skin. Thin and crazy-eyed, he looks now more or less as he did when the allies rescued him from Buchenwald – even the pyjamas look the same.

Mr Grunspan curses us and the world in a loud voice, for making noise, for his lonely misery, for the fact that he is still alive and unable to leave the life he so detests.

And because Grunspan is crazy, upsetting the neighbours with his holocaustian attire, and because we are accustomed to his weepy hysterics, and because he is spoiling the fun of Leah's birthday, we jeer at him. And because I have seen the ugly blackness showing through Carmen Phahdi's camouflage of blonde, it is I who casts the water bomb at Grunspan. Which hits him at the back of the neck.

He looks up, skeletal in his rage. '*Shkotzim*! Hooligans!' He screams. 'No respect for anything! You're worse than Hitler! What kind of a world is this! Azazel! Shit! I want to go hang myself!' He bursts into a dreadful wail.

Ten days later, on November 29, the United Nations Assembly votes on the partition of Palestine into Arab and Jewish states. Tehila makes us stand up in class to sing the *Hatiqva*: 'The soul of a Jew stirs… not yet have we lost our hope, that hope of two millennia…'.

There is spontaneous celebration in the streets. We pour scorn on Israel's enemies, on the British Foreign Secretary, Ernest Bevin, above all. We curse Haj Amin El Husseini, the Mufti of Jerusalem who has vowed to throw us into the sea.

The next day Mr Grunspan hangs himself from the banisters of the stair well. I catch a glimpse of his thin pyjama'd legs dangling in space. Too late, *Doda* Vic hustles Leah and me back into the sunlight of the street. She buys us falafel across the road, to kill time before the ambulance arrives to take Mr Grunspan away.

That morning another bomb goes off in a busy Jerusalem street. Fifteen people are killed in an attack on a bus on route to Tiberias. No one has time to think of poor Mr Grunspan; his death is simply added to the statistics of the conflict's early casualties.

I have flown through the sky in a Rapid bi-plane, and have seen the Hot Gates in my mind's eye. There is no music anymore, only the beating of drums. I feel hardened by my obduracy and locked in a shell of brass. Your image, Imogen, is obscured in smoke and fire.

* * * * *

Among Gideon's early clichés is one which he continuously demonstrates, curiously, and eventually, fatally: 'life' he says, 'is a game of musical chairs, without the music.'

What arbitrates the losses and the gains, raises one, and topples the other? Blind random chance, explains Gideon. No more to life than that? Oh yes, the fight against it, no matter how high the odds are stacked against you. Submit only to accidents of your choice.

He makes such pronouncements while scrutinising his face in the mirror after shaving. Gideon is at his most philosophical during morning ablution.

A bathroom accident terminates Grandfather's illness and he departs to Abraham's bosom, where of late he had longed to be. That same accident carries Mother and Tali to Jerusalem for a week, thus creating the opportunity for Jenni and her dog Rob to move into our home to look after me, because Gideon too, is away, already tasting warfare.

Moving up and down the country, Gideon fills in the details in the making of Plan Dalet. Conceived to gain the initiative from the Arabs once the British had departed, Plan Dalet aims at capturing strategic points along the supposed invasion routes of the Arab armies.

For once David Oren is at odds with Gideon. He doesn't believe the Arab states will intervene at all. He feels certain that they'll only posture then leave the Palestinians to their own devices, and for himself to clobber. Ben Gurion, and Gideon among others, know better.

Meanwhile it is Oren and his hard men who take a clobbering from the Arabs in bloodied encounters on the country's highways. Ironically, Gideon's scheme of unmusical chairs is destined to appoint Oren, not himself, chief executor of Plan Dalet, which, modified by him and carried out with ruthless zeal, will turn hundreds of thousands of Palestinians into refugees fleeing from their villages and from the country.

Jenni shuts her eyes to politics. She abhors violence, but violence courts her with bouquets of smashed people for her to heal.

She sleeps in Gideon and Mother's bed. Rob lies at the foot of mine. When she returns from work in the afternoon, Jenni helps me with my homework. We listen to music together. We take Rob out for walks in the hills.

I wake up to a pale dawn. Standing by the door which separates my room from the one where Jenni sleeps, I see Rob. He whines softly, wagging his tail. There's no light in Jenni's room but I hear voices, her's then a man's, speaking at a whisper. A door opens and shuts. I get out of bed to go to the bathroom. And there, at the bathroom's open door, stands Gideon, naked. We stare at each other.

'Go back to your bed, Philo,' he says at last.

I turn and go without a word. I lie in bed thinking this and that, until I hear the front door open and shut. Gideon is gone by the time I get up.

We sit at the breakfast table, Jenni and I, unable to look each other in the eye or to talk.

'Rob,' says Jenni, 'we must hurry up so as not to miss the school bus.'

'Rob,' I retort, 'I don't give a damn about the bus. I'll walk to school, and after school I'll go straight to *Doda* Vic's.'

By mid-winter the whole country is an arena for intensified clashes. Arab bands of irregulars are, on the whole, gaining the upper hand over our units while the British, no longer governing, act as referees in a match. Gideon is away most of the time. Mother relays his messages to us as she had been doing during Hitler's war.

With the first lull in the fighting Gideon returns home. He and Mother greet each other with forced exuberance. But at night they quarrel. In the morning Gideon in a god-like mood, pronounces my sentence: banishment.

The *Reali* School, he says, obviously does me no good. I have, therefore, been enrolled in the better suited school of Kibbutz Mishmar Ha'emek, in Jezreel. There my potential will be developed to a farther limit. There, with all that fresh air and vigorous living, my health too will improve. There, not least, the coming war with its attendant hardships will not touch me, and Gideon will have one less burden to worry about.

It is February, 1948. Mother and I alight from the bus at Mishmar Ha'emek's fore-yard in the midst of a cloud burst. Rivers of water course along the paved paths. We sit to dry ourselves in the warm laundry room of my class's house. Mother leaves on the next bus out. The matron takes me to my dormitory, where my new class mates of *Arava* group, arrive in delegations to look me over. *Arava* means prairie – an open wilderness. The symbolic significance of the name weighs heavily on me.

9

Imogen is in Boston, Massachussetts. I am half way between Berkhamstead and Tring, Hertfordshire, surrounded by a herd of inquisitive heifers.

She went off without letting me know. Her assistant at LSE informed me of her departure. Date of return? Uncertain. I don't know what to make of this. Was leaving without a goodbye deliberate, or had she forgotten? Either way, it doesn't bode well.

Imogen will be addressing an international conference of sociologists, the purpose of her trip.

At the about the same time, I shall be addressing an annual general meeting of the British Women's International Zionist Organisation – WIZO. The parallel in our respective activities is comical, with a bitter taste for me. I sense that in every way and from all directions, my life is reaching a point of crisis.

My invitation to address the ladies came at a short notice: the preferred speaker dropped out, and Stephen Fink, my inept and indiscreet boss, 'offered' me.

My views, I know, are abomination to these conservative stalwarts of militant Zionism, Jewish equivalent of Daughters of the American Revolution. Anyway, I haven't a clue what I should say to them. Which is why I'm here on a walk. A good walk on a lovely Saturday like today will surely act like a laxative on a constipated mind, and also stop me from brooding over Imogen.

A very English sun slants past the tower of Aldbury's church. Shadows lengthen towards the meadow where I stand. A half-hour's walk will bring me to Tring in time for the next train to London. But now the heifers are closing in on me, some blowing and tossing their heads. I flap my map at them. They back away but don't disperse. All of a sudden I have a title to my WIZO talk: Power and Spirituality – Childhood Recollections from the Birth of Israel.

As I congratulate myself, the moist bovine muzzles before me transmogrify into lipsticked mouths, the lovely cow-eyes take on mascara, the horns become hats. I address my audience:

'Dear ladies, I'm pleased and honoured to be here... The title of my talk is, on further reflection, unsatisfactory, for it will raise your expectations to something I cannot deliver. Moreover, frankly now that I think about it, I'm not sure what it means. However...

'There was this Swiss author called Robert Walser. A good story-teller. A mini-Kafka you might say. And no, he wasn't Jewish.

'Committed to an asylum for the insane, Walser went for a walk on a cold, bright winter day and dropped dead by a tree, conveniently close to a footpath. They found him deep-frozen under a drift of snow, a big smile on his face. And why not? Clean as a pin. A perfect death, arms crossed over his chest, ready to be popped into a coffin without as much as a change of clothes. Who could wish for a better end?

'"What's all this?" I hear you think. "We've come to hear a talk about Jews, and instead we get a load of you-know-what about some *meshigene* Swiss goy, a lunatic!"

'Bear with me, I beg of you. The digression isn't as random as it may seem. Now file Walser away in your minds and turn your thoughts to God. Imagine a tough, lean, ambitious God at the start of His career, a hip-on-thigh-smiting super-interventionist. A God who would make you tremble if He showed up at your St. John's Wood synagogue for the *Shobbes* service.

'Miracles dot His agenda. Angels move abroad on earthly tours of inspection, or on errands. They drop in on Sarah. "Lady," they tell her, "you're going to have a baby." And she, being an old woman well past child-bearing, thinks it's some kind of a joke. She has a good laugh.

'Angels drop in on Samson's folks. "Your kid's going to be Superman," they announce, "Give him only health food. No haircuts. And when he grows up tell him booze is definitely out. Broads are okay, though. As many as he can handle."

'Angels, ladies, come and go. Like bailiffs. Like secret agents. Like hit-men. Always with God's full back-up support: zap! a city falls; pow! a dissenting non-believer drops dead; wham! an army is routed.

'For all that, the world doesn't get any better. God is cheesed off. And bored. It's kind of lonely being Numero Uno, the Almighty One all the time and still failing to get things right.

'He hits on a new approach. Splitting himself into a galaxy of multi-faced, multi-gendered multi-formed deities, He spreads himself all over the world. Assuming diverse guises, he cross-pollinates with humanity, now as a prize bull, now as a shower of gold...

'More fun for sure. Better music. Better art. A richer, more varied polyphonic poetry. But at the end of the day, the results are hardly better than before.

'Then He gets this totally novel idea: why not abdicate power altogether? Come down in size, be a vulnerable mortal, set a personal example?

'Thus Wotan becomes the Wanderer. Powerless but wiser. His magic spear – symbol of his omnipotence – shattered by a strapping fool, he heads back to his own pre-ordained *Götterdämmerung*. Thus God & Son ostensibly die on the cross. End of experiment?

'Not quite. The idea of voluntary abdication of power, with self-immolation as the logical corollary turns out to be an all-time knockout trend-setter. Like a black hole of the mind, it blows horizons to infinity; big-bangs Man's creative genius... Here, ladies, is where the Jews come in.

'Don't believe they were stripped of power and dispersed all over the world by adverse circumstances, currents of history, God's punishment, what have you. No, the Jews willed it on themselves. Unconsciously but tenaciously. By decades and centuries they engineered their way into an asylum of powerlessness. Not to die inanely, like Walser, but in order to repeat forever the process of creation. How else were we to be a Light unto the Nations'? How else can the pretence to such a claim be anything but preposterous conceit?

'I invite you, ladies, to consider the Zionist Enterprise in the light of this argument: is its attempt at "normalising" the Jews a step forward, or a surrender of the Jews' peculiar, creative destiny? Well?

'Ouch! Oh no... Please... Ouch! Ladies, tea cakes are one thing. Cups and saucers really hurt!...'

Moon has murdered a blackbird on the flat strip outside the front window and brought it in. Feathers lie scattered all over the floor among uneaten remnants of the bird. His work done, Moon snoozes on the sofa, fluffs of down hanging from his whiskers.

I hoover the mess. On the table in the living room lies an unopened letter from Mimi beside the open last volume of Gideon's diaries. Mimi's letter will have to wait. I'm in no mood to read it. Instead, I plunge into my father's memoirs:

Holte, Copenhagen December 25, 1966.
Christmas. Dark and depressing in spite of so many festive lights in windows. K is away in Sweden visiting her grandmother in Örebro, I think. Said she would be back for the New Year. People her age shouldn't have living grandmothers. It's unnatural. Like being breast-

fed well past infancy. The old thing is a hundred and three! And lives in a Slot – an 18th century castle, converted into apartments for aristocratic widows of slender means.

Half of me is still in Israel. When I'm alone, like now, I'm reminded of this. I never talk to K about it anymore. It upsets her. Makes her feel that she's not enough to fill my life. She can't understand my peculiar kind of loneliness. Therefore, she feels guilty for being insufficient. I try to shield her from my darker moods by trying to be funny. I've learnt this from her – a Scandinavian ritual of pretence. How charmingly civilised they are.

Had a phone call from the Embassy two days ago. Not from A's daughter, who is now Ambassador (how time flies), but from a junior official from Trade, called Leshem. Never heard of him. Didn't think anyone at the Embassy remembered I existed. This Leshem said he wanted to see me on a private matter which he stubbornly refused to divulge on the phone. Mossad man, I bet. But why?

Invited me for lunch at a fish restaurant in town (acceptably kosher if you want, he promised). He is a young man prematurely old. Short, balding, with intense, suspicious eyes. The restaurant was expensive. Can junior diplomats afford such eating places?

He asked many questions the answers to which, I could tell, he already knew or thought he did. He seemed to know more about me than his position in the trade section would warrant. His face seemed vaguely familiar, but such faces always are. Mossad. Without doubt. What would the Mossad want with me?

Over coffee it all becomes clear. Tuvia Lishanski. Had I known him? In what circumstances was he executed? Who did I think was responsible? His self-control was impeccable. Like a trained professional agent. For all that, I could sense the hatred behind the impassive mask. Lishanski's son (Leshem, it should have been obvious to me from the start). Miserably obsessed with his father. On the trail of imagined past persecutors. Revenge?

I told him the truth, all I knew. But that's not what he wanted to hear. He didn't believe me. What he wanted was a hint of guilt, a clue to complicity. I told him I, like many at the time, considered the execution a shameful blot on the Hagana's record, regardless of whether or not Lishanski was guilty.

I offered to pay for the lunch, 'you be my guest,' I said. He didn't want to hear of it. I insisted on paying for my lunch. But he refused in such a way that I feared he might create a scene if I went on insisting.

*And suddenly I realised what a terrible mistake I had made: he took
my offer to pay for the meal as a show of guilt, an implicit confession!
Now he really believes that I was party to his father's murder!*

*'Happy Chanuka, I'll keep in touch,' he said outside, and walked
hurriedly away.*

The telephone woke me up. I cast a glance at the radio clock. It's
past midnight. 'Hello,' I say, trying to sound like someone who has
just been woken up.

'Hullo, honey.'

'Imogen?'

'Darling, did I wake you? Of course I did. How thoughtless of me.'

'Never mind. Is anything wrong?'

She laughs. 'No, of course not. I just thought of you and I miss you.
It was awful of me not to ring you before I went away. Can you forgive
me?'

'I'll try. How is the conference going?'

'It went. Finished last week. I'm in a lovely farm house in Vermont.
You'd have loved it. Darling?'

'Yes, I'm still here. Want me to fly over?'

Again she laughs. 'Honey, that would've been wonderful.' A pause,
then, 'I'll be back the day after tomorrow.'

The last bit of her schedule announced with less enthusiasm and
unattached to a term of endearment. I understand what I should have
known before: her affection for me corresponds to the distance
separating us.

'What are you doing in a Vermont farm house?'

'Having a wonderful time. And missing you. It belongs to a new
friend I made. A Harvard professor.'

Without further explanation which Imogen doesn't volunteer, what
am I supposed to make of this?

'Well, enjoy house and friend to the full. I'll see you whenever…'

'I'll ring you next from home. Philo…'

'What?'

'My new friend is rather senior. He has a lovely wife who's also
here. Good night, my love.'

* * * * *

I had forgotten about the monthly editorial meeting of *Kadima*. Everybody is already there when I come in ten minutes late. Mr Fink gives me a grim look and motions me to take a seat. Then, presumably for my benefit, he begins all over again with reproachful emphasis: 'Ladies and gentlemen...'

There's only one lady in the room, an American divorcee called Roberta Kemp. I've never seen her before. I've no idea why she's here either, and I ought to because I'm Editor!

'Let me first introduce a new colleague. Mrs Roberta Kemp.'

'Bobby. Call me Bobby, please.'

Fink grins. 'Bobby,' he repeats, savouring her name like a lollipop. 'In case you don't know, Bobby, *Kadima* has a long, illustrious tradition. It is, I believe, the first regularly published Zionist journal in Europe. The first number appeared immediately following the First Zionist Congress in... er...'

'1897!' Bobby chips in, raising a slim shiny pen.

'Sorry?'

'That's when the first Zionist Congress took place, in Basle.'

'Ah yes, of course.'

Stephen Fink, made in Budapest, imported to London via Newcastle-Upon-Tyne, is the supreme committee room operator, armed with the platitudes of a trade unionist, the banality of fortune cookie aphorisms, and the stamina of a marathon runner. Half of Fink's gift in committee survival tactics would have set Gideon on a steady course for a grand career.

Fink's desk is like a landing strip, edged with a battery of pens pointing outwards at an angle, like missiles. Dwarfed by his executive chair, he looks like a mini Stalin as he begins the business of the day.

I get the feeling I'm in for the chop. Let it be, I think.

There's good news and bad news, Fink announces. *Kadima*'s circulation has gone up by five per cent for the first time in twenty years, calling for the print run to be increased by five hundred – all going to Sidney, Australia, except for fifteen copies for Tokyo!

'Tokyo?' Bobby Kemp stares, wide eyed.

It seems a small community of Japanese converts to Judaism has heard of it and placed an order. Also, in the course of the past year, the magazine has been quoted internationally by several journals, notably by a Jewish publication in Vienna. Also, two articles by the Editor, who has brought so much knowledge and authority to the magazine ('hear, hear' all round) were syndicated in American and

Canadian Jewish journals. Israel's Independence Day special issue was a resounding success...

Fink pauses before the bad news.

While *Kadima* was thrusting forward, finances were, unfortunately, on the retreat. The Board of Directors, with great reluctance, has decided to slash the budget.

My self-destruction impulse takes over. 'Hear hear!' I say under my breath. Fink glares. Bobby Kemp puckers her red mouth to a point.

In short, as from the next issue, *Kadima* will be slimmed down by four pages, to twelve. That being the case, the Board is of the opinion that the Union's official organ should place more emphasis on 'communal affairs' and less on 'controversial' and potentially 'divisive' issues of Israeli politics and the Middle East. My stuff, in other words.

All the while Bobby Kemp is scribbling furiously, nodding her head as Fink rounds off his sentences. The coloured bangles rattle on her wrists as she writes. From time to time she stops to push her Christian Dior specs up her tiny ski run of a nose back into place.

The reason for her presence is at last revealed when she passes round her visiting card which, in embossed italics, says:

Roberta Kemp B.A., Deputy Editor
KADIMA
10 Whitefriars Street
London EC4
Tel: 020 88353 4312

The meeting over, Fink beats a hasty retreat, apologising that he's late for another meeting.

I face my deputy in the corridor.

'Hi!' she says.

'Hi.'

'Wasn't that a terrific meeting?'

'The terrifickest I've ever been to.'

She grins reflexively. 'You know, I really am looking forward to working with you. I have so many ideas!'

'Is that a fact.'

'Yeah, you bet.'

'Nine thirty tomorrow morning. Not a moment sooner.'

'Excuse me?'

'Never mind. Nice to have you on board.'

'Great. Hey, isn't it crazy about the Japanese? Can you beat that? Can we do anything to get more of them interested? Wouldn't that be fantastic publicity?'

'How about a free stick-on Jewish nose with every copy?'

'Uh uh, that's not nice!' She shakes a finger at me. Naughty naughty Editor! Later I learnt that she had had a nose job done in New Jersey, costing an arm and a leg.

'Say, just what exactly is your speciality?' she asks.

'Being had, I suppose.'

'Look, I don't want you think that I...' she starts, thrown off but not in the least embarrassed.

'No need for another word, Deputy. We're in it together now.'

'Okay. Hey, listen. In a year's time, God willing, I'm going on *Aliya*. I'm gunning for a job with the Jerusalem Post, so this should come in handy,' she confides with a wink.

'All power to God's elbow. See you tomorrow.'

* * * * *

Inside Mimi's envelope there's another one, a small brown envelope inscribed '*Abba!*'

Dear Philo, enclosed, a letter from your son. What I have to tell you is not happy news. I won't try to spare your feelings because I feel you share in the responsibility.

Jacob's gone off the deep end. Quite literally. Almost a year ago, he dropped out of university to join a yeshiva of born-again fanatic Hassidim. You are out of touch with reality here, so you wouldn't know just what a dreadful epidemic this has become. No one is safe! You cannot imagine what we have been through. If it hadn't been for David, I really don't know what I'd have done. We've tried, unsuccessfully to get Jacob to see a psychiatrist. He is mule stubborn, like you.

When at last he realised that God had no use for computers, he quit the yeshiva. So much for black hats and beards and side locks, thank Goodness. We thought he'd come to his senses, but no. One day, without warning, he took off to Eilat. The next I hear from him, he is on the high seas, a sailor on a foreign ship (at least it's an American ship!). We managed to radio-phone the ship. Jacob's fine, but he wouldn't talk to me. Philo, I'm sick with worry.

David is writing to all our embassies in the far east, in Latin America, everywhere in the world, in fact.

You'll let me know of anything important Jacob writes, won't you?

M.

Jacob's letter is in pencil on cheap yellow paper, probably of Third World manufacture.

M/S Rebecca April 3, 1986

Abba – You who have turned your back on so much, will understand how free I feel, at last. As free as is humanly possible. Freer than you could ever dream of being, I'm sure.

My days flow into each other with the rhythm of the sea. I do my duties like an automaton. I cultivate my emptiness and guard it against all intrusions. Only madmen can truly enjoy the kind of freedom I'm talking about. There's a lot to be said for being mad.

I forgive you for being my father – you must have suffered, not having been much good at it. I pity you for the baggage of memories you carry with you, like a tortoise trapped in a heavy shell. You see, I've thrown all mine away. Absolutely everything.

Like the empty oil drum we tossed overboard this morning while exercising a Williamson Turn. It's a routine maritime manoeuvre aimed at recovering a man overboard, or avoiding an on-coming vessel on a collision course. You swing hard to starboard, then to port, then double back. It should have brought us back to the point where we cast away the drum. But after some five nautical miles and half an hour later, the drum was nowhere in sight. This is the Pacific Ocean. Immeasurably vast, it swallows up the past sooner than you can look away.

Our skipper, a Bostonian, made excuses: it was not a navigational error but a wayward current which separated us from our drum. I might have told him what you and I know better than anybody – what you lose you never find again: love, faith, honour, strength. Only money comes and goes, sometimes.

Instead of our drum there was this dying sperm whale floating along side us. We leaned over the railing and watched it turn in the water, a spotted grey-green mass with tiny sad eyes. Its breath and spume filled the air with an unimaginable stench. You, who take delight in symbols, make something out of that if you can.

A word about the ship. It's an old freighter. American but sailing under a Liberian flag. The crew come from all parts of the world, so being Jewish and Israeli is nothing special. We carry whatever we can get: cement from Aalborg, timber from Africa, grain from America, refrigerators, micro-ovens from Japan, you name it, who cares?

This is my home. Jacob on Rebecca. Ridiculous, isn't it? Listen, everything is ridiculous. Your Zionism, Israel, the army, that pathetic Williamson Turn we did in and out of Lebanon, which left so many people dead for nothing. God is ridiculous — stupidly, uselessly, boringly. And you too, Abba, most of all as my father.

I lie in my bunk at night dreaming vacant dreams while flying fish skid on deck. I've heard whales singing like sirens. Siren songs hold no terror for me. I've seen great mountains of the sea come over the horizon, toss the ship hundreds of meters to the sky, then throw her down miles further on.

You can laugh at everything, except the ocean. Here I'll be, until one day they'll wrap my body with some meaningless flag, and chute me overboard, like an empty drum. You'll never see me again, Abba. I'm the end of your line, the answer to the empty promise it offered.

Jacob

Out in the deepening night, stars struggle with a yellow mist of urban pollution. A group of youths bellow their way up the road, with a ghetto blaster full on.

I fill a glass with the last of yesterday's bottle of wine.

'Moon,' I say, 'I salute you. You take everything in your stride. You recognise no absolutes, in love or in rejection. You're a real hero, whatever that means. Here's to your health.

'Let me tell you, Moon. I'm quitting my job. Leave it to Deputy B with a note saying "All yours, Doll You're on your own. Happy landing in Jerusalem."

'Don't ask what's next. I don't know. Except that I can't stay here.

'As for you, old friend, what can I say? From the street you came and to the street thou shalt return? No. I'll find you a good home, if I can't take you with me. That's a promise, Moon.'

Moon stares into the night. I turn on the television to watch an imported soap drama, they're all the same, with no beginning and no end.

10

Picture a wilderness. Interlocking low hills against a pale horizon. A tree here, a clump of bushes there. Withered grass and thorns everywhere, fed on by fidgety flocks of goldfinches. Rocks jutting out of the ground like broken teeth, and lazy buzzards above. Sparse pasture sustaining flocks of sheep, thin Syrian cattle, and the destructive ubiquitous black goats which are indigenous to the Middle East.

Cactus barriers flank dusty paths strewn with animal ordure that meander up towards three villages: Abu Shusha, Garbiya Al Tahta, and her twin village Garbiya Al Fauqa.

As the herds wind their way to or from the villages you hear the tinkling of bells, the cries of shepherd boys, the barking of dogs on the outskirts of the villages.

What you see, in short, is pastoral scenes straight from the bible, in Cecil B. De Mille Technicolor.

The Arab villages overlook Kibbutz Mishmar Ha'emek, which spreads across the lower foothills, girthed by a broad tessellation of brown and green expanses that pan down to the extremity of Jezreel. Fields of maize, wheat, alfalfa. Dunams upon dunams of plum, apricot, and apple orchards. While to the north masses a dense coniferous forest of mythical depth.

Three John Deere tractors, four Caterpillars, and a new Combine Harvester the size of a fort are lined up outside a metal hangar, along with an array of other modern farm machinery.

No foot-worn paths lead into the kibbutz but wide tracks, a road, all converging on tall gates that shut at night. The cows which trail out of spacious cow sheds each morning to graze in fenced meadows, are pedigree black and white Friesians. Thirty eight litres of prime quality milk per head a day! The milking parlour is scrubbed clean. Not a speck of cow shit on the concrete floor. Listen to the milking machines thrumming away as they pump liquid protein into the very heart of the *Yishuv*, the Jewish Settlement of Palestine!

The sheep and goats, of the same breed as those in the Arab villages, are fatter, larger, neater looking. A sensitive poet shepherds them daily out onto the hills. He has a Master's Degree in Philosophy and a loaded Parabellum automatic hidden under his jerkin.

Look at it all and dispel any doubt you might have as to who sows in tears and who reaps in joy around here.

I fill my lungs with the salubrious air of my new banishment, and relish it.

Here begins my exile. Here, too, is where our ways – Gideon's and mine – part, never quite to meet again. In sending me to Mishmar Ha'emek he has unknowingly set me on a process in reverse to his own: he is moving in the van of a new national destiny; I am drifting back into realms of Jewish atavism, being the stranger, the sojourner, the irrelevant outsider.

You, Imogen, a sociologist with a dependable ear for nuance and the assured judgement of a mighty empire in your bones, can you not see the irony of my situation? Born to Zionism, I'm here, unwittingly, its exemplary antithesis!

As for the kibbutz children, they are at the conclusive end of the syllogism: synthesis of the Zionist ideal. A race apart, evolved to perfection from the ancient stereotype. You can tell at a glance in the shower room where boys and girls mix together. Amir, Ezra, Yaron, Zvi, boys of my age, sun-tanned, strong of limb, hair bleached tawny from outdoor activities. Sinewy. Muscles tuned for contest. Unflinching eyes. Stoic pride with innocent awareness of their own worth, that's what their gazes reveal.

Look at Einat, Dikla, and Mayan, tossing their glossy hair under jets of water. See the soap bubbles on their budding breasts. Their happy freckled faces and healthy teeth conceal the germination of sombre feminine strength. For they are the wives-to-be of future warriors, farmers, artists, all united in the common pursuit of excellence in everything. These are children without a past, born to parents who have drawn a curtain over theirs.

Among them my dimensions are invisible. I stand there like a cardboard cut-out figure. Glowingly red-headed, with a pile of freshly-laundered clothes in her bare arms, Yula our matron, watches me, wondering probably how much fresh air, fresh vegetables, wholesome kibbutz bread, bananas, pints of milk, eggs, it would take to make me look like the rest of her charges.

I summon my mother Beth's chameleon powers. I dissemble assimilation so convincingly that a small fawn-like girl called Ayah, whose mother claims a distant kinship with Gideon's family, 'adopts' me. She takes me to her parents' room in the evenings and on Saturdays. Thus I am co-opted into the tribe, with rights and

107

status conferred and duties outlined.

Instinctively, I apply to my existence the basic rule of survival in exile: mediocrity. I avoid extremes. I neither excel nor fall below the norm but settle quietly in the safe zone of the fulcrum. It comes naturally, I need deploy no guile. I need no guidance from a Polonius, who might have been our class tutor, Yasha.

'The body,' he says, 'is the temple of the spirit'. *Mens sana in corpore sano* is what he really means. He is no earthy Roman, though, but a romantic humanist in the European tradition. A worshipper of nature, socialist ideologue down to the last cell of his enormous slack body. In fact, Yasha despises Rome, which Gideon venerates. He loathes everything Rome stood for, from her imperial might to the flat-footed banality of her art, as he sees it. And if there is one thing about the Jews of which he is proud, it's their suicidal El Alamo last stand in Masada against the Roman 10th Legion, in 70 AD, even though it brought about the destruction of the Second Temple.

In order to win his esteem I strive to edify the temple of my spirit. See me at nocturnal war games sneaking through the dark under-growth of the orchards towards the fire in the clearing, where Yigal, our group leader, crouches on the lookout for us. Look how fiercely I fight during face to face combat instruction. Wielding the staff like a samurai, I parry, feint, thrust, swing!

Yigal teaches us to set a course at night by the constellations of the stars. 'The enemy,' he explains, 'is afraid of the night. Therefore the night is our friend. Know it well. Learn its sounds. Learn how to move in it.' Sitting round the camp fire, we roast potatoes spitted on sticks. We sing songs. We listen to blood-curdling stories, to steel our spirits.

Who is that "enemy" that fears the night? What foe dares challenge by day or night the tall flood-lit water tower, the warren of trenches and machine-gun nests that surround the kibbutz behind a zig-zagging wire fence, the hidden armoury of Bren guns, Lewis, Vickers, Mauser, Enfield rifles and grenades?

The lights of the kibbutz are bright. A diesel generator floods power into them.

Oil lamps burn in the small windows of Abu Shusha, and the two Garbiyas, flickering timidly in the dark. Eyes of our neighbours and half-brothers, children of Ishmael and Esau, who greet us shyly as we pass each other in the hills.

The enemy is the enemy, a faceless, formless, soul-less force we have to fight, and therefore be prepared for, Yigal explains.

We prepare ourselves, oh yes we do. Man, woman and child.

Away from the coiled serenity of Jezreel, a war is being fought. I get letters from home. One with a photograph enclosed. Gideon posing grinning by his bullet-riddled car. Recklessly, he had driven through a road block in Balad El Sheikh, a village astride a main road leading into Haifa. The stronghold of a notorious local gang leader. The Arabs had shot at him through windows, from behind corners, right at the road block, like in a western movie. Death and Gideon are like lovers at war with each other.

'I think of you a lot,' he writes. 'So many things I want to tell you. So little time in which to do anything a father and son should do together. When all this is over, we'll open a new page. I promise. I've got something for you. Shan't tell you what it is, except that you'll be thrilled. I love you. Believe nothing else.'

One night I dream of him. Like a shaman, I summon him. The following Saturday he arrives, together with Mother, Tali, and David Oren.

It's a bright morning. The kibbutz is looking its best. A fresh breeze is driving flocculent clouds across a dazzling sky.

'Ah, the air is like champagne,' says Mother, tightening her coat about her.

I kiss her, and Tali. I hug Gideon. I shake hands with David. Gideon is wearing the hip-length sheep skin coat with a wide collar, which he wore in that photograph with the bullet-pierced car. The car has been repaired but you can see where the holes had been. His hair is longer than usual. As he bends down towards me, I see that his head is touched with grey.

When I tell him of my dream he laughs. 'Did you also dream of what I brought you? No? Just wait till you see it.'

On the back seat of the car – Mother and Tali had held it on their knees all the way from Haifa – is a cello in a scuffed wooden case.

'Not here, later,' Gideon says as I try to open it. 'It's an instrument for a real professional,' he adds earnestly.

My class mates gather round David. He stands by the car, one hand leaning on the wing. His coat is parted revealing an ivory-handled revolver strapped to his hip on a broad, low-slung belt.

'A .45 Colt,' he explains, 'belonged to a Nicaraguan General once.'

At last we are alone, Gideon and I. We walk to the children's farm which overlooks the forest.

'Aren't you cold?' Gideon asks.

'I'm all right,' I tell him.

He parts his coat to cover my shoulders. We sit on the trunk of a fallen pine, looking at our collection of fowls in the chicken run.

'Your teacher, Yasha, is that his name? He said nice things about you.'

'Yasha's a good fellow,' I say.

'He told me you were good at maths.' Gideon gives a snort of a laugh. 'Maths! I couldn't hide my surprise. The last thing I expected you to be good at.'

'I like maths. I like the way Yasha teaches it.'

'Ah.'

We are silent for a while.

'You look well, Philo,' he says at length. 'Bigger, stronger. No problems with asthma?'

'Not much. I had only one attack. They brought an oxygen cylinder from the metal workshop and piped it full pressure into me. I thought I'd blow up like a balloon.'

We both laugh.

'So much for Grendel. We got him beat, eh?'

'He's still there, lurking. But keeps his distance.'

'That's good. Very good.'

Another long pause

'Tell me, are you happy here?' he asks.

I hesitate before answering. I watch his face. 'I'm okay,' I say.

'Truly?'

'Truly.'

'I really think it's best for you, being here. But I was worried, in case you were unhappy.'

'No need to worry,' I tell him.

Gideon looks away to the forest. There's too much between us neither of us dares bring out. His mind wanders to other matters, I can tell. So I say, 'The cello is beautiful. Thank you very much. I can't wait to play it.'

He gives me a quick questioning look.

'Honestly. I missed having a cello. Now I can get on with it again.'

'Yes,' says Gideon. 'I was told it's an excellent instrument. Master it, Philo. Nothing in the world and in life is as important.'

'Except what you're doing.'

He shakes his head, takes in breath. 'No. Playing the cello, making music the way you can, if you work hard at it, is far more important than what I'm doing. I'd envy you, if you weren't my son.'

'Why do you say that?'

'Because I know. One day you will too.'

Crows agitate noisily in a distant tree top, momentarily distracting my father. Without taking his eyes from the birds, he says, 'Soldiers come cheap compared to music. Music is everlasting beauty. All that's good. Like the trees, like understanding…'

'Music won't win the war,' I say laconically, like a grownup.

Gideon laughs. 'Music wins a lot more than wars. Besides, I think the war is already won, even if we haven't really fought it yet. Don't worry about the war. Work on being what you are. That's really why I bought you the cello.'

'Yoohoo. Are you two going to sit there all day?'

Mother, Tali and David are standing on the rise above the children's farm. 'Come along. We're all going to lunch,' she calls.

'Okay, we're coming,' I call back.

'Look what I got,' David says. He is holding a black and white rabbit by its ears.

'What are you going to do with it?' Gideon asks.

'We,' replies David. 'We're going to eat it back home. A present from *Arava* Class. Beth's going to cook it. Aren't you Beth?'

Mother looks uneasily at the rabbit which hangs rigidly from David's fist, its nostrils quivering.

'I don't know,' she says.

'Of course you are. Excellent meat, rabbit.'

'Who'll slaughter it in Haifa?'

'Slaughter?' David laughs. 'You don't slaughter a rabbit. You break its neck, then gut it. Then skin it. I'll do it, don't worry. I'll kill it now and put it in the boot of the car.'

'Not now, David, please,' says Mother.

'I want the rabbit,' Tali says, with a finger in her mouth.

'See?' says David, 'Here's someone who knows what's good for her!'

He walks a few paces away. With his back to us, he prepares for the kill. Mother wants to say something but Gideon stays her with his hand. 'Let him be,' he says.

We see David lift his arm, hand flat, like a blade. Chop! the rabbit squeaks and convulses. Chop again, and again. Kicking and writhing, the rabbit refuses to die. Tali begins to cry. Mother looks imploringly at Gideon. He shrugs his shoulders as if to say, 'what can I do?'

The head of the kibbutz musical education, himself no mean arranger of choral works, has found me a teacher in the neighbouring kibbutz, Ein Hashofet. Retired and suffering from a mild heart condition, Ralph Lauterbach comes over twice a week to give me lessons. Many years ago he had been lead cellist in the celebrated *Amsterdam Concertgebouw*, and a noted chamber musician.

Ralph is not a hard taskmaster like Zena Herman, but a relaxed teacher-companion. He believes one learns best from free association of ideas, from joint exploration, from example which he is well equipped to give.

A balding man with a pink smooth face and serious eyes, Ralph is sparing with words as he is with his time and energy. Probably his heart condition accounts for that.

'I'll give you four lessons to start with,' he tells me. 'If we see that we are not getting anywhere, we'll stop.'

Fortunately, he likes my attitude. He tells me that my musical persona interests him. He likes my new cello too, not mine really, it's on loan, Gideon told me. Instruments like that are not easy to come by.

The way Ralph handles the cello you'd think it were an extension of his own large white hands. When I remark on that, he says one day, if I worked hard, I too would feel the cello was a part of me, a prime prerequisite for good musicianship.

'I couldn't have got you a better instrument myself. Do you know what it is? It's a *Testore*. I haven't seen one for a long time. Not in the same class as Stradivarius or Guarneri by any means. But a very good cello all the same. You're a very lucky boy. Listen to it.' He plays for me.

My poor *Testore* had seen better days. Ralph suspects the belly isn't the original. Nor the varnish in parts. And the scroll is certainly from another instrument. But all in all, it has been well-restored, says Ralph. It has a rich mellow sound, like warm clear honey.

Our lessons are a communion of ideas. Ralph brings his own cello. We play together. I learn from his technique the phrasing, the emphases, the musical intelligence behind it all.

'There are musicians who are just competent players with good technique, nothing more,' Ralph says. 'To become a true artist you must find your own way, in your own heart. No one can take you there. It's a long, hard, and lonely journey. And I can't even tell you what are the rewards at the end, if there are any, if there is an end.'

His words linger with me through the midnight silence of our dormitory. I think of migrating birds flying out in flocks yet alone. Each for itself, in the loneliness of its heart. How many fall and die on the way? How many would dare take off if they could imagine the journey?

I think of my father, beating wings against the odds in defiant but not blind rage. Predestined for destruction, he relentlessly fashions the style of his undoing.

There's heroism in that too, Imogen. Heroism of the loneliest kind. I see it all in my mind's eye as I wait for the first sound (a mere bar, a leitmotif?) that will set my compass on that hard long journey Lauterbach was talking about. At least loneliness holds no terror for me. That is Gideon's chief gift to me.

Loneliness? Terror? Ha! Cut! New scene. Wheel in the stage. Turn on the lights. String up the bunting. Bring out the costumes. Saddle the horses and line up the tractors! Action! We're about to have a CELEBRATION!

In that, Mishmar Ha'emek is unsurpassed. It celebrates nature's yearly rebirth when Jews elsewhere celebrate Passover. It celebrates the planting of trees and the reaping of the harvest, the downfall of tyrannies and the triumphs of Socialism in Soviet Russia, in China, in the Histadrut Headquarters, Tel Aviv.

Above all, it celebrates itself, for being *Ivri*, Hebrew, rather than Jewish. The stupendous miracle of its existence here, standing guard over the Plain, as its name implies.

Does Mishmar Ha'emek feel lonely, surrounded as it is by no longer friendly Arab neighbours? Not a bit. For in its collective consciousness the kibbutz has already reduced those villages to a footnote in its own epic narrative; bit characters in the pageant whose role is merely to help propel the hero towards his apotheosis.

It's Friday night, as it happens, also eve of Purim. The dining cum assembly hall – large enough to seat all kibbutz members and guests – is cleared of tables. Chairs are set in rows, in front of a stage. The ceiling is hung with looping chains of coloured paper. The kibbutzniks gather in, dressed in their best clothes freshly laundered and pressed.

Tonight it's something different. Not another Russian film, like *Prince Sadko*, *The Stone Flower*, *Aleksandr Nevsky*. Tonight we're treated to a real stage play by the Habima Theatre company on tour of Jezreel. They are performing *He Walked in the Fields*, by one of the country's most popular playwrights. In the lead role is Hannah Robinah, the *Yishuv's* First Lady of the theatre. Now in her prime, Miss Robinah is equal to any challenge. She will go on to play Juliet (in the Hebrew translation from Russian), Cleopatra, Desdemona – all in a ringing Russian accent – well into her sixties. Oh yes, in Shakespeare's own words, 'age cannot wither her'. At least not in the rejuvenating effulgence of our burgeoning culture, which is nowhere brighter than here, in Mishmar Ha'emek.

The play is moving. It deals poignantly with the moral dilemmas of our time set against universal values. Many an adult eye is dabbed with a handkerchief.

Afterwards, Purim cakes are served with soft drinks. The chairs are stacked against the walls, leaving but one row all round. Communal singing next, followed by dancing – Hora, Debka, Kharkovia, Polka. A pretty catholic selection, as you can see.

Taking position at the centre of the floor, Yasha squeezes out tunes on an accordion. Of course, the Habima actors are invited to join. Every man wants to dance with Miss Robinah, though perhaps not as much as with Mishmar Ha'emek's own sultry beauty, Ofra Luft.

For what male can look on Ofra, who is twenty and in the sweet enticing bloom of womanhood, and not be smitten? Some forgotten alien genes that crept into her forebears' blood in an unremembered part of the world, have been kissed to life by the Jezreel sun to wake and flower in Ofra. Behold her slender tallness, the statuesque fullness of her form, those black smouldering eyes that look at you aslant with merry mischief, and feel your heart tremble.

How many marriages has Ofra broken! Listen to wives talking in the laundry room and you will know that Attila the Hun did not lay to waste as many cities as Ofra Luft did break men's hearts. She's the honey-eating queen bee and all men are drones to her.

Tonight Ofra is looking her best, albeit a little plumper than usual around her middle. All eyes are turned to her. Yasha heaves the accordion. Sound cascades. 'Sing, Ofra, sing,' the men chant. She passes a hand through the mass of her caramel hair. She raises her chin to display the lovely curve of her throat. Smiling, she launches into a familiar song:

The pears and apples are in blossom,
Mist gathers o'er the river,
When arm in arm, Katyusha and her lover
Stroll along the gentle grassy bank...

Hey, do we know of misty rivers with gentle grassy banks, where lovers stroll arm in arm? Of course we don't. We are no more familiar with that than with the surface of the moon. Only Ofra, with her scratchy voice, can transport us to such imaginary scenes. We sing with her.

Then, surprise! Zarro, a bull of a man in charge of the dairy branch, lifts his arms. '*Chaverim,*' he bellows, 'here's an important announcement...'

Silence.

Zarro's grin broadens. He glances sideways at Ofra who smiles back at him. 'Our Ofra is engaged to marry... wait, wait, don't rush me. The lucky devil, may God have mercy on him, is none other than Zevick Moran from Ein Hashofet. Zevick can't be with us tonight. He's away on flying duty. I guess Ofra will ground him soon enough.'

Loud cheers. Louder clapping. Women exchange glances and tight smiles. Zevick from Ein Hashofet is a dashing pilot, handsome but short, almost a head shorter than Ofra, and madly in love with her. End of the affair for Zarro? Well, he is a married man with five legitimate children of his own.

Our class's Purim costumes are on the theme of fruit. I am a banana. Encased in a yellow cardboard shell with two small holes for the eyes, I hobble after a strawberry and a pear to the sun-flooded lawn in front of the dining hall, where the festivities are held. At one side of the stage a three-man band is playing. The music is relayed to loudspeakers fixed on poles along the edge of the lawn. Back stage, a cast of three kibbutz wits is getting ready to perform a satirical burlesque, authored by Mishmar Ha'emek's resident poetess and songwriter.

I move to stand behind the seated Yula. She is dressed as an eighteenth century English scullery wench or something, ready to turn us all into a huge fruit salad. Her shoulders are almost bare. I peer into her deep cleavage which contracts and expands as Yula breathes. She wears a little black spot on the mound of one breast, and it moves a full centimetre with every breath. I want to press my face to it.

Closer to the stage stand an unlikely couple: Britannia and Samson. Britannia is Ofra. Now she sits, shield against knee, spear in hand – the obverse side of a penny – filling my banana vision. Samson is Zarro. It must have taken the fleece of an entire sheep to make his Samsonite coiffure. He takes her spear, sticks it in the ground and hangs the shield on it. He stands behind her, hands on her shoulders. My hands are confined inside the banana costume. I couldn't touch Yula's shoulders even if I dared.

The entertainment is about to commence when the sound of an approaching aeroplane is heard. Flying a single-engine Auster two-seater, Zevick has come to salute his bride.

Putting the plane into a shallow dive, Zevick passes over us so low we can see his goggled, leather-helmeted face, with a stretch of white scarf trailing out of the cockpit. He waves, a Purim Red Baron. A shower of flowers descends from the sky. Cyclamen, Ofra's favourite. The plane goes into a steep climb. The engine strains. Higher and higher, then a flip backwards, into a perfect loop. Again he comes, flying upside down this time. What nerve! On the third pass, he dips the wings from side to side, an acknowledged greetings signal. Another loop, and he's away. Now the engine coughs then cuts. Another trick? The Auster goes on flying in ghostly silence. We watch it clear the tree tops and disappears out of sight. We wait for the sound of the engine to come on again. Instead, we hear a mighty explosion. A billow of black smoke rises from somewhere out in the fields.

People rush to help: Roman Senators, English bankers, Arab sheikhs, musketeers and a courtful of Rococo courtesans. Samson carries an unconscious Britannia in his arms, for Ofra has fainted. The lawn is deserted. The stage and chairs look like debris. And there, in the middle of it all, is Britannia's abandoned tridentine spear with the large metal shield hanging on it.

It is still there the next morning, mirroring the rising sun. A shot cracks the air. A bullet hits the shield with a gong-like ring. Then another, smashing through a window of the dining hall. The kibbutz goes on the alert. What has been feared is soon confirmed. Arab irregulars who have reportedly moved into the three neighbouring villages, have served notice of their presence.

That evening an hysterical special announcement breaks a programme of martial music from Damascus Radio to tell the world that heroic soldiers of the Arab Liberation Army have shot down an aeroplane belonging to the Jews.

Siege? Not quite. A nuisance, no more. Life on the kibbutz changes to a lower gear. Conservation is the order of the day; of food, fuel, everything in fact. There are sign boards in open spaces: 'Danger! Snipers.' No outdoors activities for us. No nature walks. Our education and social life take on a more sedentary nature.

Sometimes the kibbutz returns fire. Just rifles, no machine-guns. Hagana Command Headquarters have ordered restraint. They are not unduly worried by the situation here. There are more pressing matters needing attention elsewhere.

For compared to many other parts of the country Jezreel is as yet peaceful. The cows get milked. Bread is baked. Sheets get laundered. Books are read. Poetry is written. Music is made. But all the while we are waiting, and ready, for the big showdown, the God Almighty shoot out when the British leave Palestine.

Of course, Ralph Lauterbach can no longer come to give me lessons. The last I saw of him was when he played the Saraband from *Bach's cello suite No. 2* at Zevick's funeral. Even the rocks wept.

Ralph had left me with a number of pieces to practise. Later in the year, he promised, we'd do a Beethoven sonata together. I cannot look that far ahead. I play desultorily. I improvise, discovering new sonorities. The voice of my *Testore* intoxicates me, makes me imagine music beyond my reach. I browse through a wad of sheet music Ralph has left with me, and find an arrangement he made ten years before for viola da gamba of John Dowland's *Lachrimae*. The sheets are heavily annotated, including fingering. It seems that more than one hand is at work – a student? A mentor? Yet it looks private, like a diary. Did Ralph mean to leave this with me?

I play it. Haltingly at first, then more fluently, hitting the notes clean, without vibrato, as Ralph, or whoever wrote the notes, instructs. It is a new sound, dolorous; evocative but of what I can't tell. It nevertheless makes me dream of a faraway enchanting land. As I try my own variations on a Dowland theme, I have a vague sense that I'm at last embarking on a lonely journey of a sort – one small wing beat at a time.

Where to? To a world of legend, of course, whose creatures move to the prompting of my bow. I suppose you might modestly call this composing.

Legend, Imogen, will set up signposts from one eternity to another. From me here, at the epicentre of a gathering storm, to you, an immeasurable distance away in space and time, by way of your great ancestor whose music is the air which lifts my wings.

I want to tell Gideon, 'keep the wars away from me. I don't want to be a hero soldier. Guns bore me. What do I care about borders one kilometre to here or there, another hill, another village? Let me be the Jew, Wanderer Supremo in realms of beauty and sorrow. Einstein of undiscovered sounds. Master of the cello...'

This high falutin' stuff doesn't really originate in me. I'm too young at the time, too timid. There isn't yet enough of the rebel in me. It is, you might say, a retrospective reconstruction of Gideon's thinking, as he struggles to his feet from pools of blood and acrid smoke, in the Valley of the Shadow of Death, a broken, disarmed colossus.

Meanwhile, I am in the reading room of *Beit Arava*, House of Wilderness. An April evening flushed with lilac. Jackals howl in the orchards. Cicadas hum in the grass. Beyond the kibbutz the hills are darkening. Unfriendly hills, for lately the inhabitants of Abu Shusha and the two Garbiyas have deserted their homes to make room for Fawzi el Kaukgi's Arab Liberation Army. There is talk of an impending attack on the kibbutz. There is intelligence of artillery dug in behind the cactus barriers.

Four of my class mates and Yula are still at supper next door. I've no desire for food. My *Testore* is between my knees. I am practising a passage I had improvised earlier. I hear someone come in. A man's voice speaks unhurriedly: 'Yula, when you've finished here, take the kids right away to Tomer House. That's where the kids are going to be for the time being. No panic. Just go there as soon as you can. And no need to take anything. There are mattresses and blankets all laid out.' He leaves.

Tomer, which means palm tree, is the class just below us. Their home is considered a 'safe house', having a flat concrete roof, unlike ours which is pitched and red tiled.

'Did you hear that, Philo?' says Yula, poking her head round the door.

'I heard.'

'Better put your cello in the cupboard.'

'No. I'll take it with me.'

'Well, all right. Only stop playing now. Come and have your supper. We must go very soon.'

I put the cello back into its case and lay it on the floor. I join my class mates. I make myself an enormous sandwich, with hard boiled egg, cheese, tomato.

Yula stares. 'Is your mouth really that big, Philo? What are you, a crocodile?'

'Watch me,' I say. But no sooner do I open wide my jaws than there is a deafening boom. I feel the floor jump under me. I feel as though I've been clouted on both ears with hard pillows.

'Quick, children. Under the beds,' Yula shouts.

As I make for the reading room to get my cello Yula grabs my arm and pulls me so hard I'm yanked off my feet.

The lights go out. Explosions and machine-gun fire rip apart the void. Darkness heaves about us like the primeval chaos. There is a taste of smoke and dust in my mouth. I shout without hearing my own voice.

'Death will come... Like falling into bottomless blackness,' I tell myself.

'Dvora, Hagar, Dedi, Amir, Philo... are you all right?' I hear Yula calling. She sounds now near, now far. I realise that there is a lull in the bombardment. We answer her. Dvora is in hysterics, she thinks she's been hit by something.

'Where Dvora, where've you been hit?' Yula calls.

'Everywhere, everywhere,' Dvora wails.

'I'm coming. Don't move.'

I hear her crawl across a space, now terrifyingly cluttered with obstacles.

'You're not hit, Dvora. It's nothing. You're all right, believe me. Now children, just keep calm. We're safe here. Soon someone will come to take us away.' Her voice trembles a little. Then she begins to sing: *David, Melech Israel, chai chai, vekaya-am...* C'mon, children, sing with me...'

Renewed bombardment snuffs out our voices.

If you asked how long it lasted, I'd say an aeon of dark, howling chaos. Imagine Grendel multiplying endlessly, going crazy, roaring with brass lungs, hitting out in all directions with iron claws.

At last there's a real lull. Have they run out of shells? Yasha and the upper classes geography teacher, both equipped as a medics and carrying guns, arrived to take us to *Tomer* house.

Crawling from under the bed, I looked up to see a patch of jagged star-lit sky where the roof had been. The room is full of rubble and broken furniture.

'Come children, we haven't a moment to waste. Who knows when it'll start again,' says Yasha.

Holding on to each other, we walk away from what had been our home, across a landscape marked by strange shapes of smashed trees and ruined houses.

Twice the enemy had reached the outer fence only to be repulsed. From the forward trenches you can hear the moans and cries of the wounded and dying Arabs left behind on the battlefield. The defenders are taking a rest, mustering resources, waiting for reinforcement so as to launch the counter attack.

Morale is high at *Beit Tomer*. Sitting on mattresses away from windows, we listen to explanations. We sing. We are not afraid for we know Mishmar Ha'emek will prevail sooner rather than later. And as if to vindicate our faith, the following night a *Palmach* company breaks through the siege to enter the kibbutz. We see the men rest among their machine-guns, cleaning the weapons. Preparing for the attack.

In the morning a British armoured column appears at the kibbutz' main gate. Their commander has arranged a truce with Kaukgi so that they, the British, may evacuate the children to neighbouring kibbutzim and let the adults get on with the business of killing each other. No longer governing the country, the British don't seem to care much who wins and who loses.

I did not forget my cello. All the time I had been praying for its safety, hoping against hope that we will be soon reunited. A young man, armed an eager for battle, volunteers to retrieve it. He returns holding it in his arm as one holds a child. I see that the case is broken. Something heavy has gone clean through it smashing the front panel, cutting through the strings. My beautiful, priceless *Testore* is among the dead and I am too numb to grieve.

Four classes line up to board a row of British armoured personnel cars. It's a bright morning and the British soldiers are cheerful. They give us chocolates and sweet buns. From beyond the gate the kibbutz looks hardly changed. Except for the main school building on the rise, pride of the whole *Hashomer Hatza'ir* Kibbutz Movement. Three storeys high, charred, gutted and riddled with ugly holes, it nevertheless stands defiantly against an empty sky.

The APCs rumble along the road. Not an enemy in sight. The radio crackles with bits of snap conversation in English. *It's a long way to*

Tipperary... the soldiers sing and wink at us. We are bound for Kibbutz Mizra a few kilometres away, where they are waiting to receive us. I hold on to the remains of my cello. I have no feelings about our victory.

It is April 5, 1948. The first set battle of the war is temporarily suspended. In less than a week hence Abu Shusha, Garbiya Al Tahta and Garbiya Al Fauqa will be wiped from the country's geography for eternity. The children of Mishmar Ha'emek will return home by the end of the month, when, back in Haifa with my parents, I shall mark my eleventh birthday.

No longer a child, I'm not yet a man. I'm marooned uncertainly in a twilight zone.

11

I think fate brought me back home to witness a fall and a resurrection. Perhaps fate too had set us in a new comfortable flat overlooking a pleasing density of forest and the view of Haifa Bay. Accident, providence, call it what you will, seldom comes without a twist of irony, in our part of the world at any rate.

Bells chime among the cypresses in the nearby Russian Orthodox monastery, where bearded monks walk sandal-footed to matins and vespers. Their bosky, circumvallated world is impervious to outside turmoil. This is secluded Forest Road at the western extremity of Mount Carmel. On one side a row of houses, on the other the monastery.

The balcony of our flat on the second floor faces west. Flamboyant sunsets come with a taste of the sea and the scent of pines. A childless elderly couple inhabit the flat below us. We hear their radio in the evenings. On the ground floor live the Bergs. Dr Berg is a lecturer in Hydraulics at the Technion, about to retire and join his deaf wife in full-time pursuit of their common passion for gardening.

The British have left Palestine, which is now Israel, independent, recognised by the United Nations, and isolated with her paradoxes. Two days after our Declaration of Independence, Mr Azzam Pasha, Secretary-General of the Arab League, proclaimed in Cairo: 'This will be a war of extermination and a momentous massacre which will be spoken of like the Mongolian massacres and the Crusades.'

What preposterous bragging. Morally and historically illiterate, too. Nevertheless, as June begins, the war is at its grimmest for us. Cut off from the rest of the *Yishuv*, Jerusalem is starving. North and south, our troops are out-gunned by the converging Arab armies. Weapons, ammunition, food, are in short supply. Our only surplus is in morale and determination.

You, Imogen, who espouse the Arabs' cause, understand this: the Arabs brought disaster upon their own heads. They did not study us as we studied them. They committed a fatal mistake, taking on the Jews in the very area where for centuries Jews had been aching to prove themselves: on the battlefield. Tell this to your Arab friends when next you go to a meeting of the Council of Arab-British Understanding and watch their faces.

Gideon is away fighting in the north, fighting in the south, we really don't know where he is.

Leading a select unit of commandos, David Oren perfects his deadly night depredations on 'hostile' villages. Somewhere in a blacked-out stone and mud hut, an Arab mother might be admonishing a naughty child Tali's age with, 'be good, *waldi,* or a terrible *Yahudi* called Oren will come and get you!'

In the midst of all that, we are translated from the proximity of Mrs Herman's animated warmth to the warmthless luxury of our new home in Forest Street.

A foreign ship disgorges in Haifa Port a cargo of foodstuff and an assortment of broken Jews, spewed out of Europe. Among them is one Gittle Levi, a long-lost relative of the Hermans. All he has is a suitcase containing a change of clothes, a velvet talith and tefilin bag, and death in his lungs. The Hermans would like to repossess our flat so that Gittle Levi can spend his last days there, in the bosom of his family.

No problem. Enter Hai. A few telephone calls, and we have a new home. The word for this kind of nepotistic fixing is *protekzia*. Gideon loathes *protekzia* in every form. But before Mother can think of putting a pot and a pan in a tea chest, there is a ramshackle lorry outside, with four argumentative Salonikan Jews from the dock, ready to move us. A week later, Gideon arrives. He is full of praise for the flat, for Mother for having arranged everything so smoothly, for Tali and me for being good. He lolls in the deep shiny bath tub, filled to the brim with steaming fragrant water, sleeps like a log, and is gone early in the morning.

Come into our living room. It is late evening. Darkness steals in through the open window. Nothing moves on the road outside – it's one of those silent streets which will soon disappear for ever. The room is large. Books fill just about every available space along the walls – where did they all come from? Our furniture, some of it new, which looked dowdy in our former home, here creates an atmosphere of lived-in cosiness.

The old wireless, a miniature cathedral in walnut, is on, playing Schubert's *Unfinished*, periodically interrupted by news bulletins about the progress of the war. Seated in an armchair, with the light from a standard lamp on her, Mother is sewing buttons on one of Gideon's shirts. Beside her on a low table lies a novel in English I bought her for her birthday. It's called *The Robe*. Mother hates sewing. Perhaps the book, selected at random from a shelf, doesn't interest her. A cigarette smoulders away in an ashtray. Having recently begun to wear glasses, Mother has also taken to smoking.

Tali is on the sofa, reading a book of biblical stories for children. She's going through a boring "religious" phase, keeps saying she wants to be a rabbi when she grows up. It is a notion way ahead of its time; not until much later in life did I recognise my sister's amazing if rare ability to think with originality. I am sitting at the other end of the sofa, being totally idle: my inner evolution is currently at a stand still.

When the *Unfinished* is finished, Mother puts her sewing down. 'Children, bedtime,' she says.

'Oh no, you said we could stay up late,' Tali protests.

'It is late, darling,' says Mother.

Tali begins to argue.

'All right, another half hour, but no more, you promise?'

'Yeees,' says Tali.

All of a sudden the telephone rings. Turning the radio off, Mother rushes to it holding on to Gideon's shirt.

'Hello... Yes?' One arm across her middle, cradling the elbow of the one which holds the receiver, she throws an elongated shadow on the wall. 'Yes...' She puts the receiver down. Sinks slowly to the chair. Ashen faced, she sits motionless, looking smaller than either me or Tali. Then she puts her hands to her face and lets out a long shudder of a sigh. Tali and I run to her, hug her. Because we need no telling that something terrible has happened. But none of us cries

I can't tell how long we stayed huddled together. Until another ring from the telephone unfroze us. This time I answer. A man's voice asks to speak to Mother. She takes the receiver, leaning against the table for support in case more bad news will knock her down flat.

'Is that true? Are you sure?' she asks with sudden animation. 'Yes, of course. Thank you.'

She turns to us. Tears are streaming down her face but she is smiling. 'Your father is alive! They've just brought him to hospital. He's going to be all right, I know. Thank heaven! I'm going to him now. You be good and go to bed. I shan't be long.'

Bandaged from head to foot Gideon lies in bed, a spread-eagle golem with cables and pulleys attached to his limbs. Two steel bolts run through his left leg. His jaw is wired up, setting his torn mouth in a fixed sneer. Blood and pus stains show through the bandages. A stubble of beard grows between areas of raw flesh on his face. Only his eyes are totally familiar. They are alert, furiously alive. Anger burns in them, for him being here, imprisoned in a smashed body rather than out there, riding the warlike chariot of Israel's destiny. The miraculous gift of life does not mollify him.

He is a shocking sight for which Tali and I have not been prepared. We remain at the door, unwilling to approach because that malevolent energy in his eyes cohabiting with such extensive physical injury seems unnatural and is therefore frightening.

Mother is at his side. There is nowhere for her to kiss him. Gideon speaks without moving his mouth, like a ventriloquist: 'Why have you brought them here?'

'They wanted to see you. I thought they should.'

'But can't you see what a frightening sight I am?'

'No. You look much better. A week ago you did look terrible. Now it's not so bad.'

His eyes narrow in a smile. 'Come here, then,' he says.

We don't move.

Mother says, 'Philo, Tali, come. Abba wants you.'

The smell of rotting vegetables hangs about him.

'Come near,' says Gideon's ventriloquist's voice.

Tali hangs on to my arm. His fingers moves to touch mine, then Tali's. The fierce glow in his eyes dims in moistness.

'Abba needs to sleep. We should leave him now,' says Mother.

This is how Gideon outfaced the Angel of Death and lived to tell about it.

The attack on Jenin in the so-called Arab Triangle, does not rate highly in the annals of Israel's feats of arms. Potentially of supreme strategic significance, the battle – so meticulously prepared – in fact fizzled out before it actually began.

Historians blame it on deficient intelligence and over-cautiousness on the part of the operation's general commander, a certain 'M', whom Gideon never forgave. A closer scrutiny of events, however, would reveal how Gideon, in his reckless impetuosity, was instrumental in the debacle. Unlucky people – and when it comes to accidents, Gideon is bad luck personified – should not act impetuously in war.

June 3rd, 1948. Three battalions of the Carmeli Brigade are dug in on the hills north of Jenin, poised for attack. The objective is dual: to dislodge an Iraqi force of motorised infantry known to be in the area, and to take the town. Intelligence reports reveal the position and strength of the enemy. Jenin, the same reports claim, is virtually deserted.

Gideon is in command of the Hagana's sole artillery battalion, seconded to the Carmeli Brigade for the attack by the Chief of Staff personally.

He has drawn up plans for the exact positioning of the guns, the approach route and the route of retreat, should that be necessary. But on the night before the big day, he decides to reconnoitre the scene again. Alone.

'Don't. We don't need it,' says M.

'I need it,' Gideon insists.

'I'm in command here, and I'm telling you not to. That's an order,' says M.

'I take my orders direct from the Chief of Staff.' Provocatively and deliberately, Gideon begins to assemble his gear.

'We'll see about that!' says M, and storms out of Operations Room.

The night is tensely silent as Gideon sets out, armed with no more than a map bag and a Sten gun lying on the passenger seat of his jeep. A good half an hour's drive from his destination, he takes an unmarked track into the hills. No sooner has he done so than his jeep detonates a land mine. One of ours, with an over-kill charge; they call it "friendly" in army parlance. The blast is so big it is heard and seen miles away, at a rear base. By the time help arrives Gideon shows not a sign of life. Taken for dead, he is put in the back of an improvised ambulance and driven to the nearest morgue in Afula, where a watchful Shochet – a religious slaughterer – working as undertaker realises he is alive.

M swore at the inquest that he had warned Gideon about the mines, and showed him on the map where they were. Gideon claims that M, with the same incompetence that caused an important opportunity to be lost the next day, had misinformed him.

I visit Gideon almost daily. Not many other people do, apart from Mother and Jenni, because everybody is completely taken up with the war. His recovery is impressive. The face is no longer swollen. A white streak runs through his hair. The mouth is given a permanent ironic downturn at one corner by a well-placed scar. Another one crosses his forehead

Jenni takes his face in her hands and looks at him. 'You know, you're even more handsome now than you were before,' she says with a laugh. 'I can think of men who would pay to have scars like yours.'

He suffers from ringing in the ears, partial deafness, headaches and bouts of nausea, as a result of a severe concussion. But his memory is intact. In fact, he remembers much too much, he quips. Each morning for half an hour he punishes his body with exercise. Twenty push ups with his injured legs held on the bed by a nurse. Up and down the corridors, into the hospital garden on his crutches, racing the attending nurses. How they admire him, those nurses.

Why this rigour? What for all that sinew-cracking exercise, when he knows he is a prisoner without reprieve, out of the war, out of the swing of fortune? Defiance for defiance's sake; that's Gideon quintessentially. Will he, can he, ever learn the wisdom of resignation? Maybe, but not yet. Meanwhile, he learns something else: a bitter lesson in politics. He gets a free estimate of his standing in a world out of which the accident temporarily shunted him to a siding.

An armistice is in force. Oren has conquered Galilee, sending hundreds of Arab refugees fleeing into Lebanon and Syria in the process. Putting the Jenin flop behind him, M has moved on to distinguish himself at another arena. Having little more than held their own in the opening round, our fighting forces take a much-needed rest, before hostilities are resumed.

Not so Ben Gurion's emissaries. They are busy procuring weapons anywhere in the world where weapons can be bought. Not just rifles anymore. Tanks, aeroplanes, heavy artillery. Military analysts of the world pronounce that the Arabs have run out of steam. Our victory is assured. A total, crushing victory, as Gideon had prophesied already long before the first shot was fired.

A new generation of heroes has emerged, younger men with tough smiles and blunt audacity, straining at the leash, straining too against an ethos from a passing age – the "purity of arms".

But no heroes come to visit Gideon. No messenger from Ben Gurion to inquire after his 'Alcibiades's' health. Alone, he suppresses disappointment and turns his mind to other preoccupations. A table stands at his bedside laden with books. He is not reading politics or Jewish history. He does not try to salve his overwrought mind with literature. Newspapers that Mother and Jenni bring him pile on the floor, untouched.

He turns to our once relentless oppressors, the Romans. Julian the Apostate, that stubborn eccentric reactionary Caesar, becomes his hero. Thus Gideon renounces Yahweh and His "Chosen".

I know he is in pain much of the time. I overhear Jenni confide in Mother how he refuses pain-killers; I've seen Mother sigh and answer, 'What can we do? You know what he is. Nothing will change him.'

I don't know if his unpredictable moods follow from his pain or from a hardening of his soul. As we run out of conversation I feel his unloving gaze on me and I avert my eyes. My father is like King Saul, reaching for a spear of the mind to hurl at me in his savage melancholy.

In October Gideon comes home after a short period in a physiotherapy rehabilitation centre on Mount Carmel. Too early, the doctors say. A few more weeks would have done him a world of good. Only partially mobile and still in pain, Gideon would not hear of it. It will take three more operations on his leg and one on his jaw before he is pronounced as fit as he will ever be.

I move in with Tali so that Gideon can have my room, for he wants to sleep alone.

The war on the northern and central fronts has all but ended. Only the Egyptians – bravest of the Arab armies – remain entrenched in the south, from the Hebron Hills to around Ashdod. Jewish settlements in the Negev are cut off. Without help or reinforcement they face collapse. The moment of reckoning, when accounts with the Egyptians will be settled in a series of bloody battles, is at hand. Meanwhile, however, there is truce.

Yigal Alon, Commander of the élite *Palmach*, and the army's most charismatic general, is in charge of the southern theatre. A prince among men, a forthright, dashing Joshua, men will follow him through hell's fires.

The first blow against the hosts of Egypt is appositely code-named 'Operation Ten Plagues'. Alon's battalions muster to strike. All that's needed is a ruse to make the Egyptians violate the cease-fire, thus justifying a retaliation.

On October 15 a convoy of supplies is dispatched to cross Egyptian lines at the Faluja Junction on its way to the Negev, in accordance with the terms of the cease-fire. As expected, the convoy is attacked and made to turn back.

That night 'Ten Plagues' is unleashed on the Egyptians. Before the year is out Alon will have driven them out of the Negev, and himself stand at the gates of El Arish in Sinai. As a footnote to the campaign, two British fighter planes on a reconnaissance mission from a base in Egypt, are shot down in an encounter with Israeli pilots.

On the night of the first "Plague", I wake to hear Gideon pacing up and down in his room. I hear the sound of his stick on the floor. Back and forth, back and forth. Stop, then on again. I envisage the automatic Colt .45 hidden in the alcove cupboard where coats hang, and get the chilling notion that he aims to shoot himself.

In my mind's eye I see the gun, fast in its leather holster in the bottom drawer. Bare-footed, I tiptoe out of the room. I reach the alcove without disturbing Gideon. Groping in the dark, I feel the rough surface of the butt and pull the gun out. Instead of returning to my room where Tali might wake up noisily, I make for the kitchen. There, at the table, in the small light from the open fridge, I try to remember how to take the thing apart. I have seen Gideon clean the gun many times, disassembling it and laying the pieces on the table in a row. First, the ammunition clip. That's easy. But I forget the correct sequence of action. In panic, I fumble frantically with the catch below the muzzle. It shoots out of my hand sending the spring, the catch, and whatever other parts were engaged with it, flying across the kitchen to bang against the cupboard. I hold my breath. The seriousness of my folly cannot be exaggerated. Worse, it's clear to me that I can't put the gun together again, not with the pieces scattered all over the kitchen floor in the half dark. I curse myself for being so stupid! If I could find the pieces, bundle them in my pyjamas shirt back to my room, then get rid of the lot at the earliest opportunity, some time will pass before Gideon discovered the gun was missing. I might just get away with it.

So I get down on my hands and knees to begin the hopeless search, when the door opens. The light is turned on. Gideon stands there in dressing gown and pyjamas, leaning on his stick. He looks down at me in silence, then limps to the table and sits down. With his stick he points to the pieces, scattered at the foot of the refrigerator.

'Bring them over here,' he says.

I watch him re-assemble the gun. When he has done so, he pulls the carriage back a couple of times and releases it by squeezing the trigger. Before returning the clip to its place in the butt, he empties out the bullets and slips them into his dressing gown pocket.

I expect a severe telling off, but all he does is sit there, looking at me. At last, he gives the pistol a spin and pushes it across the table.

'Want to keep it?'

I shake my head. He stretches his arm and lays his hand on my head. 'No. I don't think either of us needs this thing anymore. Go get me a couple of aspirins, and put the kettle on. I'll tell you something interesting.'

Gideon has a dream. In the heart of the Carmel hills, where there are as yet no roads, he wants to build a model town. A town of unassuming beauty, visually integrated with its hilly setting, echoing in its aspect the rugged lushness of the Carmel.

Who will people this visionary settlement? A select citizenry, from all walks of life and backgrounds. A community dedicated to simplicity, to the rejection of pretence, to the common pursuit of excellence. Here, in this evergreen citadel of ideas, the creative energies of people will be released and channelled to useful purposes. A mini, rural Athens, no less. A lasting testament to Zionism's nobler aspirations. She will be called Tiv'on – a derivative of the word nature, with unmistakable biblical resonance.

In January the war is officially over. A delegation of diplomats and generals repairs for Rhodes, where in the course of the following six months, armistice agreements are signed between Israel and her neighbouring enemies.

Hai is asked to join one of the technical committees attached to the delegation.

'You should be there, on the main negotiation team,' he tells Gideon. 'We need men like you in such a complex situation. Shall I get a word to the Old Man?'

Gideon shakes his head. 'The Old Man knows where I am. The war was won without me. So can the peace.'

'No,' says Hai, 'winning the peace is much more difficult. It's a different sort of game altogether. You have to give in order to gain. We've not yet learnt how to give.'

He is absorbed in his brief. Night after night he sits in the armchair by the radio, brooding over files, making notes in preparation for the big occasion in less than a week.

Doda Vic says, 'Enough of this, come to bed now. No wonder you have headaches.'

'Life is one big headache,' says Hai. 'You go to bed, love. You can do without my snoring for once.'

Doda Vic wakes up from a nightmare, weeping. She doesn't hear Hai's snoring. Rising from bed, she goes to the next room to see Hai slumped over the side of the armchair, as cold as a stone. A massive brain haemorrhage had stopped his thoughts and life.

It is a time for remembering the fallen. Time also for new songs and new hopes. Our eyes are turned to the future. Dressed in black, *Doda* Vic reads for the hundredth time the hundreds of condolence letters from all over the world, before stashing them away in neatly tied up parcels. A retouched framed photograph of *Dod* Hai stands on the mantelpiece in the living room. 'Life must go on. For the young generation. Not for me,' she says, and once again takes up knitting she had long ago given up.

Tiv'on fills out in Gideon's imagination; her streets branch in his veins. The force of his vision commands his body to heal, so that by spring he is able to move freely albeit with a heavy limp, and, more importantly, drive a car.

The car comes with a new job. Gideon is appointed Director General of a new public urban development company, backed by Jewish Canadian interests. The Company is called Keret. It's first and biggest project is laying the foundations to Gideon's dream, Tiv'on.

Drive through Tiv'on today. Enjoy her country air and clean streets – all named after wild flowers. See the pretty but unostentatious villas set in gardens. Count the number of new expensive cars. Anyone will tell you that Tiv'on has some of the best schools in the country, the lowest crime rate, the best quality of life. Yes, prosperity, earned by imaginative application of skills and industry has transformed Tiv'on from Gideon's dream of ancient Athens into one of Israel's top Hi-Tech centres.

Gideon's name is no longer remembered here. It was forgotten even before Tiv'on became of age. Gideon always has been an initiator of things, never the accomplisher.

As it happened, barely a year from the day Keret's bulldozers began carving building sites into the hillside, when Tiv'on's first street was peopled, Gideon left it and the Company. Recalled to the army, he accepted an offer from the Chief of Staff to become Israel's first Military Attaché in London with the rank of Colonel, a covenant of a sort with the Old Man, David Ben Gurion.

* * * * *

From the stern of SS Kedma bound for Marseilles, I watch Haifa fall back, flattened into the hazy hills. Gulls scream over a wide frothy wake. A hot June sun spreads blinding light over a calm sea. I sail away with images of snow in my mind: tree branches bowed by its weight. Lifeless electric power lines drooping to the ground. Everything swallowed in hospital whiteness. Such a freak, obliterating winter it had been. And now an epidemic of polio rages in town.

12

I tell Imogen how Gideon once took the wife of a friend for a 'dirty weekend' in Paris. Then, as it is end of term for her, I suggest we do the same, escape to a farmhouse hotel in Wales a journalist I had met had told me about.

'You can't have "dirty weekends" in Wales,' she laughs. 'It's a contradiction in terms.'

Perhaps that is why she agrees to come.

When I ring the place to make a reservation I decide to give fate a helping hand. 'Does the room have a double bed?' I inquire.

'We have only one room with a double bed. It happens to be available.' the landlady says. 'Would you prefer to have it?'

'Yes please,' I say.

Not a word to Imogen who, in the course of three days before our departure changed her mind twice as many times. But at last and, as it had increasingly looked to me against the odds, we are on our way.

It is a beautiful Friday. Surprisingly, the traffic is not nearly as bad as we had feared. We arrive late in the afternoon and the landlady, a youngish woman with a pleasant smile and a vegetarian Greenpeace look about her, shows us to our room. It is not the room I had reserved but another, large, with a fine view of a meadow, and two solid single beds separated by an acre of space.

The landlady who says 'do call me Marion' apologises. There has been a mix-up. A sudden re-scheduling of reservations. Tomorrow, however, we can have the double room I had reserved. Luckily she tells me all this while Imogen is out of the room.

Imogen is delighted with this little Carmarthernshire farmhouse hotel.

'What a lovely place!' she enthuses. 'How on earth did you find it?'

She had not counted on our sharing a room, let alone a bed. For the moment she is happy, and I delight in her joy. I tell her that another thing I've been told about this charming place is that the food is outstanding and the wine list would not embarrass a five star establishment in London.

'I'm ready to be more and more amazed,' she says cheerfully. 'Why don't we go for a little walk before dinner?'

A light breeze whispers in the summer-sated foliage. Veiled in haze, the sun lowers towards distant Cardigan Bay. There are a few children playing on the grass in front of the house. Their shouts mingle with the vesperal song of blackbirds. As we take the path into the wood Imogen threads her arm through mine. I am aroused by the intermittent pressure of her breast against my arm, as by the imagining of our lovemaking later on. We do not talk. And looking at her as she bends and stretches her hand to touch a spread of campions, I tell myself that I am the luckiest, the most blessed of men to be in the company of this magnificent woman.

We've had a delicious Welsh lamb dinner and drunk more than a bottle of excellent red wine. Then at last I walk behind her, not too steadily, up the stairs to our bedroom.

She chooses the bed by the window. I watch her as she goes to the bathroom. I note the sudden grave expression on her face; is she considering the situation she has got herself into? As I lie on the bed waiting for her to emerge from the bathroom, I imagine her entry to the room, the nightie she'll be wearing that will show her neck and arms, if not more. The look in her eyes that will be my cue.

At last I hear the gurgling of the bath being emptied, and it takes another seeming eternity before she comes in. Her face is glistening with cream; touch me not, it says. The black silk kimono she is wearing which does not reveal a square inch of her lovely flesh, is the very antithesis of my imagined nightie. She comes towards me, leans over me, kisses me lightly on the cheek.

'Good night, honey,' she says.

Soon she is asleep. But not I. Thinking about her robs me of sleep. I want to wake her up and ask, 'What is it you want of me? I wish you'd make me understand why you've come here with me.' That's not all. I want to make an appeal of a sort, saying 'You told me once that you could never not respond to someone in pain. Well, I'm in pain, for loving you, for not understanding what I must do or be for you to love me.'

Not far from our hotel runs the river Cennen. High above it perches what remains of a once proud castle, dating from the twelfth or thirteenth century. I've read a note about it in a tourist brochure. I thought we might walk there, it's not far. The walk takes you through woods to a village called Trapp from where the castle can be seen.

Marion, who showed it to me on the map, says, 'It's a lovely ride. I often take riding guests on an outing to Carreg Cennen. We have a couple of horses here for trekking.'

Imogen, having been an experienced horsewoman, is keen on the idea. As for me, if I had survived a wild gallop on one of Apollo's legendary steeds across a stretch of Jezreel without a saddle or bridle, I reckon I could handle a placid trekking horse on an easy amble through a stretch of Wales. But Marion's own horse is lame so she herself can't take us out. Seeing my disappointment she says, 'Oh, look, Lucy and Sioux are as safe as could be. Why don't you try them out in the field. If you get on you can take them out and ride to Carreg Cennen on your own. Don't worry about getting lost. The two horses know the way back,' she adds with a laugh.

We pass the test. And so we set out clomping along on the road and into the woods, Imogen on Sioux, a pale light-footed skewbald gelding, I on Lucy who is white, elderly, with huge hairy feet.

Past Trapp, the castle comes into view high up, as if fixed in the sky. The car park at the bottom is fairly full. There's a café cum souvenir shop at the foot of the castle hill. A few ducks, hens, and a peacock scratch around. The manageress recognises our mounts and shows us to the back yard where we may tether them under a tree by a trough of water.

It is a steep climb to the top and the wind gets stronger the higher we climb, so that when we arrive to stand at what had been the moat, we are nearly swept off our feet.

Hundreds of feet below, the River Cennen meanders through meadows full of cows and sheep, past farmsteads and copses of deep green trees. Above and beyond the precipice buzzards ride the thermals.

Standing on the high promontory with this faraway landscape below, I suddenly understand that my love for Imogen will always be a thing of the mind, like hope, like a vision of something. Therein will be its endurance as its eternal freshness. I feel at once heartbroken and quietly elated, as though losing one thing I'm compensated with another, different but of no lesser value.

Imogen leans against me, resting her head on my shoulder. 'I hate castles and I hate everything they stand for,' she says pensively. 'It must have been unbearable to be a peasant living down there in the shadow of this place. Imagine the terror. A riot of dreadful English knights charging down on you from the heights...'

'I doubt your dreadful English knights would've charged at the peasants on whose work they depended for food.'

'All the same.'

I turn to her. 'Kiss me,' I say.

She gives me a look, her brow knotted. A few steps away from us a group of Japanese tourists are taking snapshots in all direction.

'Go on, they'd love it,' I tease her.

But Imogen smiles and moves away from me. In a moment of secret emotion I had forgotten an iron-clad rule: I can never expect anything of her on demand. She gives what she gives when she feels like it.

While we were away our belongings have been moved to the room with the double bed. There's a vase full of flowers on the table with a one word note, 'Sorry', and a bowl of fruit. I can tell right away that Imogen understands at once what the apology is for, and that it's all right, my deviousness is forgiven.

The room is larger than the one we had. It overlooks what once must have been the farmyard, and a view of the hills. On the wall there hangs a large oil painting of happy peasants toiling on a busy farm, an idyllic reference to the hotel's provenance.

'Well,' Imogen says, unzipping her anorak. 'Any more surprises today?'

'One more. We'll go out for dinner. There's a pub not far from here where the food is supposed to be fantastic. I thought we'd try it.'

'You wanted me to kiss you,' she says, putting her arms round my neck.

'Oh yes.'

The kiss she gives me is a lover's kiss. The warm breath from deep in her lungs mingles with mine. I taste the indescribable intimacy of her mouth. I feel her body against me all the way up from the knees.

It is I who take the first turn in the bathroom. I come out naked, a towel round my waist. As she goes in, I get into bed. There's a small reading lamp above the bed. I want to have it on when we make love. I want to see her, to look at her face as I enter her. I want a sexy emphatic denial from her of what I had thought when we stood up there on Carreg Cennen.

She is quick to return from the bathroom. No kimono this time.

Standing over me, she slips off her nightie. It takes my breath away to look at her, the heart-stopping beauty of a woman past her youth. She gets in beside me, her mouth against mine. And then, to my horror I cannot get an erection. The prospects of recovery recede as my panic mounts.

Imogen goes limp in my arms. She turns her back on me. There's a long moment of unbearable silence.

'I should've known,' I hear her say flatly, as if talking to a stranger. 'I shouldn't have come here.'

We lie in the dark back to back, unable to talk, unable to sleep. She struggles back into her nightie then goes to the bathroom, to take a pill, I suppose. She has pills, for headache, for relaxing, for sleep, for just about everything except compassion.

Maybe I'm wrong on this last thing, for when she returns, she takes my face in her hands. 'Philo,' she says, and kisses my eyes. 'It doesn't matter. It really doesn't matter.'

But I know that it does. And I know with equal certainty there will never be another opportunity.

'Let's try to sleep now. I'd like to start back home early tomorrow,' she says.

A layer of mist hang over the field. The sun has half risen above the sullen stone wall on the near horizon. It drives off the mist. I stand in the tall wet grass, my feet soaking wet from the night dew. I raise my arms like an Indian medicine man to salute a red morning resplendent with the best light effects in God's repertoire: 'Thank you, *Wakan Tanka*, for letting me experience such a glorious sunrise! Thank you for the journey without arrival! Thank you for enabling me to love her still with a warm sense of humour and without possessiveness! Thank you for revealing to me the simple truth that my lousy job isn't worth a moment's worry! Thank you for the faith I need to understand my father's life and death, and for showing me how unworthy it is to despair!

'O great spirit *Wakan Tanka*, help me live without doing violence to my sneaky, selfish, treacherous dick which I shall never ever trust again!'

Inside my head I hear the swell of Nielsen's *Helios Overture*.

To my surprise Imogen is up, dressed and packing when I return. There's a tight worried look on her face. I know it: her 'crisis' expression. She gives me a quick look, noting my sodden trouser legs, then says. 'It's good you are up. My mother rang while you were away...'

Her husband, exploring somewhere in Amazonia, had apparently disappeared from camp without a trace, and was feared killed.

'We must return to London at once, Philo.'

13

From Gideon's diary.
18 Manchester Square, London. September 1st, 1950

A legation! The British don't consider us as yet worthy of a full Ambassadorial mission. But the Foreign Ministry is euphoric, as though we have achieved a miracle of diplomacy: the British have condescended to recognise that we exist! For which we are to grovel in gratitude, and lower our heads in shame whenever they remind us of the explosion at the King David Hotel, and the assassination of Lord Moyne. Is their own record unblemished? Can any nation at war lay claim to having clean hands?

Ingratiating ghetto mentality. Deeply embedded in our genes. Induced by generations of being trodden upon, it'll take generations of self-rule to make it disappear even in Israel. This, for me, is what Zionism is about: learning to live with ourselves and take responsibility for our own destiny without blaming anybody else for failures. Above all, without all the time seeking the goyim's approval or trembling at their censure.

It was a mistake to appoint Sharet Minister for Foreign Affairs. He is cultured and intelligent. But essentially a golah Jew. He still thinks in terms of a Jewish Agency, rather than an independent sovereign state. I mentioned this to BG, and he scolded me, even though I know that in his heart he agrees and despises Sharet.

BG rightly says that it matters what the Jews (in Israel) do, not what the goyim think. But Sharet cares too much about what the goyim think. The English in particular; he has a thing about them. I hear his voice through Misha Shomron's mouth; I see his clever, deprecating gaze in Misha's silly button eyes.

My office is on the top floor. Painful though it is, I don't mind limping up three flights of stairs if it means that I'm spared Misha's constantly popping in to see me, or asking me to come to him. Misha's a great time-waster. Thank god he is physically too lazy to go up two floors.

He has given me a huge (no doubt expensive) relief map of the Middle East. Flanked on either side by portraits of Herzl, Weizmann, and BG, it covers almost the entire wall space behind my desk. Misha insists that I stick a conspicuous Israeli flag over Jerusalem.

Sitting at my ridiculously large desk with that map behind me, I feel like Charlie Chaplin in the film The Great Dictator. *Why should one need such an enormous desk is beyond me. Misha's desk is even larger, like an aircraft carrier! He says that most of the furniture was donated by the London Jewish community.*

Misha should have been a Zionist Organisation missionary, not Israel's Minister Plenipotentiary in London. He is convinced that heading the Legation here is primarily for the purpose of converting British Jews into active Zionists.

From the window I have a full view of Manchester Square with the Wallace Collection on one side. 'Go take a look at it sometime. See how the goyim conquered the world,' Misha said to me the other day, referring to all those knightly weapons on display, the best collection in London.

My leg is killing me. Some nights I can't sleep at all for the pain. Sir Nobby Clark, a top orthopaedic surgeon from Harley Street, who operated on me, said the operation was a success. Only it would take time and I must be patient. But I'm not a patient man. Especially when there's so much work and so little time in which to do it. He refused to send us a bill because he admires Israel 'and what you chaps are doing there'. When I insisted he said with a laugh, 'Colonel Jerusalem, next week I'm operating on a Saudi Prince. He will pay for your operation along with his.' Misha thinks Sir Nobby is a Jew with a guilty conscience. With a tiresome inquisitor's zeal, Misha looks for the Jew in any person who shows a bit of kindness!

I work long hours. I try to walk as much as possible. Although pain shoots from my leg all the way to my head when I climb up the stairs, I'm glad there's no lift here. The exercise must be good, for body and soul. Spirit over body.

Had my first row with Misha yesterday. He nearly ruined everything I've worked so hard to achieve since I came here. Getting places for IDF officers at the Army Senior Staff College at Camberley, or on RAF pilot training courses, as well as purchasing much needed artillery, tanks – eventually jets too – is not just a matter of formal Anglo-Israel relations. Goodwill must be built with War Office officials and with key senior officers in the forces, particularly since Attlee's government is not well-disposed towards us.

Army circles are clannish and hard to get into. It has taken me a lot of hard work and an awful lot of tact to make friends there. I was therefore dismayed and stupefied when suddenly I discovered that I was being cold-shouldered at War Office receptions by virtually everybody.

I rang Brig. Gen. B.H, who is friendly and more direct than most of the others, and arranged a meeting. Over lunch, I said, 'Brian, I suddenly feel I'm being treated like a leper. What have I done wrong? If it's something to do with me personally, I'd sooner pack up and go home than spoil things for my country.' He was tactfully evasive. At last he promised he'd 'sniff around' and let me know if he found out anything.

Yesterday he rang. Some of the 'fellows' who have been especially keen to help, were sore because the Secretary for War, Manny Shinwell, gave the Chief of Staff a dressing down for allegedly not being cooperative over training programmes. 'It's not done, to complain, you know,' he said.

I was horrified. I gave him my word of honour that I knew nothing about any complaints. That I wouldn't dream of complaining, even if I had a cause to. As it was, I had none. On the contrary, I was pleased and grateful for the way things were going with the training programme. He believed me. Promised he would talk to those concerned and set things right.

I was badly shaken by this disastrous turn of events. It took me the best part of the morning to work out what had happened. Then I stormed into Misha's office. The weekly reports I gave him, I said, were a formality, for his information only, not for him to act upon. He had hopelessly misunderstood the difficulties I reported on. He had no right to complain to Shinwell, and without even consulting me. His ignorance in military matters, and his officiousness had very nearly resulted in the total ruin of a very important operation I was running, and I still wasn't sure what would be the extent of the damage he caused.

I was livid with anger. Misha was taken aback. At first he affected not to know what I was talking about. Then he accused me of over-reacting, making a lot of fuss over nothing. Then he pulled rank saying that as head of the mission, everything that went on in the Legation – including my work – was his responsibility. And if my leg was making me tense and highly strung, which he understood, then I shouldn't work so hard.

I wanted to hit him! 'We'll see about that!' I told him and walked out.

This morning I wrote to Y to say that in view of the sensitive nature of my work he should make it clear to the Foreign Minister that I'm accountable solely and directly to Army Staff Headquarters, not to the Minister Plenipotentiary, or anybody else in the Ministry! Anyway, from now on, procedures or no procedures, Misha gets nothing from me. Moreover, if I get no backing over this matter, which I consider essential to my work, I'd rather be recalled home than remain here wasting time and money.

From the window I can see Williams, my chauffeur, parking my new Humber Supersnipe in front of Misha's black Humber Pullman.

That's another thing. I told Misha I didn't think we needed luxury cars when Israel was desperate for funds to deal with the mass immigration from North Africa, not to mention defence. He replied, rather pompously, that this was not a question of preference and no subject for modesty, false or real. The dignity of Israel (no less!) was the issue. Well, the car is bought. But as soon as I can drive, at least the chauffeur goes, even though I consider Williams the most decent and useful member of the Legation staff.

My birthday today. I'm 36. No longer young and not yet old.

September 16, 1950. Six weeks since I wrote to BG. His silence confirms what I've felt right from the beginning about being here: he's distancing himself from me.

Beth says I imagine things, that I'm not being ignored. Only that BG never answers letters, everybody knows that. He commits to paper only what he wants to have in his notes and diaries. Also, that on a sensitive issue like the one I raised, he would certainly not want to write. Which is not to say that he hasn't taken note.

Beth's optimism and resilience is boundless. But not useful when you need good serious judgement. She's the kind of woman who would ignore signs of an approaching storm. She would look out of the window to see clouds gathering on the horizon, and chirp: 'Red sky in the morning, shepherd's delight' even though it should be 'warning'.

She thinks I made a mistake in writing to BG what I wrote.

Ignoring her advice, I rang Nehemia (he has a soft spot for Beth. Touching, really). N sounded as though he has been expecting me to call and was dreading it. Kept beating about the bush, asking how Beth was, and the kids, was my leg getting better, did I like London, have we found a proper home yet, etc...

'Has BG said anything about my letter?' I asked. Silence. I repeated the question. 'No,' said Nehemia. I could tell right away that he was lying. 'Gideon, listen. The Old Man is so swamped with work he has no time to grab a sandwich. There's defence, laws, the stupid opposition in the Knesset, the Kosher Beard and Yarmulke Brigade who want this and that and more and more. You know. I don't have to tell you. Problems problems problems non stop.

'As for the North Africans, you wouldn't believe it! God knows how we shall cope. This country will never be the same again. Who'd have believed there were so many of them? Jews? They look and behave like Arabs. Can't read, can't write, can't do anything useful. Who'd have imagined how different they were from us? Who could've foreseen the problems?'

I said, 'I could. I did. That's what I wrote about to BG.'

N put on his famous cajoling tone of voice (he hates sharpness, it makes him uncomfortable). 'Gideon, Gideon, you are in the most exciting capital in the world, centre of the action. Centre of culture, of good taste, everything that's worthwhile. Who wouldn't envy you? You're doing a terrific job. No one could do it better. Do yourself a favour, just get on with it, and have a good time...'

A warning? A veiled threat? I hung up.

Like all great men, BG is crafty and ruthless. He hates being indebted to anyone. Not out of meanness, of course. Being a consummate politician, he realises that incurring debts amounts to squandering valuable political capital, and reducing his options.

If at some point he decides that it's feasible and politically possible to dismantle the Jewish Agency along with all its money-wasting satellites and hordes of petty apparatchiks, and transfer its functions to proper national institutions where they rightly belong, he will do it. And if the move reaped rewards, he won't even remember it was I whose idea it was.

I know I echo his own thoughts when I say that the army, having the only sophisticated organisational framework in the country, should handle the absorption, training, and settling of the new immigrants. Not the Jewish Agency, which will surely make a mess of it. But he's surrounded by too many pseudo-ideologists and moralists who would raise a great hue and cry at the very thought. On 'ideological grounds'.

Well, I've written what I've written. One day he will throw me to the wolves, if it suits him. Of that I have no doubt.

Met RS for lunch at his hotel. He is on his way to Washington for a two years stint as Minister at the Embassy. He told me two things, one of which saddened me deeply. First, the London legation is to be upgraded to full embassy next month (what a petty fool Misha is, for not telling me!). Then, the dreadful story of Ad Dawayama.

The village was captured by the 89th battalion (8th Brigade) in October '48. Apparently, the men went berserk, massacred about 100 men women and children, raped, looted, blew up houses with their *inhabitants locked inside. Such atrocities that make the imagination freeze. Dier Yassin was the work of a bunch of Etzel hooligans. In Dawayama a regular, supposedly well-ordered army unit was involved. The whole sordid, vile business has been hushed up. For 'political reasons'.*

Oren, who is now Chief of Army Intelligence, commanded Battalion 89 at the time. My friend and one time comrade in arms! How will I look him in the eye when he comes here next year for a course?

Maybe N is right. Do my job. Have a good time. Fall in love with England all over again; why keep the score when nobody else cares? Order BG's books from Blackwells, Oxford. Keep his wife Paula supplied with English moth balls – she will have no others.

After the Holy Days we're moving at last to our flat in Kensington. Beth has been simply wonderful. Managed everything without as much as a murmur. Tali is turning out to be a little like her. Only tougher, more purposeful, and very pretty. I don't think I'll ever have to worry about her. She's a natural survivor.

But I am worried about Philo. And disappointed. He is indolent, moody and rebellious. I don't think it's just his age. I over-estimated his gifts, and his character. He is, in reality, rather unexceptional, if not below average. Doesn't have much going for him. At times, he reminds me of my own father whom I can't stand. Still, I was perhaps too harsh with him when he ran away and got lost in Richmond. The police found him and brought him back. There was a short report about it in the Jewish Chronicle. *Probably the only claim to fame he'll ever have.*

I should have arranged to leave him at the kibbutz. England will do nothing for him. I'll place him in the first good school that will have him, and hope for the best. That's all I can do.

So, Williams drives us to King's Cross Station. 'Shall I be here when you return, Sir?' he asks.

'No need, Williams. Unless you have other things to do at the Embassy, might as well take the rest of the day off.'

'Very good, Sir. Have a pleasant trip, and good luck, Master Philo.' Williams grins, touching the peak of his chauffeur's cap. A professional to the bone, and proud of it, Williams served as a driver in Monty's Eighth Army, was wounded in El Alamein, was mentioned in a dispatch, and returned to civilian life at the end of the war with glowing references, and lasting contempt for Arabs. That alone qualified him for a job at the Legation as far as the security people were concerned anyway.

We are on our way to Ely, Cambridgeshire, for an interview with the Headmaster of Ely Cathedral King's Grammar School. A small public school, offering English education at its best, Gideon had explained. Not easy to get into – exclusivity equalled merit in Gideon's eyes (did he not see the inherent vulgarity of such a view?). You had to be clever to gain admission. In my case, certain strings had been pulled: someone high up in the War Office, himself an "Old Boy", influential with the School's governing body and a personal friend of the Headmaster.

Here, then, was a rare opportunity for which I must be grateful and consider myself very lucky. Were it not for this stroke of luck, I might have been going to an ordinary day school in Golders Green, like Tali.

I've read about public schools, I had countered. No, Gideon had insisted, Ely wasn't like Tom Brown's Rugby. I'm to imagine a gentler cradle of learning, yet like Rugby, steeped in English history and tradition: a school going back to 970 AD! Every stone could tell a story, of monks, bishops, scholars, knights, sacrifice, excellence... What Israeli boy could even dream of such an experience let alone be offered it! And when I'm there, let me not forget who I am, what I represent. Eyes will be upon me. After all, in Ely I too will be diplomat of a sort, representing my country...

The train hisses and heaves out of the station. Rivulets of rain race across the carriage window. Iron clangs against iron, drumming out the rhythm of our setting out. I watch the rows of grimy terrace houses process backwards through rushing puffs of smoke.

We are travelling First Class, to mark an occasion; to enable Gideon to do a spot of work when we run out of conversation. He sits opposite me against the direction of the journey, his black leather briefcase at his side. Sombre. Dignified.

Gideon is wearing a dark grey suit made for him by tailors called Jolly and Squire in Savile Row or thereabouts. His shoes are hand made, too. Because of his injury, he can't wear ordinary off the rack shoes. Mother buys his shirts and ties in Jermyn Street. Israel may be an impoverished classless state but a diplomat is a diplomat, and should look the part. Gideon does, every inch of him.

What makes Gideon look the part – not so much of a diplomat as of a gentleman born to quality and good taste – however, is not his expensive clothes but the way he wears them. Never too neat, he looks at ease in them. An understated suggestion of casualness. A light touch of contrived sloppiness which says that he has chosen what to wear that morning as one chooses what to eat, not out of a design to please or impress anybody.

He carries a walking stick. Both a prop and an adornment to his attire, the cane is elegant without being ostentatious. Thus, with his carefully studied limp, dark overcoat always unbuttoned and homburg, Gideon cuts an impressive figure.

Misha Shomron, by contrast, always looks the genial east-European Jew from a lowly social background that he is, no matter what he wears. Even as he posed grinning for the camera in top hat and morning coat beside the horse-drawn carriage that took him to Buckingham Palace to present his credentials to H.M George VI, he looked more like a football pools winner out on a spree than Ambassador.

I'm wearing my one and only grey flannel suit Mother bought me at Selfridges, a flannel shirt, and, for the first time, a tie. Williams tied it for me before we left home. There is a faint stain on the right sleeve which the dry cleaning failed to remove – a dollop of pigeon shit, souvenir from Trafalgar Square. Williams assured me it didn't matter, in fact, it made me look like a real English school boy; no one could possibly suspect that I grew up on a kibbutz.

We have the compartment to ourselves. Enthusing on my behalf about my forthcoming days in Ely, Gideon talks about the Cathedral which he has not seen but heard about – one of the most beautiful in England, anywhere, in fact. The school, he tells me, is virtually a part of it. It is renowned for music. Choral music in particular.

I think, what good is that, when my own music has been silenced?

'Are you just going to sit here with your yard-long face, all the way to Ely, as though I were taking you to a rock of sacrifice?' he snaps at me.

I think, here amidst the flowing smudged colours of a soft countryside his mind is on the hardness of rock. Surely it is a sacrifice we are heading for. Contemplating the offering I'm about to be made of, I shut myself from him. And he, irked by my withdrawal, pulls out of his briefcase the week's *The Economist* and *The Times*, and begins to read.

* * * * *

Ely Station lies not far from the bank of the Great Ouse. Darkly green, the meadows roll up the shallow slope, carrying the river's misty breath to the town; and there, dominating the skyline like a great ship, stands the Cathedral, its tower rising into an immense, grey, cloud-packed sky.

A man approaches. 'Colonel Jerusalem?'

'Hello, good morning.'

'Good morning. Mr Bullivant has sent me to meet you.'

'Most kind.'

Gideon has acquired a clipped succinctness of speech which he uses on certain occasions, like now. At other times, when he talks on the telephone to people like the philosopher Isaiah Berlin or the military historian Captain Basil Liddell-Hart who has become a friend, he draws out his vowels and stutters a little. For the Jews he lets his Israeli cadence come through unconcealed. These diverse modes of speech are no acts; they have become the natural components of his new persona, like the clothes he wears.

'This way, sir,' the man says.

An elderly but well-kept car is parked outside. 'Not a nice day, unfortunately,' the man apologises, because as we step out, it begins to rain again.

'Oh, we don't mind that in the least,' Gideon replies with crisp cheer.

Embraced by a wall on the roadside, the school is situated close to the Cathedral. Once inside, the grounds, the fields, stretch before you towards the river.

Term has just began. We arrive at a break between classes. Boys are milling about in the courtyard overlooked by the restraint beauty of the old building with its tall narrow windows and arches. They have clever cold eyes, pale faces, red mobile hands, and lifeless hair. They are dressed uniformly: grey flannel trousers, black shoes, navy blue jackets. They look at us with bored detachment, like the carnivores in the zoo.

'Have you been to Ely before, sir?' our escort asks.

'Actually, no. Beautiful place.'

'Oh, yes. I hope you'll have time to look at the Cathedral.'

'If not today, then certainly on the next visit,' says Gideon.

We pass through the portals on our way to Queen's Hall, the oldest, grandest part of the school, where Headmaster Mr Christopher Bullivant MA Oxon. has his office. Our guide knocks on the heavy door.

'Come,' a voice says from within.

A large, slightly dark room where leather bound books and oak predominate. Mr Bullivant rises to greet us. He is thin and tall. But surprisingly, he has a round, chubby face, crowned with a shock of wiry, reddish hair.

He lopes round the desk with the gait of a cross-country runner, hand stretched out. 'Colonel Jerusalem...' He seems to enjoy pronouncing the name. 'How do you do. How nice. And this is...?'

Gideon looks at me. I feel I'm about to let him down. I lower my eyes. I say not a word.

'Philo,' Gideon spits out. 'His name's Philo. After the second century Jewish philosopher.'

'Indeed? Do sit down, please.'

We sit in the settee. Mr Bullivant sits opposite, in a deep leather armchair. He crosses his long thin shanks. Hands together, finger tips touching, he looks at us over the top of his gold-rimmed glasses; at Gideon, at me, at Gideon again.

'Will you have tea, or coffee?' He offers.

Gideon declines for both of us.

'Well, I do hope you'll stay for lunch at our dining hall, of which we're, naturally, very proud...' Mr Bullivant spaces his words so that they each stand out.

His laughter is like coins rattling in a collection box.

'How good is Philo's English?'

'Getting better all the time,' Gideon answers.

'Splendid. Not really a problem, so long as it's good enough for him to follow lessons in class. We do have a few foreign boys, some of whom came here with hardly any English at all. Let me see, four Iranians, the son of the Pakistani High Commissioner who is in the Sixth, and a Swiss boy of your son's age. Did I understand Philo is interested in music?'

Portraits of headmasters, ecclesiasts, scholars, stare down in judgement at me from the walls. A wide vitrined walnut cupboard stands on one side, crowded with trophies. On top of it, framed photographs: the school's first football eleven; the cricket team – Mr Bullivant standing among them, bat under his arm; the choir, dressed in surplice against the fluted, vaulted space of the Cathedral. Captured opened-mouthed in the full flow of a choral crescendo.

Gideon is doing most of the talking. Mr Bullivant's gaze has changed from assessing to distant, while discomfort shows in my father's mien. His hands are restless. His thumbs press nervously against each other. It is he, not I, who is on trial here. What is a lion but a clumsy oversize domestic cat, when his leonine awesomeness isn't perceived?

'Yes…indeed…quite so…' Mr Bullivant says repeatedly. Suddenly, abruptly, he glances at his watch: 'Well now, shall we go to lunch?'

The rain has stopped. Instead of being driven to the station Gideon and I walk to the Cathedral. We are like strangers, walking together yet alone. United only in our common detestation of the school lunch and the cabbagey after taste it has left us with.

The Cathedral is dark and a little chilly. Not many people there, just a few tourists. Gideon's walking stick rings against the flagstones. Tap tap tap, past columns, and tombs. A stale odour of incense hangs in the air. Perennial death perennially sanctified.

We walk up and down the two transepts, once round the cloisters then out, without exchanging a word or a glance. Gideon limps ahead, the wings of his coat swelling in the breeze. I look up to see the mass of the Cathedral. Tower, buttresses and rows of gargoyles bear down upon me, as if pushed over by the sky.

Do you remember Kurtz, Imogen? The enigmatic hero of Conrad's *Heart of Darkness*? His haunted words as he dies, 'The horror… the horror'? Neither a thought nor vision, horror is a suffocating state of mind, induced by something undefined which closes on you like a trap. From which there's absolutely no escape. Its grip cuts into you. Your strength ebbs along with your will. Your life files past your mind's eye, mocking, like the gargoyles which are leering down at me from the height of the Cathedral roof.

Horror is futility, incontrovertible and inescapable. I ought to know. I am, after all, a precociously accomplished escapist. I ran away from home at the age of six, taking Tali with me, all the way to Ahuza. Defying the danger of Arab gangs lying in ambush on the roads, I bolted from Mishmar Ha'emek. Here, in England, I've already notched a neat little escape from the Cumberland Hotel where we lived for nearly two months when we first arrived. You see, the unknown holds no terror for me. But the known does. And I know that from here, once installed in the cold barrack of this school, there will be no escape. There will be nowhere to escape to, either. The medieval barrel-vaulted dormitory which one of the prefects so proudly showed us, would be my sepulchre. That's it! Finito!

The horror… The horror…

A bearded man of indeterminable age hangs around in front of the Cathedral's main gate. His clothes are tatty. He has bad teeth and one wall-eye. The light in the other suggests that his intelligence is impaired. Seeing us, he moves to position himself directly in our path. But he is not about to beg. He thrusts a pamphlet at Gideon, something religious. Gideon tries to brush past him, but the fellow is persistent. 'Jesus is a good shepherd. Why not join the flock of sheep?' He mouths, smiling.

'Sheep end up as mutton chops,' Gideon growls and limps on.

The realisation gradually descends on me like a weight of lead: my father does not care about me. He has decided to destroy me. Not in one merciful stroke but by casting me from him, like they cast scapegoats into the wilderness in the bible. Away from his sight. To a place where my cries will not be heard. A place so dreadfully alien that it makes even him quake. No guiding star or sign will point my way out of that awful realm.

And I'm innocent. Like the boy Isaac. The angel of the Lord came between Isaac's bared bosom and the knife in Abraham's raised hand just in the nick of time. No angel will come to save me. No one will notice when oblivion creeps up upon me and sniggers 'I'm Grendel's younger brother. What I can do would make him go faint. Silly boy! You thought you had us licked?'

The couple who share our compartment get off at Cambridge. Arm in arm, they walk down the long platform and are soon lost in the crowd. Boarding passengers pass our compartment, look in and walk on. The train puffs and lurches forward, gathers speed and races through the flat countryside. Gideon stares out of the window, ignoring me. The adamant indifference in his profile unlocks what I've been holding in check so far, in front of strangers. I begin to blubber. Gideon gives me a quick glare then turns his face away again. I do the same, to avoid looking at him.

As the train pulls into King's Cross station Gideon turns to me, furiously cold: 'What did you think England was, the Cumberland Hotel and Golders Green?' His voice is full of hatred. 'Well, say something! You've acted dumb all day. Now tell me why!'

I begin to snivel again. Gideon is disgusted with me. If there were a button which could make me disappear, he would have jumped on it, even with his bad foot.

'Enough of this nonsense. Wipe your nose and stop whimpering. You can forget about that school. I won't make you go there. One day you'll regret the opportunity you've lost, believe me.'

Once on the platform, he limps away so fast across the crowded station that I have to break into a run to keep up with him. At the entrance to the Underground he stops. His shoulders relax. When he turns there's a sad smile on his face and a hint of moisture in his eyes. He pulls me to him and holds me tightly for a long moment.

'Oh, what the hell!' he says, letting out a sigh.

We stop at Lyons in Kensington High Street. Gideon buys a Knickerbocker Glory for me, and coffee for himself. He glances at his watch, then at me. 'What do you say we go to the cinema?' He says.

14

Tonight we are invited to dinner. Our hosts are a wealthy couple whom Gideon and Mother have befriended at one of the Embassy's functions. They live, says Gideon, in a beautiful house, in one of the more expensive parts of Hampstead.

Yes, at last we have a full embassy. Now Misha Shomron is His Excellency the Israel Ambassador. Gideon too has been promoted, from Lt. Colonel to full Colonel – *Aluf Mishné* – accredited to Great Britain, and Scandinavia including Finland. While Misha is confined to the United Kingdom, Gideon may roam as he pleases all the way to the Arctic Circle; which puts Misha's considerable nose out of joint. He is, Gideon discovers, an envious man.

The embassy is no longer in Manchester Square W1 but in Palace Green, Kensington. A private road lined with London planes and beech trees, it marks the western boundary of Kensington Gardens. Many embassies are located here, as is, of course, Kensington Palace. Top hatted porters man the booths at either end of the road and salute you as you drive in. A good neighbourhood. Very exclusive.

How can a poor country like Israel afford a large stately house surrounded by a spacious garden, that humbles the ambassadorial premises of larger, richer countries? Misha Shomron claims credit for this coup, which cost the State of Israel not a penny.

The lease of 18 Manchester Square was about to expire. A small fortune was needed to renew it. Besides, the cramped office rooms were no longer considered suitable, now that the mission was growing. Misha confided the predicament to the good and the rich of the Jewish community, and lo, one day, the house in Palace Green, once the London residence of Sir Moses Montefiore, was discreetly offered free and in perpetuity to the Jewish State by the estate of that noble Jew who, to his dying day in 1885, held the fortunes of his people close to his infinitely generous heart. The historical reverberations are temperate, dignified, yet potent, like Sir Moses himself.

It suits Gideon perfectly because our new flat is in Pembroke Road, barely half an hour's walk, for him, to the new Embassy. Every day, rain or shine, pain or no pain, he walks to work and back, relishing every agonising step. There is in Gideon a streak of intractable asceticism even to the point of masochism. Mother says he would have made a perfect monk, provided his presiding abbot was blessed with patience commensurate with Gideon's capacity for self-punishment.

But let's return to tonight's business.

It is Friday, six o'clock. Mother, wearing her best dress, is ready. So are Tali and I. We wait for Gideon. He emerges from the bedroom groomed and besuited, and in high spirits, having had a good day at work. Lionel and Margaret Barlow live in Vale of Health, Hampstead, in a listed house once occupied by Lord Byron.

Lionel is a successful international corporation lawyer, old Harrovian, and Oxford Blue in boxing. His grandfather, Isaac Berkowitz, scion of wealthy Rigan timber importers related to the famous Jewish Russian tea merchant, Wisotsky, immigrated to England with a considerable fortune. Although totally assimilated, Lionel is nevertheless proud of his Jewish ancestry. He takes a keen interest in Judaism and professes an attachment to Israel, which he has already visited twice since Independence.

Margaret isn't Jewish. In fact, she is what Anglophile foreigners ecstatically describe as an 'English Rose': demure, willowy, with complexion like Harrods porcelain, says Mother, a self-proclaimed connoisseur of both English Roses and Harrods porcelain.

Margaret's father is a retired headmaster from Berkshire. A teacher by training, she now heads the Education Department in the London Borough of Camden Town. They have a daughter, Jessica, a year older than me who goes to St. Paul's School. She's said to be precocious and a rather accomplished piano player.

Our dinner appointment with the Barlows is between seven thirty and eight. There's plenty of time. Gideon suddenly announces a change of plan: rather than take a cab, we shall go by car. That morning the Humber Supersnipe was returned from the garage fitted with hand-operated air brakes, to ease the pressure on Gideon's weak foot. The brakes are more sensitive than ordinary brakes. They take a good deal of getting used to. Except for Williams, who can drive anything that moves.

'Shouldn't you first get used to the car in daylight, Gideon? We don't want to be late.'

'We won't.'

'Hampstead's on the other side of London. Is this wise?' Mother pleads.

'Wisdom has nothing to do with it.'

'You don't even know where Vale of Health is.'

'I've looked it up on the map.'

The more Mother tries to reason, the more obdurate Gideon gets.

'Sometimes you're worse than a mule. Honestly!' She bursts out.

Gideon is adamant.

The London A-Z in her lap, Mother sits stiffly at his side. At the first traffic light she is nearly thrown against the windscreen. Tali and I bump against the front seats. An angry voice shouts outside, 'Bloody idiot!'

A mist over Hampstead Heath thickens the darkness. It might develop into one of those notorious London pea soup fogs, and then what! The time is already 8.30 and we are hopelessly lost. Gideon has more or less got the hang of the brakes so we proceed more smoothly than before, but the silence is tense. Mother knows better than to argue. Tali and I make faces at each other. We have our own sign language for such situations. I know what Mother is thinking. She would like Gideon to park the car somewhere where we can get a taxi. Or at least stop by a telephone box to let our hosts know we are on the way.

'I think we've just passed the turning,' she suddenly says, 'I saw the street sign.'

'You sure?'

Mother is seldom sure of anything, especially when Gideon glares at her as he does now.

Instead of finding somewhere to turn and go back, Gideon decides to reverse some hundred yards to the turning. He sticks his head out. Visibility has dropped to a few yards. The car jerks backwards. We are going too fast, I can tell. The Humber lurches from one side of the narrow road to the other. It mounts curb by a street lamp. There's a sickening scraping noise. The engine stalls. Shocked silence. Then Mother says,

'There. It's over there.'

Gideon has a curious pact with accidents: they don't happen to him, he happens to them! He seems drawn to disaster with instinctive perversity, like whales that beach themselves.

By the sound of the scraping the damage to this new expensive car selected to uphold Israel's image, must be considerable. Yet Gideon doesn't say a word. Neither does he get out to have a look. After a moment of silence, he says calmly, 'Yes, I see it. How careless to have overshot it.' He turns on the engine, moves the car forward, then backs carefully past the turning.

'If you had told me you were coming by car, I'd have given you directions. It's really quite simple, but difficult to find when you don't know,' Lionel says with a hand on Gideon's shoulder.

They are charming, our hosts, and cheerfully forgiving. Our being late is not mentioned. As agreed, we tell them nothing of the accident. Parked across the street with its ravaged side to the wall, the Humber Supersnipe will keep our secret.

Fortunately, the dinner is not in the least spoilt because this civilised household is equipped with all the latest gadgets. Lionel confesses to an enthusiasm for automation, as though it were a weakness of character. A self-programming, multi-compartment oven will keep food indefinitely in a state of suspended deliciousness. We sit at a long table under dimmed light from a chandelier, as Inez, maid-cum cook extraordinaire, serves one course after another with choreographed precision. Strictly Kosher, of course. Margaret is not taking any chances with us. I can see what Mother means when she calls her an English Rose. To my surprise, this rose, as yet far from overblown, is considerably younger than her husband gardener. She could, just about, pass for his daughter.

Tali won't touch the soup. She hates soup. Mother compensates by over-praising the baked salmon, her favourite fish. Gideon elegantly acknowledges the excellence of the wine. How quickly he has assimilated even the prandial niceties of diplomacy.

'Sweetie, don't eat it if you don't want to. Would you rather have ice cream instead? Nice strawberry ice cream?' Margaret cajoles Tali, who eyes with suspicion the delicately pink lychees served with cream in a perfectly pink porcelain bowl.

'Please don't spoil her,' Mother protests self-effacingly.

'Nonsense,' says Margaret, smiling graciously.

'Yes,' says Tali.

'Of course you do. Inez, oh, Inez...'

In the tall Trafalgar mirror on the wall I can see the reflection of Margaret's back and nape of her neck. She has a long neck whose whiteness and form are accentuated by the way her titian hair is gathered in a coil on the top of her head, like a Victorian cameo. Her face is oval and soft. Her eyes are calm, deep green.

Mother says she envies the lovely skin English women have, 'like peaches and cream'. It must be thanks to the temperate English climate that everyone so unjustly maligns. Margaret laughs; she herself would rather have more sunshine and warmth, damn the skin. She loves the Israel sun, though not in summer.

155

Jessica responds to questions but volunteers no conversation. Unlike her parents she looks boldly at you. I feel a little uncomfortable under her unabashed scrutiny. There is a hint of bored arrogance in her dark slanting eyes. A large girl with a precociously high bosom, Jessica resembles neither Lionel nor Margaret. Her hair is dark, her features well-formed but pronounced. In her way, she is striking, perhaps a throw back to one of Lionel's distant forebears.

'I rather think the Tories will win the next elections,' says Lionel who, sitting crossed legged in an armchair, puffs out a cloud of Havana smoke.

'Really?' Gideon rocks his cognac glass.

'Oh yes, I'm pretty sure. Probably good for Israel. Churchill has a soft spot for your country.'

'Not much good for this country, though,' Margaret puts in. She is for Labour, proud of the welfare state created by Attlee's government, therefore distrustful of the Tories whom Lionel supports.

She listens to Gideon's stories with lowered eyes. I sense a chill growing between them like a secret. But she warms to Mother. She tells her where to shop for what, what's worth seeing in London, exhibitions, theatre, buildings of interest. In return, she wants to know about women in Israel, their standing in society, above all, in the kibbutz.

Mother is well prepared for such questions. A week of intensive briefing for diplomats' wives, by the Ministry for Foreign Affairs, pays off, she is not lost for an answer.

Jessica excuses herself, she has 'work' to do. But she promises to come down later. Tali and I are left with Reggie, a white giant poodle, who obligingly subsides in a sphinx-like posture beneath two original Rouault oil portraits of King Saul and Jesus, and submits to Tali's attention.

'Reggie is purely decorative. As a watch dog he is totally useless,' says Lionel by way of a timely contribution to common discourse. 'You could have a company of burglars ransacking the house and Reggie wouldn't bat an eyelid. All he does is eat and sleep, and sometimes play. Don't you Reggie?'

'That's not fair. Reggie barks whenever the doorbell rings,' Margaret protests with a laugh.

'He didn't tonight.'

'He did this morning. Jessica spoils him, that's the trouble.'

'What? You don't have protection against burglars?' Mother is innocently incredulous.

'Oh we do. Short of having the police on the premises round the clock, we have the best protection possible,' says Lionel. He begins to explain the elaborate electronic alarm system. All the windows are wired, as is the front and back door and the garden gate. There are hidden sensors in the flower beds round the house. An intrusion raises the alarm at the nearest police station. Of course the intruders are unaware of this. In less than five minutes the house is surrounded by police.

'Two minutes, that's the average time. The system is regularly tested.'

Gideon is impressed. 'Must be terribly expensive,' he says.

'Not nearly as expensive as the insurance would be without it. Wouldn't you have had it, Gideon?'

Gideon laughs, draws on his Havana. 'For a start, I wouldn't want to possess such things as would tempt burglars.'

'Ah that's the unmaterialistic Israeli in you speaking.'

'No, just the lazy man who prefers peace and quiet to most other things. Is the alarm on now?'

'No, we set it only when we're out, or alone, and at night, of course.'

Jessica reappears.

'Finished your work, darling?' Margaret asks.

'No, I can't do any more. Too boring.'

'Why don't you play us something?'

Jessica grimaces. 'Go on, precious, play that piece you were practising this morning. You did it so beautifully.'

'Come on Jess. Philo plays the cello, you know,' Lionel exhorts.

Jessica gives a superior smile. 'How nice. I like the cello. All right then. I'll take Reggie out first. He howls like a maniac the moment I touch the piano.'

The grand piano stands by the window, a real concert Steinway, and its size is perfectly accommodated in the space of the room. I expect Chopin, Beethoven, Mozart, Mendelssohn. Jessica surprises me. She launches into a Scarlatti sonata, which she plays with confidence. Technically, she is impressive. Musically, I find her playing on the soulless side. I am therefore awed but not moved.

'Beautiful, darling.'

We clap enthusiastically. None more so than Mother who confides to Margaret that she herself played the piano in her youth. 'I so regret not having kept it up. But there have been so many disruptions and upheavals...'

'Tell me Philo, are you liking Engleton Hall? Are you happy there?' Margaret asks me.

'It's okay,' I reply.

'I am so glad. I've never heard anybody not speak about it glowingly. Darling, didn't Heather and Bill's girl go there?'

'Did she? Oh yes, so she did. Very arty, I believe,' says Lionel.

'I think we've made friends,' Mother asserts as we drive off.

'Really,' says Gideon nonchalantly. He is tired. His leg aches horribly. The car makes dreadful noises as it moves along, as though while we were making friends, it had aged into a tinny jalopy.

'Of course. Absolutely. Can't you tell?'

'I wouldn't make a quick judgement in such matters.'

'Oh,' says Mother mocking his pomposity. 'You know, I think Margaret has taken a real liking to you.'

Gideon attempts a laugh.

'Laugh if you like. I can tell. A woman can always tell when another woman fancies a man.'

'Is that so?'

'That dog is stupid. I wouldn't like to have a dog like that,' Tali pronounces laconically.

A week later we learn that while Jessica was rippling through the Scarlatti sonata, burglars got in and made off with some of Margaret's jewellery. Searching for loot they badly damaged a priceless Queen Anne table in the bedroom. Reggie, true to form, didn't bark or bat an eyelid.

If you asked me where I fell completely under England's spell, I would answer without hesitation, in Engleton Hall. Here is where all the wonderful things I dreamed about England became a reality; where light, colour, sound, and smell all flowed into a sustained interlude of magic. A Water Babies' paradise, you might say, where innocence is, nevertheless, a victim.

As with you Imogen, it was love at first sight. Yet in a different, very private way, it was also a reunion of a sort.

Again, it is Gideon who takes me there. This time we go by car. He is relaxed. We are both in a cheerful mood. It is a beautiful day. Avoiding main roads, we travel wherever possible along rural lanes.

The contrast between this day and the one at Ely is emphatic. Therefore, I can trust Gideon, I fear no betrayal. For once we are allies, accountable to each other.

Tall wrought iron gates open onto a seemingly endless park full of oaks, elms and horse chestnut trees all ablaze with autumn colours. A herd of cattle graze in the meadows and among the trees. Large snow-white cows with black muzzles and broad horns.

Engleton Hall stands on a rise at the end of a gravel drive about half a mile from the gates, presenting a broad elegant façade of grey stone, with rows of windows glinting in the sunlight. A double stairway sweeps up to the front door, like a cavalry officer's moustache. A short distance from the Hall there is another building, a two-storey brick complex enclosing a courtyard. Above a vaulted portal rises a stubby clock tower whose white-faced clock forever shows the hour of half past nine.

Look past the house to the right, and there, flowing through the grounds is the River Avon, a band of light flanked by tall reeds. In midstream, a dazzling flotilla of swans – sailing down to Camelot!

Never, never re-visit cherished visions of your past. Now the school is gone, and with it the enchantment. Engleton Hall, described in tourist literature as 'one of England's most beautiful small country houses', is open to the public for a fee. Clock Tower House, where I lived, contains an undistinguished collection of fire engines. The hum of the nearby M1 drowns the murmur of the river, and ugly cars bring weekend tourists and litter to the park.

In another country, another time, I paid a visit to a former home. Crowded and dwarfed by newer buildings in Sea Way, my old home's dilapidation was the first thing that struck my eye. I was about to turn back when I saw Zena Herman, unmistakably a widow and truculently lonely, come out to empty a rubbish bin. She wore a faded floral cotton dress. Laddered stockings hung about her knees. A lipstick-stained cigarette butt dangled from the corner of her mouth. Aged stubborn defiance showed boldly in her eyes.

She saw me, stopped in mid-action and squinted at me irritably. 'Looking for somebody, soldier?'

'Mrs Herman...'

'Yes?'

'I'm Philo, Philo Jerusalem. Don't you remember me?'

She touched her head. Her hand was gnarled, rings cutting into her fingers. 'Philo! Why, my goodness! Of course. Come in. Come in.'

The room where she gave me music lessons was unaltered, except for the whitewash which flaked in ugly patches off the walls. The grand piano was still where it always stood, with a pile of sheet music on its top.

She brought tea in chipped stained cups. 'So you're in the army, my, my...'

'Yes. Golani. Just finished NCO's course. How are you, Mrs Herman?'

She spread out her hands. 'As you see. Yossef's passed on. The children all married. I still give music lessons... sometimes. Tell me the truth, Philo, you don't make music anymore, do you?'

'No, Mrs Herman.'

She sighed. 'I didn't think you did.'

I wanted to hug her but I knew that if I did I would weep and she would get cross.

'Are your parents still alive?'

'Yes. And well. They are in Washington.'

'Good, good. I don't like saying bad things about the dead.'

I looked at her, puzzled.

'Your parents, Philo, I'm sorry to have to say, are criminally stupid.'

'Why?'

'I'll tell you why. Every music teacher who's worth anything dreams that one day a pupil of real talent will come along. A real musician in the blood. Someone who, with dedicated nurturing, will go all the way to the top. A teacher can have no greater reward. Do you understand me, Philo?'

'I think so, Mrs Herman.'

'Well, for a while I believed you were such a pupil. I sensed it right away. I prayed in my heart that all would go well... Yes, you might have become a very good cellist, Philo... I blame your parents. They wouldn't listen to me. They didn't take you seriously. Didn't make you work. All wasted. Such waste is, to my mind, the worst kind of stupidity.'

I see your down-turned smile, Imogen. I hear you say to yourself, 'Oh yes, one day not too far off, he'll wake up from his fantasy and come to his senses. The magic will be gone and he'll see I'm an elderly woman, and ordinary.'

I tell you, NEVER. What I see in you is real. As real as I am. And so you shall remain, for as long as I am what I am. That is, until oblivion.

* * * * *

'You know, Philo, I envy you. If I were a boy again this is where I'd want to be,' says Gideon.

He steers the car slowly up the drive, over the cattle grid, and into the school's forecourt.

It is conker time of the year. Under the dead clock, Tom Partridge presents his 'sixer' to Charlie Bean, who takes a mighty swing. Bash! A cracking hit.

'Who's that just arrived in the Supersnipe?' Partridge demands.

'The foreign boy Old Fyd was telling us about, I'll bet,' says Bean.

'Hold it steady now, you're jibbing,' Partridge protests.

Mrs Fairchild, wife of the Headmaster, appears at the top of the stairway, followed by Raj and Taj, her two white and tan spaniels. She waves to us – a mere little sway of the hand, as the King and Queen do from their balcony in Buckingham Palace. Her face takes naturally to smiling; it beams warmth. Her dogs smile too. She is an elegant woman. Her blond hair is streaked with grey. Holding the front of her cardigan with one hand, she comes half way down the stairs.

'How lovely to see you. Do come in, Mr Fairchild is waiting for you in his study.'

As we drive away back home after a successful congenial interview, Gideon says, 'Remember Titus Arch in Rome I showed you?'

'Yes.'

'Remember why I took you there?'

'No.'

'To show you the figures of Jewish captives in chains. Warriors defeated in battle. Nobody had heard of the English when the Jews were already a great civilisation. Remember too, that Jews came to these isles with the Roman legions. They ate sitting at tables and washed in heated baths when the English tribes, dressed in skins like animals, still burrowed for acorns in forests.

'They sing hymns to Jerusalem, which they have never seen. They worship the bible of our kings and prophets. Just remember that.'

'So what?' I say.

'So that when they call you "the foreign boy", don't for a moment believe it makes you someone lesser than they.'

Everybody adores Mrs Fairchild. Especially the girls, a good many of whom have a crush on her. Poems dedicated to her, modelled on *She walks in beauty like the night* and *The Lady of Shallot*, are periodically slipped surreptitiously under her door.

To see her walk her dogs each morning by the river, wearing a tweed skirt, Barbour jacket and green wellies, her head sensibly scarfed, you'd think she was the lady of the manor. Listening to her dulcet accent and that gentle, slightly breathy voice, no-one could doubt she was the very personification of this very English estate, mentioned in the Doomsday Book. In reality Olivia Fairchild, daughter of a high street iron monger, hails from Bradford, Yorkshire.

Mr Fairchild is a scholar. Son of a missionary couple, he grew up in Burma, read Divinity at Oxford, and is reputed to be fluent in German, French, Greek, Latin, and Hebrew, none of which he teaches. When we first met, he greeted me with *shalom*, then quickly went on to talk about the school, before Gideon or I could say anything.

A tall, large-boned man with a ruddy complexion, Harry Fairchild, in addition to running the school, takes us for games, gives scripture classes, and stands in for the language teachers whenever necessary. He has a beautiful voice, the kind you associate with Shakespeare plays and poetry reading. His voice is the first thing you remember about him.

The boys' dormitories are in Clock Tower House, above the stables which had been converted to classrooms, laboratories, and a gym. Windows face other windows and overlook the cobble stone courtyard below. My room mates are Christopher Swift, Barney Todd, Peter Evans, Ted Mudd, and Neil Smith. The girls live in the main building where the music rooms, the ballroom, library, dining hall, and the Fairchilds' apartment, are situated.

But Mrs Fairchild is not the fairest of Engleton Hall. That pride of place goes without dispute to Frances Carr.

Ethereal Frances. Angel look-alike of the Victorian imagination, her cornflower blue eyes are the very essence of purity. Her mouth, plum red and slightly pouting, is an instrument of heavenly music, formed to produce the most exquisite notes. Oh, it does, it does! Listen to her sing the solo part in Thomas Weelkes's *Give ear, O Lord to hear a sinner's humble cry*. Like a silver flute is her voice. Watch her face, lapped by golden curls, upturned to the northern window in an ecstasy of a song, and beat your breast. Thus Frances solicits divine loving kindness on our behalf. What god could deny her?

Here, in the vaulted hallowed sanctuary of St. Nicholas chapel where some of the finest 13th century stained glass can be seen, I begin to weave a new identity for myself, wrapping the old one with layers upon layers of Englishness. I listen to Mr Fairchild's reading the lesson from Isaiah with tears in my eyes; the unbearable beauty of its English resonance.

* * * * *

My first day at school. At our House Master Mr Fydow's behest, Christopher Swift is my guide. He is a pale thin boy, good at work, articulate, and fastidious. He wants to go to Cambridge, then become a writer. On account of his weak chest Christopher is excused from games, except cricket, about which he is very knowledgeable.

I put on my school uniform, grey flannel trousers, grey shirt, green tie striped with white, and 'goose shit green' blazer with the school emblem on the breast pocket. My transformation seems complete.

'Ask when you want to know something,' says Christopher, 'and for Christ's sake don't ever call me Chris.'

In the main building we run into a bevy of girls coming out of one of the music rooms. They give us a quick dismissive look. But not Frances Carr. She takes me in, she smiles sweetly before walking on. Christopher registers my immediate infatuation.

'That's Frances Carr,' he says dryly. 'Virtue itself. Thinks she's God's gift to mankind. Try not to get a crush on her. Just about everybody else does. Too boring... John Hunter is Head Boy. He's in love with Frances, so he's training to be a saint too... That dragon over there is Mary Downs, Head Girl, alias "Black Death". Avoid her at all costs... Charlie Bean's okay. A bit thick, though. He has a temper. Catch him in a bad mood and he'd knock your block off as soon as look at you... Oh, one more thing, never raise your hand in class when old Fyd asks a question.'

'Why not?'

'If you do you'll wish you hadn't, believe me. In class Fyd is merciless, even to new foreign boys. It's death by thousand cuts to anyone who catches his attention.'

Half a mile upstream the river widens into a pool. Five cygnets in near adult plumage are practising flight. Barely rising over the reeds, they fly in a line and land with a ripple in the still, green water. The breeze carries the whirr of their wings to the open window of the music room where Frances Carr, accompanied by Mr Fairchild on the piano, is practising Schubert's *Who is Sylvia*. In English. She cocks her head. 'What a beautiful, beautiful song,' she enthuses

'Yes. Let's take it again four bars down, ready? Holy fai-e-er a-hand wise is she hee...' Mr Fairchild intones from the keyboard. A dilettante composer, Mr Fairchild counts on musical discipline to suppress a sinful longing for this, the most tantalising of his charges.

The grass is lush. Pheasants run criss-cross in the meadows. A slow ebb of translucent green washes over the landscape. Astride my new Hercules bicycle (Sturmey Archer three gears) I pedal after my friend and mentor Christopher Swift along the winding narrow, hedgerowed lane from Swinford. His pet jackdaw, Kerri, plummets from a leafy horse chestnut to alight on his shoulder as soon as we enter the school grounds.

Long hours of early summer afternoons distance memories of winter, of hoary crests on churned up playing fields that cut your raw knees as you fall, of tepid bath water nine inches deep by Fyd's water-marked ruler, in a yellow stained bath tub. Three boys in a row before the water is changed, then a quick run to ice-cold sheets in unheated dormitories. Lights out. Barney Todd's crystal set crackles like potato crisps against the muted thumps of communal wanking.

Darkness, thick as a pall.

In the lingering tea time hours Mr Jones mows and rollers the tennis courts, or puts up the nets by the cricket pavilion. I wake in the morning to the warble of thrushes, and because we are doing the Prologue to Chaucer's Canterbury Tales, I think of

> ...*smale fowles maken melodye,*
> *That slepen al the night with open ye,*
> *(So priketh hem nature in hir corages):*

Nature, Imogen, priketh me in a newly-awakened part of my anatomy. Enamoured of Frances Carr, it is nevertheless Alison Leeming who is the object of my arousal. Only recently a red-calved, gamey, schoolgirl comic book character, Alison has miraculously blossomed into a smooth-skinned, voluptuous figure of English maidenhood. We goggle at her as she charges about the hockey field, two buttons undone down her front.

The upper forms are busy on the school play to be staged at the end of term. This year it's John Webster's *The Duchess of Malfi*.

Among the invited guests of parents, friends and patrons, are a number of celebrities including the actor Michael Redgrave. Frances is cast as the eponymous Duchess. To counter her spirituality, the rôle of the courtesan Julia is given to over-flowing Alison, who is working unremittingly on her elocution. Mr Thomas, our English Master, directs, and himself plays the cynical Cardinal.

'Don't ham, Alison. Say it with subtlety, think of her inner conflict,' he instructs. In vain. Alison knows better than anyone that "inner conflict" and "subtlety", aren't her strong points.

The low-cut red velvet gown Alison is to wear is a sensation. More than that, it stirs up a controversy that compels Mrs Fairchild to consider a veto, much to Charlie Bean's dismay. Not for the world would he miss the spectacle of Leemer's tits popping out of her dress.

'With all that heavy breathing, it's bound to happen. Newton's Law of gravity. Elementary, my dear Watson,' he opines in the locker room.

In his way Bean is a good sort. At times, even witty. The school's star athlete, he is about the worse scholar, a dubious distinction I share with him. Except that Bean has no excuse, such as being a foreigner.

Bean fears neither man nor beast, only Mr Fydow who, according to Bean, is neither one nor the other. Fyd teaches, among other things, Latin, where he is at his most terrifying.

His hair is snow-white. The story goes that while serving in the Middle East during the war, he was kicked by a camel, went down for the count, and woke up in an army hospital in Alexandria with no other injury save his blanched hair. Not surprisingly, Fyd is believed to harbour a deep loathing for camels and all humans associated with them.

Severe and gaunt, Fyd is in reality a kind-hearted, fair-minded man, except, it seems, where the likes of Charlie Bean are concerned. Another legend about Fyd says that he had turned down a promising overseas career in the Colonial Office to take up a teaching job so that he might be with his ailing mother. Both of them live in nearby Swinford, in a cottage belonging to Engleton Hall.

Mr Fydow's sole contribution to Classical scholarship is an annotated anthology of Latin texts commonly known at school as the 'Blue Fyd' on account of its washy, inky blue cover.

Thumbs stuck in his belt, Fyd paces up and down in front of the blackboard. The 'Blue Fyd' lies open at page 27 on every desk. *Caesar: De Bello Gallico.* Mr Fydow faces us. His small eyes scan the class for a suitable victim. They come to rest on Bean, who immediately lowers his head. 'Now then, Bean, your father is a soldier, is he not? Let's see if any understanding of the military mind has rubbed on to you. Read out paragraph six, and translate.'

His voice is like two knives sharpening against each other.

'*Erant omnio iinera duo, quibus itineribus domo exire possent...*' Bean reads with a tremor.

'Stop! What is meant by "*Helevetiorum et Allobrogum, qui nuper pecati erant*" eh, Bean?'

'Er... they sinned, Sir.'

'They sinned! Who sinned?'

'The Swiss, Sir.'

'My dear old Bean, you must be barmy. What's going to become of you, Bean, eh?'

'I don't know, Sir.'

'Neither do I, Bean, neither do I. Report to me after tea, with the whole chapter copied out and correctly translated.'

'Yes, Sir.'

'Swifto, leave in a few mistakes. Otherwise Fyd will know,' Bean instructs.

'He'll know anyway,' Christopher says wryly.

'God Almighty! Jerusalem, there are lots of camels where you come from. Do they kick hard?'

'I don't know, Charlie. I believe they do.'

'The one that had a go at Fyd obviously didn't. Not hard enough, anyway. What rotten luck!'

We stand on the fringe of the darkening wood, not far from the games pavilion. Bean pulls out a packet of Woodbines from the folds of his jumper and lights up. 'Quiz?' he calls.

'Ego!' says Barney Todd, stretching out his hand, then changes his mind and declines. Only Bean really likes smoking; only he can inhale properly like a grown up. If caught he could be expelled. Bean thrives on taking risks. He dreams of derring-do adventures in far flung parts of the world.

A group of girls cycles past, hockey sticks slung across the handlebars. Bean cups the cigarette in the palm of his hand. A wicked grin forms on lips. 'I dare you,' he challenges, 'who will follow?'

Christopher snorts and turns away. Ted Mudd raises his hand, then Tom Partridge. Then me.

'Right. This is what we do…'

Behind the house rank weeds grow profusely. A rusty fire escape ladder goes all the way up the wall to the roof where a narrow parapet circles the house. Bean proposes to climb up the ladder, sneak around the parapet to the roof window of the girls shower room. The timing is perfect, he is sure, for us to catch sight of Alison Leeming in her after games ablution.

'Bean, this is madness,' says Ted Mudd, looking up the ladder.

'Coward!' Bean sneers.

'I'm not going.'

'Neither am I.'

'What about you, Jerusalem? Let's see what you're made of.'

I hesitate. 'I'll come,' I say at last.

'We'll keep a look out,' Mudd and Partridge volunteer.

Beans shrug his shoulders. 'Do what you like, only keep your mouths shut,' he says, and starts up the ladder.

Why do I follow him? Am I depraved? A voyeur? Is the allure of seeing Alison in her nudity so compelling for me to risk life and limb, not to mention disgrace?

No. I go because I'm a foreigner. Because Bean and the others don't know about Titus Arch in the Roman Forum, and couldn't care if they did. I'm hostage to my past and to the status it confers on me!

As I watch Bean's tight bum straining a few rungs above my head, I recall past adventures and escapes, and curse my fate.

One storey up, the wind feels strong. The ladder creaks and sways. I hear Bean's heavy breathing. 'Are you there?' he asks.

'Yes.'

'Good man. Keep up with me and don't look down,' he whispers.

I have a vision of the ladder working loose from the wall, and the two of us swaying in mid air as in some slapstick comedy film.

It almost happens, for as Bean purchases a grip on the gutter of the roof there is a sickening groan and the rusty brackets split from the wall. Bean swings a leg onto the roof, turns as quick as a cat, and grabs my arm. He is strong, he literally yanks me up onto the parapet. We lie flat on our bellies, breathing hard.

'Crikey! That was close,' says Bean.

And suddenly, as we look down at the insect-size figures of Mudd and Partridge walking away, we both realise the ridiculous pointlessness of our bravado and at once the purpose of the escapade becomes irrelevant. There's not a sign of life in any of the mansard

167

windows along our side of the roof. The parapet is a good deal narrower than either of us imagined, barely wide enough for one body to crawl along.

At this point Bean shows leadership. Calmly, as though he were considering tactics in a cricket match, he says, 'Well, one thing is certain, we're not going down that ladder. We'll crawl along until we find an open window, then get in and sneak down. With a bit of luck no one will spot us.'

'What if there isn't an open window?'

'Don't be daft. There's bound to be one.'

'But what if...'

'Then we'll jolly well have to force one open and that's that! Follow me.'

The shadow of the house creeps towards the river. Soon the bell will ring for tea. The forecourt will be teeming with people. If, failing to enter from the back, we came round to the front, someone would surely spot us. Disgrace and expulsion was staring me in the face. I'm cold and tired. I'm furious with myself for my stupidity!

'Keep your fingers crossed. I think I can open this one,' I hear Bean say.

Lying on his back he pulls at the frame with both hands, until the catch inside breaks loose and the window opens above him. We climb in.

It turns out to be an unused room full of odd bits of furniture. The thought occurs to me that the door might be locked. But I don't care. I'd sooner starve to a skeleton than return to the roof.

The door opens. The corridor is dark. Bean calculates that we must be more or less above the Head Master's study. I tip-toe behind Bean along the corridor, keeping close to the wall. We reach the corner of the house. Cautiously, Bean goes round it with me close behind. Just then I hear the high, precise, prematurely adult voice of 'Black Death: 'Charles Bean! What in heaven's name are you doing there? Come here at once!'

'Christ! It would be her, of all people,' Bean groans.

I flatten myself into a nearby door recess. Eyes shut, I pray that I am not discovered; I know that nothing would move "Black Death's" heart to mercy. I hear them talk. Mary's steely voice, stabbing out questions, Bean, clumsily attempting explanations, then growing defiant. He's alone there, and while his fate is sealed, he does not let on that I'm his accomplice, hiding in the shadow. At last the two of them walk away together. I have the chance to escape.

As I make my way along the corridor, I work out a plan. If intercepted, I'd say I was feeling ill and was on my way to Nurse Butterfield at the infirmary on the floor below. I got lost, I am after all, a new boy, a foreigner. Unfamiliar with this part of the house. Unconvincing, but I can't think of anything better.

Not a soul about as I reach the stairs. One floor down, and I'm safe at last: my story would certainly stick.

The door of Mr Fairchild's study is ajar. Voices are heard from within. His, strained almost beyond recognition, and another, a woman's? Soft yet implacable. He is pleading, his words are blurred. The woman says, 'No... This must stop... No more... Please, let go. You're hurting me.'

Silence. Footsteps approach the door. I draw back. Frances Carr comes out into the corridor. Her eyes are glistening. Instinctively she touches the front of her blouse, shakes her hair, and chin held high, walks hurriedly away.

'...He hath shewed strength with his arm; he hath scattered the proud in the imagination of their hearts. He hath put down the mighty from their seats, and exalted them of low degree... He hath holpen his servant Israel, in remembrance of his mercy; as he spake to our fathers, to Abraham, and to his seed for ever...

Mr Fairchild's voice resonates in the chapel, full of grave import and dignity. In the front pew sits Mrs Fairchild, beaming beatitude. Bean lowers his head; in prayer? Having been brought down from his seat, he awaits in low degree to be exalted at the end of his penitential ordeal. At least he has not been expelled. He bears me no grudge for not coming out to face punishment with him. 'You did the right thing,' he had said impassively, and left it at that.

I look at Frances Carr standing in the choir, her beautiful head bathed in light. I hear her voice, pure as ever, float above Orlando Gibbons' and William Byrd's choral music. I want to be healed of memories as perhaps she is; I long for the sacrament of forgetfulness.

In two weeks term will end, and I shall go home to Mother, Tali, and to Gideon whose deceits are of an earthier kind and easier to accept, who trespasses against others and forgives me who trespasses against him with ever growing deviousness.

15

There's good news, and there's bad news. Imogen has been promoted. She's now a Reader in her department. Also, the American professor she met, whose Vermont hospitality she had enjoyed so memorably, has invited her to work with him in Harvard for a year maybe two. The offer is irresistible. Among other things she will be able to begin the book she has been wanting to write. She says Harvard is very stimulating. She could get a sabbatical from LSE. She told me all this with a shine in her eyes, adding as an after thought that she had not yet decided whether or not to accept the invitation. There was Lucy to think about. And her mother whose health was deteriorating. We had dinner at her house to celebrate. I drank too much wine and got a little maudlin, which won me no sympathy. Whether I also featured in her consideration she did not say.

As for me, I am about to lose my job.

Which is the good and which the bad news, I have not yet decided.

Two events, seemingly unconnected, brought me to this point of departure from my editorship of *Kadima*. First, the lease on our offices at Whitefriars Street was soon to expire. Fink dropped in one morning unannounced, as he had been doing from time to time ever since Bobby Kemp was appointed my deputy. Then, sitting casually on the edge of my desk, coffee mug in hand, he let me have it. As from September *Kadima* as it now was, will cease to be. Re-sartored and reduced to less than half its present size, it will be a house bulletin produced in Head Office by Bobby Kemp, who was right for this less prestigious, less demanding position.

'Don't take it personally, Philo. I, as does everybody, think you've been a terrific editor. It's a budgetary consideration, you know. The grim truth is we have to tighten our belts. We can no longer afford *Kadima*. Of course, you'll get the full redundancy pay and a little more beside,' Fink told me.

The news came fast upon the arrival in London of the new Israel Ambassador. And Fink, having done the unpleasant part of his duty, now gave me the invitation card to the 'getting to know you' reception at the Ambassadorial residence in St. John's Wood. One for me, one for Bobby Kemp.

I read about the new Israeli Ambassador in an 'exclusive' interview

The Jewish Chronicle ran that week. Fink had left the copy on my desk as an implicit rebuke, I suspected, for not having got an interview in *Kadima* ahead of the 'JC'.

His name is Shmaryahu Leshem. A stalwart of the ruling right wing Likud Party, Leshem had a previous posting in Copenhagen. He is no stranger to the UK either, having studied for two years at St. Antony College, Oxford. Leshem is an expert on the "Arab Middle East", the story pointedly emphasised. With experience in regional intelligence.

He is married with two children, a son currently serving in the paratroopers, and a daughter who is studying Archaeology at the Hebrew University, Jerusalem.

I gaze at the two photographs of Leshem and his wife Yocheved. He is balding. A knitted yarmulke – the hallmark of the militant religious – tops his head. The eyes are set close together, truculent peepers. A round face with a small severe mouth. His wife's picture is not flattering. She looks, it seems to me, like the spitting image of their movement's founder, the Polish-born revisionist ideologue Vladimir Zabotinsky, in drag. London's Jewish community is in for a strictly Kosher time with these two.

Suddenly I remember; I think I know who this Shmaryahu Leshem is. And if he is who I think he is, he is sure to know who I am.

The guests to the reception are arriving on foot because, for security reasons, the police have put up no parking signs a hundred yards to either side of the Ambassador's home on both sides of the street. It is a warm early summer afternoon but overcast, with a taste of imminent precipitation in the air. Men and women are dressed formally. All except me. I don't mean my ordinary everyday trousers, open neck shirt and faded sports jacket to be seen as a demonstration of some kind. Yet I know this is how it will be construed.

But I am already out of the swim of everything connected with my work. Whitefriars had been evacuated last week, a day after publication of *Kadima*'s last issue, ahead of the date I was given and without prior warning. As far as Fink is concerned, I have passed into history along with the magazine I edited. If this is Mr & Mrs Ambassador's first social function to mostly Jewish guests with a few house goyim thrown in, for me it is, happily, the last.

At last I am in the line, only a few people away from the Ambassador and his wife who are standing just beyond the entrance of the large reception room to greet their guests. He is wearing an Israeli suit a little too tight for him. She is in Foreign Ministry regulation number, made by Israel's number one fashion house for women, Maskit.

It's him all right. There can be no mistake; there can be no other.

No one present here but me knows, nor can guess, how this man Leshem despises Britain and the British. He cares not a fig for the language of Shakespeare. London's parks, museums, galleries and theatre mean nothing to him. British courtesy and affability he considers rank hypocrisy.

A Mossad man through and through (Gideon used to say he could always spot one in a crowd) with Mossad discipline and training, Leshem probably prepared well for his mission: read British newspapers, a few definitive novels, a history or two. Then concluded that Britain's rise from a small philistine nation with narrow insular horizons, to an imperial colossus without parallel, was an historical aberration now in the rapid process of being redressed.

Yes, I know the type. Britain for him is enemy country. The British are foes and he, defiantly wearing like a battle helmet the knitted kippa, emblem of his faith, is a front-line soldier in the war for the survival of the Jewish state.

Before I leave here I must talk to him. Alone.

I now stand before him. He looks at me. Not a spark of recognition in his gaze. His handshake is limp. We exchange a few niceties. His eyes shift to the person behind me on the last sentence to leave his mouth, and I am nudged forward to greet the Zabotinsky doppelgänger, Mrs Yocheved Leshem.

Glass in hand, I 'circulate' among businessmen, journalists, rabbis, lawyers and doctors – Jews and gentile friends of Israel – thinking how to corner Leshem for a private talk.

'Philo!' Fink hails me.

I walk over to him. His eyes say 'Now really, must you come here dressed like a *shemozl*?'

He pulls an envelope out of his breast pocket. 'For you. It came to the Embassy and was passed to me this morning, as I was there for a meeting.'

The letter bears a Danish stamp.

'Also, someone called Nimrod, an Israeli, rang while you were out.'

'Nimrod? In London? Did he leave a message?'

'He said he was on his way home from Washington. Just wanted to say *shalom*. I think he was ringing from Heathrow.'

I thank Fink and move on in search of Leshem, feeling that the letter and coinciding message from an old time comrade point to some sort of a day of reckoning.

I cannot see Leshem anywhere in the room.

Two leggy security men – unquestionably Israeli former combat soldiers – are standing chatting by the main door of the reception room. They give me a quick alert look as I pass, before resuming their chat.

In the hall I turn right in the direction of toilets, double back, and seeing the two security blokes deep in conversation and unwatchful, trip upstairs. There's nobody about.

I vaguely remember the house from the days of Misha Shomron and his wife. I have a vague recollection that somewhere along this corridor was, possibly still is, the study. I head in that direction until, reaching a closed door, I hear a smoker's cough from within. I knock once and go in, shutting the door behind me.

Shmaryahu Leshem is standing behind an ornate pedestal desk, staring. His right hand is hidden in the desk's open drawer. Surprise and anger show on his face as he sees me.

'What are you doing here?' he asks gruffly.

'I want to talk to you.'

'There are set procedures for that. They begin with asking my secretary for an appointment. I will not be interviewed for *Kadima*.'

'This has nothing to do with *Kadima*.'

'Whatever. I must ask you to leave at once.'

'Not before we talk.'

Leshem's eyebrows shoot up. His mouth drops half open. 'Have you taken leave of your senses? Would you rather I have the security men throw you out?'

'I don't think you want to do that. It's not necessary. What I want to ask won't take long.'

So he sits down. An expression of tough indifference replaces the surprise.

'Just as a matter of interest, it wasn't a gun you were reaching for in the drawer, was it?'

He laughs contemptuously. 'Perhaps I should call security. You're either mad or stupid. I was looking for my indigestion pills, if you must know.'

We are talking in Hebrew. Leshem glances at his watch. 'I know who you are,' he says affecting boredom. 'Very well. Five minutes is all you have. From Now.'

'I want to talk to you about my father Gideon...'

His hands come together. 'What can I tell you that you don't already know?'

'You were in Copenhagen, working for the Mossad when my father died, weren't you?'

'Correction. I was Second Secretary at the Embassy.'

'You knew my father. You kept contact with him... Perhaps you pursued him?'

He smiles wearily. 'I think you're letting your imagination run wild. I did meet him once or twice, Copenhagen is not a big place. We met on Embassy business, as I remember.'

'Like what?'

'That I can't remember. And if I did, it's really none of your business. Look, I'm not going to be interrogated by you. Get to the point, or leave.'

'You know how he was killed...'

Leshem scratches his chin. 'So do you. It was all in the police report, and the Embassy's. He was not murdered, if that's what's bothering you. He drove his car over a bridge and drowned. An unfortunate accident, but nothing sinister.'

'Why, then, did you refuse to see me, when I arrived in Copenhagen?'

'I saw no point in meeting you. There was nothing I could add to what you already knew. I was not in any way involved with your father at the time of his death. Anyway, I honestly don't remember that you wanted to see me, or that I declined to meet you. The Ambassador knew your father personally. She was personally dealing with the matter. You talked to her, didn't you?'

'She told me you made the arrangements to ship my father's body back to Israel. The Israeli press ran stories suggesting that Gideon's death was no accident, that he was killed... I know you were with the Mossad at the time. If anyone knew what really happened, it would've been you. Yet you would not see me...'

It was all coming back to me. Sunday March 16, 1967. A brilliant morning. At the landing approach to Kastrup Airport, Sjælland appeared through a cover of cloud braced by a choppy sea, ablaze with emerald green. Red houses and verdigris towers, and still, dark woods. A land of fairy tales and friendly officials.

Yoram Carmi, Political Counsellor at the Embassy, was there, waiting for me. A soft-spoken silver-haired man with a psychiatrist's voice.

'Sorry to meet you in such unhappy circumstances,' he said, putting his hand on my shoulder. 'I've booked you a room in a nice hotel we use a lot.' 'Can't I go to my father's flat?' Carmi shrugged. 'I thought you might not want to.' 'No, I would rather stay there. Thanks all the same.'

So, to Holte, a woody suburb to the north of Copenhagen. Gideon's flat was small. I sensed it was not much lived it. Probably he kept it just so as to have an address of his own.

'Are you sure you want to stay here?' Carmi asked. 'Yes,' I told him.

He took me to lunch in a quiet inn in the woods further north. Skovriderskroen. A party of Danish men and women were having a jovial business lunch. They were laughing, having a great time. I wasn't hungry. I could tell Carmi wasn't, either. He ordered beer and sandwiches. In between eating and drinking he kept looking at me with those large brown understanding eyes of his. At last he said: 'So terribly sad. Your father was an extraordinary man... So much talent... Such a huge gift for happiness, and for tragedy.'

Outside magpies and jays were chattering chaotically among swelling buds.

'Gideon was happy here, you know. Who could blame him? Denmark is so different from our country...' 'Do you know Kerstin Dahlberg?' Carmi's eyes took on a wistful glow. 'I've met her. A remarkable woman. Like a heroine out of a great novel. She's very distressed, but taking it well. Maybe I shouldn't say this, but I believe they were right for each other, as if created to be together...I'm sorry...' 'That's okay.' 'Look, I have a letter for you from her. She's in Sweden at the moment, but I know she plans to come back to meet you.'

As it happened, she didn't. We never met. Alone that evening, I recalled Gideon's last letters. If he had been so happy as Carmi told me, why were his letters to me so heartbreakingly sad? What was he doing driving alone at around one in the morning, from Møn? So many things I wanted to ask which occurred to me only when I was flying back home, with Gideon's coffin in the aeroplane's cargo hold.

There was little in the flat that could tell me about his condition. A few unused suits in the walnut wardrobe with a jumble of shirts, ties, sweaters... After the burial I distributed his clothes among my friends. Nimrod was one of them – he had taken a fancy waistcoat. We sang 'Gideon's body lies amoulding in the grave but his clothes go marching on'. He would have laughed.

There were a few books on the one bookshelf, notably a French paperback edition of Pierre Teilhard de Chardin's writing. Gideon's last attempt at optimism? The pages were uncut; the French are cruel on pretences.

In the bathroom mirror cupboard I found little jars containing a Swiss ointment for restoring loss of hair. Tens of them, stacked on top of each other like tins on a grocer's shelves. It was there and then that I wept for him for the first time.

Tali rang from Chicago. She had got the telephone number from the Ambassador. 'Philo,' she said, 'I'm coming tomorrow on a Pan Am flight. Meet me at the airport, won't you?'

She had already done much of her crying, in Chicago, in her husband's arms. Now she was steeled to sort things out, to support, to protect family interests. She was good at all that, Tali.

'Christ, what a dump! Let's clean up and get some air in here,' she said. And later, 'Have you met this Dahlberg woman?' 'No, she's in Sweden. She's very distressed, I'm told.' 'Isn't that too bad. We're all very distressed, not least Mother, who is my main concern right now. Can we get her telephone number in Sweden?' 'I don't know. We can ask in the Embassy. They seem to know her.' 'Let's do that. There are many things I'd like to know. The whole business smells a bit rotten too, if you ask me.' Tali's reflexive suspiciousness, as always.

Carmi took me to the Jewish mortuary where the coffin lay on a slab of stone. He remained standing at the door, comically sombre in his hat. 'Did you see him?' 'Excuse me?' 'Gideon, the body, I mean.' 'No.' 'Did anyone identify the body?' 'Oh yes, I'm sure. All the paperwork has been done too. It's ready for shipment.' He gestured at the coffin as though it were a piece of merchandise.

'I want to see. I want the coffin opened. Now. Would you get those two fellows outside to open it, please?' 'I don't think you should,' said Carmi. 'Maybe. But I want it opened all the same. I insist.' Carmi began to argue, then gave up. The two attendants began unscrewing the coffin's top. Underneath there was a metal covering. They began to roll it back, sardine tin fashion. A yellowed cranium came into view. Had Gideon gone bald? At that point, Carmi said something sharply in Danish, and the men stopped. 'Look,' he said, 'this really isn't good for anybody.' Then he took me firmly by the arm and literally dragged me out. Outside Carmi took in a deep breath. 'C'mon, let's go and have a beer somewhere,' he said.

'Why do I have the feeling people are hiding things from us?' Tali said. 'And I'm sure as hell not leaving until I get some answers.'

Poor Tali, she could never apprehend camouflaged toughness. It always crept right up to her to hit her in the face.

'The Ambassador said she didn't know where that Dahlberg woman was. I don't believe it. I'd like to give her a good shaking! Damn it Philo! She's supposed to have been Gideon's friend, the Ambassador!' 'I wish you'd stop saying "that Dahlberg woman". Her name's Kerstin. They were very close, more than just friends...' 'Oh really? Isn't that touching! Listen, I don't much care what she is or what they were to each other. Gideon's dead. Mother's left alone. I'm thinking of her. Only of her. And I want to know what he left. Everything! Down to the last penny!' 'Look around. What you see is what he left. Hair restoring ointment. Can Mother use that?'

We were on the point of fighting. We both sensed it coming and held back. Tali hugged me. We stood holding each other for a long moment. 'For God's sake, let's get out of this place. Let's book the first flight back home. There's nothing left for us to do here. Let's go home, Philo,' Tali said. 'I was thinking of having him cremated... leaving his ashes to Kerstin. That's what he would have wanted.'

Tali pulled back violently. 'Absolutely out of the question! We are taking him home, Philo. No argument. Our father's going to have a proper funeral. In Jerusalem. And everybody's going to be there! I don't care what he would have wanted. Funerals are for the living, Philo.'

* * * * *

'I did what I was asked to do. If you believe the nonsense you read in newspapers, that's your affair. As far as I'm concerned, your father died just as it was stated in the report. I see no reason for thinking otherwise,' Leshem replies in his slow, deliberate voice.

'You didn't like him, did you?'

My question enables Leshem to sound superior.

'I neither liked him nor disliked him. That, in any case, is totally irrelevant.'

'He wrote in his diary that you pursued him. Why?'

Leshem took in breath. 'I believe your father was under considerable stress. I think perhaps he was imagining things.'

'My father was not given to imagining things. He was also someone who could, and did, cope with stress better than you could

177

understand. I don't think you're telling the truth, Mr Ambassador.'

Leshem glances at his watch.

'Our five minutes aren't up yet. And if you think you can fob me off with such nonsense you'd better think again, or call in your security men.'

The Ambassador leans back in his chair. He regards me lengthily. At last, he says: 'Look, as I said, I did meet your father. At my own initiative... My interest in him was, so to speak, similar to your interest in me now. A futile exercise, leading to nothing. The account is closed. I've put it all behind me. You should do the same, for your own peace of mind.

'I know how you feel. But I can tell you this, you'll find no great revelation. Most deaths are very ordinary and have little significance for the living. I know nothing about the circumstances of your father's death beyond what I've already told you.

'Let me now say something else, on a different subject. I've read what you write. You've got it all wrong. You're out of touch with what's happening in Israel. Maybe you want everything to be nice and moral, and decent so that you'd feel more comfortable living here. Maybe you want your English friends to pat Israel on the head and say, "there, there, what a nice civilised little country you are, almost like us". Perhaps the hang-ups you have about your father have something to do with this, I'm no psychologist. But I can tell you this, those who denounce us the loudest are all the while sizing up their trade balance with the Arabs. And in their hearts they know that when it comes to the crunch, what counts is this!' Leshem thrusts out a clenched fist.

'You've been away too long. If you're honest with yourself, you should now make a decision. Either cut loose altogether. Or return home, vote, pay your taxes and protest against anything you like any way you like. I think your choice of venue to express the views you hold, is wrong. And wicked.'

I force myself to check my impulse to argue. It is futile; there is nothing more to get out of him. The 'account is closed'. Leshem no longer matters.

'That was long five minutes. You will go now,' he says and rises.

* * * * *

As I cut across Hampstead Heath on my way home, I think of Nimrod.

We had been comrades at arms, we've remained friends and, in an haphazard sort of way, have kept in touch with each other. There have been times when I wished I was a little more like him: stoic, unassuming and undemonstrative.

Nimrod was the kind of paratrooper commander who dies or lives leading from the front. The supreme kibbutz born and bred combat soldier. The last sort of man one expected to leave his kibbutz for the allure of money and foreign travel.

He was stationed in Copenhagen, representing Shapira Enterprises in Scandinavia and Northern Europe. (The comic irony of it: Nimrod, a samurai from Jezreel, selling sweet kosher Israeli plonk and carpets for an extreme orthodox tycoon from Jerusalem!)

I touch the letter in my pocket. Is it his? Was there something he wanted to tell me? Is today a day of portentous coincidence?

We nearly died together, Nimrod and I, in 1973, in a war I need not have fought. Because I was on the point of decamping for England after Gideon died, after the Six Days War. Had I done so I'd have departed on an equitable rate of exchange: imported, newly-Jewed Alison Leeming; exported, me, the doubter.

Only Mimi had held me back, tenaciously. With Jacob. She wept and protested whenever we talked of divorce, of separation. Even though there was no longer love in our marriage. Even though she had had other lovers.

Love, she had pleaded, was not one thing or the other. Time spent together and children was also love. And respect. And just being used to each other. She told me the war had disturbed me emotionally – it was a well-known phenomenon. Psychiatrists throughout Israel were working overtime on cases just like mine. Post-combat depression. Unless I actually kicked her out, she would not go, she said.

She wouldn't give up her affair with Oren, either. We were stuck together, the three of us; a family in a sense, knowing each other too well; knowing how to hurt and how to heal. In Tibet, Mimi said, it was common for two brothers to share a wife. That was very civilised. Weren't Oren and I like, well, almost like father and son?

Then came Yom Kippur. Saturday October 6, 1973. Sirens tore the hallowed silence of the afternoon, bringing the sky crashing down. Oren arrived, a bearer of calamity in a general's uniform. We stood in the hallway embracing each other, with Jacob, nearly ten, huddled between us.

Oren, formerly Head of Military Intelligence, now Director General of a government-owned company, was bound for Army Staff

Headquarters, Tel Aviv – every help was needed. My reserve motorised infantry unit had been disbanded in a recent reorganisation. I had nowhere to report to. So I decided to go north. That's where my old unit had been. There I was sure to run into someone I knew. I got into my uniform, organised my knapsack.

The sirens were wailing incessantly. Someone came knocking on the neighbours' door, an army messenger, with summons for Rafi? And there was Rafi in the street, rushing home from the synagogue, stomach rumbling from the fast.

'I'll take you as far as Tel Aviv. You'll have no trouble hitching a lift from there on,' Oren said. A Pause. Then, 'You sure?' 'What a question!'

Rosh Pina in northern Galilee, looked flattened in an oppressive dusk. The familiar petrol station cum café was jammed with army vehicles, jeeps, lorries, half tracks and tanks loaded on tank carriers. Artillery boomed over the hills from the direction of the Golan Heights. Even here I could taste sulphur in the air.

Then I saw Nimrod in battle fatigues of a paratrooper major, coming out of the lavatory at the back and making his way to a nearby army jeep. 'Nimrod!' I shouted. He stopped, screwing up his eyes. 'What are you doing here?' 'Going crazy. Can I come with you?' 'I'm going straight into hell.' 'That's fine with me.' 'Don't you have a unit?' 'No. I've been lost in some list. I just came, hoping to find a unit I might join.' 'I could use an officer. Hop in then.'

The bombardment got heavier, with shorter intervals in between. In Operations Room of Brigade Headquarters, Central Section, they estimate that the Syrians have opened up with anything up to a thousand artillery pieces. But there is no movement. The analysts don't think there will be; just shelling, as in the War of Attrition.

'What do you think?' I asked Nimrod. He shrugged. 'I'm saving my thinking for later on. But I can't imagine the Syrians going for a mobile attack. Hope and pray they don't.' 'Why?' 'Because we have less than seventy tanks on the whole fucking Heights, mostly old Shermans. *Miluim* units. Let's try to get some sleep.'

But you can't sleep, not when the walls and ceiling shake all the time.

At ten o'clock in the morning the hitherto unimaginable was confirmed: the Syrians have launched a three-pronged attack from Rafid Junction with a force of over six hundred tanks. They were pushing east, overrunning our forward fortresses.

Voices of commanders from the front appealed over the

communications network: 'Come and get us out, for God's sake...'
'They're grinding us to bits!' '...all my tanks except two, are gone.
The Company commander's dead. I've ten wounded on the deck of
my own tank. What do you want me to do?' 'Just hold on. Hold on for
five minutes more.' 'With what?' 'With your dick. With anything.'
'We've even run out of prayers. Where are the bloody Phantoms, for
God's sake?'

Voices that haunted my dreams for years.

'Where are we going?' 'Towards Aleika. The Syrians have broken
through there. We're going to gather any tank crews we can find who
can still fight, and organise them into battle groups,' said Nimrod.

We set out jolting along in a half-track, Nimrod, a bus driver
reservist from Kiryat Shmone, and I.

Flashes of light illuminated the satanic mass of basalt rocks on the
plateau. There was the first day of creation, and now the first day of
its undoing. Time bombed out of sequence for ever. Alone, like crazed
wanderers, we trundle across a desolation that was already defaced
with burnt out tanks, some of them still smouldering.

A corporal emerged from behind a rock near a crippled tank, holding
his Uzi submachine gun at the ready. 'I thought you were them,' he said.
'Where's your unit?' Nimrod asked him. 'I'm my unit. What's left of it.
We got hit by God knows what.' His protective overalls are smudged
with soot. There's a stench of burnt flesh about him. 'You okay?' Nimrod
asked. The soldier nodded. He looked at us, then over his shoulder. 'Got
the driver out. He's hurt. The rest are dead.'

Behind a rock outcrop we found the driver lying on his back covered
in a torn sleeping bag. He was conscious. Complained that his foot
hurt. When we tried to lift him onto the half-track, his guts spilt out
like a tumble of sausages. Then he went quiet. The corporal slumped
on the ground and began to shake all over. Inside the tank the gunner
was dead, leaning against the gun breach, welded to it by the heat. We
couldn't get him out. 'C'mon, let's move on,' said Nimrod.

At a wounded evacuation point a gynaecologist from Haifa was
getting ready to cut – without anaesthetics – into the living trachea of
a soldier who had been hit in the face. A television crew had arrived.
Looking lost, they began shooting footage at random.

'Who the hell are you two?' a Sergeant Major barked at a young man
in fresh battle fatigues and the girl soldier with him. 'We're a singing
duo from Northern Command. We've been sent to entertain the troops.
Who's in charge here?' The sergeant major pointed at his groin. 'This!'

The Syrians are over there. Go sing to them!' The girl broke into tears.

Just then a smoke-blackened Sherman tank rolled down the slope. Ten wounded men were sprawled on its deck – heroes from a recent battle in Aleika, and the television crew closed in on them.

Again we set out into the battle zone in our half-track, like Valkyries searching not for fallen heroes but those still on their feet.

A pair of Phantom jets came silently out of the sun towards us. I raised my hand to wave, then watched with frozen incredulity as the lead Phantom fired two rockets at us, which hit the ground maybe ten meters in front of the half-track. The shock lifted the vehicle and threw it sideways. 'That's it! Gideon, here I come!' I thought, before the light went out.

Next thing I saw Nimrod's face, covered in dust and blood, looking down at me. 'Can you move?' I tried. I could, just about, it seemed such a painful effort; better to lie still. But Nimrod was pulling at my arm 'Get up, get up,' he shouted. My friend.

I make myself a cup of tea and open the letter.

Holte April 2, 1988.

Dear Philo,

I've been wanting to get in touch for many years. Why didn't I? Nervousness, inertia, also the fear of recalling painful memories. I've tried for so long to put the past behind me, though never to forget.

Gideon used to talk about you a great deal. I feel I almost know you. And if it's not too presumptuous to say, I also feel close to you, because of him. And at the same time so far apart. Gideon taught me, among other things, how to reconcile paradoxes. Of course, growing old also helps.

It must be fate that made me meet your friend Nimrod in Copenhagen. We spent an evening talking about you, until I knew that I could no longer postpone getting in touch with you. He said he would give me your address but it must have slipped his mind. So I posted this letter care of the Embassy in London. I hope it reaches you.

What I really want to tell you is that something has come up – let it be a surprise, a good one, I promise – which concerns you. We should, therefore meet, as soon as possible. In London? I'll happily come there, I love London. I remember a breakfast at the Ritz was something really special. Shall we meet at the Ritz for breakfast?

I'll contact you again to fix a date.

Yours, Kerstin.

16

From Gideon's diary

*Katmandu, April 14, 1963 – A year, almost to the day since I took
office. A most satisfactory year. I should write and tell Golda, who
didn't intend my appointment to be a prize, nor even satisfaction. A
small, out of the way country of no importance to anybody. Friendly
people. No Jews. What do they know about Israel? Nothing! Let
Gideon tell them. He's good with goyim and savages. The air is thin.
Clear his head of all those crazy ideas. Two years or so up there in the
mountains, will do him a world of good, and give us a rest...*

I can hear her Yiddishy American voice. Ignorant, tribal, vindictive,
narrow-minded and banal. That such a woman should be our Foreign
Minister! But I respect her strength of character. And I'm grateful for
this ambassadorial posting. Providential I'd have called it, if I
believed in Providence.

Everyone should have a monastic interlude of a sort at least once in
lifetime, to cleanse the soul, like an extended Yom Kippur fast of the
spirit. This is mine.

As I walk in the shadow of the mighty Himalayas, I feel liberated.
Reduced yet enhanced – like a speck of light, a dot of consciousness, a
tiny increment of infinity. Looking back, I see how futile self-
importance and self absorption are; they are barriers in the way of real
wisdom of which I have no more than a glimpse as yet.

I shall pay my debt to the full for the good fortune of being here.
Golda shall have nothing to complain about. Nor will the Nepalese.
Whatever they want, I'll recommend they get. Roads? Solel Boneh will
help. Machinery? Israel will provide. Training in agriculture,
irrigation, medicine? The Israel Embassy will be receptive. Anything. I
owe it to this gentle welcoming people. Except military. In this I will
not be forthcoming, not if I can possibly help it. How distant and petty
all the frenetic agitation of world politics look from here.

As I expect, Nepal will side with Israel in UN General Assembly
debates. That's really all Golda cares about, and I will deliver Nepal's
vote to her. And when His Majesty King Mahendra Bir Birkham Shah
Deva visits Israel this summer, he will appreciate that Israel is a true
friend; an ally who repays friendship with friendship at a high interest.

In preparation for the royal visit, I'm writing a report for the Ministry on Nepalese customs, history, government, and problems. Erland is a great help. Of all the Europeans here none knows or understands this country as well as he does. Whenever any of the ambassadors is stuck for a point of information he goes to Grev Erland Dahlberg. But they are seldom to be seen at parties and functions. They mostly keep to themselves he and Kerstin. I am grateful for their friendship, for the benefit of Erland's enormous library, and for his wisdom.

Our tiny mission works harder than the others. Hardly surprising. For other countries, it's just a matter of being here. For us, it is a long-term investment.

I have to join in the social life here. A waste of time but a part of the job nonetheless. Diplomats tend to be more frivolous than other people when they are bored, and here this seems to be the case most of the time. Dinner parties given on a rotary basis among the embassies. State functions of the Nepal government and the Court. Picnics. Rides or walks. Gossip and talk about missed opportunities which eventually slides into facile philosophising. The altitude, that must be one of the reasons. And the magic isolation: we are like inmates in an enchanted sanatorium here – our 'Magic Mountain'.

Beth is bored. Between June and September, during the monsoon season, she visibly wilts. Heights do nothing for her except make her short of breath. She will, therefore, not venture out of Katmandu to the mountains. She has put on weight. Too much cakes and tea with Debbie Merriweather. It doesn't become her at all. She looks like a plump nervous hen. Debbie has most of their food flown in from Washington. How ridiculous.

I, on the other hand, have lost so much weight I had to have my clothes taken in by the tailor Bill Merriweather employs. I eat little: a bowl of spiced rice and yak's milk yoghurt once a day. Beth says I'm like Torquemada, too lean, too ascetic with my hair cropped short. Kerstin likes the way I look. She says I remind her of one of the Kings of Israel in Chartres, without the beard, of course. I take pleasure in her liking me. She's serious, high-minded without being stuffy, and she has the most captivating smile I've ever seen. I love to make her laugh. She's a rewarding companion, in many ways.

Katmandu enchants me. Its colours, dominated by red and saffron, recall a recurrent dream I have of a place at once familiar and alien: a mythical travellers' point of arrival or departure. I take early morning walks. Invariably, I arrive at Durbar Square. Temples everywhere. I sit among the people in front of the Great Temple and let thoughts come at random to my head with the passing scenes.

As I watch the people, Newars, Sherpas, whatever, pedal past in hundreds on Chinese-manufactured bicycles, I feel there's an important lesson to be learnt from them. Simplicity of life? Spirituality? Were we ever like that?

A Nepalese official proudly told me that one of their sources of hard currency was exporting yak's tails to Britain, to make wigs for English judges. I had to laugh. The most vaunted justice in the world cosseted by the backside addendum of a primitive bovine.

One morning, on an impulse, remembering what Erland told me of Hindu and Buddhist cosmogony, I bought a mandala from a street painter. Another time, a flute from a vendor by the Temple steps. It makes a lovely sound, even when I blow on it. I saw a man bearing a stick of incense depart from a procession to insert a chit of paper in a cleft between the stones of the statue of the Monkey-God Hanuman. A prayer? A request? When I was a boy I used to see religious Jews do the same at the Western Wall in Jerusalem.

Mendicant beggars everywhere. I can tell the holy men from the rest by their deportment and robes. There's so much unaffected dignity even in their begging. Among Erland's books I came across one about the 16th century Mogul emperor Akbar. A great humanist, he abdicated power to roam his empire incognito, as a mendicant, with nothing but a staff and a begging bowl. Abdicating power must be at least as exciting as achieving and maintaining it. With us, I think only Ben Gurion understands this. I have a premonition that soon he will resign again, this time for good.

Erland and Kerstin keep two elderly, sure-footed horses on which they ride in the countryside. I prefer to walk. My leg hardly gives me trouble nowadays, perhaps because I'm lighter than I ever was, and fitter. On my outings I wear a robe, like the villagers. I carry a staff. But I have the Swiss Alpine boots Bill Merriweather got for me. The scenery changes so often along the hilly footpaths. I cross rope bridges over mountain streams. That, and the hanging mist in the mornings create an illusion of having traversed a great distance even on a short walk. Once on a walk, I passed through a village and witnessed a burial. The body of the old man was burnt in a funereal pyre. Thus Agni the God of fire freed his soul at the beginning of the reincarnation cycle.

I sat some distance away and thought about death, and the freedom you gain when you stop being afraid of it. It's the body which fears death more than the spirit. A man, having reached the height of spiritual development, can subdue vanity, ambition, even the desire for power. Like the Emperor Akbar. But the body fights all the way to the end, with appetite, and with sex. How pathetic!

Later I had a tilaka painted on my forehead. It was still there, albeit smudged, when I came to the Embassy the next day. I'm sure R rushed a private memo to Golda about it.

April 18. No Pessach for us this year. Beth has gone with the Merriweathers to Terai where Bill, murderer of animals, planned a massacre of wild life he calls hunting. I joined Erland and Kerstin in their Kakani lodge north west of Katmandu, from where there is a splendid view of the Himalayas.

Erland was having one of his chronic bouts of depression, so Kerstin and I went for walks and rides in the hills without him. Here, for the first time, she talked about Erland. He's tormented by a sense of failure, perceiving excellence which he cannot attain. Isn't that masochism of a sort, if not arrogance? I asked. No, she said. Erland has no arrogance in him at all. He is a perfectionist, and too aware of his own imperfections. She said he has a kind of death wish, and she thinks that his obsessive attraction for the east is a part of it.

Clearly, she reveres him. Does she love him? I wonder. She told me it was no sacrifice at all for her to have given up her own career as a botanist. On the contrary, travelling and living with Erland in the east has been an enriching experience, a kind of self-discovery she would not exchange for anything in the world. Sometimes, though, she felt sad about not having children. Couldn't she still? I asked. She shook her head and went silent. We were looking at the hills, when she suddenly said: 'Ever been to Pokhara? No? Ah, you have a real treat waiting in store. Why don't we go? Tomorrow!'

We took the bus from Katmandu – the 'midnight express'. Nearly 8 hours to traverse mere 125 miles. Neither of us was in the least tired on arrival. If Gan Eden really existed, this, not anywhere in the Middle East, must have been it. Upland meadows. Yak pastures. Everywhere masses of wild flowers in full bloom.

She was telling me about Annapurna, the beautiful goddess of plenty after whom the magnificent peak was named. I almost said how noble and beautiful she was herself, and how, like Annapurna, unreachable.

That night we slept together. There were no preliminaries, no explanations, and no guilt. Just pure, intoxicating joy. As though it *was the most natural thing in the world, as though it had to happen, as though we have both been waiting all our lives to be united with each other.*

It's Philo's birthday, and I can't think of anything to give or say to him.

Well? Thus Gideon in his Year of Leanness.

Roll back ten years or so. Summer, now and in England. Gideon tips the scales at thirteen stone ten pounds, a personal record. While Mother is at her slimmest. Never again will she look so pretty.

This fat summer Gideon is aeons away from cosmogony of any sort. Nor do the enigmas of life and death trouble him. If anything, it's the temporal pomp of historical continuity which preoccupies his thoughts. He has discovered Evelyn Waugh. He goes to Hatchards in Piccadilly and returns with an armful of Waugh's novels. In no time at all he even begins to resemble the author. Observe the sceptical eyebrows, the wicked irony in the mouth, the steady warmthless scrutinising gaze. Note the measured tone of voice, the fastidious choice of words. A gun cabinet stands in his study. In it, one Purdey and another shotgun of inferior pedigree. England, you are a Circe for foreign dreamers!

King George VI died that winter. Gideon bought the records – two discs from His Master's Voice – of Prime Minister Winston Churchill's eulogy. He played them again and again and, would you believe it, tears shone in his eyes! Cor blimey, stone a crow! What's Hecuba to him, or he to Hecuba that he should weep?

We watched the coronation procession: Gideon and Mother from the balconies erected in the Mall for distinguished foreign guests, Tali and I from amidst a sea of people that surged all the way from Buckingham Palace to Westminster. The entire Empire was parading through London, reminding the world that fairy tale pageants were still alive and well with Britannia. It rained buckets on the Queen of Tonga. Smiling and gigantic in an open carriage, she waved to the throngs, who cheered their hearts out.

I lost my grip on Tali. Pressed against an Australian matron who smelt of peppermint and beer, I drifted all the way down towards Embankment. The Thames glowed with the embers of the day. 'Goodness me, whose boy are you, dearie?' the Australian lady cooed, clicking her snappers. She walked away leaving me with paper flag of her country stuck in my breast pocket.

At last, a tearful Tali came home in a police car. 'How could you let go of your little sister in that crowd!' Mother gasped, before fainting. The day had been too much for her.

Summers space my years like still lagoons. The smell of rain on the grass. Human milk bottles 'overing' on cricket greens. Blackbirds' vesperal twittering out of the heavy foliage, mingling with the flat thump of tennis balls.

Tali takes elocution lessons at a drama school in Fulham. Gideon wins a tidy sum in the Derby, betting on Arctic Prince, who streaks home. Gideon again, wearing plus fours and cradling his Purdey. A terrible shot, he nevertheless bags a few grouse on a friend's moor in north Yorkshire. There he is, grinning at the camera.

And here am I, standing next to Pip Oxley on the tennis court in Barningham Hall. Pip is Andrew Oxley's son. Andrew is a writer, related on his mother's side to the renowned Colonel R. Meinertzhagen, our goy hero from the British Mandate. Sympathy for the Jews has been bred into Andrew, then deepened by his current literary enterprise, a definitive history of the genesis and development of the Israel Defence Forces, in which Gideon – friend and kindred spirit – is a valuable source of information.

But Gideon isn't here. He's in the Arctic Circle, observing Swedish military manoeuvres. I'm here because there's no one at home. Last week Grandmother died while sleeping in her rocking chair under the pomegranate tree in her garden. Mother has gone to Jerusalem for the funeral, and Tali is in Devon with a family of visiting friends from Israel.

Andrew and Diana's house in Barningham just about qualifies as a stately home, only they wouldn't dream of calling it that. Pip and his twin sister Angelica are two years older than me. He goes to Rugby. He takes me for walks along the River Greta. We ford it hopping from rock to rock across the frothy water. He and Angelica have a private language of allusions which I can't understand – public school twittery, devastatingly precocious.

We have summer pudding on the lawn for tea when it doesn't rain, and lamb with mint sauce for dinner, which Cook serves in the dining room. Inside it's freezing cold, even on a warm day. The English, says Gideon, consider cold a virtue.

'Darling, what have you been doing today?' Diana Oxley asks

Angelica, because doing things is important, and dinner is the only time when we all see each other. 'Oh, this and that.' The length of the table reduces conversation to short questions and shorter answers, with long silences in between. Tall, with dreamy blue eyes, and a drooping moustache, Andrew Oxley reminds me of Elgar. Diana's father, ninety six, once a cavalry colonel in India, sits next to me. His face is ruddy, his eyes watery yet still fierce. With gnarled hands he grasps the knife and fork as though they were weapons, and listing over towards me, mutters, 'Trouble with the Jews, never had good cavalry.' Gideon had roared with laughter when I told him that. Said it was the profoundest comment on the Jews he had ever heard. I can't reply to the old boy, since without his hearing trumpet which he quickly removes after each uttering, 'Pops' is as deaf as a post.

1954 is a milestone in Gideon's career: the Israel Airforce buys fourteen Gloster Meteor jet fighters. Now we are to have warplanes worthy of our pilots – the best. And although Gideon diffidently understates his part in the transaction all credit goes to him. Even Misha Shomron acknowledges this, with his customary hyperbole.

I come home for Easter vacation to face a moody, irritable Gideon. You sense tension the moment he sets foot in the flat. I see how Mother is terrified of him, and it angers me. She's like a rabbit in a python's cage. It is on me, however, that Gideon loosens his ire.

'He doesn't mean it, you know that...' Mother whispers to me, hoping that Gideon, engrossed in reading, doesn't hear. But he does.

He glares at her: 'If you want to say something, say it out aloud. I hate whispering.'

I am ready for insurrection, and afraid at the same time.

Behind our animosity lies one reason: my end of term report was poor; Mr Fydow doesn't think I'll be ready to take O levels in the summer. Gideon has said not a word. He pretends it doesn't matter. But I know he is disappointed. He thinks I'm 'letting the side down'. What and whose side? I want to ask, and whose life is it out there, alone, in the front line of the 'side'? But Gideon throws no challenges and asks no questions. Like an angry god, he punishes us with his moods.

To our domestic malaise we soon have an audience: David Oren arrives to begin a course for senior staff at Camberley College. With him is his new wife, Athaliah Ben Yehuda.

Suits don't suit David, they make him look rotund. To camouflage his unease he acts with boisterous joviality which, like the suit he wears, ill becomes him. At other times he preaches. That bores Gideon, I can tell from his face, and so, I suspect, can Athaliah, but not David.

'My my my, what a little gentleman you've become,' David says to me, slapping me hard on the back. 'Tali, you talk English like Shakespeare...'

That, actually, is one of Mother's stock phrases. He then hugs Mother, recognising in her a dependable, unchanging ally. To Gideon he defers awkwardly, for although senior to him in rank and an old friend, here Gideon is formally in charge. The last thing David wants is to make Gideon feel that he, David, is taking liberties with him because he is a Brigadier whereas Gideon is only a Colonel.

Athaliah is hard to make out. She looks ageless. Her face is oval and as inscrutable as a Japanese No mask and framed by smooth hair streaked with grey. Her eyes twinkle with a suggestion of laughter. They are small, chocolate brown. When she looks at you, you feel as though you are being watched from behind a screen. I sense almost immediately that she's not terribly impressed with Gideon. Moreover, she refuses to presume familiarity just because Gideon and her husband have been friends for so many years.

Athaliah teaches Philosophy at the Hebrew University. She's older than David, neither will say by how many years. He is immensely proud of her. I hear Mother say to Gideon in a low voice, 'He adores her so much, it's plain to see. But how he's changed! Must be her influence...' And Gideon answers flatly, 'Poor David, he has always adored to adore...'

Athaliah is granddaughter of the celebrated man of letters Eliezer Ben Yehuda, for which reason no less than out of the desire to underscore her independence, she has kept her maiden name. Oren, after all, is almost as common as Cohen or Levy.

Mother puts them in Gideon's study. Large and self-contained, it is the most private room in the flat. Over dinner, David announces with a meaningful wink at me, that Athaliah is not only a philosopher, she is also an accomplished pianist who might easily have turned professional had she wanted to.

Happily, their presence suspends our strife. Within a week it's like old times again between Gideon and David. We go out to see a Hollywood biblical epic at the Leicester Square Odeon. Neon lights flash a menu of colours at the night sky. Starlings hum in the trees. The Square is teeming with people, while on the pavement in front of the Odeon, two buskers are doing a Houdini act. The one inside the sack is still struggling with the chains when two policemen appear on the scene and his mate pockets the takings and makes off. The bound one unbinds himself, sticks his head out of the sack. 'Where's that sodding pillock gone?' he calls out. Some people in the queue laugh. Hands on hip, the two bobbies strike a mock menacing posture. 'Oh my gawd!' squawks the busker, and dives back into the sack.

Athaliah Ben Yehuda is not amused. For her it is a spectacle of human degradation, a cutting indictment of England's unjust class system. Nor is she awed by the theatre's opulence, the plush seats, the wurlitzer organ which rises from the pit in a tempest of sound and pink glow. David is: 'You need an empire to have things like this,' he says, impressed with his own perceptiveness.

About that time I experience a regeneration of a sort. A strange creative energy surges within me. I begin to compose music. Yes, passage by passage, whole structures and landscapes of sound rise in my mind, alive with colour and movement.

A mystical experience? A miracle? Yes to the first, half yes to the second. For while I can recall my compositions at will as though I were playing from a score – every orchestral and instrumental section vividly defined, all musical influences subtly recognisable – while I can edit, improve, and then actually hear in my mind as if played on a top-quality stereo system installed inside my head, my compositions remains locked in me without an outlet. I can't as much as whistle them. Like Moses on Mount Nebo, beholding the Promised Land knowing he'll never set foot there, I rejoice in the gift, and accept the punishment with resignation.

I confide in Athaliah. Ostensibly schematic and over-principled, she's not astonished let alone dismissive. Autism of the creative imagination, she pronounces. But I'm an artist nonetheless. We talk about art. Rather, she talks and I listen, trying to fathom my new identity which she outlines. The true measure of an artist is knowing his craft implicitly and instinctively. Understanding with the soul, as distinct from with the intellect. That's what sets apart a genius like Mozart from a supreme craftsman but ultimately ordinary artist like, say, Hindemith. And Mendelssohn? Yes, him too, less significantly. Wagner, revolting anti-Semite though he was, was dead right about Mendelssohn.

I take to listening to Wagner, surreptitiously, because he is forbidden, for which reason his attraction is all the more powerful. I succumb to his magic. I learn that art has a morality of its own, independent of social or political values.

Gideon can barely conceal that he doesn't hold Athaliah in high regard. Her didactic style bores him. He shows this most when we sit together for dinner. To her credit, Athaliah doesn't attempt to please. Never have I seen anyone ignore Gideon with such implicit superiority, as she does.

'Some men,' she says, apropos nothing, 'need a woman to stretch them to their potential. Without such a woman they remain like unripe fruit for the rest of their life. Venting pointless energy. Ultimately useless.'

David nods vigorously. Mother looks uncomfortable. Gideon demonstratively stifles a yawn and says, 'Oh, really. Beth, would you pass the bread, please.'

'What do you think Abinoam Ben Barak would have been without Deborah?' Athaliah goes on, 'Zero! Wouldn't have been able even to get a company of warriors together.'

'Maybe not. But what would Deborah have been without Barak, huh? More wine, David?'

Alone in the flat, I put on a record at near full volume. The Pye Hi-fidelity Gideon has bought booms the bass against the walls and ceiling. Understand this: when I listen to music I listen with every bit of my being; I live every bar. Thus, I'm now in the head of Arturo Toscanini as he conducts *Beethoven's Seventh*. And when that's over, I take on another guise for *Mozart's piano concerto No 27 in B flat, K 595*, with Clifford Curzon. At the last movement I sense an intrusion, and turning, I see Athaliah Ben Yehuda sitting on the armrest of an armchair by the door. She raises a finger to her lips. I try to ignore her; the intimacy of my listening is gone.

'A beautiful concerto,' I remark pointlessly when the record is played out.

'Oh yes,' says Athaliah, 'By far his best, in my opinion. And because it's so brilliant, ironically it shows up all the piano's limitations.'

I stare at her. 'How so?'

'Well, it has such a range of sonority and such a wide variety of possible nuances. While the piano is a fantastic instrument its greatness is also its weakness. You see, a pianist can play soft or loud, fast or slow, but he cannot produce his own sound in the way that a string player or a flautist can. The sound created by the bow on strings depend entirely on the player, as is with wind instruments, particularly the flute. It is a continuous sound, and the colour and quality of it depends on the musician's skill. Do you follow?

'A real musician has his own sound in his imagination. It changes as he develops. But only when he can create that sound has he reached the point where his art and skill come together. Do you understand what I'm saying?'

'I think so.'

Athaliah smiles inscrutably. 'Want a piece of good advice?'

'What?'

'If you find your inner voice, listen to it. Always. In music as in anything else.'

I'd like to know what voice Gideon hears in the silence of his soul: a mermaid's song? Siren's? The single unremitting voice in the burning bush?

The Orens are gone. He to Camberley, she to a bed-sitter in Bloomsbury close to the British Museum, where, having obtained a reader's card to the Library, she plans to research into Aristotelian influence on Maimonedes, before returning to Jerusalem. 'David has his career, and I have mine. We're close yet separate. The best kind of marriage,' she declares at their last supper with us, in an unusual moment of personal confession.

As the Orens depart, Gideon's moods return with a vengeance. He sleeps alone in his study now. A slit of light shines under the closed door well into the small hours of the morning. You can hear the BBC World Service playing softly.

Gideon's morning ablution is a lengthy affair. Mostly because it is here, in the bathroom, that he is at his most communicative with me. While he shaves, I sit on the edge of the bath and listen to him talk.

When the ancient Greeks warred with each other, Apollo's oracular shrine at Delphi nevertheless remained inviolably neutral, for all Greeks to visit in safety. Similarly, for one hour every morning, our bathroom is a sanctuary where moods and quarrels have no admittance. Here I listen to my father's wisdom, his thoughts about life, about Israel, about himself and me. Here I share his humour and his witticism.

Only now he bolts shut the door. A quick splash, and he is out. We don't see him all day, except for a couple of hours after supper, before he retires to his study.

He sits in an armchair reading. A pile of newspapers lies at his feet – *The Times*, *The Economist*, back numbers of Israeli journals, and *Le Monde*. There's music in the background – his records: French songs with Yves Montand, Edith Piaff, Charles Trenet. You see, Gideon is teaching himself French.

Why French? Because he wants to read Montaigne and Voltaire in the original. Because French civilisation is at the heart of Europe, and Israel is a mere heart beat away, he says. Because Ben Gurion is teaching himself Classical Greek. Because Gideon simply likes the sound of French and the names of wines. Inside him, a butterfly *flâneur* is already struggling out of its chrysalis.

In September Ben Gurion resigns as Prime Minister and withdraws to his beloved Sde Boker in the Negev. He is succeeded by Moshe Sharet. Lavon is Minister of Defence. Gideon, who always maintained that in a true democracy strong leaders were superfluous, is worried about the absence of strong leadership in Israel.

Fedayeen attacks from Egypt and Jordan, are countered by Israel's own retaliatory raids. Nasser has supplanted Neiguib as ruler of Egypt. 'The clouds are gathering. Our main enemy now has a dynamic leadership, and we are misgoverned by flat-footed party functionaries and committees,' Gideon reflects gloomily.

I wonder if he wonders whether his day will ever come. Or, that seen from the perspective of exile, things at home look worse than they actually are.

Come into our salon. Gideon is at his post-prandial reading. Mother is browsing through a magazine. Across from Gideon, book in my lap, I sit, pretending to read. In fact, I'm busy working on a string quartet á la Debussy. Not easy, not my medium anyway. To make things worse, my concentration is poor on account of Gideon's presence. One passage half sketched, I look up to see him glaring at me.

'What are you reading?'

I mumble something, sneaking a glance at the spine of the book I've picked at random from a shelf. 'Shaw...'

'Shaw! You didn't even know what book you have there, did you? Why pretend? Why don't you go and get your comic book? That at least would be honest. You might even learn something. Better that you idled your time away in news theatres and rubbishy films than pretend to do things you obviously can't do. Huh! Who do you think you are fooling?'

Mother makes nervous noises which we both ignore. He is livid with anger. I sense that all evening he has been waiting for an opportunity to turn on me. I reply with insolent nonchalance, 'What do you care what I do, anyway?'

He half-rises. Will he strike me? I'll fight back!

'Get out of here! You make me sick,' he barks.

So? I read *Eagle* comics, now and then. I also frequent news theatres in the West End. Do you know of lonely men in shabby raincoats, eating out of paper bags in the dark, while the world rolls past in celluloid black and white? Men for whom 'Embassy' is a brand of cigarettes they can't afford? Are you, Father, blameless for my afternoons at the local Odeon, watching B films? Or evenings spent smoking in an espresso bar in Hampstead, waiting to catch a glimpse of the waitress's ample cleavage as she bends over a table? All wasteful. All empty, and pointlessly languorous. So is my life, Abba, half the time.

In punishment, my pocket money is cut by half. Cinema is therefore out. But not museums, which offer a more demanding form of escape. I dream of joining the Colonial Service in some pacific paradise like the Gilbert Islands. Just disappearing without a word to some distant corner of the world.

One morning in the British Museum, I run into Athaliah.

'Philo! What a surprise!'

She is delighted to see me, and I her. We go for a snack in the cafeteria. Now at last on the last stage of her research, Athaliah is lonely. I can tell, although she doesn't say. She's homesick too, and she misses David whom she sees only on weekends. Neither Gideon nor Mother has been in touch with her since she moved into her bed-sitter, and that hurts a little. Being both, in different ways, victims Athaliah and I strike an alliance.

I discover that without other people around Athaliah is a terrific companion. More surprisingly, she has the catching enthusiasm of an innocent. She treats me as an equal, and since I know London and my English is better than hers, I am in charge on our outings to lunchtime concerts in St. John's Smith Square, to exhibitions, to Wren and Vanbrough churches which she wants to see.

Coming up for air, we face the sun-drenched court of the British

Museum, and Athaliah blinks and rubs her eyes. 'Aren't you starving?' she asks. 'After a dose of medieval darkness wouldn't hearty lunch at the pub across the road be just the thing? My guide book says it's one of the best in London for pub lunches.'

Half way across the court, she stops dead. 'Let's go back a minute. I think I've forgotten something in the Library,' she says.

Too late. I see what she is trying to prevent me from seeing. I see Gideon emerging from a door across the other side of Great Russell Street. There's a woman with him. She is tall, elegantly dressed, and wearing a wide-brimmed hat which half conceals her face. They stand on the pavement, close but not touching. There's a shockingly blatant air of intimacy between them. Then Gideon raises his cane to hail a taxi. Before they get in the woman turns to kiss him. I recognise Margaret Barlow.

'To think that next week I'll be back home!'
'And I back at school.'
'Wasn't it lucky that we ran into each other?'
'Can't tell you how it saved my holiday.'
Long silence.
'Philo...'
'What?'
'Look, I think what we saw earlier, your father and that woman, is nothing out of the ordinary... Just friends meeting... People often misunderstand... therefore... I don't think you should mention it to anyone. Let's just keep it between ourselves, okay?'

I say nothing. How can I explain to Athaliah what I intuitively know, that Margaret Barlow is Gideon's Gilbert Islands of the imagination, his exotic corner of the world far away from us? She would never understand.

* * * * *

'Try the Dover sole, it's delicious,' Gideon suggests, and orders for both of us.

We are at Scotts Restaurant, Piccadilly Circus, and he's in a cheerful mood, therefore I'm apprehensive. When he has something telling to announce Gideon tends to move to neutral territory. I know from experience that the importance of his message corresponds to the grandeur of the setting he has selected for its delivery.

'By the way, how did you do in the exams?'

'I think I passed in English, History, and Geography. Not sure about French.'

'Good, good. So how many left to take?'

'Four more, in the autumn.'

'Yes, that's what I want to talk to you about. The situation is as follows. I'm being posted to Washington in July. A sudden decision back home. You could come with us. But I think it would be better if you stayed behind to finish your exams.'

'Where?'

'Well, Margaret and Lionel Barlow said they'd be happy to have you. You'd like it there, wouldn't you?'

'How can I tell? What then?'

Gideon takes a sip from his wine glass. 'Well, let's cross one bridge at a time. After the exams you could join us in Washington, or go back home, stay in Mishmar Ha'emek until you're due for the army. Hardly two years you know…'

I cut into the sole's flank. The decision seems of cosmic dimension. 'What do you want me to do?' I ask.

'I want what's good for you. Only that,' says Gideon with a sigh. 'Think about it. Meanwhile, why don't we leave it open until after your exams?'

17

In Ward 33, Whittington Hospital, Highgate, you can tell that the National Health Service is just about on its last trotters. Depletion of resources and general fatigue have stamped their mark on the floor, walls, beds, and staff. A tangle of rusty ladders and pipes clutter a patch of grey sky at the window. Through this ugly reticulation flood in noises of a healthier world: traffic, voices, the never ending beat of rock music which creeps up the bed's metal legs and into my back. Next to me lies a black man from Haringey, about to have a prostate gland operation. 'Lord Almighty, you made me wrong!' He keeps groaning, but winks as he smiles at me.

I tell him, 'God over-reached himself. He should've stopped after creating the cat.'

'Right on, right on,' he replies.

A pipe from his pyjamas fly drains his bladder into a plastic bag.

It is morning. Nurses come and go, impassive and already tired.

'I had gall stones. It's nothing, man,' says my next bed neighbour.

The ward consultant assures me cheerfully that I'll be a new man after he's cut them out.

Do I want to be a new man? I cannot enthuse about this surgically-induced renaissance, even when I feel, as I now do, discarded into a purgatory of a human junk yard.

Thanks to a timely injection, the pain has fizzled out of my guts, along with the energy that went to fight it. Drugged and drained I drift into a metaphysical haze where my past is telescoping fast into the present: Anno Domini 1986. I'm on course for a collision wherein I am to be at once casualty and voyeur.

Nobody knows I'm here, except my neighbour downstairs who will feed Moon. There'll be no visitors. You, Imogen, are away for the weekend, attending a conference in Oxford. And although you've told me you loved me, in your fashion, I know for sure that you wouldn't dream of leaving a work engagement for my sake. Matched against 'Work', 'Love' for you, as in tennis, means nothing (I borrow this bitter insight from a poet I admire).

When Gideon wrote – not once but several times – about a recurring dream of a landscape at once alien and familiar, I understand what he is talking about. Why do people raised in sun-baked lands dream of dark green woods and running streams? What do kibbutz children draw in class? Not squat bungalows and fields which they know, but dream cities with steeples and clock towers which they have never seen in reality. What did the urban founders of Israel sing about? Shepherds and shepherdesses piping to their flocks in green pastures.

What are such dreams if not access into an expanding universal memory – call it God, if you like – which we shall re-experience at a later stage of our evolution, when we are tiny and free and the world is huge once again? Thus spake Gideon (more or less) in the shadow of the Himalayas.

Here and now, I want to believe it. After all, haven't I dreamt of you, Imogen, time and time again long before we met? The habit persists. In fact, I do believe it was one of your protean oneiric visitations that put the gall stones in my guts.

Like this: rosy dusk; another time, another place, but essentially England. Sandbags encapsulating a space on the roof of Sherborne School for girls, Dorset. Improbably, a beam of light probing a pale evening sky. Two men beside me, like me, wearing silly steel helmets British Army issue. While we search the empty sky, you gaze seaward, across the undulating expanse of darkening countryside. I recognise you the instant you appear, clad though you are in armour over a flowing robe, just as you were when you sprang clean as a jet of water from a god's head. 'Private John Bull, Private Tom Brown, at ease!' you command. 'By Jove, who's that alien masquerading as a bare-kneed Tommy?' 'Me? *Ego sum qui sum*, Ma'am.' You touch me in the abdomen with the tip of your lance. Oh, the pain is excruciating... And then there is Moon, crouching at the foot of the bed with anxious amber eyes.

At the hospital they ask what's my religion. I'm shivering cold. I say that like Emperor Julian, I'm a devout apostate. What's that? the man wants to know. Oh, just put down anything, for Christ's sake. So it's C of E. What the hell, Christian Jew or heathen, as a rate-payer I'm entitled to eternal rest in St. Pancras and Islington Cemetery in the event of demise under the knife.

Two books, taken in a hurry before I get carted off lie on the bedside cabinet: the Icelandic *Njal's Saga*, and Milan Kundera's *The*

Unbearable Lightness of Being. Neither will be opened while I'm here. But the nurse with a tattoo of a rose and dagger on her ankle, will look and wonder. The doctors on their rounds, too, will arch their eyebrows: well well, here lies a cultured foreigner, the first devout apostate to grace our beds, and here's the proof! How my life at times reflects Gideon's, as in a funfair's mirrors hall.

Go-back-go-back-go-back! bark the grouse on the moors. Gideon stirs from a hunting dream into an awareness of pain. Unlike me, he doesn't call for an ambulance. Grimly, he waits till dawn. He rings his specialist. Then summons Williams to take him in the Supersnipe to a clinic in Wigmore Street. Here, in a private room equipped with a radio and scented with a bouquets of roses and carnations, he defies pain. What are gall stones but a nuisance to one who had suffered in silence the agony of battle wounds?

Eventually, they end up as a souvenir on his desk: two black pebbles embedded in a mounted perspex block inscribed with *Col. Gideon Jerusalem's Gall stones. London October 17, 1953.*

On the bedside table lie two volumes of Gibbon's *Decline and Fall*. Plus Evelyn Waugh's *A Handful of Dust*. Plus a thriller by Simenon. Plus a leather-bound antique edition of Josephus Flavius' *Wars of the Jews*, this, a present. Music resonates – Hans Hotter singing Sachs's famous aria from *Die Meistersinger*.

Not bad, eh? Actually, the last is my touch, edited into the scene for effects. Gideon wouldn't have been able to tell *Die Meistersinger* from *A Night on a Bare Mountain*. Moreover, he wouldn't dream of listening to Wagner.

Visitors come to see him by the droves: military cronies, Andrew Oxley, Captain Basil Liddell-Hart. And Margaret Barlow, daily, each time with a fresh bouquet of flowers which she lovingly arranges.

The evenings belong exclusively to Mother. That's when Gideon is at his most subdued. But who does she bring along on one visit? Why, her brother Uncle Sam, he whom Gideon despises. Uncle Sam insisted, and would not be denied; family's family, even when you loathe them.

'What lovely flowers!' he says, sticking his bulbous nose into the bouquet. 'Beth, I'll say again and again. You have style!'

'Actually, it was a friend who brought them,' says Mother.

'Ahah!' Sam smiles meaningfully at Gideon, who looks away and announces that he's not feeling well and would prefer to sleep.

Because it was Sam who brought Gideon's infidelity to the open. He met them in Paris, when Gideon was supposed to be away on a military function somewhere in the north. Instead, there he was, a reposeful *flâneur*, strolling arm in arm with Margaret Barlow along Avenue des Champs Elysées in the lilac hours of the day. And Uncle Sam, himself an immaculate roué, gambler and deceiver, meets them head on, raises his cane and doffs his Panama. And Gideon cuts him dead and walks on. What is Sam to do? Back in his hotel, he rings Mother. 'Guess who I ran into this afternoon…'

There were tears. Margaret's. Mother was magnanimous in an inverted kind of victory. Followed by reconciliation. Yes, in her way, Mother has style: she's a supreme reconciler. Her instinct for resignation is overriding and catholic.

With one turn of the crank, Charlie Bean brings his 1927 Cluley roaring to life. A cloud of smoke emits from the exhaust pipe. Triumphant, he poses beside the splendid machine, one hand resting on the bonnet, the other cockily on his hip: 'How's that!'

'Bravo!' I clap.

With his shock of unruly hair and silk scarf round his neck, there's something of the Boys' Own comic book hero about Charlie Bean, and he wears it well.

The Cluley is Bean's pride and joy. He bought it for £17 9s10d in a Hammersmith junk yard, worked on it with total dedication for three months, and there it was: not quite vintage but a beauty for sure; shiny nickel radiator, black mudguards over yellow-spoked wheels, and maroon coach work. Thirty eight mph on the straight with a helping tail wind on her maiden run. This is a year of miracles.

'Right, get in,' says Bean. I climb aboard. We are off to El Vino in Fleet Street, where Cousin Luke Bainbridge, having come down from Merton College, Oxford with the worst degree possible, is holding court in celebration of having, against all expectations, landed a job with the *Daily Express*.

Kind, generous Bean is taking me along, to cheer me up, because I'm losing the war with Gideon.

I had passed my O levels. Gideon nodded with approval. I edged over the A levels barrier. Gideon congratulated with a frown: it was time for me to go back home. Home? To Israel, he said, excusing my delinquency on account of the imperfect trans-Atlantic line. No, I said, no, damn it! Not yet. Then come to Washington. Not that either. And he relented in poor grace. Gideon is a brave loser, never a good one. Then came my grand coup, the prize I most coveted: a place at St. John's College, Cambridge to read History. And my father? 'Absolutely out of the question! However, well done. I didn't believe you could do it.'

That is why I feel totally devastated, and grateful to my pal Charlie Bean for his simple, cheerful sympathy.

Having read his Washington diary, I understand. Away from the seductive charm of England, Gideon's energies are refocussed on his career, on the things that really matter. Israel's politics reach out to him. There are memos to Ben Gurion, to the Chief of Staff, to friends and allies in high position. How telegraphic his analyses have become. Curious isn't it, that Washington, geographically farther away, is nevertheless closer to the heart and soul of Tel Aviv than London is, ever was, ever will be.

Gideon attends the Democratic Convention in Chicago and reports that he is convinced Adlai Stevenson will be the next President of the USA – 'Bad for Israel'. Wrong on both counts.

Washington DC inspires him:

October 5, 1955. Had lunch with Averell Harriman, politically the best informed American I've met to date. He reminds me of a Roman senator. There's an imperial quality about Washington. An ordered criss-cross of streets. Wide avenues. Wide open spaces. So much assertive vigour that the innate vulgarity of much of the architecture doesn't obtrude. This is modern Rome at the height of her power – hub of the civilised world. By comparison Europe is effete and decadent, as Athens was during Rome's Augustan age...'

Gideon fears I might degenerate into an English 'Athenian'. What an undeserved advantage would be given thereof to his enemies in Israel. The fact that Tali, attending Woodrow Wilson High School, is already a replica of an all-American girl, complete with bobby sox, fat legs and Bermuda shorts, counts for nothing. America instructs. England transforms. And I must be saved before it's too late.

Geese are flying over the Serpentine. The trees are heavy with summer foliage. A pale haze hangs over the water and spreads to veil the white Nash terraces round Regent Park. To think that it snowed only a week ago! Mad August. Unreal year. Crouched over the wheel, Bean pilots the car along the ring road of the park, dreaming of flying through clouds.

'Sod you, Abba,' I think, 'this is the last time I lose to you.'

We put on a tie before stepping into El Vino. Catching sight of us, Luke waves his arm extravagantly. His face is pale. A lock of brown hair slants lazily over his high forehead. He has a beaky nose and deep-set ruthless eyes. With him are two young men of his own age, and a plain, sharp-featured girl called Amanda.

'My cousin Charlie Bean,' Luke introduces, 'and his friend from the resurrected Jewish State. Sorry, didn't catch your name.'

'Philo.'

'Ah. Well, Charlie, how's your fabulous car? You didn't have a breakdown on the way, did you?'

'Not on your life. She goes like a bomb,' says Bean, thumb up.

'Don't say that, dear boy, the world is full of bombs going off all the time everywhere,' says Luke.

'I'm dying for a drink,' says Amanda in a demonstratively London voice, because she lives in a poky bed-sitter in Tuffnel Park, and considers it a virtue. Bean volunteers to get the drinks.

'...There I was, sitting in front of this stunningly beautiful editor who looks and sounds like Rupert Brooke. "We are damned lucky to have Geoff Cohen, Bainbridge," he tells me. "One of the best science editors around, a terrific fellow to work with. Have you read that marvellous piece he wrote on why the male of the species is invariably more beautiful than the female?" I say no. He looks astonished in an insufferably superior way, and says "Oh, you must." "Why," I ask, "is the male of the species invariably more beautiful?" You should have seen his face! I swear his jaw dropped full six inches, he looked so put out...' Luke's laughter is like a mule's bray – hee-haw-hee-haw.

'I take it you weren't offered a job?' asks John, who is sitting next to him.

'Actually, I was. Full credit to the man. Only by the time I heard from him I had already accepted the *Daily Express* offer. Features. More fun. Better pay. Anyway, I know bugger all about science.'

'I loath and detest Lord Beaverbrook and everything he stands for,' says Amanda, pulling a face.

'My dear, everybody does.'

'I can't see how you can work for such a rag and be so chuffed about it.'

'Greed, moral turpitude, and lust for thrills. Simple as that. Look, Nasty Nasser is going to give the Israelites their comeuppance. What is science doing that's so exciting? Cheers everybody, to fun!'

'I say, why is Ted looking so woebegone. Ted?'

'Ted's in a state of shock,' says Amanda, slipping a hand in between Ted's thighs.

'Really? Tell,' Luke commands.

'This morning Ted discovered his father was Jewish.'

Ted manages a wan smile, 'Great, okay. Only... can you imagine? All these years none of us knew. Isn't this amazing?'

'Amazingly amazing! Charlie, quick, a double whisky for Ted. This is an emergency!' cries Luke.

I cease to listen. I'm day-dreaming I'm on Mount Carmel. An afternoon heavy with heat. I hear the familiar trailing sing song of a street peddler – *Alte sachen, alte shiech, eisen, lumpen, alte sacheeeen...'*. Outside, Erna is hanging damp sheets on the laundry line. A blue number tattooed on her thick arm stands out against her red skin – the Auschwitz lottery number that never got called, so she lives.

'Don't tell me, brother this will be my last path... Clouds have covered the face of the sun and it is dark...' she sings, then suddenly breaks off. 'Hey, *Alte sachen man!* Wait!' She goes inside... The radio blares out music and news bulletins... our forces held out against a Syrian armoured attack in Deganiya...

Ori Falk's window is like an empty eye socket now that he's dead.

Erna returns with a wooden box full of junk. Memories, like people's belongings, pass from hand to hand, and are recycled to take on new meanings.

Should I feel ashamed for loving England?

The Heath is breathing after a long kite-flying afternoon. The colours in Margaret Barlow's paradisal garden are merging with the gathering dark. A bird is warbling a liquid song from among the foliage of an apple tree. I'll be extravagant, let's say a nightingale out for an early rehearsal. I know that I shall not have many more evenings such as this. I know that with time they will become precious, charged with qualities they never really quite possessed, a compound interest of half memories and half fantasies. Let's settle for a compromise midway between extremes.

I'm alone, reclining in the sofa in the living room whose window is half open onto the garden. Lionel and Margaret are out for the evening. So is Jessica, I think – urgently expanding her experience.

She wants to lose her virginity in an interesting way she once confided. I turn on the wireless and tune into the Home Service. Tension in the Middle East and the Suez Conference dominate the news. Since I shall soon go home, I ought to care. But I don't.

Jessica comes in wearing jeans and a loose white cotton blouse through which her bra shows.

'Hullo Philo.' She walks over to the wireless and turns it off. 'Aren't you sick to death of all this nonsense? I am. I can't stand another word about the boring Middle East. Eden's obsession with Nasser is sick. They both deserve each other, if you ask me.'

'Probably. Nevertheless, what's happening in Suez is of major importance...'

I know I'm being stuffy, Jessica has that effect on me.

'Really? To whom is it important?' she intones mockingly.

'To the world, of course.'

Jessica throws her head back. 'The "world" is politicians' excuse for just about everything. What two nasty, vain men think of each other is not important. Brecht has died. That's important. W.H. Auden is Professor of Poetry at Oxford, that too, is important.'

I'm in no mood for an argument. I keep quiet, hoping Jessica would lose interest and go away. Instead, she sits at the piano, plays a few chords, then her own variations on the theme of *Bah bah Black Sheep*.

'So, Philo, what are you going to do about your dreadful father? Will you defy him and go to Cambridge? I see. No. You're going to be a dutiful son. You're going back to Israel to be a hero in the army. And you'll be telling yourself that you've made such a noble sacrifice for the Zionist cause, right?'

'Piss off Jessica.'

'Oh dear me, I've touched a raw nerve.'

'All very well for you to talk, how on earth do you imagine I could afford Cambridge on my own?' I throw at her, not altogether fairly, because although rich, Jessica had won an Exhibition to Newnham College, where she's reading Classics. By way of a reply Jessica thumps out the opening bars of Chopin's *Funeral March*. I get up to leave.

'No, don't go. I'm sorry, truly. I didn't mean to hurt you. Too bad I can't help.'

'Yes, so there we are.'

'Of course, you could do something outrageously romantic, like boarding a ship as a deck hand and escaping to sail the seven seas.'

'I hate the sea. I get sea sick just thinking about it.'

'Oh well... nice idea anyway. Won't you at least break your boring abstinence and have a drink with me?'

'That I could manage.'

'What'll you have?'

'Oh, anything.'

'One anything coming up,' she says, and decants whisky into a cut glass tumbler.

'A chip of Greenland glacier?'

'Please.'

For herself Jessica concocts a cocktail full of twisting colours. 'Cheers! Bottoms up, this is just the prelude.'

'You won't get me drunk, you know,' I say as I down my whisky.

'No? Oh, I forgot, you're a hardened low lifer, aren't you? Why don't you introduce me to your sleazy friends?'

When she laughs her eyes sparkle. She has Margaret's eyes, only dark, and mischievously quick. Her breasts are large, and now more enticing than ever.

'Tell me,' I say, 'have you managed yet to lose your virginity in an interesting way?'

'Not in an interesting way,' she replies blandly.

'No point in my introducing you to my friends, then.'

'Don't be coarse,' she says, frowning.

She sits down at the piano again. Undecided, she trails a finger across the keys.

'Play an A minor variation on *Chopsticks*,' I suggest.

She grins dismissively. Suddenly she is looking at me seriously, intently. 'Shall I show you something exciting? Do you want an experience of a lifetime?' she asks.

I follow her with my eyes as she gets up and makes for the door. I have a vision of her returning dressed in a silk diaphanous dressing gown, throwing it open to reveal those round, big, thrusting breasts of hers, a soft, rolling belly, and sturdy thighs. I see her doing the dance of the seven veils for me. My blood races.

She comes back carrying the most beautiful cello I've ever seen, holding it by its marbled neck, like a professional. 'Do you know what this is?'

'A beautiful cello?'

'Oh yes. A Guarneri. One of the best. A heavenly-sounding Guarneri. Daddy bought it a year ago. I daren't even imagine how much it cost. He's going to give it on loan to a brilliant young Russian cellist who recently defected to the West. Don't you wish it were you? Go on, touch it, play it. And when you are lying in some Israeli army camp, wallowing in your *Jude the Obscure* self-pity, regretting opportunities you think you lost, remember that you've held and played one of the most beautiful, perfect instruments ever made by man.'

She comes nearer, holding out the cello and bow. 'Take it. Your first and last chance. It won't fall apart and neither will you.'

Returning to the piano, she gives me an A. I tune the Guarneri. Passing the bow over the strings, my fingers remember a cunning I thought I had lost, and I tremble inwardly.

'Shall we try to play something?' I hear her say.

'It's been such a long time, I daren't...'

'Don't say that. Have another drink and dare. Call for the devil if you think it will help.'

Leafing through a pile of sheet music, she pulls out something. 'How about this? Let's give it a go, shall we? You can still read music, can't you?'

The piece is Beethoven's *Sonata No 1 in F major Opus 5*. After a few faulting starts, miraculously the music flows. What I hear, however, is not our mistake-ridden lumbering performance but a perfection of the *Adagio sostenuto*. The mind's deceptions, Imogen, aren't always cruel. Afraid that the spell might break, I give up at the end of the first movement.

'Bravo! Well done!' Jessica cries, clapping her hands. 'Enough. I'm going to put the cello away now.'

I don't think I'm quite drunk. Let's say just high... Okay, very high. Although Jessica usually terrifies me, I'm not afraid of her now as she sits beside me on the sofa. Moreover, I get the notion that if I were to reach out and touch her breast, if I were to lean over and kiss her neck all the way down to where her bosom rises, she would breathe open-mouthed, eyes shut, like in a movie love scene.

As it happens, she beats me to it. Taking my hand, she places it on her breast. First outside, then against her skin, through the opening of her blouse. We wrestle each other on the sofa. Her tongue writhes in my mouth. Her blouse comes off, then her bra, her jeans. She looms above me naked, except for her panties, a hot voluptuous maja. I say to myself, if she's already lost her virginity uninterestingly, then I haven't much to live up to. Never mind the performance, pump away and be damned!

She produces a condom from the pocket of her jeans. 'Let me do it,' she says. Bending over me, she virtually swallows my penis before slipping the rubber over it. I pull her to me and she struggles. 'Lie still!'

Thump thump in out in out squelch... I'm sucked clean into her like macaroni.

'Don't come yet, for Christ's sake,' she gasps. I try to think of funerals in order to dampen my ardour. Too late.

All at once she freezes. Have I done it wrong? Astride me, she stares at the window, horror writ large on her face. She reaches for an item of clothing to cover herself.

'Jessica? What is it?

'Police! All over the garden! It's the fucking alarm! Philo, we've set off the burglar alarm! Can you believe it!'

We never made love again after that. Nor did our moment of passion bring us closer in any way. In October Israel, backed by France and Britain, invades Sinai, the Suez war was on and ultimately the only winner was Abdel Nasser. Standing among the crowd in Trafalgar Square, I listen to Nye Bevan denouncing the invasion, ridiculing Eden for being 'too stupid to be Prime Minister.'

There is Jessica with her friends, shaking her fist, shouting. So much anger in her face, such futile energy expended on hatred. Poor Jessica had discovered an appetite for political demos. Years later she was burning expensive 38 double D cup bras in Camden Town.

I ring Gideon. 'Make it short,' he tells me, 'I'm busy. What is it? You want to come here?'

'No, I'm flying back home tomorrow,' I say.

'Good. I'll see you there, then.'

Rome is overcast. A welcoming airport official apologises, but promises that El Al passengers on a stop-over to Tel Aviv will not be disappointed with the Eternal City. I stand in the Forum. A cloud breaks over Titus's Arch and the pigeons scatter. Rivulets run down the bearded faces of the captive Jewish warriors. Aliens they were in Rome, the heart of Europe, and a stranger I'll be back home from Europe. For a while at least.

Each one of us Jews is automatically vaccinated at birth against the Alien's Depression illness, and still, it seldom works.

18

The border cuts through Jerusalem like a dead river. To the west, the Jewish part; trees and parks, stone houses set in gardens, and also many ugly housing estates connected by untidy rubbish-littered streets. To the east, the unreachable city of dreams and prayers with her cupolas, belfries and minarets, all contained by the grey crenellated wall Suleiman the Magnificent built in the 15th century.

Jews in the western part look longingly to the east, to places they imagine, or read about, or have been to; to cemeteries where their dead are buried; to the brooding stretch of wall at which they once prayed and wept, which now lizards and doves possess. Arabs in the eastern part gaze to the west, remembering homes that were once theirs, which now house Jews. The Christians are the unthanked mediators who gingerly move between the city's two separated parts. But Jerusalem, the stone conveyer of disparate prayer, looks intractably to heaven.

Strangely, this dead river of a border keeps a peace of a sort, suspending animosities and aspirations.

From behind a barrier of sandbags on the high roof of Notre Dame Hospice, I sit and watch the goings on in the Old City and beyond. Littered with rubble and rusty coils of barbed wire, the border passes right by the building. Once a busy street was here, and will be once again. I have a powerful telescope mounted on a stubby tripod. Also, a clipboard with paper for noting down movements of Jordanian military vehicles. As I swing the telescope from one vista to the next, the Jordanian soldiers perched in a look-out post similar to mine on the corner of the Old City Wall a mere thirty meters away, do the same into our part of the city.

It is early morning. Two of my men are still asleep in a room below. A haze is lifting from the hills. Church bells and the knife-like voice of the muezzin stir the streets to life.

I like taking the first watch. The truth is, I shouldn't be here at all now. My army reserves duty, the first since my discharge, officially ended last week. I am here, victim of one of the Defence Forces' "administrative delays". Still, at last a civilian, about to become a student at the Hebrew university.

I work as copy editor in a government publishing agency which translates Soviet scientific journals into English for a restricted American market. My departmental boss, Cheryl Bloch, a biologist newly-arrived from Johannesburg, is rather put out by my extra week's absence from work. Until someone at the office puts her straight: in Israel the army takes precedence over everything, a fact of life.

Cheryl is a large, serious woman, totally married and totally religious. She reminds me of school custard pie — acceptably bland. My other colleagues make up an assortment of Russian émigrés, Americans, Britons, and one Australian. Most of them have scientific qualifications of one sort or another. The Russians translate the text into what they think is English. The rest of us try to make sense of what they have written and put it into intelligible English.

Yes, I'm content. The project I'm currently editing is a lengthy treatise on the manufacture of ice cream in Kaliningrad. I love ice cream. The pay is reasonable, the company congenial. Most importantly, the management is accommodating about fitting work with university study. I rent a quiet room in Cheryl and her husband Eric's flat in Talbiya. Of course, there are strict regulations: no visitors after ten at night, and no radio or music on the Sabbath which they observe with the utmost rigour. I don't mind. I don't plan to stay there for long anyway.

Actually, what has detained me in uniform a week after I should have checked in my equipment and gone home, was a border incident. Incidents are not frequent here, but neither are they rare. Divided, the city has a tacitly recognised integrity. Violate the border, however, and shooting breaks out all along the line, immediately. Such violations are perpetrated usually by people who are strangers to Jerusalem, or lunatics, of whom there is no shortage on either side of the border.

Like this Jewish boy from Brooklyn, a familiar figure with the police, who believed he was Jesus Christ. God knows what got in to him when one morning, right under our noses, he walked bare-footed, wearing a kefiya biblical style and a grey Sears & Roebuck suit with the trousers legs rolled up, through a breach in Notre Dame's wall into no man's land.

We started shouting at him. The Jordanians waved and cursed. Oblivious to all, he raised his arms in benediction. Another step and bang! Rubble flew in all directions. When the black smoke cleared, there was a crater in the ground and all that was left of the fellow was a blood-soaked patch in the dust, a smashed foot, and the day's copy of *The Jerusalem Post*.

Soon, sparked off from another position a mile further south, shooting flared up all along the border from Pagi in the north to Kibbutz Ramat Rahel in the south. It went on sporadically all day and into the night, until a cease-fire was negotiated the next morning via the UN observers. That's the way things happen here. Nowhere in the world is the idiocy of war so bizarrely manifest as in Jerusalem.

Do you know, for example, how the city came to be unified in June 1967? Oh yes, our paratroopers stormed the Old City without artillery support, to spare the holy sites from damage. And true, King Hussein of Jordan started it all when, ignoring Prime Minister Levi Eshkol's appeal to stay out of the war, he ordered his army to shell Jewish Jerusalem.

Want to know the real reason why the Jordanians started shelling? In a word, Motti.

He lived in a run down stone house in Abu Tor, and worked in the Israel Broadcasting Service as electronics technician. A fanatic radio ham, radio was the only passion in his life. Nobody much liked Motti. He was quarrelsome and unreliable. Most of all, he quarrelled with his neighbours who objected to the bleeps and squeals emanating from his radio room at all time of day and night.

Two things happened to Motti on June 1st 1967: his wife went off with a lover, and an angry neighbour climbed on his roof and hacked down an expensive aerial Motti had erected earlier in the year. Also, Motti hadn't been called up to the army when everybody else was. That further depressed him. So he conceived of a personal protest against everything. Over the next two days he taped and edited half an hour's selection of his most thunderous farts, strung up a series of high-powered loudspeakers on the roof and on the nearby trees, and at dawn on June 5th, turned on the tape at full volume on all loudspeakers.

The effect was cataclysmic. Neighbours rushed to shelters. The rumour spread that the Arabs had unleashed a new secret weapon of mass destruction. Jordanian troops in their look-out posts also panicked: 'The Jews are attacking!' they telephoned command headquarters. '*Aliehum*! Fire with everything you've got!' came back the order.

An investigative freelance journalist unearthed this episode five years later. By that time Jewish settlements were sprouting all over the occupied West Bank and the story was killed for "religious considerations", such as the unthinkable profanity that spiritual

Jerusalem was liberated through the agency of high decibel flatulence emission!

Motti himself ended up an impoverished wretch, cleaning tables in a beatnik holiday camp on the shore of the Red Sea. It was said that Shin Beth security agents deliberately turned him into a drug addict.

Tali and her husband Ben live in a small neat flat in Beit Hakerem – a good first-time-buyers investment – for which Gideon provided most of the money. Both are studying. Ben second year Medicine, and Tali Psychology and Sociology. They have a baby daughter called Orly Hilda (Hilda after Ben's deceased mother who is buried in Newark, New Jersey). I have dinner with them on average once a fortnight. Invariably, Tali cooks roast chicken stuffed with sage and onion, an American recipe. 'The recipe for a successful marriage,' Tali pronounces, 'is not to love too much, and not to have too high expectations of your spouse. Best, in fact, not to have too high expectations of anything. Affection and trust. Lots of it. And there you have it.'

Ben smiles and twitches his eyebrows. He is a laid-back type. Both seem so grown up and set in their ways. Or is it that unlike me, they know exactly what they want out of life? Tali thinks I should also marry, a no-nonsense kind of girl, preferably an 'Anglo-Saxon' *olah* with a new immigrant's right to a tax-free car, among other things, so that we can all be family together.

I say to her, 'First things first. I want a place of my own. I'm getting claustrophobic in Cheryl's flat.'

'Yeah, sure, why not in Beit Hakerem? I'll ask around,' she promises.

Coming back from lunch break at the Alaska Café one day, I find an envelope marked 'Urgent' on my desk. In it there is a messy draft translation of an article from *Zhournal neorganicheskoi chemii*. The Chief Editor thinks it should be appended to the Ice Cream book, and wants it edited 'in a hurry.' I struggle with it unsuccessfully before taking it over to Cheryl's office.

'Cheryl, take a look at this please, it doesn't make sense to me,' I say.

Cheryl flips through the pages. 'Absolute tosh. Where's the original?'

'Haven't got it.'

'Get it then. I want to see the formulae.'

'The Russian connection is indisposed today. No access to his desk. How about a bit of informed guesswork? I mean, this is ice cream, not chemical warfare. I bet these enzymes or whatever they are, could induce diarrhoea even in the toughest Vodka-cured leather-stomached *mujik.*'

'Probably, like enema. Instant release,' says Cheryl with a dead pan face.

'I get it. A KGB trick! Shouldn't we alert someone?'

My joking leaves her cold. 'Okay, leave it with me. By the way, I wanted to have a word.'

'Go ahead.'

She tells me they need my room, would it be terribly inconvenient to move out? In a week? I tell her not to worry.

* * * * *

Washington April 18, 1960

Philo, Greetings. [Gideon never opens a letter with 'Dear...' which he considers effete and irrelevant. A charming affectation]

I salute you. Both for the subjects you've chosen to study, and for your determination. I have underestimated you in the past and belatedly, I apologise. May you never fall prey to a father's curse of not seeing his own children for what they really are, and paying the price for the deficiency. I'm humbly ready to pay the price, whatever it may be.

You know I value the pure pursuit of knowledge for its own sake, without calculations, without an eye for gain. But we live in a tough world where errors are not easily forgiven. What will you do with a degree in History? Be a teacher? An academic? Take your chances and opportunities as they come?

Remember when we met soon after you finished officers' school? I said that if you wanted real freedom to develop your mind and soul, without worries, you could do a lot worse than stay in the army. Our army is the best, the most enlightened and understanding when it comes to such things. I said I would give you $1000 for every rank you rose above captain. You were dismissive, even rude. I understood why. But I was hurt all the same. It took me a while to realise that you were right and I was wrong. Enjoy your university days. Open yourself to new experiences. I've always believed that's what university is for. The excitement of new ideas in freedom is much more important than beavering away for a good degree.

I can see that you don't need my telling you that. Please promise

213

not to be too proud to ask for help with money, should you need it.

Your new room in Ein Kerem sounds ideal. Completely self-contained? A private garden surrounded by a wall, and a view of the village? How unusual, yet how like you to find such a place. See? Already I relish your life vicariously.

Tell me more about your landlord friend. How long did he serve in the French paratroopers? Was he sent to Jerusalem by Le Monde, *or is he a stringer? Strange, that with his experience he should want to become a biblical scholar. I can see that a few rounds of Thai kick boxing at the start of the day is excellent for the circulation and for the mind. I hope you've learnt enough by now to give as much as you take.*

My term of office here is ending. In June we shall be coming home. It's been good here. Useful too. But I am glad it's over. I've been away from home for too long. Roots are fragile things; away from their native soil for too long, they wither and nothing grows in their place.

I have an idea I want to put to work on my return, and I've outlined it to BG. We shall see, we shall see, we shall see. I'll tell you about it when we meet. Happy birthday.

Your father.

Dawn in the walled garden. Bulbuls warble as Jean-Pierre Lamont and I square up to each other for the first round of our ritual routine, wearing nothing but a kind of loin cloth. Jean-Pierre is over six foot tall, lean and muscled like a long-distance runner. His movements are fluid and unerring. He reminds me of a snake poised to strike. Those dark eyes, staring fixedly from his bony monkish face, mesmerise me. I lunge at him with my fist. He moves easily out of reach. Recovering my balance, I try a kick as he had taught me. Again I'm wide of the mark, and over-balancing with my guard wide open, I see – too late – his leg scything through the air. The size ten and a half foot connects with my ribs. I go down, winded, comets whizzing before my eyes. Jean-Pierre is standing over me. 'You err nert concentrating. Zees eez a self-inflicted blow,' he admonishes, more in anxiety than disapproval. I can't say a word, let alone get up. Jean-Pierre kneels beside me, passing his hand over my ribs. I wince. He picks me up and carries me inside.

An hour later we are chugging up the hill in his Deux Cheveaux to Hadassa Hospital, where a cracked rib is diagnosed. They bandage up my chest like a mummy so I can hardly breathe. I arrive at the university just as the bell rings for one of the most popular lectures on campus: Professor J. Talmon's course on *19th Century European Nationalism.*

Lauterman Hall is full to capacity. Acknowledged as the main event of the week, Talmon's lectures are heavily attended by all who can find the time, not only by History students, either. An historian of international standing and author of many books, J. Talmon is an electrifying speaker, at once formidable and entertaining. He is also notorious for throwing students out for the slightest disturbance, real or imaginary; it's his way of keeping tension in class.

He is ready to begin as I make my way to a vacant seat in one of the back rows. Professor Talmon fixes me with a glare which says, 'all right, whoever you are. I've taken note of you!'

A cough gathers deep in my chest. In vain I try to suppress it, not least because coughing is a torture in my condition. The attempt only makes things worse, and just as Talmon launches into an anecdote about Cavour, I succumb to a protracted cackle of a cough. Coming where it does, it strikes a farcical note. A few students giggle. I look up to see Talmon's finger pointing at me. 'You there, kindly leave the hall at once!' he thunders. As faces turn to look, I recognise one of them in the row just below mine.

'Philo! My goodness, fancy meeting you in such funny circumstances!' Mimi, my childhood sweetheart, greets me outside at the end of the lecture, 'Where have you been all this time? I heard you had left the country...'

My first impression of Mimi is that she is sexy in a Parisian fashion model style. She has a willowy figure. When she stands talking to you, she arches slightly backwards, which makes her appear taller. She is wearing a voluminous black blouse and slacks with a broad leather belt. Her hair, now dark and glossy, pours out of a black silk bandeau in a thick braid over her right breast. Round her neck there is a loop of amber beads with a pendant of some Canaanite motif (Mimi is a second year Archaeology and Arts student). Gone is the precocious beady look of her childhood. Her teasing eyes which charmingly tilt upwards at the far corners, now gaze at me with coquettish good humour.

'I can't believe it! Isn't this incredible? What a strange boy you were, and look at you now...' Hugging a pile of books to her bosom, she takes a small step backwards as if to get a better look at me. Her voice has a slight burr. She's altogether the kind of girl whose attraction grows on you. You want to flirt with her, to make her laugh, she has such a lovely laughter.

'You won't believe this, Philo, but every now and then, I think of you.'

'You're right. I don't believe it.'

'Honestly, I swear!'

She laughs, and I can't believe that the skinny, snooty clever little girl who lived up the road from me has grown into this woman with an appealing neck and a voice that makes you feel you've had one drink too many.

'I bet you didn't even remember me. No? No, I don't think that's true. Tell me what you've been doing. I want to know everything. Absolutely everything, from beginning to end.'

'It'll take more time than you have,' I boast.

'But I have lots of time. All the time in the world.'

'Well, for a start, I've cracked a rib this morning Thai boxing. That's why I coughed in such a ridiculous way that Talmon threw me out.'

'Oh my god, Philo, are you in a dreadful pain?'

'Not unbearably.'

She brings her hand to her mouth and begins to laugh, 'Oh Philo, whenever we meet you seem to be hurt by one thing or another. What on earth is Thai boxing?'

Mimi shares a flat with a fellow student in an old Arab house in Abu Tor, overlooking the Valley of Hinnom with Mount Zion on the other side. She's in the east while I'm in the west, and the whole of Jewish Jerusalem lies between us. It is some distance, yet I visit her at least twice a week. We have a lot to talk about, a lot of ground to cover.

Her friends discuss J.S Bach, and medieval art such as the stone-carved Kings of Israel at Chartres, and walks in the wilderness of Judaea, or Galilee. They argue about "values", and how hypocritical politicians of all parties are. When she's with them I see how intensely Israeli Mimi is, and I'm drawn to their robust, unequivocal enthusiasm, to the simple directness of their curiosity, to a kind of innocence which excuses pretentiousness.

Years later, after the "values" had been swept aside by a tougher reality of power, when people like Mimi's friends who had spent the long evenings of their salad days exploring ways of being noble and spiritual and ascetic, woke up from a fat complacency to the dusty taste of disillusionment, they would look back with nostalgia on what they believed was 'Beautiful Israel', lost for good, like innocence.

In those precious evenings of glowing dusks Mimi prepares supper of salads and cheeses, followed by black aromatic coffee for which she grinds the beans with a quaint brass coffee mill. We listen to a record of Dylan Thomas's *Under Milk Wood* in the BBC production, borrowed from the British Council library at Terra Sancta. Then there's Gérard Souzay singing Bach's *Cantata No 82 Ich habe genug*. Intoxicated by the heady cocktail (we have a light head for cultural stimuli) Mimi inappropriately reads a passage from Charles Baudelaire's *Les Fleurs du mal* which none of us understands, then, more appropriately, a poem by Amichai who is 'incidentally, a friend'. The atmosphere thus created moves a former paratrooper who had sneaked across the border to the ancient Nabatean rock city of Petra and lived to tell about it, to reflect lugubriously on the haunting beauty and dangers of the desert.

Lightness and substance; whimsy and gravity; commitment and illusion. A kind of disjointed fiction superimposed on a disjointed reality. That's how I see Mimi's world in retrospect.

'Beautiful Israel'?

The way Mimi and I became lovers was, however, circumstantial. A freak storm prevented me from returning home one night. Half asleep with wine, we embraced to the singing of Sarah Vaughan, ended up in Mimi's bed, and woke up in the morning looking at each other as though we were Tristan and Isolde.

'Your father,' says Mimi, 'is the most attractive, sexiest man I've ever met. Should I tell him?'

'No need. He knows,' I say.

Here from Washington on a few days' visit, Gideon looks far from his most attractive. He has put on weight. It shows mostly in his face – a double chin which he tries in vain to hide by holding his head high. His glamorous Hollywood scars now look like creases.

The declared reason for the sudden visit is the death of his father. Eighty years old, senile and neglected, Grandfather escaped from his old age home and was found dead in the orange grove he once owned on the outskirts of Petach Tiqva. The funeral takes place in the municipal cemetery. His small grave is squeezed in between two other small graves. The only mourner apart from Gideon and myself is Grandfather's room-mate, a weepy old man wearing an oversize *yarmulke*.

Covered in a shroud, Grandfather's corpse stands at the gape of the grave on a stretcher. As small as a child's, how he has shrunk in his last days. Gideon intones the Kaddish prayer. After the interring, he washes his hands and casts away the paper yarmulke he took at the mortuary. We walk briskly out of the cemetery to the car park. The sun is beating down like a battle axe.

'Want to have lunch with me in Tel Aviv?' he suddenly asks. I nod. He puts his arm round my shoulders. 'I loathe funerals, and Jewish funerals are the worst. When mine comes, make the least bit of fuss. Have a celebratory dinner and remember all the fun we had together.'

In truth, Gideon never cared for his father, or his mother, for that matter. Having left home as a youth, his contact with them had always been tenuous. He sent them money, paid for his mother's funeral, then for his father's old age home. As far as I know he didn't visit him more than once a year, before Rosh Hashana, even when he was in the country.

The underlying reason for his being here is linked to the next stage of his career. Gideon is leaving the army. He has turned down several offers of directorships of diverse business enterprises. He's only interested in realising a project he has conceived which, he believes, would be of determining influence for the country's future. For his own future too. An entrance into politics could well follow a successful completion of his scheme.

Although everybody who is anybody is currently preoccupied with the latest national coup, the abduction from Argentina of Adolf Eichman (Gideon considers this an irrelevant distraction), parental funerals confer privilege, so that even Ben Gurion finds a moment to see him. I have never been able to decide which of the two Jews hold in greater reverence, life, or death.

We sit in a Jaffa fish restaurant, the haunt of politicians and celebrities.

'How about oven-baked sea bass?' Gideon suggests, as he begins to unravels his plan. 'Think of a major problem facing us.'

'Security?'

'Everything is security. Something else.'

'Tell me.'

'Inequality. Cultural, therefore social, therefore economic. Ultimately it has to affect the holiest of our holy cows, national security.'

'Abba, you're not going to preach Communism...'

Gideon laughs. 'What I have in mind would make Communism look like a picnic for liberals.'

'Go on, I'm all ears,'

'In three words, compulsory uniform education. The immigration from North Africa is, in the long term, a blessing. For the time being, however, these people are confused, disorientated, uneducated and unskilled in anything useful for a modern industrial society like Israel. Unless something radical is done soon, the division between us and them – the so-called "Second Israel" – will deepen and become permanent. We cannot afford a nation divided across a cultural-economic rift. It's immoral, not to say dangerous. It's against all that Zionism stands for.

'But look at what's happening already. The new immigrants are dumped in places no Ashkenazi Israeli would consent to live in. Instead of being assimilated they are being segregated in shanty towns, in far flung rural settlements where they are ill-equipped to cope. They are employed in useless, ill-paid, demeaning work – "black" work for our "Blacks". If, say, we were flooded with immigration from Europe, the USA, or Russia, can you imagine these immigrants would be treated in the same way as the North Africans? Of course not. They wouldn't stand for it for a start.

'And do you think the "Blacks" are so stupid that they don't understand and feel resentful? The resentment will grow, have no doubt, and it will be passed on from one generation to the next. A time bomb...'

People at the neighbouring tables are showing interest, not so surreptitiously. Gideon goes on regardless: 'There is a better way.'

'Go on.'

'Whiten them...'

The idea, he explains, is to establish a nation-wide network of co-educational boarding schools, modelled on English public schools, staffed by a corps of dedicated, highly-trained teachers. All children from the ages of seven to sixteen, Ashkenazi and Sepharadi, will have to attend by law. Enrolment will be centrally carried out with a view of achieving a balanced mix.

'There will be many doubters, I know. People will say it's too

219

expensive, too this and too that. But is there a better investment for the future? Is there a more effective way of creating an equal society from such disparate people? Think about it, we are a small country surrounded by enemies and lacking in natural resources. Our future can only be ensured by a cohesive society which is free, equal, and creative, imbued with values of excellence,' Gideon concludes with a mischievous twinkle in his eye.

I put my knife and fork down and clap.

'Well?' He asks.

'Consider two flaws for a start. One, the enforcement of such a scheme might be considered undemocratic and therefore politically unacceptable. Two, how would your "whitened blacks" come to terms with unwhitened parents and background once they have graduated from your élitist concentration camps? Besides, isn't the army suppose to do a good deal of the levelling?'

'The advantages surely outweigh the flaws...' Gideon tends to fall in love with ideas, and when he does, he refuses to see their imperfections. '...Some painful sacrifices will have to be made, I'm aware of that. Ways will be found to lessen the pain.

'Of course, it'll take a good deal of time and research to work out the details. One starts with the vision...'

'As visions go, it boggles my mind. Wouldn't it take a Moses and a half to turn it to reality?'

'The only man who is big enough to set it in motion,' says Gideon ambiguously, 'is BG. I'll have to convince him. Anyway, I've thought of a working name for the scheme: Operation Lighten Our Darkness.'

'Not to be thus presented to Ben Gurion, I trust.'

Gideon laughs. 'Oh no, this is just for you and me, a private coded reference.'

I raise my glass, 'Lighten Our Darkness!'

'In our days, Amen!'

'Amen Selah!'

'By the way, I like Mimi. Is it serious?'

'In an unserious sort of way, yes.'

'Seems a fine girl. What does she see in you?'

'Continuity, I think.'

Gideon gives a slow smile, 'Ah well, as good a thing as any, isn't it?'

I could never be really certain whether Gideon was entirely serious about his Operation Lighten Our Darkness. He never mentioned the subject again. In *Ha'aretz* of Monday July 11, tucked beneath the lead story on the chaos in the Congo, there is a little note about his impending return home. Quoting an 'undisclosed government source', the reporter speculates on Gideon's new job: a newly-created post within the Treasury, to deal with economic aspects of 'provincial rural settlements', a term used for the agricultural settlements built for immigrants mainly from North Africa, to which Gideon has objected. The story also mentioned that 'Colonel Jerusalem, a London School of Economics trained economist, has a special interest in immigrant settlements, and would be accountable directly to the Minister of Finance, Levi Eshkol.'

Gideon telegraphed not to meet him and Mother at the airport, they would go direct to their rented flat in Tel Aviv. The following Saturday we have a family reunion. Tali, Ben, baby Orly Hilda, and I make the journey there in their tiny Fiat 500.

My parents' new flat is in the fashionable part of Hayarkon Street, where many of the European embassies are situated. Small, neatly but impersonally furnished, its balcony affords a glimpse of the sea between the rising buildings of the Sheraton Hotel on one side, and the new Hilton on the other.

Mother is happy to be in Tel Aviv among friends, with so much to do and see. Although Gideon appears cheerful, I sense restlessness in him. I suddenly realise how both he and Mother have changed in relation to each other, and I can see that Tali too is aware of this.

Gideon no longer listens to Mother. His responses to her are reflexive, like a twitch. He comes alive only when talking or listening to either Tali or me, or even to Ben who has always bored him. I have a vision of long empty silences when Gideon and Mother are alone in this impersonal flat. Perhaps Mother dreads it; maybe even her resilience will not stand the loneliness of living together, no longer sharing anything. I tell myself too readily that there's nothing I can do about it. I return to Jerusalem at the end of the day alone and depressed.

The job at the Treasury Gideon is expecting does not materialise immediately. All that hot summer he languishes on paid but undefined leave, waiting for a telephone call to tell him of his new appointment. Mother makes frequent escapes, to Jerusalem, to Haifa, anywhere she's invited.

As a senior army officer, Gideon is entitled to a house at a greatly reduced price, in Zahala, a leafy sought-after suburb of Tel Aviv favoured by the defence community. His allotted house neighbours with Moshe Dayan's. Gideon declines the offer. Mother first gets to know about it from the gossip column in one of the evening newspapers. Typically, she makes no fuss even though she very much wanted the place. In a silent demonstration of grievance, she decamps for three days to Tali's home where Gideon phones and, speaking to an enraged Tali, announces that he has bought a plot of land north of Nethaniya, on a worthless stretch of sand dune where he intends to build a home. Soon, aided by three local labourers, he is busy building it – to his own plan. Friends who come to talk to him find him dressed in khaki working clothes and wearing a wide-brimmed straw hat, sitting trowel in hand astride a precariously rising wall.

'Here,' he explains, 'will be the main bedroom. Here, another, there, the study, and the bathroom...'

They have tea on what will be the lawn, and Gideon enchants them by enthusing philosophically that building the house is the most satisfying work he has ever engaged in.

The house that Gideon built is a sprawling bungalow of eccentric design, set in two acres of sandy soil where rows of fruit trees have been planted and an oval stretch of grass thickens steadily to the constant hum of sprinklers. A minor miracle in land reclamation; allotment Zionism.

Mother is grudgingly impressed, but says: 'How can you expect to be remembered if you stick yourself in the middle of nowhere?'

The first thing she did after he died was sell the place and move back to Tel Aviv.

Nevertheless, Gideon is remembered, even before the house is finished, and the long-awaited appointment is duly confirmed in the New Year. After the Holy Days he joins the Treasury as the Minister of Finance' Special Adviser for Development of Provincial Rural Settlements. A small pied-a-terre in Jerusalem comes with the job. Declining the official car, Gideon buys an old Jeep, for he plans to visit regularly even the most inaccessible places connected with his work, and, while at it, create the appropriate image.

I should have seen more of him during that period. I know he needed me. My failure to respond was not deliberate. I was enjoying life, university, discovery, and not least, the pleasure of Mimi and her circle of friends. How could I not relish all those nights we spent talking about ideas until dawn, smoking Gauloise cigarettes, listening to Ella Fitzgerald and Stan Getz, making love, and in between cramming for exams for which we were always poorly prepared?

Late one night in early summer, I return from Abu Tor to find Gideon's jeep parked outside the house. Lanterns glow in the Garden where Gideon, Jean-Pierre and his wife Margot, are half way through a third bottle of wine. They are high, Gideon more so than his hosts.

'Can you put your old man up for the night?' he asks.

I have only one bed, but the settee is large enough to sleep on.

'That'll do just fine for me,' says Gideon, refusing the offer of my bed. 'What a beautiful place! And so right for you. Lucky man. I once stayed at the convent up the road.'

'I know. And at the monastery on Mount Tabor, and at the one on Beatitudes. You always retreat to foreign religions, don't you?'

Gideon laughs. 'The trick is to use the right one for the right occasion.'

He sinks into the settee, spreading his arm on the back rest. 'Nice couple, Jean-Pierre and his wife. We should promote inter-marriage with gentiles like them, to improve the race.'

'Didn't Ben Gurion say that?'

'So he did. Jews in concentration are too much. Got any more wine?'

'No, but I could get a bottle from Jean-Pierre.'

'Don't bother.'

'Shall I make you something to eat, then?'

Gideon shakes his head.

A dog barks forlornly somewhere in the village. Gideon breaks the silence. 'I don't suppose you can remember, but years ago, you could hear the jackals howling on a night like this. We've killed them all. That's progress for you.'

I look at him as he gazes through the window into the mass of darkness in the garden.

'What's behind this escape, Abba?' I say at last.

He turns his head. 'Escape? No, I suddenly felt like seeing you. The flat in Rehavia is too oppressive. Much nicer here. Do you mind?'

'Heavens no!'

'Good. Why don't you put on a record, if it's not too late.'

It's past midnight but the walls are thick, and the kitchen separates my room from Jean-Pierre and Margot's bedroom. I know Gideon has something on his mind. I know music will help release it.

'That's okay, what do you want to hear?' I say.

'You choose. Cello. I always feel a little guilty when I hear cello music.'

'Do you want to feel guilty?'

'Just a little,' he grins. 'Sometimes guilt tastes like a pleasant after dinner cognac.'

I play Elgar's *Cello Concerto*, and turn the volume down. After the first movement, Gideon stops listening. Presently he says rather sententiously: 'The purpose of life: To look for a purpose face-to-face with death.'

'What?'

'From a poem by Gunnar Ekelöf, a Swede.'

'What does it mean?'

He shrugs his shoulders. 'I'm not really sure. I read it sometime ago and it stuck in my mind. The thing about reading poetry is that you can enjoy it without actually understanding. It leaves you with a mood... You know, Philo, I think I'm running out of options.'

'Why? Has anything happened?'

'Only that whenever I try to do something I think is original and meaningful, which I know is good, unimaginative politicians and intriguers moves in to block me.' He falls silent. 'Take the development towns and settlements. A lot could be done to correct past mistakes. I'm employed to do just that. I made plans, I drew up budgets for them, and the Minister said "Gideon, that's wonderful. Just what's needed." And I wait, and nothing happens. Then I realise what a fool I am. The government wants to keep things the way they are.

'"Don't make waves, Gideon," they tell me obliquely, "be a good fellow, drive around in your jeep, write reports, file in monthly your expense accounts – yes, don't be mean to yourself – and enjoy the perks. This way everybody will be happy." Everybody, except the poor bloody 'blacks'. And then I realise why. You know why?'

'Why?'

'Because at heart, the Party wants the Moroccan immigrants to remain ignorant, to remain forever dependent on the Party for employment, housing, for everything in fact, and believe it especially before elections. An exploitation of ignorance and abuse of democracy, that's what it amounts to. It's heart-breaking. It's wicked, not to mention stupid. I don't want any part of it.'

'Are you going to chuck it in?'

Gideon sighs deeply. 'It's being done for me.'

I see it all of a sudden: the visit, his devil-may-care mood. Before

I can say anything, he comes in first: 'You think I've been fired? Oh no, that's not the way it's done. Nobody gets fired in this government, and nobody seriously resigns. You get moved. Upwards, sideways, sometimes down.'

I dread his humiliation. I can't hide my relief, which makes Gideon look at me, eyes smiling, charged with irony.

'Which way are you being moved?' I ask.

In reply, he points his finger upwards. 'Literally. Eight hundred meters or so. I've been offered the post of Ambassador to Nepal.'

I check myself from saying 'why, that's wonderful' and ask instead, 'Are you pleased?'

Gideon shrugs his shoulders. 'Your mother is. She thinks it's a good move. At least not as bad as it might have been.' He pauses. 'I know it's banishment. I've accepted all the same. Banishment can be good, if it makes you look at things with a new perspective. Besides, I'm getting tired of fighting... I know it wasn't Golda's idea. The mere thought of having me in her Ministry for Foreign Affairs, even on secondment, is enough to give her stomach ulcers.'

'When will you be going, then?'

'In spring. Give us time enough to tidy things up, and let the house.'

I get up to turn the record over. We listen in silence to the *Enigma Variations*. After the first movement Gideon says: 'There's another thing. You might as well hear it from me. A week ago in the Knesset, in response to a barb from Menachem Begin, Ben Gurion retorted that he didn't need lessons in democracy from the leader of the right wing Herut. He then went on to tell the House that a "close associate" whom he would rather not name, had once proposed that the army take a more active part in running the country, and that the government should set up a compulsory education system based on military discipline. He, Ben Gurion, rejected both proposals "with revulsion", as smacking of totalitarianism.

'I wrote to BG asking him if he considered that scoring a trivial political point in a trivial parliamentary exchange justified betraying loyal friends. I told him that if my name ever came up in connection with these slanderous distortions, I would not hesitate to go public to set the record straight.

'His secretary rang me two days later to say the Old Man has taken note of my letter, but why was I getting so excited over nothing? Then came the offer of Nepal. Probably an attempt to shut me up. That evening I got a call from a young political columnist with *Ha'aretz* whom I helped when he was a student in George Town University. "Gideon," he said blithely, "sit down and relax before I go on..."

'A high-ranking personality in Labour has apparently leaked the story to *Ha'aretz* citing me as the said "close associate". "Gideon," he told me, "you've made some nasty enemies. But don't worry, you also have some good friends. I'm going to sit on this story. But if it breaks out with other newspapers then we'll have to run it too. Sorry. Just wanted to let you know."

'I know it's not his being such a good friend which makes him sit on the story, but someone with a heavier arse sitting on him. Anyway, there it is.'

I envisage a scandal, Gideon's name in headlines, linked with ugly adjectives, and he fighting back, laconically, disdainfully, inadequately.

'Well, that sums up my situation,' I hear him say, 'Tell me, how are things with you? What are you doing tomorrow? Goodness, today, I should say.'

We are going to the Abu Gosh Festival. Mimi is one of the organisers. I know it will be a most enjoyable day. I want to take Gideon along, Mimi is sure to get an extra ticket even at the last moment. I begin to tell him when I hear the steady rhythm of his breathing, he's fast asleep.

On its way from Shiloh to Jerusalem the Ark of the Lord rested here, in Kiryat Ye'arim. Not a Jewish shrine marks the site but a church, built in 1926 by the Sisters of St. Joseph of the Apparition. In this spacious Italianate basilica, under the patronage of the gentle nuns, music-loving Jews, mostly from Jerusalem, come once a year on a Saturday in the summer to listen to baroque and sacred music.

Picture an olive-covered hill overlooking the village of Abu Gosh, in the midst of which stands the Crusader church of St. Anne, built in turn on the site of a camp of the 10th Roman Legion. Myth and legend surround the village: was this biblical Emmaus? Perhaps also Anatoth, birthplace of the prophet Jeremiah? A cooling sea-breeze from the west fans the hill. The leaves of the olive trees turn and whisper. Across the bowed backs of two ridges to the east you can see the extremities of Jerusalem, with the derelict Arab village, Lifta, edging up the slope.

The Festival is not advertised. It receives no official grants. Audience and players come here for the pure love of making and listening to good music. My Mimi is one of its founding stalwarts. Yes, on such a day, as we pile into Pierre's battered Deux Cheveaux with a picnic basket full of food and wine, I am proud to feel she is mine. Radiant Mimi. The event is the climax of a year's hard work and she is at the heart of the Festival's organisation. She contacts musicians from all over the world, writes letters to wealthy individuals asking for contributions, sees that the programmes are printed and mailed to patrons, and liaises with the nuns at the convent. All this she does in her spare time, in consultation with the musical director, an elderly controversial conductor with whom she has been accused of sleeping. Mimi herself plays the recorder passably well. Sometimes she joins the ensemble. And sometimes she sings in the choir.

But not today, although it is decidedly her day, for the main work on the programme is Pergolesi's *Stabat Mater*. Two years Mimi had battled to stage this work. Only after she secured the acceptance of the two soloists, a soprano and an alto from Holland, did her dream become reality.

At the interval we emerge into the bright daylight from the cool, scented darkness of the church with Pergolesi's music in our souls. The sun stands at the mid-point of its course. People are spreading picnic blankets under the trees. We too find a shade-giving olive tree under which to settle down. Jean-Pierre uncorks a bottle of red wine. He slices the bread into thick slices, holding the loaf in the crook of his arm and drawing the knife across it towards him, as French peasants do. Margot's Coq au Vin is delicious.

Ari Gillon, the Festival's musical director and conductor, appears from among the trees shading his eyes against the sun.

'Ari!' Mimi cries, raising her arm.

Tall, with a shock of silvery hair, he turns, grins, then comes towards us in a bouncy gait.

'My dearest Mimi, what can I say except thank you, thank you, and again thank you?' He bends over her and kisses her lightly on the mouth. 'Forgive me,' he says archly, 'this is a great day for Mimi and me.'

On a patch of grass not far away, some members of the ensemble, together with singers from the audience, are about to sing madrigals. They are presided over by a small dark young man with bird-like features and darting movements. His face lights up as he catches sight of Mimi.

'Mimi, angel,' he calls out, 'a place of honour is reserved for you among the heavenly host.'

'Thanks, Michael. Not too soon, I hope,' Mimi laughs.

'At the end of time, not a moment sooner,' Michael cries, 'come and join us, we're going to do your favourite pavan.'

'Another time,' says Mimi, and blows him a kiss.

I cannot tell on this afternoon that six years from now there will be war. I have no way of imagining how relief and exultation will give way to arrogance and we will slowly become ugly in the carapace of contempt for the vanquished.

As I look at Mimi reclining against the trunk of the olive tree, eyes shut and smiling, slowly sinking into torpor from the wine and the food, I want to tell her that I love her. Because during this carefree interlude England fades from my mind, as does Gideon and his troubles, and I'm filled with Mimi.

She reaches for my hand. 'Don't you wish, Philo, that this moment could go on and on and on?' She says.

'With all my heart,' I reply.

And Margot, in her charmingly imperfect Hebrew, echoes a fleeting thought in my head: 'Philo, per'aps you should marry Mimi, non?'

Without opening her eyes Mimi laughs heartily: 'Never! That would be almost incestuous, not to say unromantic. We've known each other since we were that high.'

Although Mimi has a retentive memory, she is not an ambitious student. The idea of learning rather than the learning process itself is what appeals to her. Yet getting poorer results than she expected in the finals upsets her.

'What does it matter, since you don't want to do a post-graduate degree?' I try to console her.

Mimi is inconsolable. It's a matter of pride. Moreover, she blames me for her poor performance.

'When you study for yours, I'll keep away from you so that you can study in peace,' she throws at me.

'You want me to do that? Go away?'

'No,' she says, 'I want you to be good, and be patient with me.'

We are into a more rigorous regime because Mimi decides to re-take her Archaeology finals.

It is Saturday. I'm at her place. Partridges are chattering on the slope of Mount Zion. It had rained heavily the day before but now the sky is blue and full of broken cloud, an unusually mild day for late November. I'm in the kitchen preparing lunch. Mimi is in her room. I had seen her only once the whole day, when I brought her coffee. There she was, sprawled on the bed, surrounded with books, and a jazz record playing. 'Thank you', she said, without looking up.

'How can you concentrate with all this noise?' I asked.

'That's my way of studying. I don't tell you how to do your thing,' she snapped.

I walked out.

Now, as I come into her room to invite her to lunch, the radio is on. Sitting up, Mimi looks dazed.

'Have you heard the news today?' she asks.

'No.'

'It's too awful, us sitting here like two cocooned lumps without even knowing what's happening in the world,' she says irritably.

'Well, what has happened? World War Three broke out, or something?'

She looks at me, her eyes full of tears. 'The most terrible thing. They just said on the news that President Kennedy was shot dead in Dallas yesterday.'

If I am shocked, it is more at her reaction than at the news itself. I don't consider the assassination of an American president a world disaster on par with, say, a massacre of innocent civilians, or an earthquake that wipes out entire communities. But I've never seen Mimi look so shattered – she, who is bored by politics and disregards Americans!

She covers her face with her hands and weeps silently.

'End of Camelot... End of so much hope... what's the point of doing anything?' she says through her tears.

'Mimi, darling, what's the matter? You've been overdoing things. Why not break off for the rest of the day? We'll go to the cinema in the evening.'

I put my arms around her and hold her tight.

'Oh Philo, perhaps all I really want is to have children, and a garden, and make home-made jam and pickles, and cherish my friends...'

Is it weakness? A sudden surge of irrational protectiveness that make me see Mimi's homely whims as the very essence of life? Is it fate? I hold her tight. The smell of the chicken risotto carbonating on the gas ring wafts into the room.

'Mimi,' I say, unable to believe what I'm hearing, 'let's get married.'

* * * * *

Her parents' home on Mount Carmel looks much as I remembered it, only larger. Ernst Landau, now a High Court Judge and working a lot from home, has built an office abutting with the main house. It is he who greets us at the front entrance. A self-effacing man, and a listener by instinct, he seems to have grown more shy with the years.

The lawn is as meticulously manicured as ever. Splashes of bougainvillaea cascade over a new, taller perimeter wall. Theo, long since dead, has been succeeded by a Rhodesian ridgeback called Max, and Suzy, an overweight spaniel bitch. In Mimi's room, the crowned rocking swan, none the worse for wear, has kept an ageless imperious frown.

'Why, Philo, I'd never have recognised you. Imagine our surprise when Mimi told us the good news. Isn't it a funny world? You must tell us about what you've been doing, later. Isn't it a funny world, Ernst?'

Like the swan, time has hardly touched Mrs Landau. A delicate fragrance of expensive soap still hangs about her as it did when she bent over me outside her house many years ago.

'So you actually grew up in England. How exciting! And your parents, where are they now?'

'In Nepal, Mrs Landau. My father is Ambassador there.'

'You must call us Martha and Ernst, Philo. Nepal? That really is so exotic, don't you think so Ernst? I hope your parents will come to the wedding, even though Nepal is so far away. Have you brothers and sisters? Forgive me, I don't remember.'

'A younger sister. Tali's her name. She's already married and has a small daughter. They live in Jerusalem.'

'But that's wonderful! Come children, dinner is ready. You must be starving.'

Since we are not yet married we are put in separate rooms. Mimi comes to say goodnight. She puts her arms round my neck.

'Why can't we sleep together?' I protest.

'Old fashioned propriety. It's only this time. Next visit we shall be Mr and Mrs. Isn't it strange?'

'Your mother seems to think so. Life is full of surprises. I should have told her.'

Mimi slaps me playfully. 'Time for clichés, is it?'

'Why not? Goes well with old fashion propriety. Shall I sneak into your bed in the middle of the night for the last chance of illicit love?'

Mimi moves her pelvis against me and kisses me open-mouthed. 'Don't you dare. Listen, let's make a vow.'

'I don't believe in vows, they break too easily.'

'A promise then, that although we are married we shall be lovers and friends, not husband and wife.'

'I thought you wanted children and home-made jam and that sort of stuff.'

'I do. But I also want independence, and the sweet tensions which exist between lovers.'

'Your contradictions are stupefying.'

'Try to reconcile them all the same.'

'I solemnly promise.'

'I'll dream of you tonight, lovely sexy dreams,' she says.

Perhaps Mimi was right. Perhaps we both feared the binding responsibility of marriage. Over the years I learnt to read portents in her apparently casual remarks. As the date of our wedding drew near so, it seemed, our apprehensions grew. She was meeting her friends without me. I had taken an additional part time job with the *Jerusalem Post*. Finishing my shift at around midnight, I would go with colleagues to Fink's bar for a drink.

When it came to home-hunting, Mimi had more commitment than I did, but also more time.

We are standing in an empty flat which is to be our home. Large mullioned windows open onto the compound of the Ethiopian cathedral. A pretty, quiet picturesque street. The price of the lease is a bargain. It's love at first sight for Mimi.

'Well?' she asks with a hint of challenge.

I shrug my shoulders. 'Seems okay to me.'

She glares 'You don't really care, do you? The truth is you don't want to leave your Ein Karem retreat at all,' she bursts out, and there is truth in her accusation.

Mother arrives from Kathmandu a week before the wedding, apologising for Gideon's absence. Martha and Ernst put on a brave face, duty is something they readily understand. They invite Mother to stay with them but she declines, saying she has promised to stay in Tel Aviv with her sister whom she hasn't seen for ages. Besides, there are things she has to do there in connection with the house.

On a bright spring morning our wedding is celebrated at the synagogue and adjoining garden, where Café Eldorado once stood. It is a grand affair – Mimi's parents have spared no expense to provide the best food and drinks. Wearing a white silk dress of classical cut, Mimi looks at once pure and provocative. Mother and Martha are standing together chatting, their eyes shining. Tali catches my eye, winks, giving me the thumb up. Out in the street, the police are directing fleets of cars to an allotted parking space. The line of arriving traffic is endless – government officials, two cabinet ministers including the Minister of Justice, and a formidable representation from the army top echelon in cars bristling with radio antennae. Gideon's relatives show up in strength. Staid, successful, and mostly dull, they carry collectively the stamp of the hard-working *Yishuv* bourgeoisie.

Jean-Pierre and Ernst are the only men present who are wearing ties. Ernst is standing at a far corner, surrounded by colleagues. Uneasy with so much social intercourse, he bravely forces himself to act the host. Martha, having left Mother's side, is circulating among the guests. Gracious, surreptitiously assessorial, she takes in without as much as a flicker of an eye who is here, and who is not.

'Well, Philo, congratulations. Your bride is very pretty.' Athaliah has thickened and greyed in the years since I last saw her. Not David. The contrast between them is a little cruel, for resplendent in uniform of General Commander of Southern Command, David Oren looks fit, aggressively youthful for his age.

'I have a right to kiss the bride,' he declares with feudal authority as Mimi joins us, 'after all, I am a sort of honorary father to Philo.'

Mimi laughs. Stretching her arms, she turns her neck to be kissed, and David, perhaps because he has had a drink or two, makes a great thing of it, peering down her front as he leans towards her.

Suddenly, there is Gideon making his way towards us, smartly dressed in a light grey suit. There is hardly time for introductions before the wedding canopy is virtually over us for the commencement of the ceremony. Nods and smiles pass between him, Martha, and Ernst. They have never met before. Her mouth pressed, Mother shakes her head, not in disbelief but as if to say, 'I knew it!'

Having taken his position, the rabbi begins to intone the prayer.

'Thought I'd come to see you off after all,' says Gideon under his breath.

People are looking at him but he avoids eye contact. Soon after I've cracked a glass underfoot to cries of 'Mazal tov!' Gideon takes his leave. He has a plane to catch from Rome back to Nepal in the morning, he explains.

'Is Gideon always so unpredictable?' Mimi later asks.

'Yes. Too predictably so,' I tell her.

She leans her head on my shoulder. 'I love him, I really do,' she says with a laugh.

We check into a honeymooners suite for a long weekend at an Ashkelon hotel. The manager proprietor makes a good deal of fuss over us – a bottle of the best champagne for the newly-weds, on the house! The chalet next to ours is occupied by a retired judge who is recuperating from open heart surgery. He tells Mimi that he knew Ernst Landau, a fine man, good lawyer. Would we do an old man the honour of having a glass of wine with him? We sit on the veranda listening to him reminisce while the Mediterranean turns violet.

As Mimi takes a bath, I think of Gideon, gradually understanding why he did what he did: a hopeless act of defiance, a calculated snub against those among the guests whom he believes have let him down. The sadness at the thought of his futile, reckless despair weighs on me.

Fragrant from her bath, my wife gets into bed and snuggles up to me.

'What is it, love?' she asks softly.

'Nothing, a little knackered, that's all.'

I ought to share with her and I can't. We lie against each other listening to the breathing of the sea.

We wake up to the sound of voices. An ambulance stands outside the old judge's chalet, he is taken out on a stretcher, his hands the colour of wax. Another heart attack. Perhaps all that remembering had been too much for him.

19

The announcement is casually made. Well, actually, not that casually, when I think about it. Imogen rings from work late in the afternoon. 'Darling, are you busy this evening? Because I have to talk to you.'

Have to?

This morning I have been made redundant ahead of schedule but with my consent and with full pay to the original date of my departure. There was a tiny reception. I was given a generous cheque as severance pay. Stephen Fink gave an over the top eulogy. I could tell from his face he could barely repress his joy to see the last of me. Afterwards I went to the Courtauld Gallery, then to the British Museum, had lunch and returned home feeling a little depleted, a little unwanted.

'Is anything the matter?' I ask.

'No,' she says reassuringly. 'I have to tell you something that, well, may concern you. When can I come?'

'As soon as you can.'

'In a couple of hours?'

'Great.'

'Can I take you out for dinner?'

'Depends what you have in mind to tell me.'

She laughs. 'Fair enough.'

From my high window I see her manoeuvre the car into a space on the opposite side of the street. I move away so she won't see me. She doesn't come up right away; when I return to the window, she's still sitting there in the car, immersed in thought. At last she gets out, crosses the street without a glance up. I buzz her through the front door downstairs and wait for her at my door. It is two flights of stairs to my flat. Imogen arrives a little out of breath. Whenever we meet I never know whether or not I should put my arms round her and kiss her, and I am less certain now, having watched her sit lengthily in her car.

She gives me a peck on the cheek.

'Well?' I say.

'May I have a glass of wine, Philo? White, please.'

We sit opposite each other, she with her back to the window. After a few sips she puts her glass on the coffee table.

'What I wanted to tell you,' she says, 'is that I've accepted the invitation to Harvard. This morning I faxed my acceptance.'

A pause. 'It wasn't easy. There were so many things to consider, including my mother. In the end I decided it was the right thing to do.'

I avoid looking at her when I say, 'Yes, I'm sure it is. You did the right thing.'

Then I say, 'In what way does it concern me other than the obvious, that I'll miss you?'

She hesitates. 'I thought you might want to come with me.'

I raise my eyes to look at her. 'What will I do there all of, what is it, two years?'

I can see a flicker of irritation in her eyes. 'I suppose what you do here, more or less. You hate your job...'

'It's come to an end this morning.'

'All the better. You're free. You could have one or two years of total freedom to do as you like.' She stops. 'If you feel unhappy you can always come back.'

'Just like that?'

'What do you mean "just like that"?'

'Do you love me?'

She looks vexed. 'You've told me again and again that you wanted to write. Or to research into something. Well, I can give you the opportunity. Take it, with it goes my friendship, my deepest affection...'

'Do you love me?' I repeat.

She lowers her eyes. Her mouth hardens. 'Think of what I've said. But please decide fairly soon. We'll talk about it another time, perhaps,' she says.

We had supper at a local Chinese restaurant, then she returned home without coming up to my flat again.

My head tells me accepting Imogen's offer would be a fatal mistake. Another thing my head tells me as I sit in my sitting room with Moon in my lap, is that Imogen already regrets having said what she said. She had acted on an impulse, a moment of... whatever. In Harvard she would feel differently. There I would not fit into her scheme of things. She would not want to be distracted by my unhappiness. She had made an ill-considered offer; I jibbed; she was off the hook. Knowing she will probably make no further reference to it, hoping I would not bring it up.

All of a sudden the telephone rings. I rush to it, thinking it is her, but no, it is the telephone operator wanting to read me a telegram: *Meet me for Breakfast Monday 9.30 Fortnum and Mason stop Kerstin Dahlberg*.

I have the weekend to prepare myself for the meeting. I have no idea what Kerstin Dahlberg looks like nor what kind of a woman she is. I find it curious that Gideon, whose diary observations are generally detailed, is curiously vague about the woman he loved. He never mentioned her to me in his letters. Nor did Beth say anything about her except that she was a 'Swedish beauty.'

The detective in me gets to work: why did she send a telegram rather than ring? Is there a hidden meaning in her re-locating our breakfast meeting from the Ritz to Fortnum and Mason?

Among Gideon's books which I have brought with me from Jerusalem, there are two with an inscription by her. I take them out. One is *Seven Years in Tibet*, by Heinrich Harrer. The other is a coffee table book in Swedish about traditional Christmas celebration in Sweden. Both are simply inscribed: 'To Gideon, with affection, from Kerstin'.

I shall consult Imogen. A good excuse to find out if she still wants me to go to the States with her, I decide. She is not at home. Eventually I get through to her cousin Claire who tells me Imogen has gone to Norfolk for the weekend.

There is a hold-up on the Northern Line. I arrive at Fortnum and Mason a quarter of an hour later than the appointed time. I recognise Kerstin without difficulty: the air of expectation about her. She has not yet ordered. She doesn't look about searching for me but is deep in introspection. She has a serious, strong face, not beautiful. Not, to my eyes at least, the beauteous goddess of plenty, Annapurna, of Gideon's fantasy. Of course, she must have changed a great deal. When she and my father were together they were both in their prime. Now she is an elderly lady.

As I approach she sees me. Her face lights up.

'Hello, Philo,' she says getting up and stretching out her hand. She has an open smile, an honest hand. I like her immediately.

'Well, what a surprise. First your letter, then the telegram. To be honest, I didn't think I'd ever meet you,' I say.

The way she raises her chin, and her slightly full but firm mouth at once sexy and serious, and her once metallic blonde hair turned silver, remind me of Jenni of my childhood. This is what she might look like now, if she's alive. Had Gideon seized upon a second opportunity, having let go the first?

'I did say I will come to see you,' she laughs. 'Do sit down and let's have breakfast. Sorry it's not at the Ritz. You don't mind?'

'Not at all. Better here, in fact.'

I heard someone once unkindly compare the Swedes to Swift's horsey Houyhnhnms: wholly good, wholly high-minded, wholly boring.

Kerstin is nothing like that at all. She is, I get the impression, impulsive, warm, considerate, above all, fun to be with. And I love her lilting Swedish accent.

'Tell me, Philo, how is your mother?'

'She's well.'

'And Tali?'

'She's also well.'

We've finished breakfast and are on the second cup of coffee and still she says nothing about the purpose of her visit.

'Would you mind if I smoked?' she asks.

'Not at all.'

Her brand is a long slender black cigarette. She offers me one, and says 'good for you' when I tell her I don't smoke. I watch her cup the flame in her hand as she lights the cigarette. She draws deeply, hollowing her cheeks, inhales, then, closing her eyes, emits upwards a stream of blue smoke.

'Well,' she says.

'Well?'

'Gideon told me that Tali might not be friendly but that you would.'

'He was right. About me, that is.'

'I am very glad to hear that. He talked a great deal about you, Philo. That is not to say I think I know you. Nevertheless, I wanted to see you. It was not easy then, in Copenhagen.'

'I can understand.'

'Can you? Ah well, here we are anyway.'

'Yes, here we are.'

She takes out of her handbag an envelope and holds it out to me.

'This is what I came to give you.'

It is a light cream envelope, can't be more than a letter. I am about to pocket it when Kirsten says, 'It might be better if you opened it here and now, because I think you will have questions to ask.'

Inside there is a København Privatbanken cheque made out to me, for £85,000. I stare at it, incredulous.

'Soon after he came to Copenhagen,' says Kerstin, 'Gideon made certain investments. Good investments, as it turned out. They have recently matured. This is what they yielded.'

'I thought he was broke. What did he invest in?'

'Does it matter now? Let's say he had help. From good friends.'

'...You?'

She looks down abstractly into her coffee cup.

'I know Gideon would have wanted you to have the money,' she says after a pause. 'I know he would think you needed it most. But it's up to you... I mean with regard to your mother and Tali. It's not a very large sum these days.'

'What about you?'

Again she laughs, a sad laughter this time. 'I'm all right. This is for you.'

'Kerstin,' I say, 'how did Gideon die?'

She clears her throat. 'There was a report...'

'It was too vague. Tell me, please, if you can bear to.'

She lights another cigarette, then begins: 'Someone rang him. Gideon didn't tell me who it was. You see, at the time he was desperately trying to start some business. We didn't have much money.

'He said he was driving to Møn, where that man was staying for a few days. He said he would return the next day. He didn't want me to come with him. The next day, at around noon, he phoned to say that everything was fine, and he would be back that night. He sounded cheerful. Optimistic.

'The rest is as in the police report.'

'The man he told you he was meeting, who was he?'

'I never got to know who he was.'

'Didn't you try to find out?'

'No,' she says and shakes her head. 'I'll always be haunted that I didn't go with Gideon to Møn... He was difficult that day. I also was...' She stops abruptly and stares fixedly at her cup for a long moment. 'There isn't more I can say, Philo.'

We have another cup of coffee. She has a busy agenda on this, her last day in London, she tells me. There are things she wants to buy for her new home.

'Yes, I'm leaving Denmark,' she answers my question. 'Leaving Scandinavia altogether.'

'Oh? where to?'

'Greece. I've bought a lovely little house on a lovely little island. I've always longed for the Mediterranean. I shall live there alone and in peace. Trying to forget some things, holding on to the memory of other things. The end of one chapter, beginning of a new one, doesn't that sound like a nice and cheerful retirement?'

I wish her all the happiness in the world. If she is not doing anything tonight, I make a tentative offer. She thanks me. As it happens, she has a ticket for a West End play.

'Next time, perhaps.'

'Next time certainly, Philo.'

She is staying in a 'wonderful' little hotel in Bloomsbury, flying home tomorrow evening. I get up to leave when Kerstin Dahlberg says as an after thought: 'Oh there's one more thing.'

She brings out of her shopping back a dark lacquered wooden box. 'I didn't know whether or not to bring it. It is by right yours, if you want it.'

'What is it?'

'Gideon's ashes,' she says with unbelievable directness. 'Perhaps you think it's crazy. I don't know how to say this. Gideon left Israel for good. I know he would not have liked to be buried there. But I have no right to decide this. Only if you don't want it I take it back to Denmark.'

I stare speechless at the box.

She says, 'Maybe I should not have brought this.' and she is about to retrieve the box.

I sit down. I put my hand on the box.

'Kerstin, I flew back to Israel with a coffin . There was a funeral in Jerusalem, Gideon's funeral. What's all this about his ashes in this box?'

'Now you'll be angry with me, and I shall be very sorry.' She pauses. I have to prompt her to go on.

'The body you buried was my husband Erland. He died of a stroke the day before Gideon's accident. Erland would have liked being buried in Jerusalem. I'm sorry, Philo. Really sorry. I did what I thought was the right thing, at the time. Are you furious with me?

Shall I take this box back to Denmark?'

I look at her, then at the box, then at her again. Then I burst out laughing. Gideon would have laughed. But you, Imogen? What would you say?

Walking up Piccadilly towards Green Park, I clutch Gideon's black box. I think of the quaintness of his ashes being handed to me over a breakfast table in Fortnum and Mason. What will passengers on the Jubilee and Northern lines make of me, sitting holding a lacquered black box, smiling and giggling to myself?

Walking home through Highgate Wood, I feel lighter than air at the thought of having eighty five grand in my pocket. More money than I've ever had, it will change my life. No hurry to decide how.

Only after I have deposited it in my Muswell Hill bank and am walking home with a week's supply of luxury cat food for Moon, do I begin to think of Tali and Beth.

Tali is comfortably off, living in a sprawling bungalow in one of Tel Aviv's most sought-after suburbs. Beth, too, is a shade better than okay. Whereas I am needy; a fact.

Besides, could I go through the story with them? Detail by detail, recalling the past years once again, agonising over questions that had no answers? Was it not better to let things alone?

Convenient rationalising. In keeping the money all to myself I soil myself with deceit even though it was given me, not to share with Tali or Mother, that's the bottom line, I can hear you say, Imogen. So be it.

Propped up inside the box I find an egg-shaped pewter container half filled with coarse greyish powder. What shall I do with my father's ashes? Cast them from Waterloo Bridge into the River Thames that he loved? Or into the North Sea, to be gobbled up by a shoal of herring swimming east to Denmark? Or keep box and jar on the mantelpiece as a domestic shrine – Father in life, now house Lar?

I stick my finger in the ashes. The contact instantly sends a cold shiver of doubt to my mind. So I ring Miles, catching him just as he is about to leave his rooms for lunch.

'Miles, would you know someone who could do a test analysis of something for me?'

'What of?'

'Ashes.'

'What kind of ashes?'

'That's what I want to find out. If you happen to know of some forensic lab...'

'Hmm,' says Miles. 'How urgent?'

'Crisis urgent, Miles. I must know the result tomorrow morning.'

'Oh well, that's okay. Can you get it over to me?'

'Right away.'

'Great. Can't be a hundred per cent sure I can do it but I'll certainly try.'

'Bless you Miles. Oh, how accurate will the analysis be?'

'Pretty accurate, I should think. Unless the stuff comes from outer space. What is it all about, anyway?'

'Another time, Miles.'

I send it to him with a courier service. Before the day is over Miles rings back: 'Got paper and pen handy, Philo?'

'Go ahead.'

'Ingredient one: household fire cinders. Ingredient two: garlic pepper. Ingredient three: baking powder. Ingredient four: vanilla. Ingredient five and last: brown-grey beard shaving, probably from an electric shaver. Gosh, Philo, what are you up to?'

'Never mind. Are you absolutely sure?'

'Positive. A friend helped. She's a top forensic expert.'

'Thanks a lot Miles. You've been a great help. And Miles, could we please keep this strictly between us?'

'Nothing underhand, is there?'

'Nothing. All strictly above board, I swear. Not a word to Imogen, okay?'

'Okay.'

I ring the 'wonderful' little hotel in Bloomsbury; reception tells me Mrs Dahlberg has checked out.

20

Tonight I am preparing dinner.

Now, with this commission offered and accepted, I feel up-beat about it, about everything. I shall strive to create a memorable feast. For Imogen, two of her colleagues, and her American patrons here on a brief visit. All hail to Fate, dispenser of accidents good and bad.

For it was an accident that thrust this culinary challenge at me: Julia Dowland, Imogen's formidable mum, had had a near fatal fall. Not a fall actually but rather an accidental exclusion from the safety of her home during a particularly inclement night, which exposed her to the elements and hypothermia.

Imogen cut short a lecture to rush to Norfolk. With the old girl massaged back to life and in a stable condition, Imogen remembered the dinner and rang me in panic.

'Darling, I can make it back home in time but would you be an angel and do the shopping?'

She started reading out a list. I cut her short.

'Of course. No problem. But listen, why don't I prepare the dinner from beginning to end?'

A charged silence. Should she trust me with so important an occasion?

'Perhaps I should call it off... How annoying that I haven't got the telephone numbers here with me. I wonder, Philo...'

'No need to call it off. I'll take care of it all.'

'Are you sure?'

'Absolutely.'

'Make it simple, darling,' she said.

I understood what she meant: don't be ambitious, don't experiment (if the dinner is a passable flop, not a disaster, she has a legitimate excuse). Don't spend too much.

The latter slant is a touching revelation of Imogen's character. She is far from mean, in the larger sense. Yet petty meanness is ever a symptom of her anxiety.

'Don't worry. Everything will be just perfect. Trust me.'

'I do. And I'm grateful. And I can't thank you enough...'

'No need to. Concentrate on what you have to do and let me take care of the dinner,' I said.

Prior to going over to Imogen's house to begin the preparations, I need to get myself into a creative frame of mind. I take a walk in Alexandra Palace. As I pass beneath Ally Pally's now defunct radio mast, an imaginary transmission hums into my consciousness, and in my mind's eye I see not a magic recipe but scenes from Julia Dowland's ordeal.

A chilly autumn evening. The Danish voices that reach her come not from the walnut relic which is her wireless, but from far away beyond the flat meadows, from the coast.

She downs a large sherry, dons her battle tweeds, fastens the windows, locks the doors, then lugs the commode out into the garden. Throned upon it among the faded roses, she makes ready to outface a Viking invasion.

That's how Jim Slater finds her at the crack of dawn as he drives his cows out to pasture. 'Mornin', Mrs Dowland,' he calls out, and would move on knowing there was no accounting for the daft things upper-class folks get up to. But Mrs Dowland keels over and falls stiff as a board to the ground.

Frozen rigid, she is ambulanced to the Norfolk and Norwich Hospital. And while her mind turns to ether, her thawed body stubbornly resumes its slow, steady ticking on towards a centenary...

I have reached the end of the park and am standing at the edge of the road, and all of a sudden I am overcome by a grandeur of sadness. By the time I take possession of Imogen's house key from her next door neighbour, I feel at once valedictory and resigned. I step inside to survey her kitchen, the matrix of my farewell gift.

It is a large, chaotic kitchen, haphazardly equipped. How will she sort it out before she goes? So many personal items. What will she take with her and what leave behind? No, I've got it wrong: Imogen is tougher than I think. Her emotional development conveniently lags behind that of her intellect, enabling her to travel lightly through life. She will weep... then bin her childhood teddy bears along with me and put it all behind her four drinks and four hours away from Heathrow across the Atlantic.

I too must shed some ballast. To speed me up and away I shall have at least a clean £200,000, when I've sold my flat. My idea of wealth is to have enough to see you out in good style. Thus, I'm wealthy, unless longevity thwarts me.

I shall override Imogen's injunction. I shall create the kind of dinner neither she nor her friends will ever forget, and never mind what it costs. From among an assortment of cook books in the kitchen bookcase I select one that looks the most serious. It is entitled *Gourmet*. There is a barely decipherable inscription on the title page (possibly the author) which says something to the effect that unlike Imogen's many other accomplishments, her cooking needs help which this book should hopefully provide. The illustrations are mouth-watering. Leafing through, I reach a recipe called *Faisan à la Bohémienne*: 1 young pheasant;1 young quail; Truffles 2 to 3; Bardes de lard; Salt and pepper; Dry sherry; Slices of stale bread; Foie gras; 1 shallot; Cayenne pepper; Butter.

As I compute the quantities needed to banquet seven eaters, I get excited, understanding that in the making here is a feast that would have done proud the legendary banqueter Lucius Licinius Lucullus. In other words, the mother of all dinners, to be remembered and talked about by a whole generation of North London academic guzzlers. A challenge, if ever there was one!

I draw up the shopping list then ring for a mini-cab to take me to Harrods, where I reckon it is most likely I shall find all the ingredients I need under one roof.

It takes full ten minutes for two shop assistants to load the taxi with my purchases that include a range of exotic fruit, a selection of French cheeses and bread, bottles of wine and one huge chocolate *bombe*.

On the way home the driver blunders into cul de sac road leading by a pedestrian passage to Chalk Farm. A bill board displays a faded poster of some famine relief fund. It shows a stretch of bare earth cracked by drought, and a family group of skeletal Africans with clouded eyes, squatting on it. Next to it is another poster advertising a popular brand of dog food. The driver turns the car round. We start back only to get held up by a large van unloading at a health food cum art and bookshop. The shop's window is dominated by Africa Famine Aid. It features a blown-up black and white photograph of an afflicted African village. In front of the photograph stands a real open sack of mealie meal surrounded by an assortment of jugs and earthenware. *"This amount of mealie meal will feed a family of four for four weeks. It costs less than an average lunch for a family of four in London"* the caption informs.

I position the chocolate *bombe* in the fridge. I draw the pheasants and the quails and line them up on the counter. After arranging the other ingredients in their correct sequence of preparation, I step back to relish the cornucopia of expensive food heaped to overflow on the table. There is a lot of work ahead but there is time; time enough, in fact, for a short much needed snooze. I go upstairs to Imogen's bedroom. Her bed is unmade. I lie on it and dream of her.

It is three o'clock when I wake up. I descend to the kitchen where, book in hand, I commence to bone the quails, chop them up with some of the truffles, and set aside the peelings for later use. Having garnished the pheasants and prepared them for the oven (at the right temperature, that's crucial! the recipe emphasises), I stuff them with the chopped quails, then set about making the sauce.

All is going well so far. I allow myself some modest self-congratulation. I uncork a bottle of Médoc 1972 and pour myself a large glass, then another. I'm not a good drinker and in no time at all I feel recklessly light-headed. And when I turn on the radio, what do I hear? Hector Berlioz's *Symphonie Fantastic*!

I am at once transported to a medieval banqueting hall. Before me is a long table laid with an outrageous superfluity of rich exotic fare, and golden bejewelled goblets. There are shields on the walls and tapestries. In a gallery with a carved wood screen an ensemble of minstrels make music, which is all but drowned out by the laughter of the noble carousers at the table.

Who are these people masquerading in period costume? Why, they are to a man and woman eminent professors, explorers, princes of industry who chair public committees, and society water flies; Imogen's friends, English to the soles of their feet, here gathered to celebrate her.

And there she is herself, seated at the centre, dull-eyed with wine, attired in a flowing gown of pure white silk, with a single teardrop of a pearl suspended by a gold thread in her delectable cleavage.

Now the solid hall's door is thrown wide open. In canters a fearsome knight – digidum digidum digidum... His charger is jet black. So is his shield, his tunic, armour, helmet and helmet plume. A god-almighty battle axe rests across the pommel of his saddle. Slowly he raises the visor but the face is invisible; nothing in there? Nevertheless, this intruder, this unmannered foreign warrior (he must be that, how else?) throws down a challenge, in dead seriousness. Crash! right on the flagstone in front of the table.

Imogen smiles, bemused. The men on either side of her strain to see through clouds of Havana cigar smoke. They are ready to clap; they think it's the fucking floor show!

It must have been at about that point that once again I rang for a taxi and whipped out for some additional purchases at that arty-farty shop that was patronising African misery.

I'm cold sober when I return, and without further ado, get down to work. Eventually, I hear the key turn in the door. I put on the chéf's hat I had bought, and greet Imogen at the kitchen's door.

She laughs to see me. 'Darling,' she says, 'you're simply marvellous. How's it going?'

'Like a dream,' I tell her.

'Let me see.'

She gapes incredulous at my work in progress.

'My God!' she gasps at last, 'have you taken leave of your senses?'

'*Au contraire*! I've brought all my senses together, harnessed and spurred them on for a creation that'll boggle your mind,' I reply.

'But dearest Philo...'

I place my hands on her shoulders. 'Don't worry, everything's under control. This is my show, my present to you. It'll be a feast you'll never forget, Trust me.'

'Philo, I didn't mean this to be a tour de force. My friends are...'

'This is not about your guests,' I say firmly. 'This is about you and me.'

She gives a slow drawn out sigh. Then catching sight of the half empty bottle of wine, she says, 'Oh, well, if it's like that, might as well help you finish the bottle.'

We toast each other and to the evening. She laughs: 'You never do things in half measure, do you? Can I help with anything?'

I can see she is dead tired, so I say, 'No. There isn't all that much to be done, anyway. Why don't you go upstairs and take a rest.'

'Are you sure?'

'Absolutely. Go now.'

'If I lie down now I'll sleep for eternity,' she says.

'I'll wake you up in time. Don't worry.'

Through the oven's glass panel I can see the stuffed pheasants turning golden and glossy, dripping their juices onto the slices of dried bread I had placed under each bird. Soon they will be ready. The timer chimes for the gravy. I take it off the gas ring. I dip a spoon into the copper saucepan. Delicious! As the book instructs, I lay the slices of foie gras, cock's combs and kidney on a large platter, as an accompaniment to the main course. Then, standing back, I pour myself the last of the of wine and raise my glass to the crowning success of my ambitious enterprise.

The dining table is set and ready. In the kitchen – my operations room – the entire plan of the dinner from beginning to end is pinned up on a cork board on the wall besides the busy cooker: first course, half a melon filled with diced mango, kiwi fruit, pitted cherries, white grapes all shot with rum and served with chilled Alsace. Ten minutes interval for appreciative conversation, then *voila*! the main event! A quarter of an hour after the table had been cleared, the guests senses are on a high plateau of pleasure; wham! *la bombe*!

The bill for this gastronomic extravaganza is as high as its animating pretence. I'll pay it to the full. This is my sort of grand exit. I reckon I deserve it.

But at this moment of devil-may-care reflection, Gideon steals into my thoughts. The phoney ashes... Why did Kerstin Dahlberg give me the box if not to point at something, a riddle for me to work out? Is it possible that my father is alive, re-invented somewhere? I picture him ageing, overweight, sitting among the vines of a villa on some Greek island, watching the sun set in a mythical sea... Waiting for me, like Theseus's father?

'The account is balanced and closed, Dad,' I speak to him. 'Rest in peace among your vines and fig trees, Guido, your secret is safe with me. In our different ways we are both frauds. Only you, Abba, started it when I was still innocent.'

Professor Jerome Lennox and his wife Barbara are enormously tall. Afflicted with arthritis, he walks with a diffident stoop. Long-boned and long-faced, she, by contrast, is totally and emphatically perpendicular. If ever there was a living general statement about New Englanders the Lennoxes are it, from their informal footwear to their courteous, sedulous curiosity.

Jerome has already developed a kind of proprietorial affection for

Imogen. She is going to go down quite extraordinarily well in Harvard, he says. Since his voice carries, I can hear him from the kitchen as I am about to make my entry.

I come to greet them wearing my white chéf's hat. They don't know what to make of me and my unhidden familiarity with Imogen confuses them further. Barbara Lennox gets chummy. Her husband puts on a thoughtful Robert Frost expression.

'I guess this is going to be a grand production, huh?' says Barbara.

'The grandest in town,' I tell her.

Johnny Baker, a colleague of Imogen, arrives with his wife Virginia. They are younger, demonstratively affectionate to each other, and serious. Enlightened liberal socialism is stamped on their faces, a creed they back by having four precocious children at home in Islington, two Burmese cats called Jenny and Nye, and an ageing but dependable Volvo estate car which they boast never gets washed more than once a year.

Gareth Rose is last to arrive. An anthropologist and an old friend of Imogen and her former husband, he too is on his way to an open-ended stint in an American university. He kisses Imogen and holds her in a long embrace.

I gulp down my drink and excuse myself, there's work to be done in the kitchen.

The sound of conversation and laughter reaches me. I sit down and light a Sobrani Black cigarette from a packet I bought at Harrods out of sheer nostalgia. I'm no longer a smoker, having kicked the habit some twenty years ago. Inhaling makes me dizzy.

Imogen pops her head round the door. 'Everything all right?'

'Perfect. Ready in, let's say, half an hour.'

She comes in. 'I can't believe you've done all this.' She makes a sweeping gesture with her hand.

'Neither can I. But here it is.'

'Is there nothing I can do to help, anything?'

'Nothing. Go keep your guests happy.'

'They'll think you're the cook if you go on wearing this daft outfit.'

'I am the cook.'

'I mean...' she stops in mid sentence, comes over and puts her arms around my neck. 'You know you are more to me than all of them put together. Far more,' she says.

Imogen has rejoined her guests, leaving the door ajar. Jerome Lennox is in full flow recounting a recent study tour of Japan. An intriguing country, so much disciplined energy... So intrinsically alien to the western mind. The formality of its society locked in anachronistic mannerism, all concealing deep-seated contempt for other races, though you couldn't tell because Japanese politeness is an impenetrable mask. A Japanese colleague had taken him to a restaurant in Tokyo. They had lobster: 'Can you imagine? The poor creature was still alive and breathing while we were digging into its back!'

'How could you eat it?' Virginia Baker gasps.

'With great difficulty and revulsion. Actually, I couldn't, even though I tried,' he replies, adding that Man's inexhaustible quest for new culinary experience repelled him to the point of disgust. As for Japan, he could see the writing on the wall for its decline, when western consumer culture sapped its traditions.

'Isn't that the fate of all civilisations, not to mention empires? Look at Britain, not so long ago the greatest empire the world has ever seen, the hub of European civilisation. Now verging on the insignificant and falling to the bottom of the European league,' says Johnny.

'I, for one, have no regrets. At least we're still a relatively gentle, tolerant, caring society,' Virginia ripostes wryly.

Pitching in at a pause, Gareth Rose changes the subject to Ethiopia. He had visited the country the year before. The civil war was the most horrid example of mindless destruction he had ever witnessed. But it paled to insignificance beside the famine that was gripping the country, which outside help could assuage but not eliminate. On returning to England, he found it difficult to eat a square meal for nearly a month, he confesses.

My mind goes into a spin, until Barbara Lennox's full-bodied New England voice miraculously pilots it back on course.

'...Talking of adaptability, did you know you can sing all Emily Dickenson's poems to the tune of *The Yellow Rose of Texas*? Truly. Jerome's buddy from Comparative Literature told me. Jimmy Sterne, honey. He said a freshman student wrote a paper on it. Each and every darn poem! I actually tried, and it works, isn't this amazing?'

I rise to my feet. I say under my breath, 'Lady, prepare to be amazed out of your socks.'

And now at last, the full impact of what I have done and what must follow hits me like a tidal wave. I have to hold my hands together to stop them from shaking ridiculously.

The feast I have laboured to create for the best part of the day, is staged on the table: a glossy, beautiful still life, to look at but not to eat. For I have sprayed it all first with a hardening fixative, then with two cans of Windsor & Newton Artist Picture Varnish which I bought on my earlier sortie. Set rock hard, it is a piece of sculpture, to be kept and admired for who can tell how long.

What Imogen's guests are about to be served bubbles in a big African cauldron which, together with its cooking contents and an assortment of earthenware and wooden spoons, I bought for a three hundred pounds donation at that Famine Aid.

I'm ready.

I ought to be cold sober because I understand it is unworthy, even cowardly, to face the colossal embarrassment I am about to inflict and to suffer anaesthetised in whatever degree. Wearing the chéf's hat and carrying a large wooden stirring spoon, I brace myself to announce with a straight face that dinner will be ready in no more than five minutes.

My entry is greeted with an instant of astonished silence followed by loud laughter and clapping to which I respond with a bow.

'Philo, can I help at all?' Imogen calls after me as I retreat.

'No need. Absolutely not at all,' I call back.

I lock the kitchen's door against intrusion. With the cricket bat size wooden spoon that I had earlier paraded with, I give the mealie meal gruel in the cauldron one last stir. It has the consistency of diesel oil. I ladle it out into six wooden bowls and as I do so I hear Imogen leading her guests to the dining room.

The large dining table looks magnificently baroque. Imogen goes through a routine of showing each where to sit. They are jolly and relaxed. Social chemistry in conjunction with booze has made them expansive. Even though the build-up to the meal has been restrained, I can tell they are expecting something out of the ordinary yet are inclined to good-humoured forgiveness if disappointed.

Barbara Lennox is the first to note me standing at the doorway in my apron and hat.

'Woweee!' she cries, clasping her hands together, 'Hail to the chéf! Do I smell something absolutely fabulous?'

She is also the one who says with a forced smile, 'Hey, you're having us on, right?' as I superimpose the steaming wooden bowels on the gleaming porcelain before each guest.

Nobody else says a word.

Imogen, when she is displeased, puts on an expression of stony opacity which reminds me of the Queen at her regally not amused. It is on to a full effect as she gets to her feet and goes to the kitchen. She returns to an awkward silence. What will she do now? I wonder. What will she say to break this unbearable silence?

Barbara Lennox comes to the rescue. Picking up her spoon, she turns to her husband. 'Won't you please pass the salt and pepper, dear?' she says. And then, 'Is someone going to say Grace, or what?'

The dinner guests have departed, retreating ahead of a domestic crisis they think is in the air. The table has been cleared; the African demonstration – mealie meal gruel and utensils – binned outside. We stand in the kitchen among the debris of the evening, and Imogen passes a finger over the hard glossy breast of the top pheasant of my creation.

'At least,' she says reflectively, 'there was good wine and decent bread.'

I say nothing.

She walks round the table, looking at the ruined dinner as if it were an exhibit.

'What an awful waste,' she says. 'Is there anything left that you haven't ruined?'

I take it she means food. I say, 'Enough for a couple of sandwiches, perhaps.'

Her mouth twitches in irritation. 'Doesn't matter. I'm not hungry. Pour me a glass of wine, please.'

But she doesn't drink, she just holds on to the glass.

'What I really dislike,' she says without looking at me, 'what I find unforgivable, is waste. Wilful waste of useful things. Waste of a life.'

'For me this wasn't waste. I had to do it.'

'Why?'

'You wouldn't understand.'

She begins to say something then stops. Her gaze changes from being distance to sorrowful.

'No. I don't suppose I would.'

We stand looking at each other across the table.

She says: 'Do you think you're the only one to find life imperfect?'

'No. Perhaps I have less than you, Imogen, to fall back on when life isn't so much imperfect as desolate and hurtful.'

The sympathy drains from her gaze. She has become the one person selection committee that has, unfortunately, to turn down an applicant – me.

'I am sorry, Philo, that I can't be for you what you want, what you need, perhaps.'

'What about me? Can I be for you what you want and need?'

She half turns. 'I'm not someone who's obsessed with ideals. I ask for less in personal relationships. I try to accept a fairly broad compromise...'

She does not use the word "love" and I sense valediction in what she says, for her unspoken answer to my question is nevertheless a clear "No".

Suddenly, to my surprise, she comes over, presses her face to my shoulder. We stand embraced for a long while. When at last we disengage, I say to her: 'Is this the end?'

'Oh no. Oh no, Philo. There's no end. Only changes.'

'I mean, what with you being in the States and me here...'

'We'll keep in touch. We must. Maybe you'll come to visit me. And I you, whenever I'm in England.'

'Maybe. How long will you be away?'

'A year. Possibly two. I don't know yet.'

'A long time.'

'Not that long. Goodnight, honey.'

* * * * *

Jerusalem Yom Kippur 1988.

My dear Philo,

If God exists and cares at all about what Jews do or don't do, I wonder if He would be angry with me for writing on this holiest of days. Probably not. After all, this letter is an atonement of a sort.

I asked a friend who was visiting London to contact you. She came back and told me that you had left Muswell Hill without a forwarding address. No one seems to know where you are, as though you've disappeared completely.

I can't say I'm all that surprised. There's a part deep in you that always wanted to vanish without a trace, isn't there? I'm writing to your old address in the hope that somehow my letter will reach you. Rather like a shipwreck tossing into the sea a 'Save me!' note sealed in a bottle, then waiting. Such missives have been known to reach their destination eventually, isn't that so?

I haven't heard from you since you left the country. When I think of you, Philo, I ask myself if the mistakes we made and all the hurt we inflicted on each other – yes, you too! – might have been avoided. Probably not. I don't know if hurt and loss can be separated from happiness and richness, like two sides of the same coin. Except that you need balance, to stop hurting before you destroy, and we have not always succeeded in that.

Jacob has returned home confused and sick in body and soul. Like our country, you might say. So sad. My heart is breaking and there's nothing I can do. For him or for Israel. I hold his hand and talk to him, and it's like talking to a wall. I go out on demonstrations against the government, against the occupation of the territories, for peace. The police shove us around as though we were cattle. The onlookers mock and jeer at us. And I think helplessly how both Jacob and Israel began their lives on such a high note of promise. Look at the sorry pass they have come to.

Jacob needs you, Philo. And so do I. No longer as a husband, please understand. I have no claims in that respect. I mean to say I need you as someone whom I know, who grew up with me. For whom I have cared. That, Philo, forges an imperishable bond. And claims of need are forever valid when you have such a bond, don't you think?

What have you been doing all these years?

Funny how I repeat myself. Didn't I ask you just that when we first met in Jerusalem? You are such a nomad, in your heart, in your imagination. Will your restlessness never die? I want to say to you, stop wandering and come home. We are a minority here now, people like you and me and the friends we've had. Minorities have a duty to stand up for what they are, and the only way to do so is in being together.

You used to talk of a dream house on a hill, overlooking the sea, in Zichron Ya'akov. Remember? A haven! For when darkness gathers. I hope and pray with all my heart that you'll find such a haven, wherever it is.

Talking of darkness, I've had a more than a glimpse of it. Cancer. My left breast has been removed. I am well now, and working as hard as ever. You probably don't know that I'm Archaeology Curator at the Israel Museum.

My parents are well, and so is Beth whom I see about twice a year. I have no contact with Tali.

Well, that's all I have to say. I hope you have good memories of what has once been home to you. They won't bring you back, I know. Maybe they will be a tiny light at the corner of your consciousness, like a token patch of unplastered wall religious Jews in the Diaspora keep in their houses, to remind them they are in exile.

Yours ever, Mimi.

I might have told her she is that small though never fading light in my consciousness. A constant reminder, not a guiding beacon. And I would, if I could, press her wounded breast to mine in reconciliation. And I'd have to tell her that I no longer belonged to her 'minority'. They would have to make their stand without me. Mimi can, and doubtless will. An incremental reduction in her ranks wouldn't daunt her.

The wind is high, bending the grass on the fell as it howls down into Baldersdale. Standing on a rise, I see newly-arrived flocks of fieldfare turning in the wind like blown leaves. Below stretches the broad sweep of the dale, and on its other side, surrounded by meadows which slope towards the reservoir where wild geese swim, is Blind Burn, my home, an old stone farmhouse rented from a neighbouring farmer who has become a friend.

Mimi wouldn't believe, being totally urban, that here is my haven. On this brooding fell my imagination is nourished. My solitude in this place is intractable but undemanding. Here is the closest thing to home I shall ever experience.

One day I might reach out to touch what I have left behind. Then I'll say to my son Jacob, 'Everything I have I leave to you, Jacob, for better or for worse, to do with as you please. The territory I've covered – real and of the mind – I've mapped and sign-posted for you. Learn from it what you can, if you can. Or condemn me if you must.'

Night is falling over the Balder. I can hear the day's last screeching of the pheasants and the now weak, pre-sleeping bleating of the sheep in the stone-walled field beyond Blind Burn. I clear the table of my light supper and light the log fire. Shadows of the flame dance on the beamed ceiling and the walls, now lined with my books and pictures. I put on a record of Elizabeth Schwartzkopf singing Richard Strauss's *Four Last Songs*, decant a generous dram of Macallan whisky into a glass, and light a *Romeo y Juliet* Havana cigar. My acquired tastes, you see, are expensive as they are dissonant with the time, and altogether private.

I sink into this comfortable, outrageously old-fashioned armchair and I think of you, Imogen. Shut off from the world and cocooned in my thoughts, loving might seem incurable, but like diabetes it isn't necessarily life-threatening. (I am, by the way, in excellent health.)

Perhaps my sister Tali was right about love: to survive the wear and tear of everyday life, she said, it must be, and remain, ordinary. Extraordinariness is love's unfailing terminator.

Except for me, now and here where extraordinariness is the spice of my existence.

A quotation from a novel I read long ago and forgot chimes in my mind: "We have gained in terms of reality and lost in terms of the dream".

Which is the more significant? The gain? The loss?

Moon stretches and yawns, curls up on the rug by the hearth, and falls asleep.

I should have found the words to tell my sister Tali, and Mimi and friends who shook their heads to see me leave.

We were born when there were heroes. How were we to know that the inescapable destiny of heroes is defeat?

On the fields where heroes died now spread towns and settlements. Civil servants drone daily in and out of government office buildings. Diners crowd restaurants, talking of new cars and summer holidays in Switzerland, and the faraway prospect of one day towing in icebergs to slake the country's growing thirst, when the aquifers of the Palestinians have run dry.

The pontificators pontificate. The aquiescers acquiesce. And the zealots, who have risen like weeds from among the fallen heroes, vindicate Yahweh, for "Amalek" is crunched to rubble, his towns and villages made desolate. The 'Beautiful Souls' are silenced.

To understand without the ache, you need take distance from the scene. I'm not making excuses, that was how it happened for me, long ago – *Presume not that I am the thing I was.*

I sip at my delicious Macallan, I blow a fat ring of blue Havana smoke. Well? Don't I at last have my England, not extraordinary nor exciting, but secure? When all is said and done, am I not a lucky man?